To John & Judy Horwitz

Happy Reading

[illegible]

1993

THE DISCIPLES

JOSEPH J. ANDREW

SIMON & SCHUSTER

New York London Toronto Sydney Tokyo Singapore

SIMON & SCHUSTER
Simon & Schuster Building
Rockefeller Center
1230 Avenue of the Americas
New York, NY 10020

Designed by Irving Perkins Associates, Inc.
Manufactured in the United States of America

1 3 5 7 9 10 8 6 4 2

Library of Congress Cataloging-in-Publication Data

Andrew, Joseph J.
The disciples: a novel / Joseph J. Andrew.
p. cm.
I. Title.
PS3551.N414D57 1993 92-45613
813′.54—dc20 CIP

ISBN 0-671-79599-6

For all four of my parents,
but this one, in particular,
for my father,
Jerald L. Andrew, M.D.

ONE

THE PARABLES

When he was alone, the twelve, together with the others who formed his company, asked what the parables meant. He told them, "The secret of the kingdom of God is given to you, but to those who are outside everything comes in parables, so that they may see and see again, but not perceive; may hear and hear again, but not understand; otherwise they might be converted and be forgiven."

—Mark 4:10

TOP SECRET
Handle Via Comint
Channels Only

1.

WE ALL MARRY into trouble. That's what Tommy Wood told me later when he was trying to describe the feelings he had in the middle of a Wednesday afternoon in August of 1989. We all marry into some type of trouble, some family feud, some crazy relative, some financial philandering. But nobody, Tommy Wood must have thought that afternoon on an island in the Bahamas, squinting his eyes shut to ease the pain, nobody marries into the trouble *I got*.

The trouble that Tommy Wood got was the warm end of a .38, with the acrid, rubbery smell of having just been fired, pressed into the side of his forehead. While he concentrated on the circle of hot metal searing his skin, a three-hundred-pound Bahamian woman ran the fat blade of a dirty machete slowly down the front of his shirt, popping each button as she came to it.

"Who are you, Mr. Thomas Wood?" she asked so softly that our hearing devices could hardly pick up the lilt of her Caribbean-accented threats as her rum-brushed breath hissed into his sweat-caked hair.

Our miniature camera, designed a decade ago by our friends at Langley, was hidden in an ancient overhead light fixture that hung from one of the rafters of the palm-thatched hut on the small Bahamian island. The camera showed Tommy Wood swallowing hard when the gun on his temple pushed his head to one side, the muscles in his neck stretching and bulging with tension and fear. The fat woman pressed her melon-wide lips against Tommy's ear, and her red tongue inched toward his eardrum like a snake as she asked again, "Who are you?"

"Really," I remember saying like a primping Oxford don as I wiped the sweat off my forehead in the surveillance room on the big island. I couldn't keep my eyes off the small television screen that showed us the action taking place a few thousand yards away on a small island just off our shore. "Really, this is too much, Murphy. I didn't come all the way down here to watch this . . . torture. This is damn annoying. Tommy won't tell that mountain of a woman anything anyway."

"Let's just wait," Murphy suggested. His stitched-together body was hunched over the television monitor as if he were enthralled by a porno flick. "You're an analyst, boss, not an agent," Murphy said. "Tommy'll talk. He'll break. The boy will talk."

The fat woman smiled on the television screen and let the big blade rip Tommy's shirt and expose an inch of his muscular, bruised skin. She pulled the blade down slowly, as if she were shaving his blond chest hair, while two of her stick-thin black assistants pulled on the ropes that kept Tommy's arms pinned above his head. Her wide red tongue rolled out of her mouth like a wet carpet, and she licked the rib bones that showed through his skin, like the hull of a bronzed and battered ship. "Who is this Tommy Wood?" she asked, tasting the salt of the sweat that rolled down his chest.

"Murphy, do we have any more ice?" I asked. "Or did you mainline it all with those rum-runner things you were inhaling?"

"Shut up," Murphy sassed. "You're missing the good parts."

When I glanced back at the small screen, the tall man with the gun at Tommy Wood's head was moving his thumb slowly, cocking the gun. Tommy didn't tell me this later, but I know that when a gun is cocked three inches from your ear, the sound grates like the jaws of a giant fish and everything else sounds dull and muffled, as if you were underwater. All you can think of is, what next? Will I hear it, or will it just happen before I can recognize a sound or sense the heat? What next?

"I'm . . ." Tommy said softly, the air squeezed out between clenched teeth. "I'm an architect."

The fat woman laughed and pressed the blade of the knife against his pants, ripping them along the zipper and cutting the elastic on his underwear. She left his leather belt intact, opening it roughly with one hand. “Who?” she said over and over again. “Who? Who is this Tommy Wood?”

“Is this really necessary?” I asked Murphy, my annoyance and anxiety turning into anger.

“The ice?” Murphy asked, without glancing up from the screen. “Or this little play? No, of course not,” he said, standing up but still not moving his eyes from the screen. “Not necessary at all, but damn good fun.”

“Christ, thank God I'm not an agent, if this is what you guys call fun. No wonder it's so goddamn bungled. Wait a minute. I thought we told her not to cut his belt? Damn it, why did she come so close to cutting his belt?”

“She didn't cut it.”

“Are you sure?”

“Who cares about his belt?” Murphy said. “This boy's worried his balls are next.”

The fat woman pulled up her dress, past her ballooning underwear, as Tommy's pants fell away, rubbing her mountainous rolls of flesh against his naked, taut body. She closed her eyes as she moved, and the three sweating black men in the small hut all looked away, as if they could not stand the sight. Then she started talking in rhythm with her movements, her Bahamian accent sliding into Cleveland English. “Tommy, Tommy Wood. I have this, this theory,” she said.

“A theory?” I asked the television screen. “You've got to be kidding.”

“I knew you'd love this,” Murphy said. “She sounds just like you, Steele. Another frickin' theorist.”

“More of a vision, Tommy. A prediction,” the fat woman said, the sweat glistening on the folds of her black skin. “Voodoo for you. Let me give ya some info-ma-tion. Your business, Mr. Wood, the spy business, is dying, just like big, fat, rich white men's companies in the States are dying. They took on too much money, honey. Junk bonds. Poison pills. Golden pairs of chutes. Takeover artists. Makeover artists. They, they forgot about producing anything. Making anything. All they did—all they did is trade each other what they already had.”

“Stop this, Murphy,” I said softly between sips of my drink without ice, not sure if I meant it. “I can't stand here and listen to the fattest woman in the world lecture us on the failed economics and social policy of the United States. Stop her.”

"I can't," he said. "It's part of the deal we have with her. She gets three hours, and for those three hours—and she's got forty minutes left—that boy is hers."

"You see," she said, running her hands up and down his tan thighs, her long fingernails leaving thin pink scratches in the muscled flesh, "when the ice thaws, when the cold war is warmed over, my sugar-cane son, what have you spies got to show for all your work? Eaves-dropping until your eaves drop dead? What have you got to show for all the white games, all the white money, all the black dead? Nothing. Big fat nothing."

"I'm an architect," Tommy gasped between her gyrations. "I don't know what you're talking about."

She kissed him full on the mouth, her tight corn-rowed hair whipping him as she turned away from his stony face. With her dress still pulled up to her belly, she turned back to him and licked his entire face, leaving beads of saliva rolling down his cheeks. "American assholes," she said, slipping back into an island lilt full of hot rum vowels and sea-harried consonants. "Every spy from the States is ah asshole. Keeping your little secrets from us, from the people. Afraid that if we understand your game, we'll see how worthless it all is."

"Really, Murphy," I remember saying, "do we have to listen to this if we are paying her? Talk about looking a gift horse in the mouth. She knows we're listening and watching. What's her problem? Is she some kind of religious fanatic? Plus, I specifically said she wasn't to touch his belt. Does she know what she's doing?"

"Of course she knows," Murphy said, running a finger down the crease of his khaki pants leg. "That's why she's yelling about all this spy crap. For your benefit. For the spy boss down from the States who is listening in. God knows, she could care less what I think."

"Good," I snapped. "That makes two of us. Now stop this ridiculous charade. Send our men in to get him."

"Look," Tommy said hoarsely, as if he could hear me. "I'm just an architect. I'm not, not a spy."

The fat woman erupted in laughter and grabbed his genitals, sending ripples of shock up his chest. "Then tell me, honey. Tell me, Mr. Tommy Wood, American architect. How'd you end up in this predicament? Gun to your head. Ropes on your wrists. Hope in my hands. How'd you end up here?"

"I married," he said softly, just as Murphy reached to push the red button next to the monitor that was supposed to signal the fat woman to disappear into the night with her three silent accomplices, leaving Tommy to wonder why he had been kidnapped and then so suddenly released. "I married into trouble."

Six months earlier, in February of 1989, we were lucky enough to tape another conversation, but not lucky enough to understand it until months after we were lectured by the fat woman in the Bahamas. For that is the paradox of most intelligence gathering—you can use lightning-fast machines to vacuum up the entire electromagnetic spectrum and pick up more information than you imagined existed, but transforming that information into intelligence takes the slow minds of people who need coffee breaks and time to daydream about last night. Just as in this story, you have to piece together bits of information, scraps of subjects, pieces of perspectives, and quilt it all together to get the intelligence that will keep you warm during the long last nights of the cold war.

But because of luck, or fate, or paranoid overplanning, somebody at our internal security desk had had the foresight to plant a bug in the big green Ford Explorer that the local real estate broker, given the contract to sell the land at Fort Meade, next to our headquarters, was allowed to drive over the hills and valleys of the mothballed military training grounds. No matter that it was a technical violation of a half dozen provisions of several federal statutes, that miniature transmitting device hummed along for months at a time, sending out encrypted radio waves that were picked up by one of the low-orbit Keyhole satellites and beamed down to one of the dozens of radome dishes located on the roof of the National Security Agency.

"It's a wonderful location," the dyed-blond real estate broker said to the man who sat next to her in the front seat of the Explorer as she drove slowly up the gravel road to the high point on the land that was for sale. "You know, the Army was ordered by the Department of Defense to close military installations like this all across the country. Ninety-one of them, I think."

She had been contacted by the Bundt Bank of International Commerce's U.S. real estate division and asked if she would show one of the bank's people the Fort Meade land that might soon be for sale. The BBIC was one of the largest banks in West Germany and, coincidentally, the majority owner of the Equitable Bank and Trust Company, which had a branch bank inside the main building at the NSA headquarters, right between the barbershop and the dry cleaner's along Corridor C. The real estate broker mentioned to her colleagues, whom we talked to later, how nice it would be for the NSA's own bank, or so she thought of them, to be involved in developing this piece of property.

This was where she always liked to bring prospective developers, she told me later. Long ago there had been an orchard on the hill, so the old farm road went all the way to the top, where a few bald cherry trees stood like sentinels to the past. Later she described the man to me as around sixty-five, short, with wild white hair, a brush of a moustache, and a slight German accent. "Really, a great location."

It was the last day of February, and the trees were bare branched in the clear, harsh mid-morning Maryland sun, which left no room for the imagination. The lush pines scattered among the bare trees looked like small prisoners of green trapped in a tangle of brown arms, and the only birds that flew over the road were crows, which glistened black like oil—maybe from eating the road kill smeared daily across the tar and asphalt of the highway that went around the fort.

"Ja," the old man said again with his heavy accent. "But what is that over there?"

He pointed toward the tangle of NSA buildings just barely visible from the road, and she smiled to hide her cringe. She was famous in her office for selling hundreds of homes within two miles of a nuclear power plant without ever mentioning that it was there, and she had had no intention of explaining the neighboring buildings unless she had to. Now she had to.

"That over there," she said, pointing, "those buildings and the three towers? That's the NSA—the National Security Agency. Just some government bureaucracy on a little corner of Fort Meade. Really nothing at all. Say, four hundred or so of the thirteen thousand acres here. We're right next to the four-thousand-acre Patuxent Wildlife Research Center, which you can see over there, behind the water tower. Right now we are almost exactly in between Washington, D.C., and Baltimore, Maryland. A perfect location."

"NSA?" the man asked above the noise of the truck as it automatically shifted down to a lower gear to climb the hill.

"Spies," she said as if she was talking to a child, her hands probably leaving the wheel, as they did when she later drove me up to the top of the same hill, searching for a gesture that would help her explain what she was saying, but she couldn't think of anything that would show what a spy did. There is no gesture for spying. "You know, sort of like James Bond? Not many people have ever heard of them, I've found. Everybody thinks of the CIA or the FBI. But this thing, this group of people, they tell me is even bigger. But they're really quiet. They'd be great neighbors. You'd never even know they were over there. They're so secret we say NSA stands for 'No Such Agency' around here, isn't that a hoot? No Such—"

She stopped midsentence, realizing that this wasn't helping her sale.

There were scratch marks on the side of the Explorer she had been driving that day, and she explained them to me by saying that when she and her white-haired passenger got to the top of the hill she parked the truck so close to a line of old cherry trees that a few dead branches scratched the paint on the passenger side. The winter wind always comes from the west, so they walked away from the truck into the oncoming cold, which cracked against their coats and burnished their skin to the color of hot copper.

The old German had brought his own binoculars, with large, heavy matte black housing, and he said, "Beautiful for houses, yes?" as he slowly scanned the forest. Undoubtedly, the miniature camera hidden in the binoculars was so quiet that the real estate broker could not hear the tiny shutter clicking away. He probably zoomed the camera's lens to a set of receiving dishes on the east side of the tallest building's roof, memorializing the type, scope, and direction of the dishes—just in case he ever wanted to send the NSA something by satellite.

From the top of the hill you can see that there are dozens of other large buildings in the complex, all with wild hairdos of swooping long periodic antennas and angular parabolic microwave dishes that look like *Flintstones* barrettes. You can see that the whole complex is surrounded by three fences. Two cyclone chain fences, crowned with twisted rows of barbed wire, stand twenty feet apart for miles around the complex. In between them, in the middle of the green asphalt pebbles that look like grass from the top of the hill if you aren't looking through high-powered binoculars, is another fence that is almost invisible. It consists of five strands of high-voltage electrical wire that will knock a man flat on his back if it is touched. Through the binoculars, the white-haired man could easily see the hundreds of television security cameras on the sides of the buildings and on the tall fence posts. He probably wondered if their zoom lenses were trained on him as he turned away. Unfortunately, they weren't.

"Beautiful . . . ," he said, faintly on the tape. "I would put my family house here."

"Wouldn't that be nice," the broker said, her tone demonstrating that she was trying to shift her manufactured charm into overdrive. "Do you have a big family?"

"Ja," he said, and then switched to English as he put the big binoculars back to his small blue eyes. "Twelve. Twelve brothers and sisters."

"Oh," she said. "Just like the disciples."

There was a long pause on the tape, and the silence doesn't tell us if the old man swallowed hard, flinched, or nearly dropped the binoculars. The silence doesn't tell us if the broker smiled nervously at the old man, hoping that she had not said something that had offended him. It doesn't tell us if they watched a crow settle down out of the sky, like a black handkerchief floating in the wind, onto one of the bare branches of the trees that surrounded them. It doesn't tell us if they paused to smell the first fragrances of spring in the wild crocuses that were pushing their way up through the bronzed and burnt carpet of last fall's leaves. But the silence was long enough that she said, "You know, the disciples? Jesus' guys. Isn't it Matthew, Mark, Luke, and John, you know?"

"He went up into der hills," the old man said so quietly that our bug could only barely pick up his stilted German-accented English, but the listeners could guess at what they could not hear. The air was so cold that his voice was crisp and distinct, even though it was faint. "And summoned those he wanted. So they came to him and he appointed twelve; they were to be his companions and to be sent out to preach, with power to chase out devils. And so he appointed the Twelve: Simon to whom he gave the name Peter, James the son of Zebedee, and John the brother of James, to whom he gave the name Boanerges or 'Sons of Thunder'; then Andrew, Philip, Bartholomew, Matthew, Thomas, James the son of Alphaeus, Thaddaeus, Simon the Zealot, and Judas Iscariot, the man who was to betray him."

Again, the silence ate up the tape, until the broker cleared her throat and simply said, "Oh, I guess I got the names wrong."

"Yes," the old man said, louder, his voice relaxing. "They are hard to remember, yes?"

"I guess you'll need a big house, then," she offered, in a voice that showed she was more confused as the conversation went along. For a moment she was afraid of the old man, she told me later when I interviewed her up on that same hill, and she wondered if she had her Mace spray in her purse. She had this instinct about people who really weren't interested in buying property but looked at it all the time. She told me later that at that moment she suddenly felt that the white-haired man had no interest in this property at all. "Shall we go? It's beautiful to look at, but we should get back to my office to get you all the appropriate information before your plane leaves."

He reluctantly got back into the truck with her for the drive back down to her office, where they would talk for an hour about what type of investment might be needed. "Yes," he said, hoisting himself up into the truck with a grunt. "Beautiful place for a house, yes? Now I just need an architect."

"You know," she said, starting the Ford's big engine, "real estate brokers can always recommend good architects. You should let me give you a list of—"

"I have my eye on one," the white-haired man said, reaching for the truck door. "I've identified my architect. For my family."

The truck door slammed shut with a whoosh of air, a snap of a Chekhovian cherry branch, and a crash of metal against metal—popping the earphones off the listeners when they finally got around to the tape months later, after the whole world had changed.

2.

THIS IS HOW I usually begin my reports. I ruminate for hours and then pick two points in time, two events that seem to give meaning to the story, as a frame adds context to a painting. Then, from the third point, where I sit when I begin my report, I fill in what happened in between those first two points: taking its measure and weight and remembering my old fifth-grade teacher, who explained to me that a line is the shortest distance between two points. Then I pick another two points and fill in the line between them, until all the points are connected and a story appears like a picture in a coloring book.

I take out a yellow legal pad and a slightly chewed pencil and scribble "TOP SECRET UMBRA" in large letters on the top of the page. Then I drop down a line, as I have done for twenty years, and print "HANDLE VIA COMINT CHANNELS ONLY," just to protect even those first few precious thoughts. Next, I search for a code name for the entire report, checking with my computer files to make sure I don't use a name that has already been taken. "Discipline" has been used, I see on my computer screen, as has "Disciform," but to my surprise there is no "Disciples."

On the left-hand side of the warm, sunlight-colored page I write as neatly as I can "CODE NAME: The Disciples." Then I underline the name, "The Disciples," and pick my two starting points. Point A: "I married into trouble." Point B: "He went up into the hills."

But from that moment on, this report is different from any other report I have ever written or you have read. Different for a thousand reasons not worth mentioning, but for this: this report may be circulated beyond our circle, my fellow spooks. This one is for the history books, someday. You need to know how this all developed. You need to know who I am and what my biases are. You need to know the details that mattered so much—the smell of the flowers, the look on her face, the gargling sound of the boat motors far, far off. You need to know these things because my report deals with nothing less than why what was once our most powerful enemy casually disintegrated before our very eyes.

I start explaining my report here, between these two points in 1989, because there isn't any way to tell this story in chronological order. I'm not sure anyone in the organization really knows in what order these things happened. I start here because this is when I was pulled in: near the end. I was brought back after all the bureaucratic decisions had been made, all the strategies schemed, all the usual tactics tried out. I was brought back, as old executives forced into early retirement are always brought back, when it was too late. I was brought back when the business, to use the Bahamian woman's metaphor, had nearly gone bankrupt. When Congress was cutting our budget and the experts and pundits were calling for an investigation into why we were so wrong about so much. Only then was I brought back to explain what had happened and to untwist the parables locked in the recent history. Only then was I brought back to figure out Tommy Wood's wife's troublesome family.

I have often been criticized for my vivid sense of imagination and my prurient interest. But, as I always used to say, those are the very qualities that make an analyst so valuable to any intelligence agency. I'm paid good, clean tax dollars to reconstruct events. To take old yellowed documents, twisted reels of tape, and disorganized files and breathe enough life into them to suggest motivation; to come to conclusions; to develop theories.

I read, I listen, I watch, and then I make up the parts we don't know. I spy on the spies, reconstructing their actions, telling their stories, trying to relive their lives so that we don't miss a thing. Of course, we miss much, because so many things at the time don't seem to be worth recording or reporting, let alone remembering. Like any big organization, we fall into the habit of doting on orders and hierarchy and salary adjustments. But it is my job to not lose the forest for all the trees. That means that sometimes I have to guess. I have to suggest a range of options. I have to pull my fingers through my graying hair, close my eyes, and imagine what some spook might have been thinking the moment of some fateful decision.

I supply the human touch, the motivational angle to the dry information that we suck up out of the air. I was the HUMINT man in a SIGINT agency—one of the analysts who specialized in supplying the human intelligence in an agency of technical collectors of signal intelligence that is pulled from the sky by satellites and by a host of the other technical marvels of the twentieth century. I was the man in the middle of a century-long dispute between human intelligence and signal intelligence. The Ph.D.s, who were dismissed as mere "techies" but who ran virtually every one of the agency's ten components, believed that HUMINT was subject to all the subjectivity, all the mental aberrations, all the social bias of the source as well as the interpreter of the source, while SIGINT had no such failings. The intercepted radio communication, the decoded satellite transmission, or the tapped microwave transmitter has technical aberrations that give it away almost immediately if it is not legitimate. Men are fallible, machines are not, or so the theory goes.

But the best SIGINT in the world can be understood only if you know the context. Even if you've tapped the right telephone and the information is in a breakable code, you still have to speak the language, know the nicknames, feel the pain, remember the relationships for the signal to be made into intelligence. And if you're not sure who is making the telephone call, or if you get only part of the message, or if the code the message is sent in is confusing, then you have to speculate from what you do know to get to what you must know.

That is what I do, along with thousands of others in the world's largest intelligence organization. I just happen to have done it longer, and risen to the awkward position of being the storyteller to the boss: the personal analyst to the director of the National Security Agency, known on the government charts as DIR/NSA, and pronounced by the forty thousand employees in the agency as if it were one word: dernza.

Which means I usually got the ones where something went wrong.

Before the cold war ended and the Soviet Union exploded into dozens of parts, my boss, the dernza, wrangled down the hall in that gait he got from wearing cowboy boots under a judicial robe for all those years. He may have received his three stars in Air Force Intelligence and been appointed to the federal bench, but it wasn't until his prep-school buddy became president that he became the dernza. He wrangled down the ninth-floor hall outside the executive offices known as Mahogany Row, and as he threw open my door he said, "Steele, tell me a story on this one.

"Tell me a story," he said. To his friends and his inner circle, he was known simply as the Judge. "Lay it on me, Steele."

He tapped his feet in time with his Texas twang, and the tassels on the loafers he wore, in deference to Washington society, slapped the shiny leather like a crop on a polo pony's side. "And, Steele," he said, with a lockjawed smile that dripped of sarcasm and nose-picking good humor, "try not to make up too much of it this time.

"I mean, why in Jesus' name," he said, as if we were sitting next to each other on a fishing boat instead of in the small, dark office I got when he was made the dernza, "do all of your cases end up in sex and drugs and rock-and-roll, huh? Can you explain that, Steele?"

"Only so you'll read them," I supplied, reaching for the pipe I kept on my desk just for those occasions when I wanted to make him think I was the embodiment of the wizened Ivy League spy don. For it was in these moments that he liked to think of himself as the political appointee and me as the intelligence agency professional, although in retrospect the roles seemed to get reversed.

"No," he said, with a thin smile that would again be on his face when he asked me to come back from early retirement to save his behind, "I don't think so. It's your imagination. You see adultery and dope where every other analyst sees faulty flow charts and mismanagement."

"Thank you," I said, with the hint of a fake yawn, "for the compliment, Judge."

"Is it because you're so damn rich?" the Judge asked me, always fascinated with my wife's money. "Is that what rich people see all the time? Because you married money? Is everything just sex and drugs and booze to you people? I can't stand you."

But I knew that he liked me, he liked my wife, he liked my wife's money, and he liked that I made him look good, so he put up with my impertinent behavior for years before he handed me a pink slip over a good lunch in December of 1988, mumbling about Gramm-Rudman budget cuts while he apologized that it had to be done. His voice was so quiet that I could hardly hear him. We had avoided the giant cafeteria on Corridor C, the Judge's armed guard driving us down the Baltimore-Washington Parkway through the rolling, forested Maryland countryside to a small restaurant just off the road that the Judge frequented. For special occasions the Judge had a table set up in the restaurant's basement, so we could talk freely, without worrying about what other diners might hear. I remember sitting in the back seat of the roaring Chevy, chatting with him about some turnover in personnel in the A Group of the Office of Signal Intelligence Operations, and noting how nice it was that Maryland prohibited big trucks on the parkway. His armed guard, part of the Federal Protective Service, came in and ate with us, his eyes scanning the dark basement room while his ears tuned out our conversation. He was trained not to eavesdrop on the eavesdroppers.

"Damn," the Judge said, handing me the pink slip in the damp basement room. "I hate this part of the job."

"What's this?" I asked him, staring blankly at the pale pink piece of paper in my hands. The windowless room began to spin slowly around me as I tried to focus on the paper. I saw the word "retirement" in the middle of a paragraph, and the phrase "pursuant to top secret umbra report HJ238I by Code John X" at the bottom of the page. The top of the thin piece of paper was stamped with inch-high red letters whose ink had bled down onto the black print below. "TOP SECRET UMBRA/HANDLE VIA COMINT CHANNELS ONLY," the ink wept. Even my firing was secret, I remember thinking as I shook my head to clear it of the rush of memories that was pushed up into my mind by the surge of adrenaline squeezing my fists tight.

"You're retired, Steele," the Judge said, and then took a bite of rare steak and chewed loudly. A bit of bloody beef caught between his giant white teeth, hanging there as he spoke. "Early retirement. As of next Friday, you're out of here, my friend. And nobody will ever know about that report John X did on you. You're scot-free. You're gone on some trip to wherever rich people go, wearing that gold watch from the No Such Agency."

"Watch?" I remember asking, my brain refusing to comprehend what he was saying. What was this about John X's report? I was just hitting my stride. Even if the Judge used all his connections to have the president reappoint him, with the help of my wife, Carolyn, *I* could have the Judge's job in the president's second term. The Judge was the one whom everyone expected to retire and let his friend appoint a new dernza. He was the one who said over and over that he needed to go out into the private sector and make some real money for his family. Jump over to the big suppliers of computers and satellites that would love to have the Judge's influence and expertise.

"I guess you have a Rolex," the Judge said, with his mouth again full of meat. "So how about letting me wear that ol' retirement watch, huh, partner? How about giving me that gold watch?"

But then he choked on his food, and after several deep coughs, watched closely by the armed guard, the Judge simply said, "I'm sorry. Really I am. Look, none of this crap they have on you amounts to much more than a hill of beans except your involvement in that Mexican thing with Carolyn. Everybody wants to help their wife, but when your wife is the CEO of a damn multinational company and you work for the NSA you just can't assist her out of a little industrial-espionage jam she's in. You can't help her train a team of vigilantes to fly into Mexico and free some exec that's been kidnapped by a competitor. They're pressuring me, and pressuring people up the line in the White House. You understand?"

I didn't understand. Everything I had done to assist my wife in organizing the rescue of a company executive who had been kidnapped while investigating a Mexican operation that her company had been interested in taking over had been cleared and perfectly legal. Still, I could find no words for my defense. If the Judge wanted me out of the agency, then I was out. He nervously put down his fork and rubbed his manicured hands over his drooping jowls. "Let's not let this thing affect our friendship, all right, partner?" he said. "I mean, you don't need the paycheck, and I've got it all arranged so that no one will know a thing about it. You and Carolyn just ride off into the sunset. Buy yourself a ranch and invite Helen and me out for a ride."

He smiled broadly at me, his mouth stretched into a tortured grin that reminded me of a wood sculpture of a laughing mermaid that Carolyn had brought back from her mission to Mexico. Just like the torrid red-and-green face of the wooden carving, the Judge's strained smile masked his true emotions, at which I could only guess. Relief that he had finally got a competitor out of his way? Sadness that a friend and contemporary had to be put out to pasture early? Satisfaction that my good luck, which he envied so, had finally run out?

Then he invited my wife and me to join them for dinner. A good dinner, not in some basement, he said. Just the four of us. Sometime soon. Real soon.

It was nearly a year before we could fit that dinner into his and my wife's busy schedules, and on that Tuesday in August of 1989 he was sitting in Washington's most expensive restaurant ordering Dom Perignon and asking me to come back.

"Why do you want me to come back?" I asked, watching the sparkle in my wife's eye. I had talked to him so many times that day that I knew exactly why, but I played the good, solid actor. We had decided that if I was to come back we had to do it publicly and provide a good cover story in case we were being watched. Every word must be phrased with the knowledge that we might be listened to. It was all I could do to not look under the table for the telltale bug, the tiny chip hidden in the rose, the long-distance microphone shaped like a rifle and aimed at us from the coat closet, or the van with an infrared laser sensing tiny motions off the window that could be reconstructed later into the sounds of what we had said. However, I was also determined to enjoy the ritual. "Why do you want me to come back?"

"I want you to tell me a story," he said quietly, with that thin smile that was as much a tightrope as a curve. "A big story. A tricky story. One that can't be screwed up."

"Are you paying for this dinner?" I asked in response.

"Does that make you happy?" the Judge barked. "Rich guys like to see poor guys spend their money on them, is that it?"

"Order the oldest brandy on the menu and I'll think about it."

Taking that as an acceptance, he turned to my wife and said, "Carolyn, tell him for God's sake not to screw this up."

She leaned toward the Judge in her impeccable silk dress and took his big Texas paw in her small pearl-colored hand. Then she said, in a voice trained at Smith and aged with the money that her family had been steeped in since before the Boston tea party, "My dear, he never, never has."

I leaned back in my chair and saw my own image in the mirrored walls of the restaurant. I was tall and still thin, with a shock of graying hair and a tan, chiseled face. Even when I took off my glasses I could see the twinkle of a whitecap in the ocean blue of my eyes, and the threatening gleam on my gold bullet cufflinks. Sometimes I felt like an imposter in the well-tailored clothes Carolyn bought me—like Jimmy Stewart dressed up as Cary Grant. I was more comfortable in jeans and a flannel shirt, or the old suede jacket I used to wear into the office every day until my secretary joked that she thought my skin was suede. But Carolyn wouldn't have me pretend to be anything other than I was: the husband of one of the wealthiest women in the country. I turned back to the Judge in his cheap, rumpled suit and stained tie and wondered what he saw when he looked at me. How did it feel for him to need me, I wondered as I promised myself to be less cynical and more caring with him. I never stopped to think that there might be more to the Judge's request than that he truly needed me. I made a fatal error the moment I agreed to come back, almost screwing up the story before it had begun. I trusted someone.

But how do you screw up telling a story? Logical consistency is important. Establishing premises before you leap to conclusions is crucial. But on the whole, reconstructing events after the fact isn't all that hard unless reality butts in and makes dead files rise up and haunt again. Spooks don't die unless their files get lost. Mission summaries and conclusions don't get screwed up unless *the thing* isn't really concluded. And that was the problem the Judge got me into. He wanted a story before the thing was over.

That's my theory about where we first went wrong. Call it theory number 407 or so of the vast storehouse of theories an old man accumulates: The difference between fiction and reality is that when faced with reality you can't ever say The End.

So this, then, is the beginning.

3.

On the hot day, late in August 1989, when I came back to the agency, I put the Rolex watch that Carolyn had given me in a bureau drawer in our bedroom. Then I put on my wrist the cheap gold retirement watch the agency had given me a year before. I wound the watch and rolled the tiny gold knob on its side until the word "Tuesday" popped up in a window on the watch face. Feeling like Lazarus back from the dead, I loved to check the time and date on that retirement watch. Its very presence made me feel young again.

By the date hand on that watch, I came back to the NSA the Tuesday before the Thursday we took Tommy to the Bahamas. I start the story in that island hut because the prescient, languid words of the fat woman with the machete fit neatly into a theory of mine, let's say theory number 327: The business of intelligence is stupid. Everyone else, even fat women on islands in the ocean, knew what was going on; it was only the professionals who didn't see the massive changes in the world coming. Twenty-two thousand miles above the earth our dish-shaped geostationary Magnum and Aquacade satellites, costing more than one hundred million dollars each, eavesdropped on every communication that entered the air, and yet we couldn't see what was happening right before our faces. I think of it now as if it was a lifetime ago, even though it is really only a matter of years. Regardless of glasnost, the Soviets were still our enemy, and the public perceived them to be a powerful, worthy match for our military and our intelligence machines. In my view, Gorbachev's reforms were not much more than window dressing, the Berlin Wall stood strong and tall, and Soviet and American submarines chased each other under the seas. For those of you not involved in governing, but only in politicking, in May of that year Lithuania and Latvia announced that they were leaving the Soviet Union, and all our intelligence told us that it was merely a matter of time before the Soviet tanks rolled through their cobblestone streets and put an end to all this foolishness. But that isn't what happened. That fall Czechoslovakia returned to democracy, the Berlin Wall came down in November, and one by one the various Soviet republics decided to be free.

So when people who don't know what I do ask someone in earshot of me how the world changed so much so fast, I am tempted to say, go ask Tommy Wood. How did the Berlin Wall come down without the Soviets invading? How did the Soviet Union survive a military coup and throw out communism as if it were garbage, without a civil war? What led to the collapse of the East, the defeat of Iraq, the death of the Soviet Union, and the renewed efforts for peace in the Mideast, all so quickly and so close together? What happened in 1989 that made the world suddenly embrace freedom, democracy, human rights, and some semblance of peace with a fever that knocked the wind out of analysts all over the globe?

The answer is a love story. This love story. This love story about the stupidity of intelligence operations.

The eleven sister institutions in the United States espionage family all got fat in the last decade. The well-known sister CIA got three billion dollars last year, and its very basic information, to say nothing of its very basic purpose for being, was wrong, out of touch, and seemingly irrelevant in our changing world. The ugly sister Defense Intelligence Agency hadn't a clue that the East was about to crumple. The fat sister FBI was too busy chasing communists in Cleveland or St. Louis to notice that the real communists went out of business in Moscow. My own agency out in Fort Meade, Maryland, got so caught up in installing new laser-disk encrypted satellite telecommunications systems that we didn't bother to try to understand what we were telecommunicating. We were all stupid about intelligence. All too busy playing cops and robbers to realize that there wasn't really anything to steal.

That was the first of my theories that Tommy Wood seemed to prove—as if his very existence was to act out my fantasies to see what would happen if a man progressed from point A to point B at *x* time at *y* speed. I saw Tommy Wood as not much more than a story problem—until I saw him sweat and bleed.

His file read like a novel even before I got my hands on it. He grew up in the Midwest, he told her the first time they had dinner. Her name isn't even in that first report, she is just *her*, the *she*, the *woman*. And that is somehow fitting, as if naming her would make her less universal, less powerful, less the essence of Eve offering the forbidden fruit.

It was a small restaurant in New Haven with plastic red-and-white-checkered tablecloths and candles with glass hurricanes wrapped in plastic nets. It was the first week of May, almost four months before I came out of retirement, and the restaurant was empty of students because they were busy pretending to be studying for their final exams. Rebecca and Tommy were three-quarters through the second bottle of Chianti, and she was leaning forward toward him, her elbows on the table, her dozen bracelets twinkling in the candlelight, and her eyes riveted on him in a way that made him know that he had won. As he started to stumble over his verbs as he talked about Indiana cornfields and high school basketball, he knew—absolutely knew, he told me later—that she had fallen for him.

I've seen the video. It was masterfully done. You wouldn't even guess it was from a hidden camera. There was hardly enough light in the restaurant to focus on anything, but Bobby, whom the Judge refers to as just a techy but who has two Ph.D.s and is in line to run the NSA's R&E group, pulled it off again. What came out of the can looks like a grade B movie, full of romantic shadows and muffled conversation. She always requested tape on the first meeting. She wanted it so she could make sure they followed up on their "agreements" later.

Her eyes were aglow in the dark corner, and everything he said seemed to seep into her soul. She held her wineglass to her mouth long after she had taken a drink, and her left hand stroked a long strand of thick auburn hair as if it were a purring cat. As he talked about his senior architecture project, I'm sure he ran through a checklist in his mind: Was his apartment clean? Was his roommate in the city tonight? Had he made his bed?

As he was constructing a floor plan with his silverware, she reached out and touched his hand.

"You have calluses," she said with admiration.

"I'm a carpenter," he said. "In the middle of all this Ivy League architecture and these pompous professors, that's what keeps me sane—and pays the rent. You know, I really like to build things."

"I like that," she said softly, pretending she didn't know. Then she laughed a little too loud, showing that she was a touch more drunk than she reported she was. "My family would like that," she blurted out, and then looked embarrassed, as if she was worried she had scared him off, but Tommy Wood took her hand across the smoky candle flame and said, "You know, you are one beautiful woman."

She just smiled in response, leaving her mouth open and breathing in his very soul.

"I'd like to take you to Indiana," he said suddenly. "I'd like to show you where I grew up. The corn. The hogs. Big, flat fields that just go on and on, you know. That just go as far as you can see."

"I'd like that," she whispered, her fingers touching his palm.

"I'm thinking about going back to visit in August," he said quickly, but then a look passed over his face as if he had just realized that he was inviting a woman he had barely met to go to Indiana with him sometime months later. There was nothing on her face that showed any surprise, or any interest, but as soon as I heard his suggestion I wrote one line in my notes that still haunts me. "He's the actor," I wrote, meaning that Tommy was not sitting there passively being recruited by our agent, but rather, he was planning on taking her to Indiana. From the very beginning we underestimated him.

"The last weekend," he continued, talking faster now, as if he were paddling a boat against the current. "We could make it a road trip."

"Sorry," she said wistfully, her eyelids slowly closing as she continued to rub the center of his palm. "But I have plans."

He smiled at her and took her hands in his, saying, "Now what could be more important than driving across the country to Indiana with some guy you just met?"

She laughed. He rubbed the bridge of his nose with one finger, without letting go of her captured hands.

"Family reunion," she replied, exhaling in a way that made him remember her lips moving, but not the words for a long, long time. "First week in August I have to go to a family reunion."

"Shame," he whispered. "A real shame."

"I'll never," she said, leaning across the table so far that their foreheads almost touched, "never live it down."

It was a masterful performance by a true professional. For the She, the Her, the Eve, the woman, sultry, tempting, with a rogue feline complexity and a flame of deep red hair, worked for us. She was, as we say, leaving behind our personal identities, National Security Agency. She was agent Rebecca Hood Townsend. Code name Hot Blue Wax.

One could argue, ladies and gentlemen who read this little document, that at that moment the first domino was pushed that led to regimes tumbling, the Iron Curtain crumbling, and the graffitied German Wall succumbing to the laughter of a generation of people who just didn't see the purpose of it all. Tommy and Rebecca were the straw that broke the camel's back. These two lovers inadvertently lit a fuse that has probably cost half of us spies our jobs and all of us our security. Domino, straw, fuse, they were beyond mixed metaphors and into the realm of the metaphysics of causal relationships that I can contemplate only after many mixed drinks. This little love story answers the big question of our time, and thus must bear this "YOUR EYES ONLY, TOP SECRET UMBRA/HANDLE VIA COMINT CHANNELS ONLY" stamp.

The story of these two lovers explains—I believe brashly and sincerely—why the cold war ended so quickly and mysteriously. Why Gorbachev folded when he could have fought. Why country after country became more democratic, more capitalist, and more free within a few short months.

It wasn't something in the air or in the water. It wasn't something beamed down from a satellite in space. It wasn't a historical necessity following some unknown but well-documented pattern. It wasn't the Reagan buildup of nuclear forces or the failure of the Soviet economy. Only Hallmark cards would dare to print the truth. The truth that love and laughter conquer mistrust and suspicion every time.

4.

WHEN I SAW their files later, listened to the mountains of tape, and watched the clandestine video until I could mimic their every move, I saw the spark that set the whole thing aflame. The project was doomed from the beginning because she lost control. The project was certain to explode because Rebecca Hood Townsend, under her smooth-acting, trained double takes and feigned interest, was truly in love. She might not have known it at that first dinner, and Thomas Joseph Wood was too busy concentrating on his conquest to notice, but she was a goner. And why not? She was a cynical federal agent who had probably lost all sense of reality, and he was a young, funny, honest, and good-looking man. She was told to pretend to fall in love with him, and she did just that. But the pretending became the reality. The files do not show, and we never knew, when Rebecca told Tommy that she was a recruiter for the

NSA. But when she stopped pretending, she obviously told him that she had been assigned to recruit him by making him fall in love with her, and that the love became paramount, not the recruiting.

What is amazing to me is that no one at HQ saw it sooner, particularly her section chief, the assistant deputy director of the Office of Administration, John X. But John X got his own emotions in the way. Like a dozen other men, John X was in love with her, or at least his watered-down vision of her, and that muddied his judgment. In retrospect it seems so clear. She didn't pretend to fall in love with him, any more than she pretended to be one of our own agents. She was ours and she did fall in love—and she was not ours and she was pretending to be in love—all at the same time.

The setup was comic in its stupidity. Many of her superiors had been nervous about her, so she was brought out of our asset inventory in Manhattan when she was only twenty and set up at our old back yard at Yale as a junior VP in an import-export shop. Later I discovered that the import-export shop did business, by pure coincidence, with the "Big C" Consolidated Shipping line, which my wife owns, but at the time HQ just wanted her close at hand. She had been recruited through our northeastern recruiting office behind the blank solid wood door of Room 406 in the old McCormack Post Office Building in Boston.

At first we thought we could watch her better there, at our old college stamping ground. But after a year or two her business at the import-export shop was virtually forgotten. Our business took over. Her mission was to assist in recruitment and to keep an eye on a couple of professors in mechanical engineering and physics who were doing work on compression in fiber optic telecommunications systems and were on the NSA's scientific advisory board—which was a way in which we plumbed academe for ideas without inviting them into the front door of Fort Meade. The boys up the line in the organization asked the right question for once: What was in it for her? The salary wasn't great. She was too good-looking. Too smart. Too young. Her background, or at least what we knew about it from the full vetting, was too much a blank.

But she was damn good. She recruited some of our best, and seemed to have fun along the way. She enjoyed the role of prostitute for the cause. Took it up as if she were part of the French underground, doing what she had to do for some movie-star revolutionary hiding out until it was safe to come back to town. Her methods were out of the movies and her expenses were way out of line, but several promising young agents who were promoted fast remember some very pleasant evenings in New Haven with Rebecca.

She may have started out as the company's whore, but as the years passed and she kept her good looks and the promotions of her catches came fast and furious, she had so much dope on her pimps that she became the highest-paid asset in her division. She damn well did what she wanted to do because she had delivered—delivered the very men who now ran the agency. She was rewarded not just with money but with information. As her target catches got bigger and more important, her "need to know" increased. She received the coveted red card: a color-coded, computer-striped plastic-laminated security badge with an attractive full-frontal photograph that got her into virtually every part of the giant spy city at Fort Meade. The more she succeeded, the more codes to cipher-locked doors she retained. She was given virtually complete access by John X, because she wasn't some Ivy League snob, but an agent who had worked her way up from the bottom and proved her worth. It was a story the Texas general turned judge turned dernza just loved.

Auburn hair. Green eyes. A lilac tattoo on her thin left ankle. Five foot seven. One hundred and twelve pounds. Thirty-four years old. (All Connecticut data show twenty-four years old.) Family in Philadelphia. Her home address in the file was a house in Philadelphia that her father had sold three years earlier. But we never were good at updating our records. Father doctor: general practitioner who had retired early. Father German national who came over before the war. Mother: German national with nurse's degree, but not employed out of the house. Siblings: five, four male, one female; she was the middle child. Brothers Erik, Jan, Joseph, Fritz; little sister Margert was at Brown, studying comparative literature. Languages French, German, Spanish. PIN number 97302. File code name Hot Blue Wax.

Her file was perfectly normal, except that it had been reconstructed twice, I noticed the day it was delivered to my office for my review. Two times bright young hotshots from Yale, both good-government types who stayed for a while and then went on to State, had had her file expunged and redone. I doubted very much they had spilled coffee on the carboned pages. Hot Blue Wax had some good connections.

5.

WHEN I AM TRAPPED in some characterless white-walled dentist's office, waiting forever to see my white-suited friend who is doing battle against my age and decades of pipe smoking, and I ruffle through a *Boy's Life* because that's all there is to read, I imagine Tommy Wood growing up. Because Tommy Wood's life is a small slice of American pie. Orphaned by a teenage mother, he was adopted through a Lutheran church agency. His adoptive father was an insurance salesman and volunteer fireman who was killed trying to save a neighbor's barn. His adoptive mother was a schoolteacher who died of breast cancer when he was in college. Born and raised in the little town of Ossian, Indiana, he won a spelling bee in sixth grade and got his name in the local paper. His high school yearbook shows he ran track and wrestled in high school, did well in math, was a ribbon-winning 4-H marksman, worked as a carpenter every summer, was runner-up in a triathlon. He went to Indiana University, where he majored in math and took some of the very logic courses that Herb Yardley began in the thirties when he taught there, but Tommy spent the second semester of his junior year in Munich, studying architecture, and did very well. Then, by some quirk of fate or luck or geographic allotment by the admissions office, he ended up at the Yale School of Architecture. His well-insured insurance-salesman father had left him enough money that he could attend, so long as he was careful with it and had a part-time job.

Once there he was a decent student, the file shows, but uninspired. He was a little too earthy for the rarefied art history world of Yale. His work was derivative without being historical, and the one professor's critique that made it into the file said, "This obsession with blending into the environment, qua late Wright, is a seventies preoccupation that I wish you would get over. We've got urban problems that cannot be addressed by low-slung earth-covered caves littered with architectural gymnastics. The cantilever is not freedom—order is freedom."

But even after that diatribe he still got a B.

According to Rebecca's first report in his file, a "family friend" who had known Tommy's parents suggested to Rebecca that she show him around New Haven when he arrived at Yale. She never bothered to call him until "word got around" to Rebecca that Tommy Wood was "a casual rebel without a cause," and while he was a small fish compared with her usual targeted recruits, she had seen a request for architects by the L Organization, the Office of Installations and Logistics, so she requested permission to go after him. "Why bother?" John X had noted in the file that he asked Rebecca. "I don't think he's a likely prospect for L. Don't they just want engineers? So why him?"

"Number one: Humor me. Number two: Trust me. Number three: Because I'm bored," she had responded. "And I think he's not such a bad prospect." John X approved it reluctantly, noting to his assistant that he wasn't used to Rebecca's actually wanting to go after someone. Lately, John X mumbled, it was like pulling teeth to get Rebecca to do any work.

Indiana has always had a special place in the hearts of NSA recruiters, since it was the home of the father of American code breaking, Herbert Osborne Yardley, who grew up right where the small Eel River meets the wide White River near the town of Freedom, in southwestern Indiana, and later taught at Indiana University. But Tommy grew up in the north, about equidistant from Garrett, Indiana, the birthplace of the modern-day father of the NSA, the longest-running deputy dernza, Louis William Tordella, and Fort Wayne, Indiana, home of the first director of the NSA, Major General Ralph Julian Canine.

He had it all. A Hoosier. A Yalie. Both parents dead. An only child. Great physical shape. Voted in Republican primaries. Needless to say, regardless of what John X thought, if Rebecca wanted him, the organization had an immediate interest. We have—or should I say had?—projects all over the globe, designed and built by our L Organization, that needed his innate sense of camouflage. The L Organization's supervising architects and engineers had never had a Yalie, but they knew they could buy some brownie points upstairs with their Ivy League bosses if they landed one, and this one sounded like one they could stomach. No postmodern naïve wimp, they reported after seeing the student projects Rebecca brought them. This guy was a carpenter, not a showman. He'd fit right in.

But Rebecca had a different idea. She didn't know it when she was assigned to get him, and I'm not sure when she got the idea, but Tommy Wood became her ticket out of the organization at the same time we thought she was trying to sell him a ticket to get in.

The first thing to note is that he was very good-looking. Tommy's solid, midwestern charm was often overlooked in the analysis—probably because he overlooked it himself. He didn't consider himself good-looking. He wore plain clothes, and, unlike most professional art and architecture people, he never made what he wore a fashion statement. They were just jeans, rumpled khakis, a beat-up leather belt with a heavy brass buckle an artist friend had made for him, tennis shoes that had never seen a tennis court, and an assortment of old white work shirts that made him always look as though he had a farmer's tan.

Six weeks after meeting Tommy, Rebecca took him to Nantucket, where she had gone with many of her catches. He read a beat-up paperback copy of *Moby Dick* out loud on the nearly empty ferry over to the island, and she helped him unbutton his shirt in the hot afternoon sun. The photographs show her running her hands down his shoulders and V-shaped torso, each finger tracing the taut curves of his muscular workingman's back. Then she pressed her mouth to his shoulder blade and licked the L-curve of the bone beneath the skin.

Note: She did not kiss his back, but licked it. Attention to detail is important. If you look closely at the photograph, taken by the men John X assigned to follow them, you can see her tongue pressed against him, tasting the salt of his sweat as he read aloud from the rail of the ship. You see the book in his hand, raised so that he can see it, and his mouth open wide, declaiming some rushing Melvillian sentence.

Tommy was a romantic. He drew pictures of castles on paper napkins at taverns on the island, which our men dutifully collected after he left. Our men reported watching through binoculars as he sang to her on the beach and raked his large hands through her long, wild hair. They talked late into the night, the French doors of their hotel room thrown open to the sea breeze and to a boom microphone lowered from the room above.

My theory number 198: God made most people fall asleep right after making love so they wouldn't say stupid things. For example, the first audio tape in the file, recorded in Nantucket, captures how absurd reality sounds.

"Becky," he said hoarsely as he kicked the sweat-wet sheets off them and she rolled into his arms. "I love you."

"You do," she said, not asked. "I never would have guessed. I thought you treated every gal who came your way like this."

"I *love* you," he repeated sleepily. "But I don't *know* you. You're so damn secretive."

"It's part of my allure," she said, sounding younger than she did when she was in a briefing session at HQ. "If you knew me better you wouldn't fawn all over me like a damn teenager."

"I do not fawn," he said, laughing.

You can hear them kissing then, over the soft sound of the long drapes sweeping across the floor as the night breeze buffeted the lace in and out of the room.

"I want to meet your family," he suggested abruptly.

"Why?" she asked, a little too quickly.

"Because I want to know where you come from. Who your people are. How you grew up. I want to see embarrassing pictures of you as a kid with braces and bell-bottom pants."

"I never had braces."

"You see," he said, "that's my point. I don't know you. I don't know if you had braces or acne or a dog when you were growing up. I don't know who your best friend was. I don't know what your favorite Saturday-morning cartoon was. I spend all this time with you—hell, I'm ready to marry you—and I don't know how many brothers and sisters you have. I know your dad's a doctor who has retired to be a farmer, but I don't know if he farms corn or catfish. You've got all kinds of things, all kinds of clothes, and I can't figure out what it is you really do for a living."

He talked on for another minute, but listening to the tape you hear those words "I'm ready to marry you" hang in the air while he went on talking. The drapes stopped their noisy swoosh right as he said those five simple words, as if all the air had been sucked out of the room. Rebecca didn't make a sound. That invisible barrier that exists in all dating relationships was broken, months earlier than it should have been, and there was no going back. He had said the words "marry you."

What was she thinking? She had been brought down to HQ just the week before and told that she should turn Tommy over to another operative if she was going to get involved with him—as if she hadn't gotten involved already, I note for the cynical and for the record—and she had told them to shove it, that she had delivered before and if she wanted to take a little bit longer with this one then she damn well would. He wasn't going to spoil, she told them. He'd still be there when she was ready to hand him over. And then she added to her section chief: "Just as you were, John."

The conference room went silent. "The point here," John X argued, "is that this Mr. Wood is taking up all of your time and nothing else is getting done. We haven't had any reports about your contacts in artificial intelligence, physics, or anthropology. What have you been doing? The year is only half over and you've used up all of your vacation time. This can't keep going. Something has to give."

"That something is you," Rebecca offered. "I've asked for more time. Give me more time to get Tommy in the door. He's worth the extra time."

Then her section chief and former lover John X, who was also a Rebecca find, cleared his throat and gave her the extra time she wanted. The Judge had already approved it, he noted. His look showed a certain disgust at the Judge's seeming tolerance for Rebecca's antics, but then he ran a hand over his face and gathered up every last ounce of professionalism he had left. He asked her how Tommy was taking the pitch. She said fine, Tommy seemed interested in helping his government. Tommy talked about it all the time, she said. He'd probably walk in and volunteer for no pay.

Theory number 435: The only good liars are the ones who don't think they are good, because confidence leads to arrogance, which leads to exaggeration. Rebecca was too confident.

As soon as Rebecca left the meeting, planting kisses on the cheeks of half the men in the room, Bobby the techy stopped John X in the hall and told him that he had accidentally taped an entire three-hour conversation between Rebecca and Tommy when Rebecca had borrowed a company car for a drive up to New Hampshire. According to Bobby Rickhouse, during the entire drive there and back there had been not a single positive mention of the organization.

"Accidentally taped?" John X asked, his Diet Coke can shaking in his hand. Taping one of your own agents' conversations without his or her knowledge was something that clearly violated agency procedure unless it was approved by the Judge or the deputy dernza, Paul White.

"We had a bug in the car tuned to a recorder hidden in the trunk," Bobby explained loudly, completely unaware of the implication of what he was saying. "It was a mistake. We didn't know it was there, she didn't know it was there. The car's manifest said the bug had been taken out."

"Did she check the manifest?"

"Of course," Bobby said, playing with a coaster on the long conference-room table. "She's good. She always wants to know who had the car last and what they did with it. To tell you the truth, it was a miniature that I worked out at home and was testing out on the car when I checked it out. I've been having problems with the microphone transmitter, you know. It tends to go out if you bump the mike, so I checked it out on myself and, well, I just forgot."

The recently chided section chief turned gray, left the room, and listened to the tape-recorded surveillance on one of his own.

"When can we go visit your family farm?" Tommy asked over the whine of the car's engine. "I really do want to meet your folks. You know, as an only child I always wanted to have a big family. Lots of brothers and sisters, like you have. What was—is—it like to have so many brothers and sisters? Loud, crazy dinners? Pillow fights every night?"

"Not so idyllic," she answered, her voice far off, as if she was thinking of something else. "Fighting for your parents' attention. Always feeling like no one paid as much attention to you as they did to your brothers or sisters. Getting beat up. Losing games because you were smaller and younger. Doing incredibly stupid things because you were trying to be cool like your older brothers and sisters. It's not all roses, you know."

"I still think I'd like to be part of a big family."

"Then join the NSA," she said with a laugh.

"Right." He laughed. "I think one spook per family is enough. And believe me, after what you've told me about the place, I wouldn't touch it. I'd rather spend all my time touching you."

"That's my boy," she said with a sudden southern drawl. "That's why I love you. You wouldn't fit into that organization, with all its stuffed shirts, if you faked it. You would not believe some of these guys. They actually think that what they do is important—like, really important. As if the future of the world hangs in the balance with each of their decisions."

"Your boss sounds like the worst," Tommy said. "John X? What kind of name is that? His last name must be really embarrassing."

"He's embarrassing," Rebecca joked. "He's a security freak. He doesn't want everyone to know his last name. He's one of those paranoid Vietnam vets—and a perfect example of why you wouldn't fit in, my boy."

"Frankly, Scarlett, I don't give a damn," Tommy said. "Never join a club that's not already in your golf bag."

"Huh?" she asked.

"Hoosier humor," he replied, kissing her again. "Just made it up."

"Stick to architecture," she said. "Forget about comedy. I think your talent, Mr. Wood, is in building big houses for big families. Lots of bedrooms."

"With lots of beds?" he asked.

"Only if we can try them all out."

With a dispatch that our organization can muster only when intra-agency backstabbing and posturing is involved, Tommy's phone and Rebecca's phone were both tapped immediately. John X, in a fit of jealousy, simply signed the deputy dernza's name to the request sheet that was faxed to London just for show, asking our English chums to tap the phone for us, since we are not allowed to tap phones within the United States. The NSA was not legally allowed to intercept domestic telephone calls without a warrant, so John X did what section chiefs had done for years before him: He called his English counterpart at England's counterpart to the NSA, the Government Communications Headquarters, or GCHQ, and asked him, pursuant to a secret treaty known only by its initials, UKUSA, and his forgery of Paul's signature, to intercept the phone calls made by Tommy or Rebecca and forward all interceptions to him as quickly as possible. No one in London questioned the legitimacy of the order; they just routed the tapped calls back to John X. Because the recordings were not encrypted in any way, they were easy to spot and transfer.

That night, listening in on her phone, John X—jealous? envious? scared she'd turn on him?—heard her ask Tommy to go with her to Nantucket. The next morning, without consulting anyone, John X ordered that they be followed by agents hired by the Federal Protective Service and that every conversation they had be recorded. Even though it was clearly illegal, but still accepted practice, to list the names of American citizens, he alerted G Group to put their names in the watch lists for the computers and listeners that searched for key words in the intercepted communications that involved areas other than the Soviet Union and the Pacific communist countries.

"Did you," Rebecca asked softly, her taped voice barely audible over the slow whisk of the curtains swinging in the Nantucket breeze, "did you just ask me to marry you?"

"I don't know," he said after a long pause.

"Because," she went on slowly, each cool word clinking into the next like small ice cubes in iced tea, "if you didn't, I mean, if you did not ask, then I want to ask you."

"Ask me what?" he whispered, in warmer, stronger tones.

"I want you to ask me to marry you." She paused, stretching the tension. "Now."

"Now?" he asked.

"Now."

"Rebecca," Tommy Wood of Indiana said, his voice strong and warm with nearing slumber, "will you marry me?"

I'm sure that the counterintelligence agents in the room above, who were holding the boom mike and listening through their big, boxy earphones to the panting and irregular breathing that led up to this conversation, were holding their breaths at this point, not quite believing what they had heard. They had expected clandestine trading of top-secret information, and what they got was a marriage proposal. All they knew was what John X had told them, that whoever this broad was she was suspected of being a double agent who was messing around with a guy who was faking being a new recruit. They noted that John X's story seemed preposterous.

Their report back to John X at HQ was short and to the point. Nothing to worry about. The woman is genuinely in love. A handwritten postscript said, "Per your request, we exchanged his leather belt with the exact match you gave us."

But, of course, that was exactly what everyone should have been worrying about. Only John X was worried that they were in love, and he was worried for reasons that had absolutely nothing to do with national security.

"Yes," Rebecca Townsend answered. "Yes, Tommy. I'll marry you."

Then, according to the report, the most amazing thing happened. Agent Hot Blue Wax acted like a normal human being. She cried, she laughed, she made love all night long.

6.

THERE ARE A MILLION THEORIES about why she did it. Most depend on the angle you take. Did she coerce him into asking her to marry him? Or did he coerce her in some subtle fashion? Who was the motivating actor here, as we say in the trade. How did she know he'd ask her? Why did she risk saying yes? How early on did she plan this? Who planned it for her? Could it have been any guy who just happened to come along at the right time?

You can probably guess my theory. For those of you who aren't trained in the subtle arts of intelligence gathering, play my job for just a moment. Imagine that you are me. Think about what you know about me, even though I haven't really explained myself at all. Think about what you know about me so that you can guess my conclusion. You know I'm an old romantic who is in love with his wife. You know that I believe in loyalty, friendship, patriotism, but that I believe people do things for reasons that cannot easily be explained on some bureaucrat's form. I enjoy good food, good drink, good books, and an occasional good pipe. All of those attributes make me old-fashioned, yet I work with an annoying computer terminal in my office and have a perfect memory for the curve of a woman's leg.

You know enough about me to know that I think she simply fell in love.

My theory is premised on that photograph of her licking his back. Besides the obvious animal attraction, she was acting as though she was in love even when she didn't have to. Rebecca was leading the life of a high-class intellectual prostitute who was given the assignment of corrupting a straight midwestern farm boy, who, instead of being corrupted by her, lifted her out of her corruption. He was honest. He was strong. He was one-dimensional in a way that is attractive in architects, artists, and Prince Charmings who come unexpectedly to rescue you from a confusing situation. That is why I think she did it.

The answer she gave to HQ was even simpler. "John," she said on a recorded phone call from Nantucket, "I'm going to marry him. I know you will find this amazingly funny, but I've decided I want to have kids."

"So go to the sperm bank. You don't have to marry the kid," John X sneered.

"He's not a kid and—"

"Does he know how old you are?"

"Oh damn you," she screamed in a most unprofessional way to her boss. "What does that have to do with it? So what if the old biological clock is about to wind down? So what if I decide I don't want to miss out on whatever it is that comes over people when they have children?"

"In other words," John X said, "he doesn't know."

"Lighten up, John. It doesn't mean anything to the organization. I'm expendable to you—but I'm not to him."

"You," John X said, too loud and too fast, as if for a moment he forgot the call was taped, "are *not* expendable. He *is* expendable."

"I think you're jealous."

"Jealous!" John X shouted into the phone. "Jealous of a kid cowboy and a—a—a prostitute? In 'Nam, honey we'd—I mean, what do I have—"

"That's my point," Rebecca said with stiletto words. "I'm not some whore in Saigon, like you want to believe. I'm not yours. I'm not the organization's. I'm mine. Only mine. Send my pension check to my parents' address in Florida. I'll be back in a month for separation interviews and debriefing."

"Becky," John X pleaded, "let's not get excited. Once a year for ten years you've threatened to quit. More money, more time, less work, now it's for some guy you want to have kids with. Let's not go through this all again. I've talked to the Judge. Against my advice he said you can have anything you want. You'll go on disability for a year. Have a kid. See how you like it. You can stay in New Haven. We'll get your cowboy a job designing safe houses and—"

"He's not working for you, and I'm not working for you. I've just had it. I want to have a life. I'm tired of talking college boys into joining the ranks. Get a new recruiter. Hell, get a new life yourself, John. The party's over. The war's over. Vietnam's over. We're over. Try to save your own marriage before it's over. Stop living in the past and get on with it."

Then she hung up.

John X punched another line on his gray phone, which was only for classified conversations, and called Bobby Rickhouse in the intercept-equipment division of the Office of Research and Engineering, which was known simply as R Group, probably forgetting that the phone and not the line was tapped. "Bobby—let's go with your new toy. He's got—our suspect has the new belt on. The project's a go. Make sure there is no trace, Bobby," he said. "This is between you and me. No records. No clearance. You get promoted, I get the tapes."

"You got a deal," Bobby agreed, with a faint whistle. "I'm proud of the damn thing. Like I told you, I built it myself—mostly at home. State of the art. You've got to have a microscope to see the wiring in the thing. Maybe I should get overtime? Prove to my wife that all the money in that home workshop was worth it?"

"Don't push your luck," John X said. "It doesn't work that well yet."

Theory number 293: It's all in how you handle it. The organization had handled her poorly. Fourteen years before, when she was twenty, she had dropped out of Vassar and showed up at the organization's front door asking for a job. Most of us in management are transfers from other intelligence outfits, and I doubt that one out of ten of us even knew the organization existed when we were twenty. But she had done her homework. Her recruiter had been attracted to her, allegedly because of her proficiency in several languages and interest in computer science. When she came through our northeast office in Boston, where she had literally walked in and asked for a job, she got good references, and then did exceptionally well on the PQT, the Professional Qualification Test.

The Bureau was too law-enforcement and bureaucratic, she said in her first interview. And Langley, she said, was too crippled by congressional restraints and a lack of credibility. Military intelligence was all big guns and boot camp. She wanted to be someplace where she could make a difference. Where good, honest government did not conflict with intelligence gathering. She liked telecommunications. She liked breaking codes. She liked figuring out how to move information to where it needed to be. SIGINT was her bag—she loved the sight of a Cray supercomputer, she said. Just give her a keyboard and let her loose. She wanted to work for the president of the United States of America. She wanted us; how could we not want her?

Her recruiter was a new man from the South, brought in during the first months of the Georgia debacle to review the organization's operations. He was a friend of the Judge's, but this was years before the

Judge was brought into the organization. But the coincidence is interesting and worth noting. The southerners all knew each other.

This man from Georgia wrote "Yes!" and "This is the type we want!" next to these quotes in her transcript and recommended that "this young woman is the type of recruit we should be looking for. Let the FBI have the cops and let the CIA have the neurotic accountants. The NSA needs people who are clever, polished, yet willing to buck the system. We don't just need more engineers. This is no yes man." Then in the column where suggested assignments were listed he wrote, and I can still hear his small-town southern politician's drawl, "Hell, put her in recruitment so she can get more like her."

He gave her the highest rating possible and wrote a letter directly to the upstairs of the old Executive Office Building when the Pentagon's Defense Investigative Service seemed to be moving too slowly on her Special Background Investigation, and, like magic, Rebecca Townsend became an employee of the National Security Agency without enough of a check, I now see in retrospect, to justify even a secret clearance, let alone enough to send her into daily contact with top-secret sensitive information. Why so easy? Why so quick? My guess is that Rebecca charmed this southern lawyer with round glasses and a rodent for a wife the same way she recruited lanky boys from Yale when we started to train our own—she sneaked up on them and told them what they wanted to hear. She took the southerner and an SBI officer to Philadelphia to meet her parents, and they came back with reports of patriotism and psychological well-being that made Beaver Cleaver look like a communist. Her father was a respected doctor in the German community in Philadelphia. He and his wife, a nurse who escaped Nazi Germany with him immediately before the war, had few hobbies, except traveling. They had not visited any Eastern bloc or Southeast Asian communist countries and had been citizens since 1949. After changing their lives dramatically in midcourse, they craved, according to the southerner's report, domesticity and normalcy. Their children were all college-educated. The two oldest boys had served in Vietnam. They reported no close relatives who survived World War II. They had no close friends, but everyone interviewed spoke admiringly of their strong, good-looking family. Their dream was to retire to a farm in western Pennsylvania where they could "grow things."

Rebecca passed the battery of psychological tests with flying colors, and when the day came for her lie-detector test she was seen laughing on her way into FANX III, one of our annex offices near the Baltimore airport, while her colleagues who were waiting for clearance sweated out every day. The chief of polygraphy helped attach the electrodes to her long, thin fingers, then strapped the thick black belts tightly around her chest to measure breathing. The tester wrapped the heavy blood-pressure cuff around her arm and questioned her for nearly two hours while the chief disappeared down the hall, but then decided to stop and watch some of her interview from behind the one-way glass in the room. When questioned years later, he said that he just had a feeling he should watch the tiny needles bounce along on the graph-paper printer that was in the room behind the glass, but my guess is that he frequently watched the tests of attractive young women. I guess that there was something stirring about watching this athletic, red-headed twenty-year-old strapped down and asked embarrassing personal questions.

Thirty pages into the report on the test she was asked, "Have you ever had a heterosexual experience as an adult?"

"Regardless of the relevancy to the position I am applying for," she said, the tension line only slightly elevated, but still straight and true, "the answer is yes."

"Would you categorize those experiences as frequent or infrequent?"

"I would categorize those experiences," she said, with a knowing voice as polished as marble, "as not frequent enough."

"Have you ever had a homosexual experience as an adult?" the tester asked, reading from a script.

"No," she answered without a flinch. "Nor as a child—or doesn't that count?"

"Have you ever had a sexual experience with a member of your immediate family?"

"No," she answered, again without hesitation or nervousness. She told the tester that she had four brothers and one sister, that she had never been blackmailed, that she had never worked for any foreign government, and that her favorite color was red without the slightest indication of ever lying.

"How long do you intend to work for the NSA?"

"As long as they will have me—but I do intend to have a family . . . children."

"How many?" the questioner asked, veering from the script.

"Now, how do you answer that question truthfully?" she responded in good humor. "I don't even have a father in mind yet for these prospective children, so it's a little hard to tell you how many I plan on having."

"So you have no plan on how many children you wish to have?" the dry, bureaucratic voice asked in all seriousness, unaware of the question's absurdity.

"No," she said with a laugh, which probably ended with the pursed-lipped smile that I later learned to recognize. "You could say I have no plan."

"No plan . . ." The questioner's voice drones on as you can hear him turning the pages of his list of questions.

"Yes," she said. "No plan."

The only blemish on Rebecca's amazing record was that she seemed to show up at the wrong place at the wrong time. When the Heilbrun affair happened, there was Rebecca: one of the few people who had access to the lost information. When we lost our best contact recruiter in Afghanistan, Rebecca was the courier for the information the Soviets eventually got through one of their agents. She was never formally investigated, because she never appeared to be in the wrong. Just coincidence. Just at the wrong place at the wrong time. A dozen men covered for her. A dozen men were promoted, like her section chief, John X, for the good work they did together.

Rebecca seemed always to be the exception to the restriction that all intelligence organizations live by—the need to know. She was always being brought into projects at a higher level, with more access than she really needed to get her mission accomplished. More than once she was the exception to the elaborate information classification systems we have put in place, always, at some higher-up's order, finding a way into compartmentalized information that she normally would not be allowed access to.

Nothing could ever be traced to Rebecca, and her work was solid. In retrospect, maybe her work was too good. Three years in New Haven. Two in Cambridge. Four in Manhattan and then five more in New Haven. While a couple of old guys were suspicious of this successful upstart, her new recruits raised her salary every year and gave her a furnished house and an expense account with virtually no questions asked. She brought in eleven professors in her last six years. She was able to make two shippers and three import-export businesses very friendly to us, with a little help from the IRS. She ran three smuggling operations to bring political prisoners from the East, and landed the Peruvian chief of staff's son with help from the DEA.

And in walks Tommy Wood. Architect. Recruit. The future father of her children. A man with a miniature microphone hidden in his belt buckle.

"Tommy," she said, in a voice like a smooth Merlot as she lay in his arms in the house the agency got her on the coast of Connecticut. They had just returned from a Fourth of July party, and the sound of fireworks was still ringing in their ears. "You're not in love with me for my money, are you?"

"Money?" he answered, his voice amazingly clear for a miniature microphone and broadcasting source. Bobby the techy's work was ingenious but unreliable. "What money? I thought you spent it all on this thing you call a cottage, or on that French coffee you drink. I thought you were broke."

"No, really," she said.

"No, really," he repeated. "I am really not in love with you for your money. Your money, or at least your things, scare me. You own so many things. So many knickknacks from around the globe. Everything about you is in quantity. Lots of family. Lots of clothes. Lots of furniture. Lots of secrets—one of which, I think I'm about to find out, is that you have lots of money."

He paused. When she didn't say anything, he went on. "That is all so totally different from me. I mean, I've got some clothes, some books, a drafting table made of plywood, and a ten-year-old Jeep. You've got a dozen rooms here full of stuff. Honey, I love you in spite of all your things."

"Let's get rid of them then," she suggested excitedly. "Let's sell it all. Give it away. Anything. Let's just leave it behind and move to the country. Let's move to Pennsylvania—back to my folks' farm."

"Wait a minute. What about my career, my potential career down there in the big city? Manhattan, here I come."

"Philadelphia," she continued, as if she didn't hear him. "It'd be a great place to be an architect. The farm's just—not far from Philly. We'll get a place in between. We'll get two places. You can build a house on the farm and we'll have a condo in the city. I've got two brothers in the city. It's a great place."

Her voice rises and falls on the tape in a near-hysterical cadence that I had never heard her use. She was convinced on a bottle of wine that this was a brilliant idea.

"But what about your job?" Tommy, the practical midwesterner, asked. "What about the job that pays for all of this luxury? What about your career? The career you are supposed to be recruiting me into? Look, we've talked about this until we're blue in the face, and you know I want you to quit working for the government. I just can't picture living with a spy, even if all you do is recruit new spies. You know how much I distrust—is that the right word?—the whole concept of working for some secret spook network, but can you really just quit on them? I mean, is that how it works? You know, I don't see you as a housewife."

"I'm tired of it," she responded, probably pouting. "I may just damn well be a housewife for a while. Or paint. I want to paint giant landscapes. Paintings so big that they almost look life-size. Landscapes so big you can just walk into them. And we can do it. I have some savings we could live on."

"Money," he said. "I knew you were hiding something. Everything about you tells me you're hiding something. It's like peeling an onion, always a new layer. A big ol' Indiana onion. And the whole thing, the whole process, makes me want to cry when I'm peeling your secrets away."

"Hey!" she shouted. "I work for an intelligence agency. Of course I act like I'm hiding something. It goes with the territory."

"And so does hidden money," Tommy said, over the sound of her laughter. "What have you got, a secret Swiss bank account?"

She had $104,000 in her pension fund and $72,000 in the stock market. For fourteen years she had lived on the organization's expense account and invested most of her salary. She must have told Tommy about the cash she had hidden, although we don't have that on tape. But I am somehow sure that he did not marry her for her money. When he asked her to marry him and move to Pennsylvania he probably guessed she had some money, but nothing like the $507,000 she had in cash in a safe deposit box at the Bundt family bank's Manhattan branch.

The dream house may be the smoking gun. The dream house may have been part of his motivation. What young architect without a job, fresh out of school and brimming with ideas, wouldn't marry an older, beautiful, wealthy woman who wanted to have his children and build his first house? The real estate market was bad and no one was hiring new architects. She was his ticket out of uncertainty, just as he was hers.

That summer, he worked late into the night on the house plans. She stayed in his small apartment near campus, reading sophisticated computer manuals while he bent over his drafting table, his face getting closer to the big scraps of paper as each night went on. Later Tommy told me that Rebecca had said that if she was going to quit her job and go back out into the job market she had better fine-tune her computer design and programming skills, so she read while he drew, both of them scribbling notes to themselves.

"Becky"—he had begun calling her that as he dreamed of their future together, cutting her name short as their summer days grew long—"I know it is not only silly but sacrilegious to design a house before you've found the place for it, but that picture that you have of you and your mom on the hill at the farm seems to capture what I'm looking for. Just for argument's sake, let's think about a house on that hill. See how the light plays on the trees—that must be the west, this side the east, and up and down the hill north and south."

"Yes," she whispered, and then repeated the word loudly so it said so much more. "Yes."

That was where he set the house, slung out low and long from the top of a Pennsylvania hill that sloped down to a stream that he had never seen.

"You know," he said clearly through the miniature microphone, "this would be a lot easier if I'd seen this place. Why don't we go visit? What's the big deal about visiting your family? Did they disown you when they found out that you were a spy?"

"I'm not a spy."

"Okay," he said. "My mistake. You just talk people into being spies."

"I talk people into using their engineering skills, their computer designing skills, their technical skills into working for the United States Government. Is that so bad?"

"No," Tommy answered. "Look, I don't want to fight about it. I just want to know what I'm getting myself into. Is it the Addams family or the Cleaver family? That's all I want to know. What about that family reunion you mentioned a long time ago? Whatever happened to that? Huh?"

"Family reunion?" she asked quietly, her voice trailing off as if she had just walked from the room.

"Or was that all just part of the act?" he said. "You couldn't go to

Indiana with me that weekend in August because you had to go to a family reunion, remember?"

"No," she mumbled, and then cleared her throat. "I don't remember telling you that."

"I wish," he said, his voice growing louder as the sound of his shoes pacing across the room became a background beat to his lament, "I just wish I could replay the first half of this relationship—like on video tape—the half before you told me about your true occupation, and after each statement you made ask you if it was true or false. Was it part of the act or was it really you? Was it part of the NSA recruiting gig to say that you had a family reunion in August, or was that a little snatch of truth that sneaked out over the wine?"

"Tommy, Tommy, Tommy," she said. "I love you even when you're mad."

"How reassuring," Tommy snapped, stopping his pacing.

"Stop it. Hoosiers can't do sarcasm. You just can't pull it off. There *is* a family reunion. It is in August. I am planning on going."

"And you won't take the guy that you are going to marry to your family reunion?"

"That's right," she replied after a pause.

"Okay," he said. "I see I should have gone to law school so I would know how to cross-examine you. I can't get a straight answer out of the woman I am planning to spend the rest of my life with. Would that worry you? Just hypothetically, if you fell in love with a beautiful—but older—"

"Thanks," she interrupted.

"If you fell in love with a person who first revealed to you that she was at first just pretending to be interested in you because a bureau of the federal government that she worked for wanted to recruit you, but now she really did love you, and then told you that, surprise, she was rich, and then told you, surprise, she was older than she had mentioned, and then told you, surprise, she didn't want you to meet her family—wouldn't that, just hypothetically, make you a little concerned?"

"Stick to brutal honesty," she suggested with a laugh. "Or gentle concern. I'm telling you, you just can't do sarcasm and irony. It's not in your blood."

"Rebecca—" Tommy said sharply, but with a tinge of exasperated love in his voice. "I'm going to that family reunion. I'm going to meet these people you've been trying to hide. All right?"

There is a pause in the tape, only the sound of tense breathing recorded.

"Yes," she said again. "All right. You win. You're going. We're going. Yes, yes, yes."

Tommy told me later that Rebecca was gone for long stretches of time that summer. Some of those absences were for her many meetings at HQ with John X, two or three were meetings with her contacts among the professors who supplied us with information, and the logs show that she met with the Judge three times. But there were days at a time when John X could not get hold of Rebecca. He didn't press her on where she had been, assuming that she was off somewhere with Tommy. The very thought of her in his arms, I presume, would have made John X sick with envy. So he undoubtedly did what most people do to avoid pain: John X simply didn't ask. Whatever he didn't know couldn't hurt him.

But again, in retrospect, we gave Rebecca much too long a leash. Because she worked almost exclusively with students and professors, we always assumed that she wouldn't accomplish much during the summer months. But that summer she hardly worked for us at all—there are no records of new recruits, new agents, or new relationships with professors. She was playing with Tommy, trying to convince him that life with her wouldn't be so strange, or maybe planning for her family reunion. But there were no notations in her file that anyone complained about her frequent absences. The NSA is not the kind of agency that monitors whether field operatives are putting in their forty hours a week, but the lack of supervision of Rebecca was amazing. Everyone just assumed she was working on special projects because John X was allegedly supervising her activity. John didn't complain, so no one else did.

"It's time to go there," she said the Friday before the Tuesday I was brought back to the agency. It was nearing the end of August, when John X was just about to close down the agency's surveillance operation because he found nothing even the slightest bit suspicious about her behavior.

"Where?" he asked, without looking up from his drafting table.

"To that hill on the farm. It's time to meet my family. Time to tell them about us. It's time to go to that family reunion. Next week. Let's try to go on Monday. Let's take the whole week, okay? My brothers and sisters are all coming early in the week, then we'll all go together to meet the rest of the family. First my family, then all the aunts and uncles. That way you won't have the shock of meeting all of them at once."

That night, on that same hill on her parents' farm, a man lay flat on his stomach with an Israeli Timberwolf .357 Magnum carbine in front of him as he scanned the fields below with infrared binoculars with nitrogen-filled lenses and a high-gain 25-mm intensifier tube. He skipped over the few deer he caught in his eyes' sweep from woods to woods and stopped when he saw the amber glimmer of a warm upright figure rising out of a trench near the road. He could see the outline of the M-16 with an M-203 grenade launcher in the man's hands. He assumed the man was one of the family's guards, but he called in just to make sure. He cupped his hands around a miniature Motorola telephone and spoke slowly, the location's coordinates already memorized.

Theory number 504: Everything can be justified. Even before I heard Tommy's side of the story, I knew he had only the best of intentions. He was in love. He was the luckiest guy on earth. She had dropped out of the sky: caring, witty, attentive, rich, and in love with him. Of course, he didn't ask as many questions as a sane man should have asked, but he was by definition not a sane man. He was in love, or at least so heavily into lust that the distinction doesn't really matter. He was caught up in the whirlwind of romance. The cliché of overbearing passion. Don't count your chickens before they hatch. Don't ask a question you do not know the answer to. Don't look a gift horse in the mouth, or you may see what he has been eating.

7.

THE FIRST DISCIPLE'S CODE NAME was Simon, but after two and a half years of research—poring over thousands of files, listening to hundreds of tapes, organizing a team of thirty analysts to probe every nook and cranny—I know the given name of each of the disciples. I remember when I learned that the first disciple's family called him Peter, and his real name was Luke. I stared at his birth certificate in my office while CNN was broadcasting the collapse of the Soviet military and the failure of the coup in the Soviet Union in 1991. Why did the Soviet military lose their nerve? Luke could have told you, if he were alive today. Luke could have taken off his mirrored sunglasses and Walkman earphones and given you a rap, in Spanish, English, or Japanese, that you would not believe. I choked on my coffee as my eyes moved from film of Boris Yeltsin standing on top of a tank to the faded, maize-colored birth certificate that said Luke was born in 1970, which made him only nineteen years old in 1989. He had seemed older, I told myself, but then I had to admit, not much older. He was just beginning to live a life without shadows and secrets and fear. But there it was, his true name, typed out neatly in the midst of all the Spanish I had had translated earlier, Luke Mendez Bundt III.

In the summer of 1989 Luke followed the footsteps of the old man in front of him, each sandaled foot carefully placed in the center of the moss-encrusted stones that wove through the Japanese garden. A slight drizzle sent chills down his back and made the stones gleam black in the sea of green moss and waves of gnarled and twisted dwarf trees. He stopped when he saw the rock.

The meandering path in the garden of the Yabunouchi School of Tea in Kyoto was empty but for the two men. The landscape was pale and heavy, the burlap-colored sky thick with the spring-morning smells. The air was still and full of oxygen, and Luke could hear the drops of rain roll down the manicured leaves and splatter on the carefully raked sand designs. Luke had been told to follow the master of the tea garden to the place of contemplation and sadness. The paths guided visitors to different places that were designed to evoke different moods, but the small paper map that Luke had been handed when he entered the garden was incomprehensible to his Latin American–trained eyes. The Japanese characters that bordered the broad outlines of rocks, ponds, sand pits, and flower gardens looked like the blood-red slashes left in the hide of a bull in the ring, and he momentarily lapsed into comparing the different rituals of his country and the one he was in.

But as he turned the corner around a stand of tortured pines he saw a small rock that was wrapped with a rough straw rope. The rope was wound around the oval rock and knotted at the top. The wrapped rock was balanced on top of another, larger, flat rock, which sat in the middle of a path that went off to the left of the one he was on.

It was the sekimori-ishi he had been told to look for: the sign that no one should go farther on that path. He looked up at the hunched back of the old man who had led him into the garden.

"Isn't this it?" Luke said in English. "Isn't this the place?"

The old man, who had spoken English to him when he had arrived and given his name, did not turn around. Luke watched him walk on into the mist, each footstep carefully placed on the meandering stones, as if he were stepping through a minefield. The old man did not look back.

Luke ran a hand through his long black hair and unbuttoned his tight Day-Glo nylon jacket so that he could reach easily for the Argentine knife that was holstered in the armpit of the jacket. He had left his gun in the big car at the entrance with his two Japanese stepbrothers, who were leaning against the car, waiting, watching and listening. The car was black, as were their loose-fitting suits, which shined in the dreary weather as if they were made of the same material as their mirrored sunglasses. The tea garden was small enough that one shout from Luke and the two of them would be with their stepbrother, who after all these years still spoke Japanese haltingly, their polished guns drawn.

Luke stepped carefully around the wrapped rock and moved quietly down a raked gravel path. He came to a gently curved wooden bridge, and as he was admiring the perfect curve of its support, he saw another old man sitting on a slab of granite that was laid across two boulders to form a bench.

The old man's eyes were closed, and his veined hands were touching the side of his bald head, cupping his large ears. He sat in a flowing yellow robe, tied at the waist with a knotted rope.

"Luke?" the old man asked in English.

"Yes," Luke responded, and then, remembering the code, he whispered, "Do you know how the weather will be today?"

"Like yesterday and the day before," the old man said, his English perfectly pronounced. "But it will be different tomorrow."

"Then I will stay until tomorrow," Luke answered. "Shantell."

The old man kept his eyes shut but gestured for Luke to come and sit by him. Luke scanned the small open space where the bench was, and after peering into the shadows under the flowering trees he came and sat next to the old man.

"I am Shantell," the old man offered when Luke sat down on the cold stone. Luke shuddered once, wishing for sun and the grassy range he came from, and then the old man spoke again. "I am a translator for the bank and the uncle of your stepbrothers. I was very sorry to hear about your father. He was a good man, and he went for a good cause. Now his father's mantle is passed from him to you."

Luke remained silent, staring past the blind old man into the trees of the garden around them. Had he seen something move, he asked himself, imagining ghosts of his father. No, he decided, just raindrops falling from the leaves. They were alone. He was alone. The new first disciple.

"Tell me what you look like," Shantell asked.

Luke opened his mouth and then thought better of it. Why should he describe himself to this blind man, he thought. "It is better that you are not able to describe me," he said.

"Yes," Shantell agreed. "I understand. Did you bring anything for me?"

"Yes," Luke said, taking the film canister out of his pocket and putting it in the old man's outstretched hand. The microfilm detailed the access code numbers to three secret accounts at the bank that Shantell could withdraw his payments from at three inconspicuous times.

"Then I have something for you," Shantell said. He brought a plastic compact disc container out of his robe and handed it to Luke. The cover was of Simon and Garfunkel, but when Luke opened the case the compact disc inside had no name or markings on it.

"Be careful with that information, young man," Shantell stated firmly. "Seven men have died to bring that silver platter to you."

"I will be careful. Their lives were not in vain. They have contributed to peace."

"No lives are in vain," Shantell whispered into the mist. "And peace? Peace we already have here in this garden, yes?"

The old man gestured to the beautiful trees and flowers that sprang from the rocks around them.

"This is the control that nature has over man," Shantell said. "This garden shows the subordination of humankind to nature. We try to put order to nature, but nature shows again and again that she will order our lives, and not the other way around. Here nature is peace. Man is war himself, and man is at war with himself. I do not have faith that the information that you have in your hands will do good anywhere or for anyone. But it is not my place to judge that. You have it now. Go then and get it to your family. Let them use it as they see fit. Let the first disciple be the first to end the family's business. The first to get us to our goal."

"Don't worry," Luke replied, to a question that had not been asked. "I'll make sure that it happens. For all those who have died getting this here. For my father. For the family. My brothers and I will make sure."

Luke stood up to leave, his trained eyes circling around him before he moved. He put the compact disc in an inside pocket of his brightly colored clothes and walked away through the cherry trees, heavy with languid blossoms, without saying a word. Moments later a car engine roared to life, followed by the loud, pulsating sounds of Japanese rap music. Then car doors slammed outside the wall and a big car screamed away.

The raindrops continued their slide down the rich green leaves, and the old man pulled a small silver pill case from inside his robe. He felt each pill, measuring the size and shape of each one. He placed the film canister inside his robe and then selected a red pill from the case. He fondled the pill for a long time and imagined placing the poison on his tongue, where he would let it dissolve until it stung. Then he would swallow, he imagined, smelling the cherry blossoms for the last time.

That was the plan that the family had detailed in case the transaction had not gone according to plan. If something went wrong it was his obligation to swallow the small oval pill with the indentation on the side. But it had gone well, he thought, staring blindly at the small red pill. Luke would not let them down.

He had always supposed that something sometime would go wrong and he would swallow the pill. But now he could return to his normal life. He could shed the clothes, the fear, the hiding, the lies. He could return to his gray-haired wife and never lie again. He was free of the family ties at last. He could return to his bland job at the big bank, debating the philosophic differences between the abacus and the computer sitting side by side on his cramped desk. He craved, he told himself as he rolled the red pill around in his hand, the mundane.

He dug a small hole in the gravel with his toe and leaned over as far as he could. He dropped the red pill into the small indentation and then covered it with gravel with his foot. That would keep some unsuspecting bird from picking it up, he thought. Yes, he thought, standing up and feeling young. That was the first life he had saved for the family. He hoped it would not be the last.

8.

THEY TOOK THE TRAIN from New Haven to New York City early Monday morning. She leaned on his broad shoulder as they sat next to each other, her reddish hair thrown over both of their shoulders and tangled into his sunburned blond hair like weeds in September wheat. Until that morning John X did not believe she knew she was being followed. The surveillance operation had been all but shut down—her jealous section chief humbled by her true-blue American proclivity to settle down and have a family. Then the morning bundle brought a classified request from the Direction de la Surveillance du Territoire.

While the DST thinks of itself as a counterintelligence agency par excellence, I am constantly offended by their typical French smugness. The request that was forwarded to John X's desk was typically obtuse: "Identify Rebecca Townsend of New Haven Connecticut."

"Why?" John X ordered a teletype operator, known as a commotech at the agency, to shoot back instantly over a coded message transmitter.

The new laser disk for our communications with the DST dropped from the machine known as "the jukebox" into the player and whirled out the identification numbers of the "tune" on the DST's laser disk that would be used to read the encrypted communication. The laser disk contained thousands of different tunes, which were simply randomly generated numbers that signified letters in the alphabet, that could be used to code a typed message. The jukebox contained ninety-nine different disks, so there were more than one hundred thousand different ways a message could be encrypted. Different disks were sent to the many embassies, and other intelligence agencies, around the globe every month to be used for decoding NSA communications. Nothing that the CIA, the FBI, or the Defense or State Department had came close to being as sophisticated or as fail-safe. Handling information was what the NSA was all about.

The commo-tech typed in the message, which was translated by the jukebox into gibberish and sent through a fiber optic cable from HQ at Fort Meade to a satellite dish on the edge of the fort by the Patuxent National Wildlife Refuge, beamed up to a National Reconnaissance Office satellite twenty-two thousand feet above the fort, beamed across the curve of the atmosphere to a French satellite, and then down to the dish at the DST, where it was decoded by an identical whirling laser disk that bore the legend "USNSA August's Greatest Hits."

"Because DST needs to know" came the gamesmanship answer seconds later.

The section chief literally pushed the young commo-tech out of his chair and sat down in front of the glowing machine and typed with two fingers. "Is this international cooperation or your perverted sense of humor?"

The machine shot back, "She has been identified as associated with your agency by an informant. We will share further Level 5 info with Paris-based HQ with your approval. Courier on way to USHQ."

Something was up.

John X granted approval and sent a man to meet the French courier within the hour. Two good men were following Rebecca within a half hour. Within a quarter of an hour, John X ordered a review of all audio tapes that had not been listened to.

Now John X, the bald, spurned lover of Rebecca Townsend, could continue his eavesdropping and spying with a suddenly clear conscience. He didn't order the action just because he was angry at her, although he admitted he was angry, but because the French had found something that made her actions suspect.

That was when he called me.

I was in the garden nearest the house when I heard the phone ring. I paused in my summer Monday-morning ritual of hedge trimming to listen to one of my wife's servants' one-sided conversation, which ended with the sound of footsteps coming out onto the veranda to get me.

John X had been one of my best employees as the chief analyst for dernza's personal staff, and, considering the nature of the activity, it did not seem strange for him to call me for my advice, even though in retrospect it is amazing that he would so readily break NSA rules to contact a former staffer. But rules were made to be broken when a mission wasn't being played by the rules. The rules were something that we bureaucrats made up—it was the laws of the land, in their dusty law-book glory, that we had to make sure we did not step over. The first thing that you learn when you enter the hallowed halls of Mahogany Row is the difference between the rules and the laws.

"Steele, it's the sudden exit," John X explained to me in his Monday-morning phone call over the gray phone for classified conversations. By this point it was clear that he thought the intercept was off the phone. He was wrong. "The sudden falling in love. Sure, maybe I overreacted because I've been seeing, oh Jesus, sleeping with her off and on over the past three years." As he told me this, admitting the sin, and NSA policy-breaking activity, which we had all known about for years, I imagined the sweat breaking out on his wrinkled forehead.

"Maybe stealing the boyfriend's belt was too much. But damn it," John X whispered on the phone to me, his hand gripping his fourth cup of coffee so tightly that the techy in the room with him told me later he was afraid it would break, "I was right.

"But Jesus," he then interjected over the safe line. "Don't tell anybody about the bug in the belt buckle. Please. The Judge would have my hide for that one. Sure it broke every rule in the book, but damn it, my instincts were right, Steele. The stupid irony is that the damn bug keeps going on the fritz anyway. We lose half of what is going on."

"John," I said as calmly as I could, standing on my veranda overlooking the acres of perfectly trimmed grass and rows of olive-green hedges, "you were okay until you put the bug in the belt buckle—whether it works or not. Right then you broke FISA, and there's no going back. Everything else was just breaking department policy, which they can fire you for. But Jesus, John, with that bug in the belt you're breaking the law. Congress could have your hide—not just the Judge. The judge you better worry about is a sitting federal judge who could put you away for five to twenty-five years for that little stunt." FISA is the Foreign Intelligence Surveillance Act, which prohibits electronic eavesdropping within the United States on foreign embassies, diplomats, and federal agents without going to a secret federal court, known as the Foreign Intelligence Surveillance Court, or just the Star Chamber to those of us with a sense of history, and asking for permission.

"Yes," John X said quietly. "But it's safe with you, right? You won't tell a soul? My instincts were right. Right?"

The piece of pale pink paper announcing my early retirement floated around in my mind. I remembered those words buried near the end of the single piece of paper: "pursuant to top secret umbra report HJ238I by Code John X." I had to be bigger than he had been,

I told myself. His career was in my hands now, and while revenge has its own sweet justice, it simply seemed too primitive. His secret would be safe with me.

"You have my word I won't tell a soul. But you can't run an operation just on instincts," I replied.

"Something is up. I just had to talk to somebody," he said, accepting my chivalry without comment. "Somebody who wouldn't jump my ass and ask me to justify all the surveillance."

"You should have brought the Judge or Paul in from the beginning," I told him. "Now you're out on a limb without a ladder."

"I didn't think, I admit it," he told me. "I just didn't think it through. But I knew, I just knew there was something going on."

He was right, I thought, half listening to him tell a story about how when he was in military intelligence in Vietnam they had a double agent who had been caught just because her man on the inside noticed she was distracted and didn't want to have sex with him as she did before. But there was no question in my mind that he ordered the surveillance because he was jealous of Rebecca's new love. Neither he nor any of his fellow section chiefs would have taken the gamble and ordered the blitzkrieg that followed. He was willing to blow his budget because the woman he was fascinated with had left him for another lover.

If reason, logic, caution, and bureaucratic rules had been followed, Rebecca would have gotten away with it. But John had that gut instinct that you get from being out in the field, and even though I am critical of military intelligence guys, John had seen action. For all his veneer of tense gentlemanly paranoia, he was still basically the grunt missile mechanic who had top-secret clearance in Vietnam because he had to know where the missiles were to fix them. And as a grunt he was in the front lines and experienced the full horror of the thing. The thing others loosely refer to as war. Those two base instincts, jealousy and paranoia, broke open the case.

Rebecca and Tommy were followed from the remodeled train station in New Haven to Grand Central Terminal, where they filled a cab with her many pieces of luggage, too many for a week-long visit, and from which they drove, our men presumed, to Penn Station to catch a train to Philadelphia. But Rebecca insisted that the cabdriver take them for a spin around Manhattan so that she could show Tommy some of her old haunts. Tommy pointed out that they might miss their train, but she protested that he complained that he didn't know much about her and then complained when she tried to play show-and-tell with her past. He couldn't have it both ways, she said with a kiss.

Our men grabbed a cab and kept up with them for nearly forty minutes, noting the addresses where their cab slowed and Rebecca stuck her arm out the window to point at a particular apartment building or brownstone. Even now when I read their scribbled report, the pencil marks as gray as a ghost, I quiver with uncertainty. Why did Rebecca take Tommy on a tour of the many places she had met our agents to hand over a new recruit from academia? Was she trying to cleanse her soul by revealing all to Tommy, explaining what she did to get each professor into Manhattan to talk to an NSA representative? Or was she just playing with us, knowing that we were following her? We still don't know. Chalk it up as one of those mysteries, one of those loose ends that happen in real life.

Our men at Penn Station were confused when Rebecca and Tommy did not show up for their scheduled train and then, showing off her talents, Rebecca and Tommy got onto the next train without our men seeing them get on. Only by our men's committing an obvious sin and waving ID under the nose of the conductor did we find out they were on the train before it pulled out of the station. With only seconds to spare, two of our men, who were rented just for the occasion, got on board and found seats in the bar car.

Again, luck was on our side.

According to Tommy, Rebecca was able to do all of this without even raising his suspicions. He was not surprised, he told me later, by her sudden changes of heart or direction. That was part of her charm, after all. Her verve. Her ability to slip into a pair of jeans and take off for destinations unknown, picnic basket in the back seat and champagne in the front seat as she shifted her car up into overdrive and sped to wherever she was going.

When our men were walking through the narrow train aisle for the tenth time they overheard her talking and Tommy saying, "I don't know how you're ever going to settle down. I mean, you talk about kids, but every other word out of your mouth is about starting a business or building this or doing that."

Rebecca was all get-up-and-go in her new transformation to domestic striver after bliss and plenitude. She talked about children in an oblique way at first. "Don't we need more bedrooms than that?" she said, looking at the house plans. Then "I don't want the master bedroom so far away from the others." And then "Shouldn't we just finish the basement off right away? A rec room, you know." Finally, the day before they were going to visit her family, when the section chief was still taping but no longer having nightly transcriptions made, she said, "Look, because of my age, we may have to speed up this, this family business."

The night before they had called her folks, after she told him not to say anything about their engagement because she wanted to do that in person.

"Mom? This is Becky—"

"It's Dorothy, Becky. My, my, even her own grown-up daughter can't tell the difference between her mother and her housekeeper on these damn phones. The sound is so bad on them."

In fact, there was a scrambler on the phone that made the recorded conversation sound like waves of static. Two days later one of the techies in the phone lab in P Group wrote John X a quick analysis: "Chief, I thought this was just a bad phone line until I sampled it and did a spectral analysis of the signal. There's no way this can be line noise. But notice the patterns I've circled on the plot. It's there too often to be noise, but the human voice just doesn't work that way. It's got to be from a signal processor digitizing her voice and squeezing high-frequency information onto a regular 3kHz phone line. This is a high-class machine whose signature I haven't seen before. Also, to top it all off, the pattern changes midstream and I can't figure out the second half to save my soul. We have enough recorded samples of her voice that I could probably make sense of it if you approve some time on the Cray. Without more horsepower, it might take me days or weeks to get this done. Can I send it to R Group for analysis?"

The answer was no. John X was playing this one close to the vest.

"Dorothy," Rebecca said, "I'm so glad to talk to you. You do sound just like Mom, and you're not the housekeeper and you know it. How's your arthritis?"

On the filtered tape you can hear Tommy in the background saying, "You have a housekeeper? What kind of farm has a housekeeper?"

"Not so bad, darling," Dorothy answered, with a German accent. "But I can't push a mop. Nor can Martha, so the boys have it bad. They have to do all of their own cooking, since you know your mother wouldn't lift a pot to save her soul. It's wonderful to have everyone home for the get-together. They can all help out."

Rebecca laughed and said, "So the cook can't cook and the housekeeper can't mop and Mom won't do a thing. Sounds like home."

"You have a cook?" Tommy asked incredulously in the background.

"Is Mom there?"

"Just a second, Becky. I'll get her."

"You have," Tommy asked, close to the mouthpiece, "a housekeeper and a cook? What kind of farm has—"

Rebecca put her hand over the mouthpiece and said, "And a gardener, a driver, three tenant farm families, and a dozen hands. It's a big, working farm, Tommy."

"I thought this was a real farm. Like an Indiana farm, you know? Cows and chickens. I didn't know this was the set from *Dallas*. How many acres is this place?"

"About five thousand," she responded reluctantly, as her mother got on the phone.

"Five thousand!"

"Becky, how are you?" a woman's voice asked on the phone. "We're so looking forward to you visiting us."

"Thanks, Mom. How are you?"

Her mother's voice had the soft, smooth roll of real pearls. It was unhurried without being slow, and warm without being maternal. It didn't sound at all like the German-accented voice of the housekeeper.

There was obviously some code being used.

"I'm fine," her mother said. "But we do need you to visit."

The word "need" sticks out. Why would they need their daughter to visit?

"I'll be there soon—and I'm bringing a friend to the family reunion."

"A friend?" her mother asked, too quickly.

"A boyfriend," Rebecca replied, lowering her voice, which was tinged with a shade of left-over adolescent guilt. "I told you about him. He wants to meet the family."

"Oh. Well, we weren't expecting anyone else—just family," her mother said, letting the words sink down. "Is it the one we thought we'd like? Not the married man, but the young one? The one from Indiana your uncle knew of? What's his name?"

"Yes," Rebecca answered firmly, and then paused. "His name is

Tom. Tommy Wood. You'll like him very much. Put it this way, Mom, you better like him very much."

"Oh really?" her mother almost whispered. "Well then, you do what you think is best. Will you be in on the usual train? I'll have your brothers meet you. They'll already be here, of course."

Do what you think is best? The usual train, to a woman who never went home to visit and hardly did anything but fly? The one from Indiana that your uncle had heard of, when Tommy hadn't been in Indiana for three years?

"Yes," Rebecca said. "Here, say hello to Tommy."

"Hello, Mrs. Townsend," Tommy mumbled, with the receiver suddenly forced into his hands. There was a two-beat silence before Rebecca's mother said, "Yes. Hello. Hello, Tom. Just a second, please. I'm looking forward to meeting you. Just—"

And then the static blossomed and their voices were lost in what the techy, in a burst of poetic license, described in his report as white noise in a dark pattern.

Theory number 39: Don't worry about what you can't control. Why, for example, was Rebecca so seemingly open on the phone, which was so easy for us to tap, and yet so elusive when she went out? Why allow us to know her plans and then take elaborate diversionary measures when she took the train home? In hindsight the answer is obvious. She wasn't worried about us. She knew we could tap the phone with a little help from GCHQ; we're the government, after all. But outside, anyone could follow her. You don't need just cause or a permit to follow someone down the street.

To whom was she trying to give the slip, then? And why take them on a tour of Manhattan in the process? At the time one of our men said it was just habit. Once a spook, always a spook. She had scared herself into believing that she should follow the textbook even if she was leaving the organization to be a housewife.

Two hours later the whole thing began to unravel.

Theory number 379: One difference between art and reality is that art separates the comic from the tragic, the happy from the melancholy, while in life there is always one within the other.

It must have happened like this: Tommy was drinking wine and eating cheese on the train as it stopped in Philadelphia before going on. Our men saw them sitting together in Philadelphia. They didn't have to change trains, so our men watched them waiting, talking, laughing, kissing. Our men did several walk-bys and caught parts of their conversation.

"How am I going to keep your brothers apart if they all have red hair and are tall?" Tommy asked.

"Okay, just concentrate. Erik is the oldest, he's a little heavy. Probably eats too much while he's grading papers. He's the professor. Then there's Fritz. He has a moustache and he dresses conservatively, probably because he's with IBM. Then Jan, who is the tallest. He's a really skinny guy. Joey is the youngest. He has long, curly red hair—really red—and he's in advertising, so he's always looking pretty good."

"Brothers, parents, sisters-in-law, nieces and nephews—I'm never going to remember who all these people are."

"Just wait until we add all the aunts, uncles, and cousins later in the week," Rebecca suggested. Then our man walked on, scribbling down notes of the conversation as soon as he sat down.

At the same time, a techy was decoding the tape of the conversation Tommy had had with Rebecca the night before, the pertinent part of which goes like this:

"Sometimes I wonder how this all happened," Rebecca said. "How we met and, you know, fell in love. From what I hear around campus, you've been falling in love with anything in a skirt that happens to glance at those corn-fed muscles of yours. And then this Rebecca chick that you've been talking about all year happens to run into you on the Old Campus. Just because some long-lost aunt or something told you to look her up when you got to Yale, you strike up a conversation. Some relative wants to set you up and you get hooked before you even meet her. Don't deny it. I've heard rumors. Following her around and hoping that she would just happen to ask your name. You've been following this woman for months. Now your ultimate love object is yours. Jesus, you've been gone before, but now you are beyond help. Isn't that right?"

"I love Rebecca," he dramatically swooned to her, talking to her in the third person just as she talked to him. "Rebecca is my love. Nurturing. Loving. And secure in who she is."

"Yeah, that's a good question," Rebecca said. "You're thinking, who the hell is she? Do you know anything about her? She's gone for days, weeks at a time. Just disappears and leaves you moping around, pretending to work when I know all you're doing is marking time until she shows up again. What the hell does that import business import, after all? I mean, you are going to marry some woman when you haven't met her mother? You gotta see her mom to see what a hag she'll be when she's fifty. You gotta know that."

"That's why I'm going to meet your mother," Tommy said to Rebecca. There was a moment of silence and then the sound of a long, soft kiss.

The decoding linguist wrote a hurried report on this conversation, which was sent directly to John X. "This shows all the signs of a coded conversation," the linguist tensely wrote in miniature script. "Repeated phrases. Obtuse references. Questions with no direct answers. The caller Tommy is trying to communicate that something has happened to the subject woman that is similar to some activity that has happened before (falling in love before with 'anything in a skirt') and will entail Tommy's traveling. Rebecca is warning Tommy to find out more information, and Tommy is telling Rebecca that something central to their plan, something that cannot be changed, is about to go wrong. I recommend further analysis."

Because no one wrote "Total crap" across the top of this so-called analysis, it was taken as the truth. What no one—the analyst who listened to the call, John X, or Paul, when he listened to the tapes—noticed was the obvious: Tommy had been following Rebecca, and not the other way around. Unfortunately, I didn't listen to the tapes until it was too late, and only then did I realize that the NSA's prey had been stalking the NSA's hunter. Tommy had been trying to meet Rebecca from the moment he had heard about her from some relative, who was unnamed and unknown to us. But then again, in retrospect, even the most innocent coincidences take on the patina of a conspiracy. At the time the crazy analyst probably saw nothing strange in a relative's suggesting that a young man look up the daughter of an old friend when he moved to a new city. There was nothing unusual about a young man's becoming infatuated with Rebecca once he saw her. There was nothing unusual about a young man's trying to find a way to casually run into an attractive young woman he had seen on campus—even if the woman was being paid by us to find ways to casually run into this same young man. Even the jealous John X believed at first that there was nothing going on here that lust couldn't explain.

After reading the analysis, John X, finally playing the role of bureaucratic section chief, called his supervisor, the deputy dernza, Paul White, to report what had happened. After that tentative, apprehensive telephone conversation, John X ordered a Lear jet to stand by and requested more men. The deputy dernza decided not to bother the Judge right away. This could wait until the Judge got back from his fishing vacation tomorrow, Paul told me later he had reasoned, obviously relishing being in charge of a fast-breaking action; the Judge had been tired before he went and had not looked well. Paul wondered whether, if he called the security line and talked to one of the Federal Protective Service guards the Judge had taken with him, he could find out what kind of mood the Judge was in. But, he told me later, he decided that might look as if he was going behind the Judge's back, so he didn't make the call.

"Don't talk to anybody," the deputy dernza told John X. "And I mean nobody."

"Okay, Paul," John X agreed, his voice cracking. "But, but I did talk to Steele. I know I shouldn't have, but I wanted some advice outside of the food chain, so I—"

"Jesus!" Paul shouted, without realizing that John X was taping all his calls now, in direct violation of organization policy. "The guy is retired. He was fired. He's out there playing country squire, living on his wife's money. Why the hell are you talking to him before you're talking to me? Are you crazy? I'm above you on the damn food chain, and I'm going to have your butt for lunch."

"This one is tough, Paul," John X said quickly. "I wanted to make sure that I wasn't, wasn't overreacting. Just checking my instincts. Just—"

"But Steele? That rich old son of a bitch doesn't know the difference between reality and his own daydreams. Who else knows anything about this?"

"No one. Nobody."

"Any techies?"

"Bobby," John X admitted reluctantly, undoubtedly thinking about the stolen belt buckle. He must have decided again at that moment not to tell anyone else about the belt buckle. "And whoever works with him. And the surveillance team 14-A in M Group. I've had them follow her, a bit. But all of them only know pieces. None of them know the big picture."

"A bit? Follow her a bit? Your ass is grass, John," the underdeputy said. "This may be your last case if things don't go a hell of a lot better from here on in. Just because you were doing this chick does not mean you can flout the rules around here. You understand me?"

"I do," John X mumbled, his voice cracking again.

"Don't do anything until I get down there. Do you understand? Do you?"

"I do," John X said again, probably looking at his watch and measuring how much time he would have before the deputy dernza arrived at the office. Enough, John obviously decided.

John X ordered our men's base operator to contact our men and have them call in directly to him on his private line. He told the base operator that he had to tell the men about a communications device that needed to be placed near Rebecca's elusive destination.

When their train slowed to a crawl for no more than twenty seconds at a small station almost two hours west of Philadelphia, Rebecca suddenly shot up, grabbed their bags, and in a fit of laughter dragged Tommy off the train. One of our men saw them crossing the old wooden walkway of the station as the train's three-foot-tall wheels began to roll faster. It was gray and drizzling, and Tommy and Rebecca were reflected in the wet wood of the old platform. Seconds later, the two agents threw themselves off the moving train into the scrub brush twenty feet past the station, one severely spraining his ankle, the other ripping his suit pants as he fell in the mud against the hard butt of his automatic revolver. Neither had time to grab their empty luggage. Neither had time to use their mobile phones and call in. Neither had time to stand up.

For when they rolled to a stop, nearly on top of each other, our men looked up to see Rebecca staring right at them through the leafy underbrush between them and the station platform, her hand pushed down into her large purse, which she had drawn in front of her. She flipped her hair over her shoulder and took a step toward them so she stood between them and Tommy. Tommy was busy examining the train station and hoisting a bag on his shoulder while her eyes narrowed into sights zeroing in on their prey. She seemed to say something to them, her thick lips moving as she shoved her hand deeper into her purse, which was large enough to hold an Uzi, but they could not hear her over the roar of the accelerating train screaming six feet from where they crouched. They had been warned that she was a good shot, so neither reached for a phone or a gun. They stayed crouched on all fours. Their hearts raced as they stared at her, panting like dogs, waiting for her to shoot right through the side of her bag, the gun never visible to the passengers watching them out of the windows of the speeding train.

But the eye-to-eye standoff was over as quickly as it had begun when two lanky men in long raincoats, looking as if they had just stepped out of a John Wayne movie, walked out of the trees by the track and asked the two agents if they needed any help. Both of the tall young men let their coats fall open to show sleek black pistols in their hands, which reached through openings in their pockets to hold the guns. Two other men rushed out of the small Swiss-chalet-looking station and surrounded Rebecca and Tommy, looking like nothing more than brothers meeting their sister at the train station.

"Hey, sis!" one of them sang to Rebecca. "Welcome home! Man, you look great."

"Erik," Rebecca said to him, "you're the one who looks great. You've lost weight, haven't you? This is my friend Tommy."

"Glad to meet you, Tommy. Can I help you with your bags?" Erik asked with a crisp, joking efficiency as he shook Tommy's hand. Erik's eyes never strayed toward the trees where behind the cover of thick August leaves the two mud-covered NSA men imitated crouched dogs.

"Joey," Rebecca said to the other man, reaching up and ruffling his red hair. "How's my little bro, huh?"

"Welcome home, Becky," Joe said to Rebecca. He took Tommy's arm and gently led him off the platform toward two waiting Jeeps, their engines idling loud and high. "I'm Rebecca's brother. We are all Rebecca's brothers. I'm so glad you could visit us. We've heard a lot about you."

"You have?" Tommy asked, looking over his shoulder at Rebecca as she walked in the other direction.

"I'll be right there," she shouted back. "Let me just check the times—the train schedule."

Our men reported later that, over the receding noise of the train, they did not even hear the two fat men walk up behind them and kick them gently in the rear. They both jumped around and stared into the ends of two shotguns aimed in their general direction.

"Howdy," the fatter of the two grunted, showing his sheriff's badge. "What do we got here, Fritz?"

"Some strangers," Fritz responded, nodding his red-haired head to the sheriff as he dropped his pistol into the deep pocket of his long raincoat. Fritz rubbed his moustache and nodded at his taller brother Jan, who dropped his gun into his pocket with the nod.

"You boys get off at the wrong stop?" the fat sheriff asked our agents, who began to wipe the mud off their faces while remaining on their knees.

"Sheriff, I'd like to file a complaint against these men!" Rebecca shouted across the wooden platform, the train now only a rumble as it turned a bend. "That man exposed himself to me."

The sheriff and his deputy looked from our men to Rebecca to her brothers, and the deputy said, in a voice that sounded as if it had come up from a Pennsylvania coal mine, "Which one of 'em, Becky?"

She paused for a second and then walked along the warm train tracks and down the embankment to them and pulled the mobile phone out of one of their pockets. "Indecent exposure, my oh my," the round sheriff said as Rebecca examined the phone. Our men saw her push the automatic redial number, study the red numbers that appeared on the LED screen, and then speak quietly and tersely into the mouthpiece. Then she threw the phone hard against the rocks on the embankment.

The number was the direct line to the section chief.

"Hello," John X bellowed when the mobile line rang in the situation room he had set up at Fort Meade. "What's up? Where are you guys?"

He was shocked when he heard Rebecca's voice. The words were short and sultry. They stung like spit in your eye.

"Can't a gal go visit her folks without being followed by your goons, you asshole? This is the final straw. I'm breaking your camel's back."

Then all he heard was static.

"Oh, I'm sorry," she said, kneeling to pick up the cracked-open phone, its wires now exposed. "I hope I didn't break it. It was this one, officer. The one with the moustache."

"Now, Rebecca," the officer whined, as if talking to a schoolgirl. "I don't know if we can—"

"And," she interrupted, "they told me they were both federal agents of some sort. Which you know, Sheriff, is unadulterated fraud. I'm a federal agent, my friends, so you picked the wrong woman to harass." She flipped out an ID that neither had ever seen before and added, "So book them, Sheriff. I'll be down tomorrow to swear out a complaint."

"Hot Blue Wax," one of the men said suddenly, thinking that maybe she didn't know who they were and by using her code name he would alert her that they were on the same team.

That was their first mistake.

Rebecca put her deep red lips within inches of his ear, breathed heavily on him so he could smell the wine, and then said loudly enough so that everyone could hear, "Book him for indecent exposure—although his indecent exposure is hardly a crime, because what he exposed is indecently small."

Then she looked up at the sheriff and his deputy and smiled and said, "I can't wait till somebody has to write that up in a report." The deputy chuckled and lowered his gun, and as he did so our other man made a move for his gun.

That was their second mistake.

The county sheriff, who had just happened to be at the tiny station in the middle of nowhere, slammed his boot like a sledgehammer into the man's back, pinning him to the ground, and inserted the barrel of his shotgun into the man's ear, saying, "Now, get down and taste some mud."

Rebecca took their wallets, their guns, and the other phone. "Sheriff, I'll call into HQ and check these guys out. I'll return their things tomorrow, when I come down to the station."

"Nice to have you back, Becky," the sheriff replied to her.

"I'll tell the boys back at HQ to get you a raise." She laughed, and walked away with Fritz and Jan as if nothing had happened. Tommy remembered that when the three of them walked down the steps from the platform to where Tommy was talking to Erik and Joe, by their Jeeps, Rebecca was punching Jan in the arm and laughing so hard that tears came to her eyes.

Of course, Rebecca never called in to check on our two agents' identification.

The agents, covered with mud and burrs, were thrown into the back of a county van and driven to a McDonald's outside of Philadelphia, where the sheriff left the back door of the van unlocked while he went in to get a cup of coffee. They escaped, which was exactly what the sheriff wanted them to do. Days later, when we hauled in the sheriff and his deputy for questioning, he said that he had had a few errands to run along the way but was taking them to the county lockup, where they would have been able to make phone calls and straighten this whole thing out. But before he even had a chance to help them, they escaped. And Rebecca? The sheriff went to church with her family, and he thought she worked for the FBI, so when she said book them, by God, he told us, he was going to book them. Particularly after one of them was so stupid as to try to pull a gun on them. "You don't just pull a gun on me in my county and then get treated like royalty," the sheriff told our investigators. The sheriff said he did not see any guns in the possession of Rebecca's brothers, who were, he added, model citizens of the county. None of them had had so much as a traffic ticket.

Theory number 97: People want to believe simple, straightforward explanations of strange, suspicious situations.

Tommy told us that he didn't see any of this after he was led off the platform, but what he had seen of the four big men who helped him into one of the Jeeps was enough for him to say to Rebecca when she walked to the Jeep, "Strange way to get to your folks' house. Can't you at least get the train to stop at the station for more than three seconds?"

"Erik," she said, patting the driver's shoulder as she slid her bag in and then climbed into the back seat with Tommy, "tell him our family's a little strange."

"Our family's a little strange," Erik responded, with a hearty laugh. Before they left the station Rebecca introduced Tommy to her brothers Fritz and Jan, who explained that they had driven separately to the station and arrived a few minutes after the train.

Rebecca sat close to Tommy in the back seat of the Jeep Erik drove, with Jan in the front seat. Fritz and Joe followed closely in the other Jeep. As they bounced along country roads, the brothers and sister talking about relatives whom Tommy claimed later he could not keep track of, his head hit one of the two semiautomatic rifles that hung in a gun rack across the back of the Jeep.

Before the 4-H marksman could ask about the rifles, Rebecca said, "There's bear in the woods."

"But M-16s?" Tommy asked. "Are these bear armed?"

"You know your rifles," Jan commented, looking at him closely in the rearview mirror. "Were you in the service?"

"No," Tommy answered, looking at the unfamiliar scopes mounted on the guns. "Just my dad. He was a fanatic about it. A collector. I spent a lot of years shooting at soup cans on the back fence."

"That's good," Erik asserted, without explanation.

"Yes," Jan said. "I'm glad."

"Glad about what?" Tommy asked Rebecca quietly.

"Our dad is the same way," she responded. "Tell him he needs a new car and he's bound to buy a Corvette. Tell him that we should have a gun and he buys an M-16. Last time he decided he needed a new tractor he came home with a bulldozer instead."

Tommy told us later that Rebecca started asking about her brothers' wives, and she took Tommy's arm and put it around her when she began asking about their children.

"Wild, single Becky," Erik said, slowing down to go over a one-lane bridge. "The only one not married off. You're in for quite a treat, Tommy. Mom and Dad will be measuring you for a tux and ring by the time you've got into the front hallway."

Rebecca laughed, with a knowing smile to him. "He can handle it."

"I'm sure he can," Jan said. "But believe me, it's rough. Rebecca is the black sheep of the family. Refusing to deliver those grandchildren that Mom thinks are her due. That's the full-disclosure report. Just so you know everything."

"So," Tommy said when a moment of silence settled on them as the Jeeps bounced across miles of country roads. "Rebecca tells me that you're all into computers."

"But I didn't say 'into computers,'" Rebecca interjected with a laugh.

"Computer science," Erik said, steering the Jeep over a series of ruts in the country road. "Artificial intelligence is my hobby. We're all computer geeks. Hackers. The whole family is 'into' computer science or electrical engineering in some way or another. But that's just work. We all summer here. We get to see our family. The accommodations are great, and, even better, Dad picks up the bill. A free vacation is always the best kind."

"We all have our own places on the property," Jan said. "You'll see. We all grew up in Philadelphia, but when Dad retired and bought this place a couple of years back we all started to spend more and more time here, until it just seemed like a good place to spend a couple of weeks every year. So Dad had places built for all of us. The kids love it. It's like a summer camp for the whole family."

"How many people live on—on the property?" Tommy asked, watching all their eyes meet again, the brothers waiting to see what Rebecca said.

"Forty-seven," she answered, watching her brothers' eyes. "With one on the way."

Erik and Jan suddenly seemed relieved, as if, Tommy thought, Rebecca had given them a signal that they could speak freely in front of him, and Erik said, "That includes most of the regular farmhands. We have guests this weekend, so the head count is a little higher."

"I guess it wasn't all *perfectly* normal," Tommy told me later, when he was sitting in my study talking to me and a tape recorder about his trip to Rebecca's family farm. "But then, what family is perfectly normal? I know mine wasn't. There was nothing so strange about what I saw that I was suspicious. I mean, I was fascinated by this big, robust family. All these tall, good-looking brothers coming to meet us at the station. Everybody with big families and lots of friends. I mean, to a guy who was an only child, it was great. It was exactly right, you know? I couldn't wait to be a part of it all. I couldn't wait to tell them that Rebecca and I were engaged. I couldn't wait to be part of the family."

"Here we are," Rebecca sighed as they turned off the gravel road onto a blacktop lane, suddenly facing the bright setting sun. The early-evening clouds bloomed pink across the sky, like a thousand lilacs falling open in full summer heat.

Note: Tommy remembered the clouds. I didn't make that up.

9.

I REFUSE to dictate. I refuse to type. I refuse to let them put a computer on *my* desk; I insisted on having another desk put in my office for the silently throbbing green monitor. But now, every time I pick up a number two lead pencil and let it scratch across the page, I tell myself that this will be my last case. I am only fifty-seven and still fit and trim. I hated being fired, or early-retired, but I will quit when this is over, because I have two personal characteristics that lead inexorably to leisure and a brutal sense of honesty: I have grown out of my youthful ambition and late in life I married a very wealthy woman.

My lack of careerist ambition and Carolyn's money make me quite unconcerned now about what my superiors think of me, which in turn makes virtually all of them dislike me. Conversely, I think that is exactly what now makes me good at what I do. As you know from reading my file, for twenty years I was a loyal soldier at NSA, slowly moving up the ranks, but then I married money and was passed over for promotion, and suddenly I was not worried about giving any of you the answer you wanted instead of the answer I believe to be true. Nor am I willing to tell it to you in the sterile bureaucratic format that you ask for it in. My boss, and even dearer friend, the Judge, was absolutely right. Where other analysts see periods and commas and the breaking of rules, I see romance, envy, irony, and the grand moral complexities that make us as a species so damn interesting. You tell me who tells you more of the truth, the guy who gives you charts or the guy who gives you character.

This story involves so many of you, my dear friends, that had the Judge accidentally assigned it to one of my younger colleagues from the military or to a civilian with two kids and a mortgage, you might have heard something quite different. But as I have already made clear, Rebecca recruited too many of you for you not to be involved. She reached into too many executive committees, and into too many executive pants pockets, for her story not to move up from the front line to the White House.

But don't get me wrong. I understand how most of you fell for Rebecca. She wasn't just beautiful, she was available. She was a hunter. She was looking for you, and she let you know she wanted you. She was attractive, because she made you feel attractive. She was smart, because she made you feel smart. She was easy to talk to, because she made you feel at ease. You told her things that you would never tell your wife, because she did things your wife would never do—and she was part of the family. She shared your work, your worries, your suspicions of the world. Too bad you weren't suspicious of her.

She was trouble, but you weren't marrying her, so you had no fear. You loved her the moment you met her, and couldn't resist telling all your college pals about her. Later, when you were a young hotshot in the organization, you went back to her to boast of your successes, to tell her of all you had done, and she listened attentively and slowly unzipped your pants, not the least bit fazed when the zipper stuck or when you had to call your wife first to tell her you'd be home late. Rebecca was perfect, understanding so very well all that you had done and against what odds you had succeeded. She was the princess of empathy. She was the queen lover of spies.

That is what I have on so many of you. I have Rebecca. Now let me give you Carolyn.

Let me tell you how I met my wife, Carolyn, because that will show you that I understand what was going on, and will give you something on me, just as I now have Rebecca on you. Then you'll trust me. You will know that I do not intend to chortle when I see you in the halls. For when I was nineteen and a sophomore, the year the president was a senior, I had flat feet, thick round glasses, and an invitation to a swank party in Manhattan. The party was in honor of one of my professors who had just written a biography of Samuel Gompers that was climbing up the *New York Times* best-seller list. I didn't know it at the time, but on the premise of researching the book on this famous labor leader, my favorite professor was doing a little domestic spying for the Bureau. He had asked me to spend the summer helping him proofread, and my good work got me a referral to a recruiter at Langley who was hot on my tail the next fall. But I was invited to the party because I helped on the book.

I took the train into the city and walked the long twenty blocks over to the then new Tavern on the Green, which was ablaze with lights. The party was packed with posh, rich, and seemingly important people, but one girl stood out. Just as I walked in, after a waiter had given me the first martini I had ever had, we caught each other's eyes.

She was bursting with sensuous energy and willful abandon as she danced and drank with one man after another. I ran a shaking hand through my hair, and moved toward her. I tried to stand near her, moving closer so that I could casually ask her to dance, but she kept being whisked away by some other man—only her long, light hair touching me as she was twirled by me. As she danced and drank, she let a champagne glass slip from her sweaty palm and crash to the floor. I moved to help pick up the pieces, but a dozen waiters moved between us, descending on the shards of glass. I watched her through the crowd of white jackets and white gloves, and I couldn't help but think that she kept looking at me. Just when I thought that my teenage imagination was playing tricks on me, she swirled out of the arms of a tuxedoed gentleman, grabbed my arms, and put them around her waist for a slow dance.

Her eyes were on fire with liquor, and her arms were all over me before I had said a word. Her whole body melted in the rhythm of the music, and she moved with graceful, athletic swoops of emotion and muscle in an obviously expensive dress that was damp with sweat. The band played jazz, and my hair fell in my face as our hips met and I looked down at her upturned lips. Before I even knew her name I was in love with her.

"Don't tell me your name," she mumbled very close to my ear, her breath hot on my neck. "I don't want to know—yet."

Her white teeth sparkled under the crystal chandeliers, and when she spoke her mouth lingered open after each word, savoring their sounds. Her nostrils flared then, and her eyes closed as she said, "Don't say anything. Just dance me out to the patio and take me into the trees."

She let her forehead fall onto my chest, and her hands moved up my back to the breadth of my shoulders. "Take me into the trees," she sang dreamily. "Into the . . . the night."

I stopped dancing, stunned, my nineteen-year-old throat drying into a desert as sweat wet my body. Was she suggesting what I thought she was suggesting?

"I love ties," she whispered suggestively, touching my faded striped rep, which had been handed down to me from my absent father's closet. "And you make such a good, tight knot. Take me into the park. Teach me how to tie, how to knot a tie."

"I, I"—I stuttered; oh, how I remember that stunned, uncontrollable stutter—"I don't know—I don't know your—I don't believe we've met."

God knows what stupid sense of inappropriate decorum sent those inane words from my brain to my mouth, but the moment she heard them she took a step back, looked me in the eye, smiled, and walked away. She adjusted her shoulderless white evening gown and, scanning the faces of the men staring at her beautiful figure, picked out someone tall, dark, uniformed, and ten years older than I.

Furious at my lack of courage and ambition, I watched as she ran her hands up the back of her tuxedoed partner, their black and white silhouettes whirling past the tables full of candles burning low. I followed them out onto the patio, watching her close her eyes and talk to him, her forehead falling onto his broad chest and then one hand reaching up to touch his black satin bow tie.

My glasses fogged over as I saw the two of them suddenly step off the patio and walk into the dark shadows of the trees. I went back to the bar and ordered my first double scotch, straight up. It burned going down hard and fast, but after a second one I found myself walking back out onto the patio and stepping into the trees. I was a spy even then.

I stumbled through the trees, imagining that I was silently creeping up on them, but probably making enough noise to scare away anyone or anything. The dark trees held up a black canopy of leaves that rustled in the summer breeze. I got dizzy craning my neck to look up at the stars that crept between the layers of the canopy, so I leaned up against a tall oak and closed my eyes.

I imagined that I found them in the moonlight a hundred feet from the lights of the party, the orchestra's music still louder than the muted night songs of the crickets and birds. I dreamed that they both knelt half naked in the grass, pieces of their clothing strewn across the grassy incline of a small embankment. When I closed my eyes tight I could see him touching her while she stared open-mouthed at the starry sky, her arms pulling him toward her. Then, as I drifted out into the sea of my drunken unconsciousness, she offered to him her outstretched bare arms, her wrists crossed together. I dreamed he tied the shiny black bow tie around her wrists, slowly knotting it. He lowered her into the grass, her white body quivering in the moonlight. In the alcohol sea my mind floated in, I dreamed they moved together slowly, her tied arms outstretched above her head, pillowed by the thick waves of her long hair.

Then, in the whirl of my sleeping mind, as the music swooped into a jazzy waltz she turned her head toward me and smiled, her mouth opening and closing to the rhythm of the tan muscles working above her. In my drunken stupor I thought she smiled as if she saw me; as if she knew that I was there, so close I could see him shudder. She smiled as if she knew my virgin eyes were jumping out of their sockets and riveting on her knowing face.

The image knocked me back into consciousness, and I shook my head and dashed on through the trees and bushes, no longer caring if anyone heard me. I thought of shouting out her name—hoping that my imagination was not right, that she had merely taken a walk with the tuxedoed man and then gone back to the party—but I realized I did not even know her name.

I stumbled out of the trees, wandering through the loud party, looking for her everywhere. But after an embarrassing hour of staring into the face of every woman there, I walked slowly to the line of waiting cabs. Tears welled up in my eyes as the cab shot through the park and went south to Grand Central, the bright lights of the city refracted in my angry tears. I tossed and turned on the train to New Haven, sick with myself and paradoxically sick with what I imagined had happened. A wave of prudishness swept over me in my deep pit of rejection, and for half the trip back to Yale I cursed her for acts that I didn't even know she had committed. How could she do this with someone she had just met, I asked myself. Someone she would probably never see again. But I was not only imagining things, I was wrong.

Eight years later, after a stint in the Army, when I was in my third year at Langley, I saw her at another party, with the same man—but now he was a freshman Democratic congressman and she was his beautiful, rich wife. My heart still ached when I saw her high cheekbones and her mane of thick blond hair, coiled over an exposed, fragile shoulder. The same professor was there, and he brought me into her circle. When she offered me her hand I joked, "I don't believe we've met."

She smiled politely and replied, "Yes, I think we have."

I was stunned into silence, wondering whether her smile meant, yes, I know you imagined watching me as I lay in the grass, or she had mistaken me for someone else.

"You were at a party in New York a long time ago," she said to me and to her husband, who had a growing reputation as a man of integrity and promise. "We danced. You had on a very nice tie."

"That's my Carolyn," her broad, smiling husband boomed in a politician's voice. "You ought to be in politics, honey, or intelligence, like Mr. Steele here, the way you remember faces, names, and things." He patted me on the shoulder and asked, in a way that didn't call for an answer, "Isn't she just great?"

"Yes," I said, not able to take my eyes off her. "Just great."

Theory number 3: Everything is related to everything else. In some Zen sense, everything is connected. What this tells you about me is that I am risk-averse, cautious, moral to the point of prudishness, but that I am a voyeur, and that I feel bested by men who act with their hearts or their impulses. Men who grab what they want; get the girl; go to Congress; get money, power, success.

All of which led me to take the job as an analyst at the NSA. I am drawn to peering into other people's lives, particularly when they are so much more exciting than my own. I am drawn to collecting dirt on those powerful, impulsive men who rule the earth.

For example, for the next twenty-five years I ran into Carolyn and her congressman more and more. I lusted after her at every party, I compared my first wife to her as we lay in bed. Her wit. Her beauty. Her money. Every time we met I said, "I don't believe we've met," and she smiled, never letting on whether she remembered or knew all that happened that night.

I arranged to sit next to her at dinner parties, always sharing with her some sexy secret that I had found out, or spinning out a yarn in the best James Bond manner about what the agents assigned to me were doing. I would do almost anything just to keep her attention, even if it meant stretching a regulation here or there. From the very beginning I trod on the edge of what would eventually lead to my being early-retired by the agency.

Her jolly ox of a husband became a senator, and I watched her business career take off after her father died and left her a portfolio of some two dozen companies. I watched her career and her husband's career very carefully, checking his files, calling up the background reports, making official requests for surveillance, putting their names on the watch lists so the acres of computers in the basement would shoot out any tapes or papers with their names. I broke no rules. I followed standard procedure. I just had no reason to make him a target. No one asked questions, since he was of a different political party from most of my bosses. I did nothing illegal. But suddenly, one afternoon shortly after my fortieth birthday, I realized what I was doing. For years I had been trying, for reasons that I would not admit to myself, to find something that I could use on Carolyn's husband. Something that would bring him down, stop his meteoric rise almost to the presidency, and make her run back into my arms.

The point is, without really being a theory, that fascination can be stronger than love and stronger than laws and rules and regulations. The intoxicating taste of a woman, or maybe just a whiff of Rebecca Townsend's perfume, may have led some men in this agency to bend the rules, to use information in perfectly legal but morally questionable ways. For we all watched Rebecca, even if we didn't have her ourselves. We watched her seduce our young recruits, as if it were some strange tribal custom that the young warriors would be brought into our little secret club by this woman. We all listened to the tapes as she unbuttoned the shirt of some college senior, or breathed into some professor's ear. We had women in Cambridge and New Jersey and Stanford who all recruited without taking their catches to bed, but if there was an important catch, one we couldn't afford to lose, like some foreign diplomat's son, we flew in Rebecca for the kill.

There is a spider-web-thin line between eavesdropping and voyeurism. A line so sticky that it is easy to get caught on. So many of you who control this agency were voyeurs of Rebecca's exploits—and rather than cheapening her, her grace, professionalism, and success made her more desirable in your eyes. You may not have actually slept with her, but you knew what she was capable of, just as I had seen Carolyn that first time, so to keep your options open you were nice to her. You gave her what she wanted, with a wink and a lingering glance when she walked away from you down the hall.

There are well-fingered pictures of Rebecca in the file. You've seen them. In a white bikini on a beach, crouched over the rippled chest of a young man who had his hands in her long hair. Another photograph of her just in jeans, the front unbuttoned, and her bare breasts pressed against a prospective recruit's black leather jacket. The photographs have been passed around, and I know you've listened to the heavy breathing on the tapes. She entertained us all and brought a different type of danger to jobs that we all wished were as glamorous as they are made out to be in the movies.

So Rebecca gets files without clearance. Rebecca gets access without approval. Rebecca touches you and smiles and you tell her what she wants to hear. Once we started counting the cases of Rebecca getting something classified top secret umbra or other sensitive compartmented information while she was on "special assignment," I was shocked. The simple fact is that she got whatever she wanted.

Carolyn got what she wanted, too. Rich, beautiful, well connected. She was a society columnist's dream.

Carolyn would dance with me at some formal dinner dance and I would tell her anything just to keep her entertained. I would always wonder but never ask what she had done with her husband-to-be the night they met at the party in Central Park. I would gossip about people and reveal tantalizing information just so she'd invite me to another party, or sit me close to her so I could turn to her and say, "I don't believe we've met."

You were promoted. Rebecca was promoted. Carolyn inherited a fortune and used it to help her husband organize a presidential campaign. But the difference between the two is that Rebecca was a spy, while Carolyn was a wife. Rebecca is causing all of you problems because we were voyeurs, adulterers, wishers of deeds we weren't man enough to commit. Carolyn still makes a pretense of at least acknowledging my secret dream of having a wife—someone loyal, supportive, a breeder of confidence, a partner in the storm.

Rebecca, I don't think we've met. I know we have not gone off into the trees and made love. And yet my hands are tied by you.

Carolyn, we have met, all my playful kidding aside. Carolyn's husband died of a heart attack three weeks before the Iowa caucuses. Three years later she called me on my fiftieth birthday, said she had heard that I was divorced, and asked me to dinner. We dined. We danced. We laughed. We drove to her mammoth house in Virginia and talked all night long. She thought she was just going out with me because I was in the intelligence business and she needed some assistance with an executive who had worked for her and had been kidnapped while visiting a potential takeover target in Mexico. She told me that her intent was to try to hire me, or at least buy my expertise, to help her out of the jam her company was in. She was hoping to rent me to solve the kidnapping, which was clearly part of some nefarious industrial espionage. But once I was with her, I refused to let go. In the midst of training her to save her kidnapped employee I asked her to marry me. She put me off, not saying yes or no, until she returned from Mexico.

I married Carolyn five years ago, on my fifty-second birthday, and I have still never asked her if she knew I was there that night, looking for her, imagining her drunkenly making love in Central Park. The odds are that what I believed happened did not happen. The odds are that she gave him only a little peck of a kiss and her phone number, and, like the nice little rich boy that he was, he called her up a few days later and they made a date. The odds are that Carolyn is simply too controlled to abandon herself as I imagined. But I'm not a betting man, so I simply don't ask—still not sure what I want the answer to be.

As I sit in the study she decorated for her first husband, I smile and wonder what she remembers and what she knows. I spend hours making up stories about what her motivation is; why she seems to love me so. I spend hours coming up with theories to explain the turns of fate that have brought my life to where it is, intertwined inexplicably with her life. The only answer I know to why she loves me so is that I love her.

She also loves what I do, although not so much that she married me for it. But from those first dinner parties back when her husband was alive and I was telling her things I should not have said in order to keep her entertained, she has been fascinated by the business. Her eager interest in it is where she shows that wild side that springs up in the midst of tension or too much wine. That disregard for the stifling rich-girl decorum she grew up with, or the laws of civil society she has grown into. She loves me because I'm a spy, even if I am one who sits at a desk and directs others who see all the action. After we married and she was forced to deal with terrorists, con men, and industrial espionage, she threw herself into training programs: learning how to fly, how to shoot, how to decode simple messages. It was as if she could protect herself from the harsh world of international business by learning the skills to protect herself in the jungle. She could hire lawyers and accountants, she told me, but she needed to know how to shoot a gun. Because I knew how to shoot a gun, though I rarely did it, and tap a phone and hot-wire a car, I encouraged her. I knew nothing about law, accounting, or economics, so this was a way that I could be of value. A way for me to pay my share of the rent, so to speak. With my help, she became a true amateur spy, like Ernest Hemingway, who helped us with Cuba, or Moe Berg, the baseball player for the Washington Senators who became a great linguist and spy. She spent money like water on gadgets and toys until she was a one-woman information bureau and industrial-espionage expert.

Our wedding was full of her employees, senators, the media consultants who are politicians' only true friends, millionaires, a smattering of my relatives from Boston and New York, her flight instructor, her martial arts teacher, her lawyers, her hairdresser, and a hundred spies. Her maid of honor was Helen, the Judge's wife, and in a fit of perverse honesty my best man was the organization's former top agent, a forty-year-old named Murphy, who had been kicked out of the organization because he had announced that he was gay.

As all of you homophobes know, Murphy and I worked together on a hundred cases, and he had taken two bullets, a mouthful of poison, three broken arms, and a stabbing all trying to accomplish missions I ran from my cozy office. Murphy is the only person to whom I have ever told the story of Carolyn in the park, and as my first gesture of independence I put him in a tux and asked him to hold the rings. Everybody was shocked, not only that I would make such a grandiloquent up-yours gesture to the agency but that Murphy brought an eighteen-year-old weightlifter as his date.

The organization had one on Murphy, but they didn't fire him until he went public. They told him they would keep him if he signed an agreement that he would tell his friends and family, and in particular his mother, dying of cancer, so that no one could blackmail him. But he not only refused, he hired a lawyer and announced that he intended to sue the NSA. Unfortunately, he gave an interview to a local gay newspaper, called *The Blade,* and mentioned two inconsequential but restricted code names. They knew he was out of their control at that point, so they fired him for violating the Internal Security Act and threatened to prosecute him for treason. In order to protect their anonymity they decided to let him go, even though the new dernza, the Judge, thought they should simply have kept him. But on Paul's recommendation, the Judge signed Murphy's pink slip—and then proceeded to hire him for secret projects on an as-needed basis. A week after he was fired, on my recommendation, Carolyn hired him to help her settle once and for all her dispute with the Mexican company, which she intended, now more as a matter of principle than of economics, to take over and dismantle or drive out of business. I admit I helped Murphy organize the mission to free Mike Carter, the president of Carolyn's holding company, from the Mexican terrorists, but I cleared all my actions with the Judge and didn't use a bit of secret information that the agency would not have given to any U.S. company in a similar predicament. I sat at my desk while Murphy and Carolyn went off to save Mike Carter and bring justice to a little town south of Mexico City.

Murphy and I were much alike. Once Murphy was out of control, he was kicked out of the No Such Agency. Once I became out of control—honest and confident with my wife's money—I was retired to my rose garden.

Out I went with a few well-chosen words by John X. John X was one of the golden boys who had that intense Vietnam vet veneer that the Judge only pretended not to be taken in by. John X had the translucent, ephemeral skin of good southern interbreeding. The type of skin where you can see every vein pulsate in his rigid weed-thin body. A body that had allegedly been tortured in Vietnam when he was a POW for ten days before his brigade swarmed over the town where he was held. However, I believe the only scars were in his mind. John X craved order, organization, and loyalty—which, at least superficially, is what made his actions with Rebecca so out of character.

He became the Judge's personal assistant in D Group at a young age, and I was the Judge's best friend. Naturally, we worked together daily, but the tension and the competition for the Judge's attention grew after I married Carolyn and my insecurities began to disappear. I reappeared, like a snake who has shed its skin, as a man confident that I could, and someday might, run the whole agency. That attitude did not set well with John X or with the deputy dernza, Paul.

At the same time, Langley got this crazy idea, which has captured every American intelligence agency now, that the NSA should concentrate more on industrial espionage and helping American companies compete in the global marketplace by tracking down foreigners who violate our copyright laws, who flout our trade agreements, and who consort with terrorists and drug dealers. But in order to do that we had to make sure that no one within the organization had an economic interest that would lead them to favor one company over another. The internal security division, which was trained to find Soviet moles, was suddenly also given the mission to be our ethics police. And lo and behold, on the ninth floor John X was made the grand inquisitor of conflicts of interest. The captain of the ethics police. I was, of course, a likely target from the beginning. John X, only a week later, submitted to the Judge a report, which I have never seen, that detailed the many violations of organization policy and regulations, approved by Congress, that I had flouted in my pursuit of discovering what happened in each and every case brought to me. The key alleged violation was that I told Carolyn too much, and Carolyn's competitors circulated a story that she was trading on agency information to make deals. No one understood that I was simply too rich to even accidentally let loose with any information that could have been helpful to Carolyn. I simply did not have any motive. But then again, I was a trained analyst, so motive was important to me. To the Judge, appearance was everything. I had helped Carolyn with Murphy's mission to Mexico to rescue Mike Carter. He knew all about that, because I had told him every detail so that there wouldn't be any misunderstanding about what I was doing. But because he knew about it, and had approved it, he didn't want anyone to pry into it. The Judge didn't want the story investigated, he just wanted me out.

My guess is that I did commit every technical violation that John X listed, but that was why I was good at what I did. But there was no truth to the story that I told Carolyn information that she could use, let alone did use, to further her economic interest. That was merely sour grapes from competitors who had been beaten at their own game by this thin, fragile-looking woman. What I told Carolyn, before we were married, were things that I thought would make me look interesting, because the information was interesting. I was guilty, but not as charged, and my motivation was love, not money.

But that little report was the grounds for the Judge to retire me. The morning after the lunch at which the Judge handed me that little slip of pink paper, John X called me on the gray phone, nearly in tears, to apologize and explain he had no idea how the information would be used and if he had it to do all over again he wouldn't ever put anything in writing without my reviewing it for political land mines. But it was too late. Ever since then he made a point of taking me out to lunch and consulting with me on difficult issues that his office had to address. But until the day he called and told me about Rebecca and the recording device he had put in Tommy's belt, he had never risked talking to me on an outside telephone.

I suppose it was guilt, then, that led John X, the man with skin so thin you could see through it, to contact me with top-secret information that no one else had heard. He told me everything as if I were sitting on the other side of the grill in the confessional. I remember him saying, "Of course, if you tell anyone about the bug in the belt buckle they could have me fired—even worse, if you're right about FISA—have me indicted, probably. I mean, this is no technical violation, like the ones they got you on, Steele. This is big-time, go-to-jail kind of stuff. So there, I guess you've got one on me, pal."

Now you all have one on me, pals. But that seems only fair. It seems only fair because I have one on so many of you. It's fair that I tell you this so you don't think I'm blackmailing any of you in any subtle way. I'm not angling for your jobs. I'm not maneuvering for your turf. You'll have dinner at my wife's mansion, because she loves to invite spies over, and as she passes the wine you'll imagine her hands tied with a black satin bow tie, and as you pour your wife a glass I'll imagine telling your wife about your last night with Rebecca and the files she took off your desk.

I have no reason to lie. I have the documents stacked around me in my musty corner office. The world around us is changing faster than we can keep up with. Ah, gentlemen, the truth—I don't believe we've met.

10.

WHEN THE AGENCY'S MEN on the train did not answer HQ's calls and did not show up at the next stop on the line, John X had Bobby tap into the railroad's radiophone line so they could call the engineer of the train. They learned that Rebecca and Tommy might have got off the train at a small station somewhere west of Philadelphia. The engineer said they made no unscheduled stops, but they did have to slow to a crawl when a faulty sensor on the tracks told them that something, maybe a tree or a telephone pole, had fallen across the tracks. The sensor must have been broken, the engineer said, since they never saw anything lying across the tracks.

"Oldest trick in the book," Bobby the techy suggested to John X. "She had the sensor fixed so that she could just hop off when they slowed down. This dame is really something."

"Yes," John said. "Rebecca is really . . . ," and he paused, searching for the right word to describe that wild red-headed grandeur that he believed she had. Not finding any word that wouldn't sound silly, he settled for repeating, "Really something. Rebecca is really something."

Then John X left the agency rules completely behind. He got on the phone and started ordering action that he had no authority to order, moving men and spending money without approval, and not bothering to even look at, let alone fill out, the mountain of paperwork that what he did would have required. He went out on his own and didn't come back.

By the time he got a general location from the engineer of where the train had slowed down, John X had sent his geographically closest men, two former Bureau boys who had retired in Philadelphia, out to the nearest airport with a faxed map. It was a CAD drawing, whipped off the computer, based on the sketchy details that we knew of the general area where we thought Rebecca's family farm was. For the record, John X, who was usually very good about noting things for the record, noted that it was very unusual that we did not have something somewhere in the organization's collective wisdom about exactly where Rebecca's family lived. Langley, he duly noted for the benefit of the agency boys, would never have let this kind of sloppiness go unchecked.

But that is just where the sloppiness began.

The two retired Bureau boys loaded up a rented Ford Taurus with doughnuts and coffee and drove to a quiet, nearly abandoned airport. The files show that John X had a rented Air Force cargo Lear jet skid to a stop on the nearly too-short strip of asphalt, and while the tower berated the pilot and the three-man ground crew berated our men, the pilot taxied the jet to within twenty feet of their car. The section chief's new number one man, Bobby the techy, jumped out of the plane before the stairs were completely down, with a heavy, square black box in his hands.

They shook hands, and former agent Johnson passed his jelly-filled doughnut with a bite out of it to former agent Morris so he could take the black box from Bobby. The analysis done later showed his sugar-stained fingerprints on the side of the black box.

"What is this sucker?" Johnson must have asked, turning the forty-pound box over to examine all sides of it.

"I have no idea," Bobby reportedly lied as he handed them the folded twenty-four-inch parabolic antenna and the small black keyboard. "I'm supposed to tell you to get it as close to the subjects as possible and hide it in a dry, high place. Like at the top of a tree. Then screw the antenna into the hole there."

"But it's already got an antenna," Johnson grumbled, pointing to the wire-whip antenna that came out of its side.

"That's for receiving," Bobby said, probably realizing that he was talking more than he should. "The parabolic antenna is for sending. Now, once you get someplace good, check the coordinates on this map and type in your location. The keyboard plugs in here. Once you type in your location, the parabolic antenna will rotate and aim at the nearest MILSTAR satellite. Don't worry if the location you type in isn't exact, it's got a backup to the GPS receiver that's built into the thing. Bring the keyboard back with you, all right?"

Morris patted his belly and shouted to Bobby as Bobby turned to get back on the plane, "Climbing trees is something I've kinda forgotten how to do! Former agents don't have to climb trees, buddy boy!"

Bobby caught his eye, ordered, "For this kind of pay you can remember," and got back on the waiting jet. To the screams of the ground crew and the recorded curses of the tower, the jet was off without any further notice, less than one minute after it had landed.

Johnson and Morris put the black box in the front seat of the Ford and spilled coffee on their maps and on the black box's cryptic directions, both of which we recovered later, as they drove fast into the late afternoon. They got farther and farther into the mountains, searching for a road with no clear name, when they suddenly thought they found it. They were in far western Pennsylvania, on the edge of the west side of the mountain range, in stony, soiled land where few people lived. The map said they were in the right place, and the small red light on the side of the box flickered on and off, which they took as a good sign. The fading sunset made it hard to see, so they were creeping along when they came to a small stone bridge. They turned into a heavily wooded dirt lane on the other side of the bridge and came face to face with a bearded man sitting alone in a jacked-up Bronco, with a reefer in his mouth and a rifle slung across his dashboard.

Agent Johnson told me later that he didn't think much of the guy at first, so he hiked up his polyester pants and began to get out of the car to ask directions. The bearded man shouted out his window, "Just stay in your car!"

"But I'm—"

The bearded man laid a hand on his gun, and Agent Morris, bald, sixty, with a case of perpetual flatulence, stuck his badge out of the car and said, "Federal agents!" in his best deep voice. His shout was answered by a rifle shot out of the dark woods that exploded the Ford's back left tire. Johnson, who was on the other side of the car, rolled his fat body out into the darkness, pulling the black box and antenna with him, and crouched with his pistol out behind a big pin oak. The oak took most of the shotgun blast that followed his door after it swung open, but two pellets dug into Johnson's left ankle, which later qualified him for a month's disability.

Morris ducked low and threw the car into reverse but hit a rock ledge on the side of the entrance to the dirt lane. He got two shots off at the Bronco as it charged his car before he saw four rifles pointing at him at close range from all sides.

"Okay," he suggested in his best grandfatherly tone. "Everybody stay calm. Nobody shoot."

Four men in ski masks in August surrounded him as he stepped out of the car and dropped his gun. He stood in the Bronco's headlights, waiting for orders.

"Tell your friend," Johnson told me the shortest of the masked men said, picking up Morris's handgun and weighing it in his palm, "to come in out of the dark."

When Morris made no sound or movement the short man moved closer to him and said, "Or we blow your head off."

"Johnson," Morris shouted weakly. "They've got guns on me. Come on in."

Morris was sweating hard, he later reported, because he knew what standard procedure for the Bureau was. He knew that Johnson would be crawling away farther into the darkness in a matter of seconds, keeping his gun and going for help.

"He'll run," Morris said. "My partner. He'll run. No matter what I say. It's procedure."

The men's eyes glanced back and forth at each other, and the short one asserted, "Radio up. Tell them not to worry about the fireworks. We've got it under control."

He then looked closely at Murphy's badge under the headlights of the Bronco and said, "You boys aren't with ATF?"

"What?" Morris asked, stalling for time and hoping that, as in the movies, he would figure out a solution to this sudden crisis.

"Alcohol, Tobacco, and Firearms, you bastard!" another bellowed.

"No, no, no," Morris nearly whimpered, seeing the script in his mind. "You can just forget about that. We don't care. You got a still or something, that's not our business. You don't—"

"How'd you know we had a still?" another of the men asked.

"I don't," Morris gasped, grasping at straws. "I mean, we're not looking for stills."

"Let's mow these trees down," the short one said to the others as he flipped on the automatic below his trigger.

"Radio it in," another man snapped. "Don't want anybody to be getting spooked."

The man in the truck radioed in something, and then they all pointed toward where Johnson lay flat on the ground with the box and the antenna, afraid to move his bleeding ankle.

Seven men unloaded their firepower into the woods in what Johnson later estimated was eleven seconds, mowing down enough saplings and branches to cover Johnson and the black box with three feet of splinters, vines, branches, and leaves. He realized, he told us, that if they found him they would find the box, so the only thing he could do was leave the box and give himself up so they wouldn't search the woods. He quietly cleared some of the branches away and screwed on the antenna. There was no time to use the keyboard, so he had to hope the GPS receiver could find the location. Then he crawled a few feet away from the black box and gave himself up.

"All right!" he shouted. "I'm coming out if you agree to let us go! We don't want any of you boys' moonshine, okay?"

There was a short conference between the men, and then the short one said, "No, we don't agree to anything. Just come out. Now."

Johnson began to think what his chances were if he tried to make a run for it, but before he had summoned up the courage to even make the decision he heard a branch snap and turned to look into the muzzle of an automatic rifle. "Come on," said a man in a ski mask who had sneaked up on him from behind, giving a diabolical snicker. "Let's go see our friends."

The man had walked within two feet of the hidden black box, Johnson estimated. He took Johnson's revolver out of his hand.

Johnson came out with his hands up, limping with the pellets in his ankle. One of the masked men frisked him, took his wallet, pocketed the cash and his badge, and tossed what was left of the contents to the short one. Two others went through the rental car carefully, in a way that made Johnson wonder, he reported later, what they were looking for and whether they were really dumb hicks making moonshine in the middle of nowhere.

"Do you boys have any tattoos?" the short one asked.

"Tattoos?" Johnson told me he repeated, thinking that they were trying to decide whether he and Morris could be identified if they were left to rot on the forest floor in the middle of nowhere. "No, I don't," he had to admit.

"No," Morris answered, certain now, he told me, that they were going to be killed.

"Well, let's see," the short one snorted. "Strip, or we'll strip you."

"Everything?" Johnson asked when he got down to his decade-old boxer shorts.

"Everything," the short one said with a hint of relish.

After they were carefully examined in the cooling evening air and no tattoos were found, Johnson and Morris were made to change the rental car's shot-out tire in the nude. They were then ordered to drive off, without their clothes and without their lights on. The Bronco followed them for about a mile and then pulled off the road and disappeared, and the two retired men told me they looked at each other, their bodies covered with mud, sweat, and mosquito bites. They laughed until tears ran down their faces.

"God, that was horrible," Johnson remembered saying.

"But thank Jesus we're alive," Morris answered. "Where's the box?"

"Back there in that goddamn woods. But I sure as hell ain't going back to get it."

They tried to drive all the way to the Philadelphia office, but they got pulled over by a deputy sheriff in the next county for speeding and were arrested for indecent exposure and driving without a license. After about two hours the sheriff decided he believed their story, gave them some clothes, and let them go. Johnson and Morris acquired new nicknames from the escapade. But Moonshine and Mosquito Butt aren't in the records, and God knows I wouldn't want to stray from the records, after all the hell I've gotten for my allegedly creative analysis.

The black box, hidden under a pile of branches, began immediately to receive encrypted communications from Tommy's belt and to transmit a 9600 baud frequency that was picked up by an orbiting MILSTAR intelligence satellite, which looked for another MILSTAR and, not finding one at the right angle, automatically sent the transmission to a ground station at Buckley Air National Guard Base, near Aurora, Colorado. The ground station sent the encrypted recordings by coded fiber optic telephone lines across the country, rather than by one of the AT&T, GTE, or COMSAT satellites that carry most other long-distance calls, to a cassette recorder in Bobby's office. By 10:00 P.M. the box had found a MILSTAR and begun to send its encoded transmission from satellite to satellite and then down to HQ. By 11:00 P.M. John X was listening to tapes that made his eyes bug out and his mouth fill the room with expletives.

"We've got to get ahold of the Judge," Bobby whispered when he got back from the airport and heard part of the tapes that were delivered to John X. "We've got to tell him what we've found."

"No," John X said, knowing that through pure luck he had cracked the biggest case in decades and ended his career at the same time. "We get ahold of him, but we don't mention the belt buckle. I don't want him to know we went that far. All right?"

"Man," Bobby exhaled. "I don't know. I think we—"

"I'll do the thinking," John X said, with a panic in his voice that comes across perfectly on the tapes. "You just follow orders. We don't know how big this thing is. We don't know who is in on it. This is bigger than you can imagine, since you don't know the half of it. So play it my way. Do you understand? My way. I want knowledge of that belt to go with us to our graves. I don't want either one of us brought up on charges, because that's the only thing they could get us on. If they don't know about the belt, the worst thing they can do is fire us. No indictments. No congressional investigations. No Ollie North bullshit. Let's just play this quiet and tight. You know, with the lips of dead men."

"All right," Bobby said. "Your way, man. To the grave. Blue lips."

11.

THAT MONDAY NIGHT I was brought into the action, but what happened to me during that Monday day explains much of what happened later. Theory number 780 may be peculiar to the spy business. It goes something like this: You can tell more about why people react the way they do if you study the time before the crucial event, rather than spending so much time studying the crucial event. People do things differently if they've had, or perceive that they have had, a bad day. There is always a predicate act, an event that supplies the crucial missing link in people's behavior at a given time, that happened the day, the hour, the moment before.

So let me tell you about my day.

An hour after John X called me for my advice on how to proceed with Rebecca I put on a suit and did something I hadn't done in the year I had been retired: I had lunch with my wife.

The sprawling corporate headquarters of the holding company she controlled sat on a beautiful green hill in Virginia. The building's light gray Indiana limestone twinkled in the midday sun, which refracted off its cut edges. I waited in her assistant's office while she continued a meeting with her in-house counsel and a gray-faced contingent of her lawyers from the firm that had fired the Judge when he worked in Washington as a young lawyer. Fortunately for the organization, he had returned to the Army, for if he had succeeded at the firm he would be wealthy but unknown now.

"Big meeting?" I asked the pretty young woman whom I talked to on the phone all the time, but whose name escaped me as I stood before her in my too-tailored suit and slightly scuffed expensive shoes. The way she looked me over made me wonder if she had picked out my clothes.

"Yes," she said with a patronizing smile. She was dressed in a perfectly tailored and obviously expensive suit that was in the same style as the outfits favored by Carolyn. "May I get you some coffee or tea while you wait, Mr. Steele?"

"No," I sighed to her deep blue eyes and perfectly trimmed blond hair, refusing to be so overtly patronized by this woman. "I'm sure it won't be long."

"I certainly hope not," she said, showing me her perfectly white teeth and the tip of a wide red tongue. The tone of her young voice said that I was being absurd to think that I wouldn't be waiting for hours. "But it has been a very hectic day."

She smiled at me again as if I were her grandfather, while making it clear that she did not believe Carolyn would break up her meeting just because she knew I was waiting to go to lunch with her. I ran a hand through my gray hair and retaliated against this athletic young woman by imagining her without any clothes on. I hoped she saw me looking at her, imagining her naked, so that she knew that I was not simply going to obediently follow her implied advice about my own wife.

But then I realized how foolish I must look and reminded myself that I always felt hostile to everyone who worked for my wife. That hostility was undoubtedly caused by a combination of all of them being so damn nice to her, so much more attentive than I had ever been, their ability to spend more time with her than I did, and their obvious envy of me for lucking into sharing her opulent life without working for her affection, as they did. All of these insecurities had been aggravated by my being suddenly unemployed. She was a success, I was a failure. She guided a billion-dollar group of companies while I guided a remote-controlled toy sailboat on her immense swimming pool.

"I think I will take you up on that coffee," I said five minutes later, trying to put on my best smile. Then, spying her name on a piece of stationery on her desk, a name I should have remembered since she called my wife half a dozen times a day when we were on vacation, I added, "Laura."

She smiled back, too quickly. "Of course, Mr. Steele."

I knew that this was the woman who probably had chosen half the gifts Carolyn had bought me, including that little sailboat, and knew better than I did how much money we had and what Carolyn was planning to do with it. I wandered a few feet down the hall of the top-floor executive offices, looking at the art, but smartly dressed executive types kept stopping me and asking if they could help me. Laura finally had to save me from a pinstripe-suited security guard whom one of the executive types had obviously called when I had been noncommittal about what I was doing there. Ever since Mike Carter's kidnapping, Carolyn had had Murphy's little private company train all of her top people in terrorist prevention. Apparently I matched the profile of an industrial spy.

"Where's Mike Carter's office?" I asked Laura as she was walking me back to Carolyn's waiting room.

"Right around the corner." She pointed. "I believe he's in today."

What I didn't realize when I walked into Mike Carter's office was how his life was a sign, a symbol of what was to come. Theory number 1389, which is hardly worthy of its own number, is that foreshadow and eyeshadow are inexplicably linked in the twentieth century. Young women for decades have worn too much eyeshadow, realizing only years later, when they looked back at old photographs, how silly they must have appeared, hiding their insecurities about their appearance by drawing attention to themselves like flowers blooming for the nearsighted bumblebee. Only later, when we look back at things, do we often find the half-hidden, nearly forgotten times that give us a tint of how our lives would turn out. The weaknesses masked by the mascara of youth or the early promise of one talent that soon faded away under the weight of dealing with the everyday.

One of those moments for this story slipped by me without my even noticing it the day before I returned to work for the NSA. If I had concentrated then, as I have now that the world has changed, on the minutes I spent leaning against the wall in Mike Carter's office, or the half hour I spent lying on Carolyn's couch in her office, my life, and maybe even the world, might be a different place. For Mike Carter was one of those old photographs that you wish you had the courage to throw away. A reminder of a failure that I, that we, were bound to repeat.

When Mike Carter had been kidnapped in the midst of an international corporate acquisition that had gone very sour, Carolyn had hired Murphy and his men to try to spring Mike from the small band of drug-selling terrorists who were demanding two million in ransom. There was little question that they had been hired by the owners of the Mexican company that Mike Carter was looking to buy, but it was impossible to get the local officials, who were no doubt also on the company payroll, to act. Carolyn had at first considered simply paying the money, but I had insisted that she had no guarantee that the money would get Mike back, so she and Murphy's gang had flown into a small village outside the small town of De Tela de Rio, several hundred miles south of Mexico City. She'd get Mike, and that company, she vowed.

"Hi, Mike," I said, knocking on the door to his small office.

He looked up at me blankly, the left side of his face marked where the bullet had grazed his head before cracking the side of his skull. He could concentrate now for only minutes at a time, and his speech was slow and stilted. Carolyn had, of course, kept him on at his full salary for all these years, but he did very little except read the paper and talk to his wife on the telephone, asking her questions such as when would she come and pick him up, and what was it that was his favorite food.

"Teele," he said, unable to pronounce the *S* at the beginning of my name. But he said it with a smile as he recognized me. I smiled back, feeling the warmth of his personality still there in that toothy grin. "Well, how the hell are you? I haven't seen you in a year"—and then he added, always recognizing that he simply might not have remembered—"hasn't it been? You tell me."

"You're right," I agreed reassuringly, sitting down in the one chair in front of his small desk, but then, realizing that if I sat down it might be hard to leave quickly, I instantly got back up to look out the window and then lean against the wall. There was a computer game on the screen behind him and a newspaper spread out on the desk in front of him. He had little index cards typed out and sitting on the desk to remind him what he was going to do today.

"My daughter is—is," he said, and then paused to gather his thoughts and force his mouth to work, "getting married next week. I—I hope you—you and Carolyn are coming. Won't—I won't be able to walk her—her down the aisle, but it will be—be beautiful."

I saw the pain in his eyes, even though he sat there dumbly smiling in front of me. It was in the dark clouds that floated above my reflection in his pupils, like grumpy demons unable to get out of the glass bubble they were trapped in. He knew that he should say something to me, a reminder of what he had been through, but he simply couldn't quite connect to what he was supposed to say when he saw me.

You must understand the causes of that look in his eye to understand part of the complexity of the story of my pursuit of Rebecca and Tommy. That confusion trapped in the glass bubble of his eyeball was the result of nothing more than bad business decisions. For all of this, in the end, is about business. About bureaucracies dedicated to making money. Rebecca's family business was what led her into a position to change the world. Rebecca's NSA business led her to where she could meet and try to recruit Tommy. Carolyn's business sent Mike Carter to Mexico, and the Mexican business she wanted to buy was willing to do anything to remain independent. I'm sure the Mexican owners had a thousand rationalizations when they hired that bunch to kidnap Mike Carter to scare off the big bad American company. Rebecca's family had their rationalizations too for what they did, and their conversations probably were not so different from the conversations the Mexican businessmen had when they decided to kidnap Mike Carter.

Carolyn would never bring herself to tell me all of the details of what happened in Mexico. But I do know that the ranch where the kidnappers held Mike was named the Mermaid. Maybe, I speculate, it was because it was on a river and next to a Spanish Catholic convent, where the Europeans had taught the local people about mermaids hundreds of years before. When Murphy's team approached the ranch, there was a pucca-wood sculpture of a green-and-red mermaid hammered into the rough tree limbs that made up the gate. But the mermaid looked as though she was screaming more than laughing, undoubtedly due to the religious rapture or drug-induced confusion (the pucca tree has a hallucinogenic bean, which the sculptors often chew while they carve) of the man who was forced to decorate the dilapidated ranch.

The result of Carolyn's mission was not good. Her pilot was killed, Mike was shot in the head, Murphy broke an arm, and three of his men were wounded. On their way out Murphy pulled up the wooden mermaid and brought it back to Carolyn. It sits in her office at home now, on a table with lights underneath, its smiling face stretched to a scream.

The day Carolyn returned to the States I met her at the Washington hospital where they had brought Mike, and she held me very close. For the first time, she sobbed uncontrollably in my arms.

"Never again," she said simply and flatly when she pulled out of my arms. "Never again."

I didn't have to ask what she meant. I knew that she felt she had been unprepared for the task she had set out to accomplish. Unprepared for a task she should not, could not, ever have imagined she would ever need to accomplish. I asked her again to marry me, and she let only one tear fall when she agreed. I wonder sometimes whether she married me out of fear that maybe she couldn't accomplish anything that she set her mind to; that there were times when she needed to be protected. Maybe she saw the world of spies and intelligence as the one area where she was not the master, and married me for my perceived strength, not knowing that I was really just an analyst and therefore farther away from gunshots and midnight plane rides than she had been. Maybe she would have married Murphy if he had not been gay. Maybe she would have married James Bond, if he had been around. But I was in the right place at the right time, so I had to do as her protector, her teacher, her lover.

For years she was always inquisitive about my job, but never expressed an interest in getting involved in the thrill of the chase again. She loved the spy business, but she abhorred the thought of my risking my life. Only after she learned what I actually did—made up stories to explain away the unexplainable—was she happy. But later that Monday night, when Murphy called, something popped inside her head, telling her that she should grab the opportunity to be on the front line again.

"How have you been, Mike?" I asked.

Before he could answer, Laura poked her head into the office and said, "Mr. Steele, your wife will be finished momentarily."

I shook hands with Mike, promising to have lunch with him sometime, and went back down the hall, breathing heavily. The brain was so frail, I told myself, and yet personality is so strong. Mike Carter was still there, not able to tie his own shoes but still there, like pieces of a broken puzzle.

If only I could put that puzzle back together again, I told myself as I followed Laura down a long hall. If only I could put his life back together so that one bullet would have moved an inch to the right and missed him altogether.

I had come ten minutes early, which is something I had never done in my life until I was retired, but it was nearly fifty minutes later when Carolyn burst out of the giant oak doors of her office with a half dozen men in tow and stopped for just a fraction of a second to kiss me on the cheek and tell me that she would be only a minute longer. The crowd paused behind her, smiled at me as if I were an unusual pet, and then followed her behind another closed door on the other side of Carolyn's assistant's secretary's desk.

A gentle buzzer went off on Laura's phone, and she got up and went into the meeting behind the giant closed doors, leaving me alone in the spacious antechamber. I brushed the dandruff off my shoulders and pulled at a thread that hung from a trouser cuff. I memorized the headlines on the dull business magazines fanned out over the coffee table. I began to plan my retaliation for having to wait for nearly an hour. Then Carolyn came out of the room, followed by Laura, still smiling her perfect smile.

"I'm sorry, honey," Carolyn said. "This takeover is—"

"Carolyn?" One of the lawyers gestured behind her, his eyebrows raised and his voice scolding.

"This is my husband, Ralph," Carolyn said. "T. C. Steele, meet Ralph Katskill Winter, distinguished, overbearing partner at the firm of—"

"Oh, stop it," he snapped, shaking my hand. "I'm sorry, Mr. Steele, it's just that we have advised Carolyn not to talk to anyone about this—this transaction. This proposed—possible transaction. Security and secrecy are very important in these types of things."

"Of course," I said, uncomfortable that someone was telling me about the importance of secrecy and security.

"And what do you do, Mr. Steele?" Ralph asked.

I paused for a moment, reliving the dozen moments when I had risked my life for my country, but then said simply, "I'm retired."

"How nice," Ralph mumbled. He smiled at Carolyn. "I'll see you in half an hour, Carolyn?"

"Yes, yes, yes," she said, obviously annoyed. "Laura, would you get Matthews and Kronski up here in half an hour for a conference call and tell them to bring every damn bit of information they have on—on this project?"

"But—" I started.

"I've had lunch brought in," Carolyn said, swinging open the door to her office, which stretched across the front of the building like a football field. It was full of leather couches and sleek conference tables that floated like jetsam around a desk the size and color of an old mahogany Chris-Craft speedboat.

"But I have, or at least had an hour ago, reservations at—"

"I'm sorry, honey, but I just don't have time," she responded, closing the door behind us. "There is just so much going on here. I just can't leave right now. But look, I had Laura get all kinds of great things. Shrimp, a little lobster salad. She had the caterer do it up right."

"Carolyn, Carolyn," I said, sinking into one of the couches and putting my feet up on a pillow just to show that I felt as though I owned the place, even though I probably had been in her office only half a dozen times since our marriage. "Maybe I ought to work here, just so I could see more of you. I could be your assistant. I could be Laura's assistant. I could be Laura's secretary's assistant's driver. I could be Mike Carter's assistant and help him find the bathroom."

"Mike's doing fine," she said defensively.

"I know," I offered. "I just stopped in and talked to him while I was waiting."

Suddenly she looked up at me, a sandwich in one hand, one page of what she was reading in the other. She looked as if she had just realized that I was there—as if my bad choice of words had forced her awake.

"When is the last time we had lunch together?" she asked.

"I have no idea. I think this is the first time this year, if you call this having lunch together."

She smiled and said, "You know, I don't think we've met."

I looked up over the side of the couch, examining her fine cheekbones and wide, loving lips. "Take off your clothes," I slyly said to my wife.

"Oh God, we do have to spend more time together," she mumbled. "How about I quit doing this? Just let the place run itself and you and I start a business together. Something exciting. Maybe become mercenary spies. Like Murphy. Intelligence agents to the highest bidders. There might be a fortune in it. We could be the first married couple to do it. Trailblazers."

"We already have too much money, don't we?" I asked, feeling that shiver come on again. She was determined to exorcise some demon she had and do something dangerous. "And besides, we wouldn't be the first ones. There's millions of sleazy married people out there selling what they know. I see it all the time. Why don't you just be a housewife. Stay home with the kids. Go shopping. Do gardening."

"We don't have any kids," she said, sitting down in a tangled mess of chrome and leather that passed for a chair. She never talked about children with me, maybe because she had never had any and now it was too late. She pushed a long lock of blond hair tinged with silver out of her face and said, "I already do go shopping, and if I did the gardening what would you and that bevy of people I hire do all day?"

"Good question," I said as Laura popped her smooth young face into the room. Her lips were pursed as if she had just sucked a red popsicle.

"Matthews and Kronski are here," Laura piped. "And Mr. Winter is holding on two."

"Wonderful lunch," I said, bounding up from the couch and spraying bits of lobster salad all over the floor. "The best apple I've had all week."

"Oh, Steele," Carolyn called, pulling on the handmade Italian shoe that had slid off as she sat in the chrome chair. I was halfway out the door before her words brought me back. "I've messed this all up. Let's go on a vacation. Someplace dangerous where only young, crazy people go. Let's have an adventure."

TWO

THE BEGINNING OF SORROWS

As he was leaving the Temple one of his disciples said to him, "Look at the size of those stones, Master! Look at the size of those buildings!" And he said to him, "You see these great buildings? Not a single stone will be left on another: everything will be destroyed." And while he was sitting facing the Temple, on the Mount of Olives, Peter, James, John, and Andrew questioned him privately, "Tell us, when is this going to happen, and what sign will there be that all this is about to be fulfilled?"

—Mark 13:1

12.

THEORY NUMBER 47: If someone is trained to look for something, they notice that thing to the exclusion of everything else. Hairdressers see a person's hair. Shoe salesmen look for a person's shoes. Architects notice buildings. When Tommy pulled up to Rebecca's family farm at the end of a late-summer sunset he noticed first the low rails in the road that the Jeep drove over, to keep cattle from wandering out across the road, and the dozens of beehouses lined up across the field in front of the large farmhouse. The dual lines of the three-foot-high boxes, each with a halo of returning bees glinting in the rays of falling light, stood like sentinels on the field that stretched from one edge of the forest, across the hundred-acre clearing, to the other edge of the thick Pennsylvania woods.

The fifteen-minute drive from the train station to the farm had taken them almost an hour as the brothers raced around the countryside, making sure to get Tommy lost, no matter how good he was at memorizing directions. "This is the scenic route," Rebecca explained as she relaxed during the bumpy ride, becoming more animated with each mile, until she was beautifully radiant when they arrived. "Like a sunrise," Tommy told me later. "With her auburn hair with golden streaks and peach-colored cheeks. The half-conscious purity of dawn."

The Dutch colonial farmhouse rose out of the clearing like a clean white whale beached on the edge of a steep hill. It was surrounded by a jumble of crisp white outbuildings, all of which had oversize emerald green shutters. There were big pitched-roof barns and long, low-slung stables on both sides of the house, shouldering up to it in a protective way. They were all perfectly normal except that they were connected by an eight-foot-high whitewashed brick wall.

I'm sure Tommy recognized it as a classic European farm layout: Each building had a distinct purpose, and all were huddled around the house, forming a walled compound. Every building appeared old but immaculately cared for and handsomely landscaped. The shrubbery was trimmed in long, straight geometric patterns, the gravel walks were raked, and flowers bloomed everywhere, tumbling out of the brick-lined beds.

Around the corner of the hill Tommy could see four smaller houses grouped around a large central space, which he guessed were the brothers' homes. Before he had even stepped out of the Jeep he saw a simple, understated wealth everywhere around him. There was no ornamentation, but a strict neatness that spoke silently of an attention to detail that only money could breed. This was a very rich farmer's home, Tommy knew, remembering the ramshackle farms of his hometown in Indiana. There were no scrawny chickens pecking around the yard, he noticed, no thin old cows, but big, bounding German shepherds and sleek grazing horses.

"Looks like everybody's here," Rebecca commented, seeing the dozen cars and trucks in the driveway, none of them the color of the Jeeps they rode in.

"Looks like a family reunion," Tommy said, measuring the beam of the house in his mind and not paying much attention to what she said, every sense he had suspicious of everything he heard, smelled, tasted, and felt.

"Family and some local gentry—hunters," Jan mumbled, and then he spoke up. "Dad's buddies are all going out early in the morning. Going to try to get some deer. The last big hunt goes forward regardless of whether there's a family reunion going on. They're staying the night, but Mom won't have them to dinner."

"You must have a lot of beds," Tommy suggested, locating the bedrooms in the floor plan in his mind.

"They'll stay up at the hunting lodge," Erik said, bringing the Jeep to a halt in front of the big wooden doors of the house. "Which is quite fun. In fact, maybe we should camp out there, Rebecca?" He paused and looked at her before he opened the Jeep door. "Maybe you and your friend Tommy here should camp up there and enjoy nature, since you're such a city girl now. It might be quieter up there."

"A hunting lodge?" Tommy asked.

"Dad has a lodge up in the woods," Rebecca explained with a smile. "Mostly to get away from Mom." Then, as she flung open the back door of the Jeep, the wide oak front doors swung open and an elderly man and woman came quickly striding down the steps, their arms outstretched to Rebecca, their daughter. Rebecca's father was balding, with Einstein-like tufts of white hair ringing his tanned head, a white mustache framing his beaming smile. He wore a gray cardigan even in the heat, and carried a big-bowled pipe in his hand. Rebecca's mother was small, athletic, and freckled, her bright eyes almost hidden behind thick gold-rimmed glasses. They looked like half of a country club bridge game on a Saturday evening.

"Welcome home!" her mother sang, just as the first shots aimed into the woods at Johnson, lying under the oak tree with the black box, rang out far in the distance; the sound nothing more than a hammer hitting a nail that no one noticed except the black box as it dutifully sent its signals up into the sky. Rebecca's mother hugged Rebecca and then offered her manicured hand to Tommy, her bespectacled eyes carefully examining his face. "I am Anna Townsend, Rebecca's mother. I'm so glad to meet you." The tone of her voice expressed approval and appreciation of Tommy, like the grumbling hum in an auctioneer's voice when he assesses the value of an object.

"I'm glad to—" Tommy began, but Rebecca's father stepped around Rebecca and gently took Tommy's arm, leading him into the house. "Quite a place," Tommy said amid all the hugging and kissing.

"So, you must be Tommy," Rebecca's father asserted, as if Tommy had not said a word. "I am called either Dad, Pop, son of a bitch, or Doc around here, yes? Take your pick."

Tommy's eyes shot at Rebecca asking a thousand questions without words. "I suggest 'Doc,' " she said. "I'd be afraid that if you called him Dad or Pop people would think you were genetically related to all of us, which would certainly be an insult to you."

"Becky!" her mother said, touching her perfectly combed gray hair in feigned surprise. "You haven't changed one ounce."

"My Rebecca is soft on you. I know, yes?" Doc said. "She hasn't said so, but she brought you home. And this weekend of all weekends—a family reunion. You know, you're the first one she's brought home since college. Just put your bags down there. I'll have one of the boys bring them in. Jan, would you take Tommy's bags here up to their room?"

"Of course, Papa," Jan agreed, with a smile and a tolerant wink to Rebecca. Jan was the tallest of the brothers, with bright red freckles that made him always look as though he was smiling. He laughed out loud when he leaned over to pick up the one bag Tommy had brought, and one of his three-year-old sons ran out the door and jumped on his back. "Horsey, Daddy!" the boy yelled.

"Anna won't mention it, but we decided to put the two of you in the same room, yes?" Doc said, picking up a grandchild in a pink pinafore who came running out the front door. "It's always an issue when a daughter brings home a guest—but she never brings anyone home, so we didn't know what to do. Isn't that right, Jessie?"

The little girl nodded, wiping chocolate on her dress. Doc stroked his white moustache and said, "Jessie, this is Tommy. Tommy is your Aunt Rebecca's friend. Jessie is Erik's youngest, and a bit chubby like your daddy, yes? And this is Sandy, Fritz's wife, and Jennifer, Joe's wife. This is Tommy Wood, Rebecca's mystery guest."

"Hello," Tommy said to the women, whom he could barely describe later. "It's nice to—"

"Would you like something to drink?" Doc asked, steering him down the front hall of the house. He stepped over two Matchbox cars and a half-dressed Barbie doll and kept talking. As Tommy was pulled through the house he was introduced to more and more grandchildren, but they all whirled by in their parents' arms, virtually indistinguishable until they began to cry.

"A beer, yes? Anna, some of the good beer, please. My wife has to get drinks," he said quietly, as if he were speaking only to Tommy, who, still in a daze, lowered his head as if he were listening. "Because the cook won't cook and the housekeeper won't keep, or whatever it is that we hired her to do. You do drink, yes? Good, never trust a man who doesn't drink. Who doesn't have things to forget, yes? Rebecca says you're an architect. That's good. You can design a barn while you're here. A bull barn. After dinner we can go look at the bulls. They need a new barn. More space. Some new fancy watering system. You've never designed a barn, yes? That's all right. I know what I want, I just need some—let's say, some professional help."

And so the evening went. A whirl of Doc Townsend's words that Tommy, in his heightened awareness, remembered very well. What he didn't remember the black box began to pick up, the sounds going from the microphone in Tommy's belt to the black box, up to the scrawny conglomeration of metal circling twenty-two thousand feet above the earth, and then beamed back down again directly to Fort Meade and then by fiber optic cable to the situation room at HQ, where John X had the sense to tape everything.

Doc Townsend, retired internist and gentleman farmer, talked to Tommy through three beers, a dinner of Wiener schnitzel and carrots and peas from the garden, six bottles of Gewürztraminer, and an introduction to the entire family. While Rebecca was constantly led away for private conversations with her brothers and sisters-in-law, Tommy met all eleven nieces and nephews, Uncle Albert and Aunt

Ethel, who were really not related to the Townsends, the cook, the housekeeper, Otto the driver and gardener, and seven of the farm employees who lived on the farm full time and their four wives and eight children. The rest, Doc explained, were up at the lodge entertaining their friends, who Tommy noted had been introduced as Doc's friends.

"And a toast," Rebecca's mother offered over a rich caramel-colored dessert of apple strudel, her voice as smooth as tanned leather on the tape from the bug in Tommy's belt. "Please pass the wine here, Sandy."

"Another toast," Jan said, pouring himself another glass of wine as the bottle went by on the way to his mother.

"Yes, another in a long line of toasts!" Fritz shouted, holding up his glass.

"To Rebecca," her mother said, her eyes moist and loving. "For this idea to have a family reunion and for organizing it all."

"To Becky!" Joe shouted.

"Yeah, rah!" Erik's wife laughed.

"To the family—the whole family," Erik stated more solemnly. And then they all touched their glasses, the dozens of clicks beating out a joyous, syncopated rhythm on the tape.

Theory number 602: Communication is an essential part of the human condition. It is not natural for people to keep secrets, which is what we at the NSA must wrestle with every day, and what gives us our purpose. Because people have an almost uncontrollable urge to share their observations, to tell someone what they believe they should not tell, professional eavesdroppers like us are kept in business. Eventually, virtually every twisted tale gets told. Eventually, even those trying to control their urge to tell drop enough clues to give you someplace to start your search for the truth. Even Rebecca's mother could not help but leave clues when she toasted Rebecca for organizing a family reunion that seemed to have taken no organization at all. Her brothers came regularly to visit the farm, they said. Her sister wasn't able to join them. Rebecca simply announced to Tommy that they were going one day. No, it is clear to even the simple-minded, and the professional, that Rebecca was toasted for organizing something much more than drawing them all together around this table. Rebecca was toasted for something much more than Tommy knew as he poured himself another glass of wine and tried to remember the name of Jan's wife, who sat next to him.

There were more toasts and stories about when the brothers and sisters were children growing up in Philadelphia. Jan had shot a neighbor boy in the buttock with a BB gun. Fritz had gotten his father's car stuck in a ditch when he was parking with a favorite cheerleader. Rebecca's sister, Margert, who had not yet arrived, had insisted that she couldn't have overdrawn her first checking account because she still had checks left. Erik met his wife-to-be when Jan took her as his date to their high school prom.

"You know," Tommy told me later, "sitting at that long dining-room table with Rebecca and all her family members, I don't think I ever loved her more. I didn't know what to expect. I didn't even know that Rebecca had organized this family reunion. But they were all so warm, so friendly. All of them tan and rested. The picture of health. It was like a Norman Rockwell painting. Everybody drinking good wine and kissing their mother when they got up to get second helpings of this heavy German food. Teasing each other and kicking each other under the table. They were so normal. So different from the quiet little house I grew up in. I mean, Steele, these people actually liked each other. They had fun being together. I ate it all up like a drug. I just couldn't get enough of them. But I'll tell you, the thought did cross my mind that nobody could be this happy unless they were hiding something."

Doc put his pipe in his pocket after dinner, and with a wineglass in one hand and a two-year-old granddaughter perched on his hip, he gave Tommy a tour of the house, pointing out the stuffed ten-point deer head he had got just last season, the rocking chair that was a replica of the one President Kennedy had loved, the basement toy room that was littered with wooden blocks, slides, Lincoln Logs, and a battered toy train. Doc ran his hand lovingly over the dusty bottles in his wine cellar and talked and talked and talked.

"This is the life, isn't it?" Doc asked the dusty bottles. "Good land. Good family. Good food. All of us together. I like to show this to an outsider, like you, yes? It makes me realize what I have. What we have. I hate to leave this—I'd hate to, but I won't, you understand. Families should stay together, yes. Though it's money, I understand. Careers. I left my family to make my fortune. So I understand. But I've done right here. This country has been good to me, yes? Just fine, so I want my family to be happy. I want good health for my family. I want peace for my family. Health and peace."

He stopped for a moment, and Tommy almost said something, but then he realized again that this wasn't a conversation. Doc pulled out a bottle, its dusty glass dark green with the old red wine inside it. He held it up to the light and brushed off the label. "Yes, here you see, the year Rebecca was born. Petrus. Good wine. Things have never been the same since she was born. But like this wine, she has improved with age, yes? When she was a little tyke she was bossy, always telling her brothers and sister what to do. But she has become confident as she has grown up. Rebecca is very, very independent. This one has a mind of her own, and once she sets her mind on something, she won't let go. She is the activist in the family. The one who gets things done, yes? When I said I wanted to buy a farm when I retired, and said that year after year, yes? She finally went out and found one for me. She found this farm. The boys would just listen to me complain, but not Rebecca. No, she gets going and there is no stopping her. Like this family reunion. All her idea. She is something, yes?"

"Yes," Tommy managed to squeeze in as Rebecca's father slid the bottle back into the rack. "Yes, she is."

"Now tell me, is my Rebecca happy? I know the answer. I know you make her happy. I can see that in the way she takes your arm, yes? Do you notice that? I think you can tell the way a woman feels about a man by the way she touches him in front of her parents, yes? No hesitation here—she is not embarrassed by you, my boy. She is not concerned what we think about you, because she has already made up her mind. She is ready for a normal life, I believe. I see a husband and children in her eyes. She is tired of all this government business. All this running around the globe. She wants you. She takes your arm, yes, and she doesn't let go. You can tell how a woman feels about a man by the way she touches him in front of her parents."

My fellow spies, you will learn later how Tommy came to be sitting in my study in my wife's house at some nameless hour in the middle of the next night, Tuesday night, telling me and a hidden tape recorder named Sony about that hot rainy evening when he wandered the rooms of the sprawling house listening to Doc Townsend talk about his family. I tell you this so you know that I didn't make up the details. Tommy filled in the details that the microphone in his belt could not pick up—the colors, the smells, the look in someone's eyes when they spoke. Tommy paced the floor of my study and explained every second he was there, every nuance in every phrase, every glimmer in the old man's eyes. While they were on their tour Tommy remembered stumbling across Rebecca and her brothers and mother in the study, and one of them was saying, "This is really an inconvenient time to come here, let alone leave—but bringing him? I mean, I understand the heat, but why bring him here? This thing may have got out of hand." But their tone was so calm, he told me, that he assumed they were talking about some business transaction that he simply didn't know about yet. The problem was that his assumption was right.

Doc steered Tommy to another room, talking louder, quicker, and asking more questions. As they looked out a kitchen window at the barns, Tommy noticed that every window in the house was shut and that the glass he was looking out of was an inch thick. Having designed prisons for a project, he knew what bulletproof reinforced glass looked like, but before he had a chance to say anything Rebecca was at his side with two cold bottles of German sparkling wine. "It's time," she whispered to him. "It's time to tell them."

"But—" Tommy grunted, his garbled voice obviously trying to say that he had a million sudden questions and a hundred sudden doubts after all the unexplained strangeness of the evening, but she was off rounding up the family before he could say anything.

All the children were in bed, the brothers' wives taking them to their cottages, and the assorted employees and friends had all gone to their quarters, so Rebecca gathered her brothers and parents in the front study and made Erik open the wine for toasts. They stood in a haphazard circle together, Doc, his wife, Tommy, Rebecca, Erik, Jan, Fritz, and Joe, their heavy crystal glasses raised and reflecting the dancing sparkles of light from the electric chandelier above.

"My toast is simple," Rebecca said slowly. "I would like to welcome Tommy to the family, for he and I"—and her voice broke for a second on the formality, as if she were afraid to say it or wanted to make sure that she said it just right—"are engaged to be married."

There was a silence, without a raised glass being moved. The brothers' eyes all riveted on Tommy's nervous, twitching smile, until Doc said, "Well, as they say down at the feed store, hot damn! Hot damn, yes?" Then there was hugging and shaking of hands and toasts that went through two more bottles of champagne brought up from the cellar. The brothers gave Rebecca bear hugs and shook their heads at her, saying, "You scoundrel," "You're in trouble now," "No, Tommy's in trouble now," "How could you keep this a secret?" And Rebecca's mother took her glasses off and wiped her eyes, saying "Wonderful, wonderful," over and over again. "What a wonderful way to start a family reunion. This will be the most wonderful week."

"Tommy," Doc sighed, well past midnight. "My boy, you have much to learn about us. We are a peculiar family, as I know you've noticed, yes? Don't protest. I've seen the look in your eye. You are much too polite. I would have demanded an answer—but there's time enough for all that. First, let's design that bull barn. Let's go see those bulls, boys."

"Now?" Jan asked, yawning.

"Of course. Of course. Let's all go."

"Papa," Erik said, "it's almost one. We'll do it tomorrow."

But Doc was already at the back door, his half-intoxicated fingers fiddling with the massive lock on the door.

"Pop," Fritz repeated, "not tonight. We've got enough troubles."

"This is a celebration!" Doc said loudly. "I will not live afraid in my own house. Let's go. To the bull barns. To the bulls."

"All right," Jan acquiesced. "Erik, Joe, let's go with him. Papa's got to go see his bulls in the middle of the night. Come on."

Tommy was out the back door with Doc before he realized that all three brothers picked up rifles out of the closet by the door before walking into the back yard and that Jan was on the telephone talking to someone about what was happening before they were ten feet from the door.

"Wait up, Pop!" Joe shouted as he trotted up to his father's side. A fully automatic Berretta 144 clip rifle casually slung over his shoulder.

"What's with the firepower again?" Tommy asked. "M-16s in the back of the Jeep when we drove up here, now this. What's going on? Isn't that a Berretta?"

"Knows his guns, yes?" Doc said proudly into the starry darkness as they walked among the barns. "Fate, destiny, some perfect arrangement of the stars that my Becky would fall in love with a man who knows his rifles."

"Wild animals," Joe offered, answering Tommy's question. "When you're out here at night, you always take precautions."

"Come on," Tommy said. "In Pennsylvania?"

"We're in the middle of nowhere," Fritz interjected.

"Bears and cougars," Joe said. "They are out here, trust me."

"Total bull!" Doc shouted back at them. "But there's no time to explain everything. Oh, yes, we have so much to talk to you about. So much to explain. Just trust us a little while, yes?"

Doc began to tell Tommy the history of each building, when it was built, what it was built for, and why it was placed where it was. Then he threw his arm around Tommy's shoulder and said, "It's wonderful to have an architect in the family. Now we'll get some things built. We'll expand. We'll grow. We'll need a house for you and Becky. Plenty of room for your children, yes? Nothing will stop us now. We may have to move, you see, so you can design a whole new place for us. I have this place in mind for a new house."

Erik was the first to hear the sound. He was walking twenty feet behind the others, yawning and not listening to his father talk. At first it was a distant rumble, maybe a thunderstorm far away. But as they walked among the farm buildings, the animals rustling awake to their voices, it entered his consciousness that the sound was a plane.

"Pop," he said, "Joe—"

But by then they had all heard it coming down the small valley, its blinking red and green lights aiming right for the farm. They all stood silent for a moment, and then Doc was transformed.

"Hit the bell!" he shouted to Joe, who was already running flat out to the nearest building. "Get to a radio!" he screamed to Erik. "To the lodge! Everyone!" He pulled Tommy into the shadow of a tall barn and shouted, "The lights! Damn it, someone turn off the lights! Get the house lights out!"

Tommy stared into the dark velvet sky, seeing the blinking lights of the plane level out over the front field, hearing the sound roar directly at them. The big house was lit up from inside as if it were on fire—their celebrations late into the night keeping all the downstairs lights on.

"Damn those lights!" Doc shouted as Erik appeared, running toward them as he spoke into a walkie-talkie. Suddenly the air was split by one blast of an air horn that seemed to come from the top of the tallest barn, and a second later the lights began to blink off in the house, one at a time as someone ran from room to room.

As the plane came over the front field, men and women came tumbling out of the buildings and the trees all around them. Most were pulling on shirts, or running in unlaced shoes, but all had rifles aimed at the sky. Erik shoved an M-16 into Tommy's hands and asked, "Can you shoot?"

"Yes," Tommy said. "I think—"

"Can you?" Erik asked again, his voice full of orders.

"Yes."

"Don't unless the plane drops something. Then aim for the drop or for the blinking lights. All the men on the ground are probably ours. Stay with Doc and me. Keep your back to Doc. He's the safety. Keep the butt square on your shoulder and—"

"I know how to shoot, but—"

"If there's an explosion, just stay down on the ground. Don't shoot unless I do or unless Doc tells you to. But whatever you do, stay with Doc."

The plane was big, Tommy thought, seeing its shadow cast by the moon as it came across the front field. Sweat sprang out on his forehead, and he wanted to say "What's going on? What the hell is going on?" but there was no one to ask.

"Too slow," Doc said, moving out from behind the barn to face his enemy. "Way too slow to do this right. Radio ahead to hold fire unless it drops explosives. Keep the antiaircraft gun hidden. Radio now!"

Erik talked feverishly into the radio, and Tommy heard other radios echo throughout and beyond the compound. Suddenly he remembered that Rebecca was still in the house. "She's still in the house," he said to no one in particular, fear in his voice. But then he saw her running across the side yard, a flak jacket flapping over her cotton dress, with one arm around her mother and an M-16 gripped in her other hand. The sight was so shocking that Tommy did not realize that the plane was nearly over them until he heard Erik shouting into the radio, "No bazooka! No anti! Hold your fire! Hold your fire!"

Red tracer lights from night laser sights beamed up from a dozen rifles to the fat silver belly of the slow-moving plane. The thin red laser beams criss-crossed the sky in a wild hallucinogenic disco light show as they circled and locked in on the plane.

Suddenly, with a great whoosh of air, the bottom of the plane sprang open and a thousand gallons of fire-engine-red paint dropped right on the roof of the house, striping it like an open wound.

"Hold fire!" Doc shouted at the circle of men around him as Erik shouted into the radio, "Hold fire! Hold your fire! Don't let them see how many we are! Hold fire!"

The now lighter plane shot up over the steep mountainside and disappeared.

Tommy looked around him, turning his head slowly in the silence that followed. Men and women were crouched all over the back yard, behind cars, behind walls, standing in open doorways, every one of them holding a rifle. They wore running suits, nightgowns, jeans and polo shirts. They were young and old, fat and thin. Every one of them no different from the people walking down any Manhattan street. But they had a look in their eye that said they were trained. They held their rifles the way chain smokers hold their cigarettes. They knew what they were doing—it was only Tommy who held the rifle out in front of him as if it were a screaming wet infant.

Doc ran toward the house, shouting, "Code B! Code B! Erik, send out reconnaissance. Get a read on the radar. Code B, everybody!"

Tommy, too shocked to do anything other than follow, jogged along with the old man toward Rebecca.

"This is just a warning, yes?" Doc said, gasping for breath, to the group of men who huddled around him by the back door of the house. "You don't start an attack like this. They just want us to know that they could blow this place off the face of the earth if they wanted to. Just a warning. They'll wait to see if we agree to pull out. But let's take no chances. Jan, fan the men out. Joe, get everybody not part of a team up to the lodge—securely, yes? Assume they know that's our plan. Stephan, stay with the house team and call the sheriff. Rebecca, secure the computer and communications equipment. Remember, we are going with code B, so get your story straight, my friends. We'll worry about supplies once we have everybody secure, yes? Radio the lodge that we're coming. Rebecca? What does this mean?"

"I don't know," she answered wearily. "A sign. Maybe a sign from the twelfth one. A sign that he can stop us. Stop us here and now."

"Let him try, yes? Just let him try," her father said. Then Doc turned to Tommy, his eyes as bright as rockets in the night. "Tommy," he said, reaching out his hand, "welcome to the family."

Tommy shook his hand and nodded in disbelief and turned to Rebecca as she walked up to him, a dark dirt smear across her face, her open flak jacket showing the sweat-stained dress beneath.

"We have to talk," Tommy suggested, his voice cracking. She took the gun out of his hand.

"Yes," she said, kissing his cheek and watching his eyes. "Yes, we should talk."

When they hugged, her large decorative Mexican belt clasp pressed into his belt buckle, jarring the miniature circuits of the transistor microphone that the jealously inspired John X had sewn into a perfect replica of Tommy's favorite belt, along with four cadmium watch batteries and an amplifier the size of a quarter. A thick wire along the length of the leather strap made the belt its own antenna. Then all we could hear was the sound of metal scraping metal, and the muffled sound of voices far, far off.

As long as we could keep a black box within five miles of him, and he was not behind too much steel, we could hear at least half of what he heard. The only trick was he had to keep his pants on.

13.

YOU MUST ALL UNDERSTAND THAT, unlike a good analyst, I have an agenda. I want to do more than explain, I want to make you understand. This is too important to simply report the facts, and to this day, going on three years later, we don't know all the facts. We know only what I've patched together, found here and there with the help of our government's computers and vast research teams. But the process here is part of the substance. The process of piecing together, of finding things out not in some neat chronological order, but in a strange, nonlinear, Faulknerian stream of having your consciousness changed by the events you run into like loose logs in the river. And that real-life method of finding only parts and pieces of stories through real-time eavesdropping influences the way that decisions are made. John X made choices on the guesses and assumptions he made when listening to the fragments of Tommy and Rebecca's conversations. The Judge decided strategies based on loose narratives scribbled hurriedly from transcripts and half-assed guesses made in foreign reports that were translated in the middle of the night by tired men and women who knew nothing of the context from which the messages were sent.

Life is too complicated to happen in chronological order. Only individual lives happen sequentially, or so my theory number 165 goes. Life, with a capital L, happens in a scattershot, jumbled-up, rushing river of events that lead people to make bad decisions on information that is later suspect at best. That is what began to happen that night, after the plane roared over Rebecca's family farm and John X spilled his coffee as he listened to men and women running feverishly around Tommy with automatic weapons.

"Oh my God," John X, the analyst on the scene, said, recording his own observations on the multitrack recorder as he listened to the events in real time as they too were recorded. The multitrack recorder is used by analysts who want their comments to be spaced along with what they are hearing on a matched tape so that analysis can be done more quickly and precisely. What is fascinating about those first few tapes is hearing John X's voice along with what he was hearing, as if you were watching someone watch a play, hearing his running commentary as the action unfolds. John was more administrator than analyst, so I'm sure he was uncomfortable with the device and methodology, and thus he used it only sparingly, and after a while he became too entranced to use it all. But his voice still speaks to me when I listen to the tapes. A voice that I don't hear anymore. A voice summoning me back to the immediacy of the action. "Oh God," John X said on the parallel tape. "I can't be—what the hell. Oh, mother Mary shit. This is unreal. Oh God."

Only with time can a more cogent analysis than John X's take apart and put back together what seemed to happen. But you need to see how I learned it all to understand why I did what I did. Your justifications, all my friends, will have to come later.

Theory number 192: Whenever something dramatic happens in a woman's life, she changes her hairstyle. Forgive me this sexist generalization, but when her husband leaves her, when she is promoted to a new position, when she finds out her best friend has cancer, she cuts her hair. She curls her hair. She dyes her hair.

I'm sure that men would do the same thing if society would allow them the same individualistic expression of taste and design. But men's choice in hairstyle is shackled by convention and receding hairlines. A woman is allowed to express herself through her hair—to design her hair as a silent reflection of how she is feeling or how she thinks about herself.

The morning after Tommy's first night with her family, Rebecca cut her long hair right at her shoulders. The first tape I heard was fast-forwarded to when Tommy rolled over on the hard double cot at the lodge, rustling the starched sheets, and saw her through the two-inch opening between the open bathroom door and the doorjamb. The microphone in the belt buckle sputtered to life, then stopped again, not yet fully reconnected. From the darkness of the windowless bedroom he watched her stare at herself in the brightly lit mirror, one finger tracing the wrinkles below her eyes. He told me later that he thought about shouting at her, telling her to stop, but he could tell by the look in the reflection of her eyes, or so he told her later as he was putting on his belt, that she was determined and that her mind was made up. In the dark fog of having just woken up with a hangover and too little sleep and in a strange place, Tommy knew without thinking about it, he reported, that Rebecca would get what she wanted.

He watched her naked back as five inches of her auburn hair fell to the cool concrete floor. Just as she finished, her eyes caught him watching her from the bed where he lay. She put the scissors down on the gleaming white sink and walked into the small bunkerlike room.

"I love you," she said, sitting on the edge of the cot, one foot kicking the pile of his clothes by the edge of the bed, jarring the miniature transmitter into action for a second time. The sharp crack of the microphone in the belt striking the concrete floor woke up John X, who had put his head down on his desk with the headphones still on, hoping that somehow the belt would begin transmitting again.

"I love you too," John X responded hundreds of miles away in the fluorescent-lit situation room in the basement of HQ, Rebecca's voice whispering through the headphones.

"I love you too," Tommy said, too quickly and too automatically.

"Do you really?" Rebecca asked. "After all I've told you? Do you want to be a part of all this?"

Her hands gripped the sheets tangled over his naked body, waiting for his answer.

When Tommy was safely ensconced in my study he told me he remembered every detail of that moment because it was at that point that there was no going back. At that moment he could leave or he could stay, and he knew even then that somehow his life depended on making the right choice. He lay in a hard bed that was bolted to a concrete wall, with a rough sheet soaked with sweat around his torso, staring at the beautiful naked woman whom he hardly recognized with her new short haircut. The fluorescent light from the bathroom streamed in from behind her, silhouetting her taut muscular features but obscuring her face. All he could see was the glint of her green eyes searching his face for an answer to a question she hadn't asked.

Then in a sudden dash of Freudian mental seasoning he remembered his mother's eyes. When Tommy sat in my inherited study twenty hours later, comfortable in the dead senator's Danish leather chair at three in the morning, he said to yet another hidden tape recorder that looking at those faceless eyes staring at him out of the darkness of her silhouette made him remember his mother.

"I remembered waking up in my bed in my room on the farm with my mother sitting next to where I lay, her palm lying on my forehead as if she was taking my temperature. But you see, I wasn't sick. I was feeling tired and groggy and wondering why it was so dark when it must be time to get up and do my chores. It was my job to break up the ice in the big water tanks for the cows and slide the feed trays in for the chickens. But the winter mornings had been getting lighter, and here was my mother sitting on my bed in the dark, with only the light from the hall lying square and flat on the floor of the red, white, and blue kid's room.

"Funny how you remember things like that, isn't it, Steele? Things like that flat, square piece of light lying there on the floor like a rug. Do you remember things like that?"

"Yes," my bourbon-bored voice says on the tape. "Yes I do."

"Your daddy went out on a run, my mother said. I didn't remember, you see, I didn't remember hearing the volunteer firemen's bell ringing. I didn't remember hearing the telephone ring calling him to help—the volunteer fire chief rallying his farmer brigade to battle some barn that was going up. I'm still a sound sleeper, you see. I remember that square of light, but I don't remember anything that led up to it. It was as if my life started all over with that damn square of light."

He paused then, his hands rubbing the soft leather of the chair.

"I remember her voice. My mom's voice. 'He's not coming back,' she said softly, her voice breaking ever so gently on the last word—'back.' He's not coming back. It must be a long run, I remember thinking. One of those ones that goes on into the morning, so that I'd have to pull down the hay by myself for the cattle, brush out the rabbit cages, and then not have enough time for target practice before school. I hated it when I had to do all the work and didn't have time to practice, particularly when there was a 4-H meet coming up in just two weeks.

" 'He went out on a run,' my mother repeated, probably trying to convince herself, 'and he's not coming back.' The next sentence she said I heard while I was staring at that square of light. She said, you see, she said, 'He's dead.' Just as simple and as flat as that square of light. 'He's dead.'

"That's what I remember, Steele. I know you want the damn name and number of every person in that lodge. I know you and your cronies think I'm some spy master or something. But what I remember is staring into Rebecca's hard, salty eyes and thinking about that night a burning two-ton barn beam the size of a tree fell on my father in his fireman's hat and broke him in two. That's what I remember, and that's when I said yes."

"Yes. Yes, Rebecca. Yes, I love you," he said on the tape originally monitored by John X, who winced with pain at every word. Tommy's response sealed his fate as he lay in a strange bed in the lodge. "I love you, damn it. I love you and I'll stay with you."

"Forever?" she asked, crawling toward him on the bed. Crawling out of the dark silhouette and into the bright light of the lamp above their heads. There was a long silence on the tape. Then Rebecca said very softly, "Give me your hand.

"Will you take this woman to be your wife?" Rebecca whispered. "To have and to hold until death do you part?"

"I do," Tommy said, his voice stronger than hers, but still quiet in its solemnity. "Will you take this man to be your husband, for better or worse, in sickness and in health, to have and to hold, until death do you part?"

"I do," she said.

"No rings."

"We don't need them. There are—are stronger bonds. Yes?"

"Yes," he said, with a voice that either broke or was so soft that it was overwhelmed by the static. "Yes, Mrs. Wood."

She pulled herself up into his arms, and he held her tight until there was a knock on the door.

Five minutes after the plane had flown over the neat Dutch colonial and dropped a thousand gallons of red paint on its roof, Tommy told me, the compound of buildings was ablaze with lights. Halogens burst from the peaks of the barns, and roving searchlights crisscrossed the forest around them. Each bee hut spaced across the front field emitted beams of light that lit up a forty-acre swath across the front of the property. Pathways up into the hills behind the house glowed with low-wattage footlamps.

Trucks and Jeeps and station wagons with blacked-out windows were driven out of barns and garages and loaded with people and supplies. Barn doors and windows were shut and locked from the inside, to the braying of restless cattle and awakened horses. The peaceful farm turned into an armed camp in a matter of minutes.

Tommy stood holding Rebecca's hand as the sounds of radio static and staccato orders filled the night air. Everyone around them, he told me in front of a roaring fire in my wife's house later, seemed to know exactly what to do. Whatever was going on had been planned for and rehearsed. Plan B was in full action. He told me they talked for a long time, he asking Rebecca questions and she trying to explain why she shouldn't answer them yet. She just tried to calm him down, while he got more and more upset.

Forty-five minutes later Tommy probably bumped his belt buckle against the edge of the kitchen counter, and the transmitter went back on. John X's headphones felt like a vise squeezing the sides of his skull, and the loud crack from the microphone tightened the vise down. "Jesus, Rebecca," John X heard through his headache, "you've got to tell me something or I'm walking out of here right now."

"Okay!" she shouted into the steam that rose from the hot water pouring into the kitchen sink, where she was washing her hands. "Where to start? What can I tell you without permission? I want you to understand. I want you to stay. To stay with me. I would do anything," she said, turning to him, water dripping from her hands, "to keep you with me."

"Then tell me what's going on," he said, sitting down heavily in a kitchen chair.

"You know, if I don't tell you, it might be easier for you to get out. If you don't know anything, you might be able to just walk away?" When Tommy didn't answer her, she went on, her voice strained and cracking. "They're protecting themselves," she said, sitting down at the kitchen table and taking one of his hands. He told me later that he could tell by the look in her eyes as they sat across the table from each other, still sweating and dirty, that she hated telling him what was going on. Each word seemed to hurt her, as if pulled prematurely from her mind before she was ready. "They're protecting themselves against somebody."

"No shit," Tommy said, knowing, he explained to me, that he should be kinder, more understanding, but feeling as if he had been misled. "Who?"

"We're not exactly sure," she answered. "Now don't get angry. That's the truth."

"Does this have something—" Tommy started to say. "Of course this has something to do with your working for the National Security whatever-it's-called. The NSA. Right?"

"Well," she said, "not directly. You see—"

"Look," Tommy interrupted, obviously frustrated. "Are any laws being broken here? I mean, am I participating in—"

"Absolutely not," Rebecca's father said from the door behind them. He came into the room, his eyes red with lack of sleep, and said to Rebecca, "If you're going to marry the man, tell him what he needs to know, yes? He'll either be with us, with you, or dead in a week anyway, yes?"

"Dead?" Tommy shouted. "Now wait a minute. I'm—"

"Let's take it slow, Papa," Rebecca said, taking off her bulletproof vest and drying her hands on her dirt-smeared skirt.

"All right. I'll tell him," Doc offered tiredly, putting his buzzing walkie-talkie down on the kitchen counter and pouring himself a cup of cold coffee as men ran by the kitchen window. "I'll give you an abbreviated version, since we're in a hurry, yes?"

"Yes," Tommy said, his voice riddled with impatience.

"You see, we are in the information business, my family is. We buy and sell information. Like brokers. Like holders of patents. We get it from here or there and sell it to people who find it useful. That is what has paid for all of this." Doc raised his arms and pointed at the elaborate kitchen. "Now you know I'd rather farm, yes? But farmers, Tommy, cannot buy good Bordeaux."

"But a farmer's overhead," Tommy said, patting the semiautomatic rifle in his hand, "isn't so high."

"That's true," Doc agreed with a chuckle. "I like this boy, Rebecca. He has spunk, yes? He is angry, yes?"

"Yes," Tommy said. "Very. If you expect me to stay here, to stay with you, I think I deserve an explanation. What is going on here?"

"Several years ago, my father," Rebecca said quickly, as if speed would make her words make sense, "bought the names, the location, the supply routes, and the bank account numbers of one of the drug cartels' most powerful families."

"An acquisition," Doc suggested unconvincingly. "Simply business. One of dozens of deals we have done. I hardly remembered this one, until I was so rudely reminded about it, yes? Just more brokering of information people needed. Men in business suits in my lawyer's conference room, yes? Drugs had nothing to do with it. I bought maps, names, account numbers, codes, management charts."

Tommy told me later that he could feel his blood pressure rise as this explanation began to unfold, not simply because of what they said, but because of how they said it. "I knew it was complicated—but it was complicated because they weren't telling me everything," he said. "You know how you can just tell that there is more to the story than what you're told? You know that feeling that you're having trouble following what's going on because the story has leaps of faith and twists of logic that your brain just can't get over, while the person telling the story just goes on as if they're making perfect sense? My mind kept dwelling on each jump while Doc and Rebecca charged on like they were in a steeplechase."

"Then I sold the information for three point seven million dollars," Doc said with a touch of pride in his voice.

"Sold it to another powerful family in the Medellin cartel," Rebecca chimed in.

"I sold it to another bank," Doc said. "I won't pretend I didn't know who owned the bank, yes? I didn't investigate, but I knew. But you must understand, Tommy, that was not my business. My business was supplying the information they needed at the terms I set."

"All just business," Rebecca repeated, as if the constant repetition of the phrase would reassure Tommy of the normalcy of what they were talking about. "Just your usual international industrial espionage, except the industry is producing cocaine and the businessmen carry automatic weapons. The rival cartel apparently used the information their bank obtained and stole four of their competitor's cocaine shipments and turned the rest of the information over to the DEA, who caught two sons and a son-in-law and—"

"Yes, a son-in-law," Doc said, nodding toward Tommy. "Even sons-in-law must watch out in this business. But you must understand, turning over the information to the DEA was part of the deal. I would not have made the transaction without that agreement. These drugs here in America are devastating. I'm a doctor, yes? This was my way to help stop this curse."

"And the DEA apparently botched the arrest of the son-in-law and one of the sons, but they were able to arrest the other son, we believe. The son of the chief financial officer is hidden somewhere in the DEA system. Are you following this? The DEA were also able to freeze most of the family's bank accounts. All of this eliminated them as a serious competitor in the region and made them very, very unhappy at their rival cartel."

Tommy remembered staring blankly at her, not sure he heard her voice through the buzz of anger, fear, and confusion that rang in his head. He told me later that after a while their voices began to blend together in his mind, the entire business complicated enough, and disconnected enough from anything he recognized as reality, that he was lost.

"Justice was done," Doc said, raising his coffee cup as if giving a toast. "American interests were furthered by this commercial transaction, yes? I am a patriotic citizen. I am a capitalist. I like to see my country win at capitalism. Particularly when I win, too."

"But the problem," Rebecca continued, her voice racing into the explanation, "is that three years later, after it's all over with, someone tells the Medellin cartel that my father was the one who obtained the information and sold it to their competitor and the DEA."

"But these men are businessmen," Doc concluded. "Revenge is not good business. Plus, they would never risk attacking an American citizen in America, yes? Or flying planes into the middle of Pennsylvania to drop thousands of gallons of red paint on my beautiful white house?"

"I don't think—" Tommy said, starting to get up out of his chair, but then sitting back down again when he realized he had nowhere to go. At the same time, John X may have stood up from his desk in the basement situation room at HQ, desperately seeking some way to understand what he was hearing, in that futile gesture of grasping for inspiration that every intelligence analyst knows. "I don't think I understand."

"I know I don't understand," John X said.

"Someone else is trying to stop us," Rebecca said, getting up and looking out the window. "The timing is too perfect to be coincidental."

"The twelfth?" Doc asked.

"Maybe."

"I just don't think it could be him," her father said. "I do not see him able to accomplish all of this, yes? Wouldn't we have found some clue? Some trace? Why would federal agents be driving around here?"

"Who?" Tommy asked.

"What the hell is going on?" John X screamed in the basement of HQ, the headphones jostling on his head, his chewed-fingernail hands scribbling desperately on a pad of paper that was filling with questions for the research team to answer. "Bobby? Shit, are we getting all of this? Are you sure?"

"I don't know," Rebecca said, her voice almost a whisper, avoiding answering the questions heard and unheard. Tommy remembered her touching the window with one finger as a few scattered raindrops hit the thick glass. She stared at the foggy impression of her fingerprint, wiping it away before she spoke. "I don't know if he is capable of this. Hiring all these people without me finding out. Cloaking it all in some Hollywood drug war. I don't even know if he wants to stop us. He still pretends that he is with us, that he supports us, that he'll take our money and be happy and quiet the rest of our lives. But then again, Papa, he is not to be underestimated."

"I understand," Doc said, his voice low and solemn on the tape. "It could be any of them, yes? Not just the twelfth one. Any of the family could have decided that they don't want to go out of business. Any of them could be selling us out behind our backs."

"Who?" Tommy asked again. "I mean, what? What is somebody in your family trying to stop you from doing? Is that the twelfth one, whatever that means?"

"Very good," Rebecca commented, her voice brightening. "I knew you would be a good agent. You get the picture. A mole. Our own mole turned against us. Another relative."

"A weak man," Doc said with a sigh. "Either one. The twelfth or our middleman, an actuary in France that we should not have trusted. But the deal was very good. I've been trying to amass some—some capital for a bigger deal that you're learning about at our family reunion. Family reunions cost a lot, yes? I'm paying to fly in all these people from around the globe. Expenses are skyrocketing. Money for computers, for all this security. Greed and need make me take risks, and now, three years later, look what happens, yes? The family needed the money for the reunion, so I took the risk. It took them years to find us, but they found us. Now we have to wait and see what they plan to do. Fortunately, some other relatives tipped us off that they were close, so, as you see, we are prepared. But we must get out of here. Do you understand? Are you following us?"

"Absolutely not," Tommy concluded. "This is all—all gibberish. What is going to happen now? What about the family reunion? I thought the rest of your family was coming. What are we going to do?"

"We're leaving," Rebecca said, her voice flat and final. "We're going to meet the rest of the family someplace else."

"We're getting out of here?" Tommy asked. "It looks like you're settling in for a battle."

"Just the immediate family are leaving," Rebecca said. "The rest will stay and fight if they have to. We won't leave until things are more settled. We wouldn't leave at all if there weren't some complications."

"You see," Doc offered, wiping his hands with a linen napkin left on the table, "this is all very messy for us. We're not used to this type of thing. We don't use guns. We don't break laws. We hired consultants to tell us how to do all this, yes? We are not terrorists—like some of our relatives—we are honest brokers. We are businessmen forced to protect ourselves from people the law will not protect us from."

"The local county cops seem awfully friendly," Tommy said.

"Oh, yes," Doc said. "Those are our policemen. They are paid by us—by our tax dollars, since we own three-fourths of the county. So yes, they are very well trained. As are our farmhands here. And our hunter friends. They are all professionals. Handpicked by Rebecca and the boys here."

"By Rebecca?" Tommy asked.

"Rich people have bodyguards," Rebecca said, ignoring his question. "This is no different."

"This is different," Tommy argued. "We're in the middle of Pennsylvania, of all places, and these people look like they are ready to go to war. Was that a Stinger missile launcher I saw out there?"

"Stinger?" Doc asked no one in particular. "I don't know what weapons we have. I have left that to the experts, yes? Stinger, AK-47, Uzi, recoilless rifles. They are just tools. We here, Tommy, are the architects. You understand, yes?"

"No," Tommy said. "Why don't you all just leave? Just go somewhere else? Hide. You can't live like this forever."

"It's the principle of the thing," Doc explained. "This is our home. It has been our home for years, yes? It may be that one of our relatives has turned on us, and if so, we don't know which one. If they are willing to turn on us, we are safe nowhere. Wherever we go we will be found out. We must secure this place first, then we must go hunting."

"Hunting for what?" Tommy asked.

"For our sour apples," Doc said. "Only moles eat them. They are spoiling the whole family."

"But—" Tommy said. He paused, the fatigue creeping into his voice over the adrenaline that had sped it up for the past hour. "Let me get this straight—is the twelfth one a member of your family? A relative? The twelfth relative, or something? Somebody related to you is sending you a sign that you ought to stop something?"

"Yes," Doc suggested. "Perfect. Now you understand everything—"

"Understand everything?" Tommy shouted, shocking the transistors in his belt. "Jesus, I don't understand anything! The more questions I ask, the more confused I get. All I want is to get out of danger, you know. Get us, Rebecca and me, out of danger. And if that means getting out of here, then I'm all for it."

"My father is a rich man," Rebecca said. "He'll make this place safe."

"I bought McDonald's stock," Doc said with a sigh, as if the weight of his wealth were wearing him down. "And then Apple and Nutrasweet. I bought the first issue of Microsoft, and before there was Coca-Cola—I loved that one, yes? Now I invest in cable television companies in the South. Ted Turner is my hero. I love CNN. You know of it? It is my favorite, because of all the information. Things that it used to take us weeks to find out—information that would be valuable because no one knew it yet, now everyone knows almost instantly. More and more information to more and more people. It may put all of us out of business. I love this country. I am a true American capitalist."

"And a patriot," Tommy almost snickered, his lips sounding as if they were in a tight, straight line. He knew he was being impolite, but he told me that the scene did not call for politeness. He felt he had been lied to, or at best misled. "You said you were a patriot."

"I see we will have to convince you," Doc said. He rubbed his eyes, undoubtedly feeling the same twinge of a hangover that Tommy reported feeling. Their wine, champagne, and celebrating had been so rudely interrupted, and the shock and adrenaline were now wearing off. "I came to this country right before the war, and it has been good to me. While my family belongs to no country, this one has been very good to us. Very good to us."

The three of them stared at each other across the kitchen table, as if they were all sizing each other up in a poker game. Who was bluffing? Who had the cards to back them up? Whom could they trust?

"You see," Doc said slowly, a finger stroking his white mustache, "I am taking a risk telling you this. A risk that your love for my daughter is not as strong as your love for your own self-protection. A risk that you will try to use this information against my family—but that would be using it against Rebecca, yes? That is the risk I take. But I believe, Tommy, that it is a small risk, because no matter what you feel right now, I believe you would lay down your life for my daughter. I believe that you will do anything to protect her, and you will find that the only way to protect her is to stay with her and to stay with us. You are part of the family, yes? And we wouldn't want you if you didn't have questions. If you weren't suspicious, yes? Rebecca has selected you like she selected these bodyguards—and so, like these men outside with guns that could kill us all in seconds, we must trust you. We must trust you, Tommy Wood. And you must trust us, yes?"

"You really haven't told me anything," Tommy said.

"Yes we have," Doc asserted quietly. "But you just don't understand it yet. It is all out of context. That is how most information comes to us. It is our job to find the context. To create the alphabet that matches the sounds. You can do that, yes? Remember this, a family. A family reunion. A family business of selling and buying information. A family mole. That is all you need to know to make your judgment. Either you are with us, with Rebecca, or you aren't, yes? Yes?"

Tommy did not answer on the tape, but my guess is that his eyes must have answered, that his body motions must have made it clear that he was with them.

"Now," Doc said, "we must get to the lodge. Whoever they are, they will try to negotiate before they attack, but eventually they will attack when they understand we are going ahead with our plan, and we must be ready, yes? Who knows if they know about the feds? So who knows how their plans might get screwed up, yes? We can't count on anything going as planned. We must be ready for anything. I want my family safe. My men will take care of the rest."

"Feds? Federal agents?" Tommy asked. "Oh Jesus, what now?"

"It seems that some of Rebecca's friends—her coworkers, shall we say—have been out looking for her and have stumbled across our home. While we sent them on their merry way, letting them think we were just some hillbillies protecting our still, yes? But I am afraid it is only a matter of time before more arrive, unless the twelfth one has arranged to keep them from showing up."

"Rebecca's friends the federal agents?" Tommy asked. "This is getting too much. Are they after you?" he asked Rebecca. "I thought you quit. Have you done something wrong? Are there twelve feds out there after you? Did you steal this information for the drug cartel? I mean—"

"Shit—they know," John X said to himself thousands of miles away, writing the words "the twelfth one" in his listening journal, which was stuck under his right arm as he drank cup after cup of coffee.

"Calm down, honey," Rebecca said to Tommy. "It's no big deal—"

"No big deal?" Tommy said, standing up.

Tommy remembered that right after he stood up he bumped into the butt of the rifle Rebecca had picked up. Once again something jarred the microscopic mechanics in the belt and the microphone went silent. John X cursed Bobby the techy and picked up the phone to call the deputy dernza. He knew, he told me later, that he was playing ball in a bigger league than he was used to and he'd better bring in the first-string team right away.

"Paul," John X mumbled into the telephone with a sigh. "Sorry to wake you up, but I've got a hot one I need your help on. I know, I know the time. I'm really sorry, but you've got to come down here now. Yes, right now. I'll send a driver."

14.

THAT SAME NIGHT at three in the morning, when the baby-faced deputy dernza, Paul, and John X decided to call the Judge, Paul insisted on first making a list of what they knew and what they didn't know. John X would do anything to stall for time, and the deputy dernza wanted to get his speech to the Judge down perfect before he woke him up on the last night of his vacation.

While Paul made his list, John called home from the telephone that he carelessly did not remember was bugged and connected to one of the dozens of reel-to-reel recorders in the telecommunications center.

"It's me, honey," he said softly.

"What time is it?" his wife asked groggily.

"Late. I won't be home again."

"Jesus, John, I thought that was all over with?" she questioned, her tone of voice expressing disbelief.

"What do you mean?"

"You know what I mean," she said angrily. "I thought she was out of the picture. No more working late with her."

"This *is* work," he responded testily. "Do I have to live forever with your suspicion now?"

"Then what's going on?" she said, moving the phone from one hand to the other.

"You know I can't tell you that."

"Yeah, yeah. Same old thing. You've got to get home some, you know. Your son is prowling around this house like some deranged lunatic, and the dog doesn't even recognize you anymore. Pretty damn soon, John, you've got to choose between work, whatever her name is, and me."

"Honey, you've got to understand that—"

"I do understand," she said. "I understand all too well. I just hope that you understand that my understanding, my stupid compassion, my amazing idiotic forgiveness, is just about used up."

"But—"

She hung up. John X's sigh on his end of the phone before he hung it up had the far-off tortured sound of a tire rolling over dry leaves. John poured himself another cup of coffee and went back to the table, where Paul was going over his lists and charts.

"Here's what I think we know. Or at least you know from your goddamn secret source of tapes."

"It's a good source, Paul," John X said, thinking about his oldest son, who had been arrested for drunken driving the week before and now refused to go out of the house, while his legal bills, which John had no idea how he was going to pay, kept growing and growing. "You've heard it yourself."

"But you won't tell me how you got these tapes?" the deputy dernza asked. "This is very suspicious. How did you know to bug this farmhouse? Did you get it out of her file? Her home address? And then when did you do it? Did you get a warrant? Did you go through Legal? Or did Surveillance handle all the details? What are the technical aspects? Is there a bug in every room, and how is the whole thing rigged?"

"I don't think those issues are important right now," John X said. "What is important is what is on the tapes. What's important is what we know."

They knew that Rebecca's family was involved in treason. They knew that Rebecca's family was surrounded by armed professional mercenaries whom Rebecca herself had helped pick out. They knew that Rebecca had access to files that would tell her the very best men for the job. They knew that these men had sophisticated weapons and that Rebecca would have known how to get those weapons, courtesy of the black market weapons specialist in the organization, who had been recruited by Rebecca and remained very friendly with her.

They knew that Rebecca could have gotten into those DEA files that were passed on to the organization whenever there were national security questions, and gotten the very information that her father was telling Tommy about. They knew there had been a dozen different drug busts in the past year that could have resulted from stolen information from the DEA being fed to the Coast Guard or some other agency that might act before asking.

They also knew, they had to admit with a collective wince, that Rebecca knew she was being followed. They had no idea where the two men who jumped off the train were, and the two agents sent into the area with the black box had also disappeared. But the black box seemed to be working, except that its own homing device was not functioning, so the techies Paul had asked to find the source of the transmission couldn't tell him where it was either. But somehow Rebecca's father knew that there were federal agents in the area.

Most troubling, they knew that there was a mole somewhere in the family organization who was feeding information to groups that were trying to stop Rebecca's family reunion from going forward—but they didn't know what, why, or where the family reunion was.

They knew that they would have to contact the DEA and the Bureau to make sure that there weren't other organizations involved in this action, and that hurt, because they would have to make up some explanation for why they were asking. They also knew that the French DST knew something about this whole affair, maybe about the French middleman who had squealed about the family's deal, but that they wouldn't know what the DST knew until the personal courier arrived in the late morning.

The talk of families sounded like Mafia or drug cartels, but the computer search showed no known activity of either in the area. There were no local police they could trust for information, because they were owned by the family, so they would have to rely on the Organized Crime Strike Force in the local U.S. Attorney's office, which wouldn't be open until the morning.

Rebecca's family could be attacked at any time by an army of alleged drug dealers, or she could disappear into the night along with her family and never be seen again. So the deputy dernza, Paul, and John X both agreed something had to be done that night. They had to take some risks, get some of our men into the area and get Rebecca out of there alive.

No matter what option they discussed, they kept coming back to the same conclusion: They had to get Rebecca. She could be a Soviet mole. Or this could all be some big mistake, although it was impossible to imagine any innocent explanation for what had already occurred. She could have been selling information for years. The organization had to know what she knew and to whom she had told it. They had to get Rebecca.

At three forty-five in the morning they called the Judge at his fishing cabin, where I occasionally had visited before my so-called retirement. The deputy dernza spoke very slowly and carefully, explaining to the sleepy Judge what they believed had happened. Paul tried to simplify the story as much as possible so that the Judge would see, even in the middle of the night, that something had to be done right away. "They're expecting a group of Colombians to attack them," Paul said, not mentioning the hundreds of details and doubts that they had learned. "Because of a failed deal for drug information. And it sounds like Rebecca might have some help inside the NSA. There might be a mole."

"How the hell do we know this?" the Judge asked, getting up out of the bed and probably feeling the tingling pain in his groin that had kept him from falling asleep until only a few hours before the telephone rang.

"I'd rather not explain it on the phone, sir," John X whispered, his tired voice breaking with the tension. "But you can be certain it is good, rock-solid information. The question now is whether to proceed to go in and get her."

"Goddamn it," the Judge bellowed on the phone, which was still tapped by the forgetful John X, "you're talking about planning a damn invasion. What do you think this is, war games? You going to call the National Guard and have them invade? For Christ's sakes, stay calm. Now here's what I want you to do. Nothing. Absolutely nothing. If you call in the Bureau, she'll end up dead or she'll see them coming and get out of there. If you try to send in our own men, somebody's goin' to end up dead as a doornail. There isn't going to be any massive invasion of dope dealers. Hell, we'd have known about that. A bunch of Colombians can't just drive into Pennsylvania and start shooting people. We just need to drive up there in broad daylight tomorrow and ask to see Rebecca Townsend and arrest her. She's not going anywhere tonight, right? Isn't that what you told me she said?"

"Yes, sir," the deputy dernza said.

"Well then, let's just keep this thing under our hats. The last thing I want is Langley or Foggy Bottom hearing that we've got moles in our midst. Again. Let's try to take care of this thing quietly, all right?"

"Yes," he said again, his baby face no doubt red and tired.

"And who the hell knows about this?" the Judge demanded.

"Myself, Paul," John X said. "And Bobby Rickhouse, who's a techy from Section Four."

"And Steele," Paul said on the speakerphone, without inflection, not showing whether he relished ruining John X's career or not.

"Steele?" the Judge boomed into the telephone. "T. C. Steele? Who the hell talked to him, and what the hell for? He's out. He's retired. He's gone."

"I felt it necessary to discuss strategy issues with him," John X said softly. "I believed he could add a perspective that my immediate supervisor did not have."

Paul turned white, and his hands trembled in anger.

"Goddamn it," the Judge said. "You bunch of backstabbing idiots. This is a serious security breach. I ought to—oh hell, get me a bird in the air right now. I'm not going to sleep a wink after all this ruckus. Send them to come get me now. The fishing sucks, anyway."

What the deputy dernza and John X did not know was that as soon as the Judge hung up he searched through the small black book he kept with him at all times, through the calendar that showed the doctor's appointment he had that day to the list of phone numbers, his tired hands struggling with the well-worn pages, which glistened under the little light by his bed. His wife, Helen, had pulled her pillow over her head to hide from the light and the noise. She thought the Judge paranoid for all the extra security precautions he had been taking—doubling the number of Federal Protection Service guards they traveled with, making plane reservations under false names, changing their children's phone numbers—but he said that with all that was happening in the world they couldn't be too careful. These late-night phone calls suggested to her that maybe he wasn't being paranoid. Maybe every NSA bureaucrat had to be more careful these days. She told me that she didn't hear a word of his telephone conversation. She had become a professional at not listening. He dialed a long-distance number and said into the phone, "Murphy? This is the Judge."

"Kiss my ass," the gruff voice on the other end of the phone said, a slight whisper in the background revealing to the expert that Murphy was taping his calls. "Do you know what time it is?"

"Your time or my time?" the Judge asked, as if it mattered. "I need some help."

"Wait a minute," Murphy said, waking up. "What's that goddamn little dance we're supposed to go through so I know it's really you? Oh yeah, I say 'What's the decision, Judge?' "

The Judge sighed, probably angry that he had invented this little game when he had reestablished a line to Murphy. "The decision is guilty, the man loses his longhorn cattle."

"Then I'll appeal," Murphy argued, remembering the old code. "Because I'm a Panhandle man. Now kiss my ass again and tell me why you're getting me up from my cozy but lonely bed in the middle of the night. And why haven't I heard from you in three months?"

"Lonely?" the Judge asked. "I can't imagine you in an empty bed. Is the fleet out to sea, or have you decided to stop risking catching the big A?"

"Not funny," Murphy said. "You fired me, you homophobe, so I don't have to listen to your fat-assed voice if I don't want to. I'm an independent contractor. Go back to sleep if all you called me for was to remind me how much I don't like you or your kind."

"I need you with a team, five to ten men, your best men, in Philly first thing in the morning. Fully outfitted for a kidnap mission."

"Heavy armor?" Murphy asked, all business, accepting the assignment without a single word of reprise, the sound of a pencil scratching coming through the line.

"The heaviest you got," the Judge concluded. "Don't worry about the budget. Just get there."

"The last time you said that you complained about my bill for six months. I want a price tag. An upper limit."

"Three hundred thousand," the Judge said quickly.

"I see you're serious," Murphy said, surprised at the number. "Only one problem—how do we get there? I can get the men around town. I've got the armor. But I need a plane at some GA in the area as early as you can get it. How about one of those slick Air Force jobs? Land it out at Republic Field on Long Island—one of their two runways is long enough. It's a general aviation airport between Islip Airport and LaGuardia. Just cruise an Air Force baby right in there. Not only do I love their uniforms, you dick, but that's the fastest way to get this operation on the road."

"No dice," the Judge said. "We'll have to sacrifice some time. This one is off the books right now. Completely off the books, do you understand? Any government agency catches a whiff of this shit and the leak is dead—and I mean six-feet-under dead. We need a private plane."

"You get the plane. I'll get the men. I don't have time to do both," Murphy said.

"Here's what you do," the Judge said, sealing my fate. "Call Steele and get his wife to send one of her jets to come pick you up."

"What is this? Revenge of the lost and forgotten toys? I thought he was out of it, just like me. Retired or something," Murphy said gruffly, pretending he didn't know exactly what had happened to me. "I don't think you can kick his ass out of the ball game and then ask him to spend his wife's dough on flying your friends around."

"We're not friends, you and I," the Judge said to Murphy. "But Steele and I are. He'll do it. I can't think of anybody else who would do it. Just tell him I said I needed it. He already knows about the circumstance. John X, that idiot of a section chief, told him part of the story. You tell him that I need it and that I want to have dinner with him tomorrow night."

"So we're not friends, but what the hell am I? Your goddamn appointments secretary? Make your own dinner plans, you asshole."

"Murphy," the Judge said, as if talking to a baby, "it's a code. He'll get the plane to you if he hears the code."

At 4:00 A.M. I got a call on the private line that I had just not gotten around to having disconnected. I recognized Murphy's voice before he repeated the code, and my heart began to race as Carolyn reached to turn on the light, awakened by the coded double ring of the phone she hadn't heard for a year.

"Where have you been all my life, Murphy?" I said.

"Bailing your ass out of trouble," he replied. "I need your wife's jet up at the old hangar in Newark pronto. The fastest one that will fit ten or so. According to the Judge, you're back in the game. It's the matter that the idiot and soon-to-be-fired John X discussed with you earlier. The Judge is pissed as hell that ol' Johnny boy called you up for your advice. The Judge wants to have dinner with you tomorrow night."

"Honey," I said to Carolyn, who was staring at me with a worried look on her sculptured face, "this is our old, dear, sweet friend Murphy finally calling us to see how we are at four in the morning. He says the Judge needs a plane and he wants us to have dinner with him tomorrow. Are we busy?"

She smiled and then fell back on the soft linen pillows piled luxuriously high on our giant bed. She slapped the sheets with a laugh and kicked me under the covers. "So much for our travel plans."

At that moment I was reminded how young Carolyn makes me feel. Even though she is only two years younger than I, she has an energy, a spark, that knows no bounds. She has an unconscious way of charging into things, of not respecting the boundaries that most people erect around themselves. She ignores social decorum and cultural walls and jumps right into every controversial issue without fear of being naïve, uninformed, or ridiculed for a lack of understanding. She'll walk up to perfect strangers and ask them if they are happy. Are they fulfilled? What do they need to do to get to where they want to be?

Those who don't know her well think of it as innocence, but it is really more like confidence. The secret of Carolyn is that she believes in herself. She does not believe that she is smarter or better than others, but she believes that she can make a difference. That she can talk people into doing what she thinks is the right thing to do. That she can converse in languages that she does not really know, that communication can be accomplished if you just try hard enough. She has that American entrepreneurial attitude of never giving up or giving in.

Which is why she is a success. She takes risks that make the coterie of M.B.A.s and lawyers who work for her cringe, simply because she refuses to believe that things can't be accomplished if they are good ideas. She asks more questions, so she gets more information. She knows everyone, so doors are open to her that are closed to others. She doesn't dwell on failures or revel in successes, but concentrates on the task at hand.

And all of that makes a wild brew of sexual zeal, deep ties to friends, and a laugh that sounds like molasses poured on fresh peaches. Her golden blond hair is graying, but she still wears it long and tousled, like a coed who ran out of the shower because she was late for class. All of that made Carolyn laugh and poke and kick me under the linen sheets of her giant bed.

"I don't think we have anything planned, darling," she said in her faked rich-bitch voice. "Just some gardening and bike riding. I think we could fit dinner in."

"Tell the Judge," I suggested in my best imitation of a pompous Yale voice, "that Carolyn and I would be happy to join him and his wife, Helen, for dinner at eight tomorrow evening at his usual place, or at my club, whichever he prefers."

"You don't belong to a club," Carolyn reminded me, easing up to the phone so she could hear more of the conversation.

"Better make it at his usual place," I said to Murphy.

"Screw you," Murphy replied. "Do I get the damn plane or what?"

"What color plane should Mr. Murphy expect?" I asked Carolyn with a barely suppressed laugh. "He needs something fast that will seat around ten men. You probably also want those little bags of peanuts, don't you?"

She took the phone out of my hand and said into the receiver, "Murphy, I'm sending a King Lear jet, white with a Consolidated Lines company logo on the side. Remember the big blue C? It will be at the old blue hangar by nine, and you better damn well be ready."

"So nice to talk to you again, Carolyn," Murphy whined. "When was the last time we saw each other? Ah yes, I think it was when you threatened to throw that drink in my face when I asked you how Mike Carter was doing when you were at my party. Did you ever recover any insurance on that plane you wrecked?"

"I love you too, Murphy," she said. "I didn't wreck the plane, I just brushed some trees. And as for that party, just because your date decided he liked me too, no reason to ruin a beautiful gown—to say nothing of your career. But it's nice to be back in business with you."

"Don't sound so pleased," I whispered. "We don't want to sound desperate to get back in. Let them beg."

"Murphy, if you drag my husband back into this," she said into the phone in her best silken voice, the vowels rolling off her tongue like a hand stroking lingerie, "I want you to take good care of him."

"He's too old for me, Carolyn. We just want the boss for his money," Murphy said.

"My money," Carolyn corrected him.

"Make sure the plane has a bar, will ya?" Murphy asserted. "If you guys are going to be involved in whatever the hell this thing is, I'm going to have to start drinking in the morning again."

"I can't imagine you ever stopped," Carolyn said with that slippery voice.

"All right," Murphy said, his voice like sandpaper and cigar smoke. "Just send the plane. Good night."

Carolyn reached over me and put the phone down on the cradle, her arm settling across my bare chest. She kissed me as she looked in her address book for a phone number, and said, "You know, part of the reason I always liked Murphy is that he got to have all the fun. Being shot at. Sneaking across borders. Rushing to the scene. You were the boss, of course. You got to plan the things out, or at least figure out what happened later, and I—what did I get to do? Running the company just isn't that exciting. Besides, it doesn't involve you at all. You could care less that I'm going to initiate a hostile takeover tomorrow morning and risk a quarter of what I have. You're just not involved in that. Come on. Like I said at lunch, let's do this together this time. Huh? Let's be a spy couple. What do you say? My money, your brains?"

That moment was when I saw in my mind Mike Carter's face as the laughing mermaid, his twisted smile plastered on like a mask hiding his pain. That moment was when I wondered what Carolyn's true motivation was in getting involved with Murphy again. "You've been through this," I said slowly. "You know it isn't all fun and games."

"I know," she responded, trying her best to be light and cheerful, but revealing her straightforward honesty in her comments. "But I want to do it right this time. I want to show that I can do it right. You and me. A couple of spies out saving the world. Rescuing the repressed. A team."

"Darling," I said, my heart suddenly light and beating oddly. "That is a preposterous, absurd, obscene, and stupid speech. Particularly in the middle of the night. Let's go back to bed, and talk about your takeover or whatever in the morning. I'll drive you to work. Or fly in with you."

"It's my plane," she said, squeezing me. "It's my bed, my car, my helicopter, my house, my money—all mine. We're going to do this together. You, me, and Murphy."

"Darling," I repeated. "When you put it that way, that is the most brilliant idea I have ever heard."

She kissed me, and reached for her phone to order the plane with the ease of someone ordering a pizza. Laura would make all the arrangements while we slept.

"By the way," Carolyn said, hanging up, "what is this all about? What great mystery do we get to solve?"

"The mystery of Rebecca," I said, closing my eyes while thoughts raced through my mind. "The mystery of why Rebecca Townsend, agent extraordinaire, is leaving the organization."

"Who is Rebecca?"

"That is the only real question," I suggested. "She used to work for you, sort of. She's the one we set up at that export company outside of New Haven that your company owns. They use your logo—you know the one I'm talking about? The same thing you described to Murphy. She's a lioness with a mane of red hair who has run off with a cub of a boy. She has cheekbones like boulders and a body that has more curves than a camel."

"You're in love," she said. "You're going to run off with a younger woman."

"Not this one," I offered slowly, leaving my options open. "She's already run off with a new recruit and disappeared."

"Is that all?" Carolyn asked. "That doesn't sound like the kind of big thing that they'd bring you back in for. Why would they need someone on the outside to find that out?"

"I don't really know that yet," I mumbled, asking myself the same question. I had not yet heard the tapes that John X had made from the transmissions from Tommy's belt. I knew only what John X had told me that very morning when he called me for advice before I went to have lunch with Carolyn.

I wondered whether John had told anyone else about the miked belt and guessed that whatever was happening was related to that belt. "But Rebecca is a very special person," I said, belatedly answering Carolyn's question. "A special agent."

"So why aren't we going to get her right now?" Carolyn asked, turning off the light. "Why wait?"

"I don't know that either," I said, trying to pretend that I was falling asleep, in the hope that I would sleep if I pretended to be sleeping. Carolyn's voice saying "Why aren't *we* going to get her?" ringing in my ears. "But I'm sure it's because she's . . . because she's a very special agent."

"Steele," Carolyn said, running a hand through her graying hair and leaning over my back, "I know you too well. You just don't want to talk about it because you don't know what you can tell me and what you can't tell me. Well, that's bull, because I'm in this thing with you this time. I'm exacting my pound of entertainment this time. So you better let me in on the show, okay?"

"Okay," I agreed, without commitment, hoping that in the morning Carolyn would get busy enough with her business to forget all about this wild idea.

"I look forward to meeting her."

"I hope I'm there if you do," I said. "That would be some sight."

"Why?" Carolyn asked. "Wouldn't we get along? Strong women and all that rot? Or do you think that I just wouldn't mix well with traitors?"

"No," I said. "I don't know why I said that. It's just that—hell, let's get some sleep. Let's talk about it in the morning."

"And," Carolyn said, refusing to let go, "I'm not going to stop asking questions. I'm going to be supersleuth. Carolyn the inquisitor."

"Yes, Nancy Drew," I mumbled, trying to feign sleep again. "This kind of stuff, you remember, was what got me fired in the first place. Me and you trying to help out the government, like it was some charitable organization that needed your management skills."

"If you weren't my husband," she said, "I'd fire you."

"If I weren't your husband," I responded, "I'd still be fired."

So the Judge, pulled out of his bed in the middle of the night, not feeling well, given incomplete information, swamped with whirling world events, and concerned about how his organization would be perceived if other intelligence agencies knew we thought we might have a mole in our agent ranks, slowed the whole operation down and gave Rebecca her chance to escape. I'm sure that I would have suggested the same thing at the time. What were the chances of a small war breaking out in Pennsylvania? His logic was impeccable. There was so much serendipity in our even knowing that she was up to something—and so much uncertainty in what we knew and how we knew it. John X was making it very hard to evaluate the quality of the information by refusing to tell the Judge or Paul where he had got it.

But I'm not sure I would have the guts to do what the Judge did almost as a reflex, without pausing to think more than the two minutes between the phone calls from John X to him and from him to Murphy. As if he did it every day, he took the bold step of simply skirting the rules to protect his agency and country. The Judge showed that intuitive risk taking that made him so good—if there was a chance of an internal problem, someone inside the NSA feeding Rebecca information, then hire a team of outside former agents who are not on the payroll to go grab your errant agent. With that one snap decision the Judge changed world events.

The irony is that, if not for the paranoia of a spurned lover, Rebecca probably would have gotten away with it. If not for the coincidence that she took Tommy home that weekend, when he had the miniature microphone in his belt, he probably would not have found out anything about her family. Rebecca could have retired with her stash of cash and raised a family with Tommy. She was within days, maybe hours, of escaping from her fast-paced life of deceit and distrust. But she didn't make it. She didn't escape from her life to Tommy's life, but rather dragged Tommy into hers.

15.

THE LODGE was a granite fortress built into the side of a steep hill. It was low-slung and linear, with a few narrow windows and only one visible door. The few walls that were exposed were made of rough-hewn granite boulders that angled out so that there were good sightlines for shooting from every corner. The small courtyard of the building had a tennis court, with a helicopter sitting on it, its blades observable when you walked up to the building. The low roof lines were covered with solar panels, telescoped security cameras, and a rainwater collection system. Small buildings that looked like half-buried stone doghouses stuck out of the hill around it, the lone eye of a gun peering out of each one into the night.

The first thing Tommy remembered thinking when he walked out of the dark woods in the middle of the night and saw the shape of the dark lodge in the clearing was that it looked like a building that he could have designed. The simple, organic shapes appealed to him and weakened his angry skepticism over being drawn into this strange situation. It was as if some modernist had designed a feudal castle—like the Rudolph buildings he had lived with, but not loved, at Yale.

It is, I have to admit, one of the most interesting defenses I've heard in my time in this business. Architecture, Tommy said, sitting in my living room after talking for hours, clouded his judgment. His comfort with the lodge clouded his judgment. His need to see the interior of the building, and measure and weigh its spaces, kept him from bolting. His love of architecture and his love of Rebecca kept him from running into the woods and repeating all this to the police. In addition, he said, "you don't just run into the woods, you know, when you are surrounded by armed men and women and when the woods may be filled with crazed drug dealers intent on revenge. Once I got inside the lodge there was no getting out. I mean, that place was, in all senses of the word, a fortress."

The extended family gathered that first night in the large central room, and room assignments were made. The children sucked their thumbs and rubbed their sleep-filled eyes, the tension in their parents' voices enough to keep them awake. Rebecca and her brothers entered and left the communications room in the first basement, the bright LED lights and the hum of computers sneaking out whenever the steel door opened momentarily for one of them to enter or exit. Tommy overheard long discussions about whom to contact in the family, about weather conditions and flight times, and the constant nagging questions to Rebecca. What do you think they know? Why are they following you? Is it standard procedure?

Half an hour before the Judge was awakened by Paul and John X, Tommy and Rebecca fell exhausted onto the hard bed in their small, concrete-walled room. They were too tired to talk and too tired to worry, but Tommy had one question that the black box barely picked up, the signal like a faint, quiet sigh. "Who is following you? How are you involved in this?"

"My business," she said softly, her voice loose and languid without sleep, "gave me access to information. Allowed me to help my family.

Not any government or person, but help what we wanted to achieve without hurting my government."

"Okay," Tommy argued. "Let's just assume that's true. Were you involved in this drug deal?"

"It was not a drug deal," she said testily but without any bite, her fingers separating strands of knotted hair. "Drugs really had nothing to do with it."

"Then why in the hell are you all planning to go to goddamn war with members of a Colombian drug cartel?"

"It was a deal for information. Not drugs. We don't care if the information is about a new computer chip design or the directions to buried treasure. It was information that someone was willing to pay for, so we supplied it—and helped our government's efforts to stop drug smuggling at the same time. Besides, you know I think that this may have all been set up as a way to stop us. All of this—getting the information and then squealing on us—could be a setup to encourage a bunch of paid thugs to attack us. This doesn't smell, doesn't feel, like a narcoterrorist attack to me. After you've been playing this game for a while you get these instincts that tell you when you're being set up. Maybe these really are the hired guns of a Colombian drug family. Maybe some other member of the family has paid off the Colombians to stop us. Maybe the Colombians don't even know who they are working for—they just know the faces on those dollars they are paid. Just working for thousands of Washingtons and Lincolns, as they say. Just mercenaries sent to stop us."

"And stop you from what?" Tommy asked, exasperation strangling his voice.

"That's complicated," she said. "That will take some time to explain."

"Is this why you quit your job? I mean, did you quit your job because of me or because of all this?"

"The answer is yes, sort of."

"Sort of?" Tommy asked, taking off his pants. "Sort of what, Rebecca?"

"Yes. You see, I'm—" and then he dropped his belt to the hard concrete floor and the signal went out.

"Damn it," John X said, taking off the headphones and tossing them aside. At that moment he had been so close to finding out what the hell was going on. Now he'd have to wait, and the waiting, he told me later, was the real torture. Waiting and wondering when the voices would suddenly pop back on and come drifting out of the headphones.

By 5:00 A.M. there was a thunderstorm moving into the area west of Philadelphia, but deep in the side of the hill Tommy and Rebecca, asleep in each other's arms, would not have heard the sharp crack of lightning and deep rumble of thunder. When they woke an hour and a half later, the rain was falling steadily under a dark morning sky. Rebecca asked Tommy if he loved her. She had cut her hair and kicked his belt. He said yes. She asked if he would love her forever. He said yes, forever, remembering his mother telling him that his father was dead. She curled into his strong farm boy arms and he promised to marry her and stay with her and her family. He realized then that there was no turning back.

Then there was a knock on the door.

I have this theory about why we didn't know about Rebecca's extended family and their activities. It is a simple theory, and therefore probably not completely accurate, but it is one that I want to believe. I want to believe that our agency was not simply incompetent. I want to believe that our relationships with our European counterparts were not so strained that they failed to pass on to us crucial information. I want to believe that all of us, spies around the globe, analysts and agents, politicians and technicians, didn't just completely botch the whole job.

But maybe we did.

But maybe we didn't. Maybe Rebecca Townsend did more than simply take information that was valuable and sell it for profit. Maybe she took information that would have led us to investigate her and her family. Maybe she stole, modified, or destroyed the very bits of evidence that would have led us to her family. Files disappear all the time. Agents receive orders to drop investigations that their supervisors, we presume for reasons of security or butt-covering, deny ever having given authority to begin. In this crazy world it might be possible for one well-placed individual, with other connections that would feed her information from all over the globe, to destroy enough evidence to keep us off her scent.

We intelligence gatherers live in a world where there is another dimension that some people can travel into and out of without anyone else even knowing about it. A dimension of international information that can keep them one step ahead of the rest of us. If

Rebecca knew politicians who would tell her things—and she did; if Rebecca knew spy bosses who would tell her things—and she did; if Rebecca had a family that could supply her with information gathered by other intelligence operations—and she did; then she could not only gather information, she could erase her family's tracks.

For all intelligence information is compartmentalized, letting people into compartments strictly on a need-to-know basis. There is almost always something that you don't know and someone else does. Whenever you think you know the four corners of a subject, a wall rolls away and reveals an entirely new room of knowledge. Knowing which wall might fall away is the mark of a true professional. Guessing where the exit is out of the reality as you know it is what the professional intelligence agent must be able to do.

For example, take the case of George Anderson. You probably don't remember George, but he played a damn good game of squash and refused to play this racketball game that all the macho guys on staff now play. Sometime in the mid-eighties, a year or two before he drowned on vacation in the Upper Peninsula of Michigan, George told me in the locker room that he had run across some strange large money transfers between former German nationals who were now in several different countries. Hundreds of millions of deutsche marks wired to Switzerland and then out again, under the cloak of Swiss law, to a dozen different tax havens. George mentioned it only because this girl Rebecca had stumbled into the case, claiming one of the professors she was assigned to bring over ended up receiving a thousand-dollar wire transfer from the same account directly, without the Swiss cover. "Who is this woman?" he asked. "Man, she is hot. Really, really hot," I remember him saying. "And good." He really looked forward to working with her, he said, with his hungry eyes twinkling in the locker room.

We always cooled off by taking a couple of laps in the pool. George was a very good swimmer, but on that day he kept stopping to talk to me about Rebecca. He was clearly addicted to her, and I counseled caution, a cold shower, and a weekend in the country with his wife and kids.

Life may be full of coincidences, but Rebecca Townsend's life, tight and controlled as a piston waiting to fire, was not. She was a brilliant strategist, we now know. But her life was empty but for those strategies. In fact, until she met Tommy Wood, it was empty of anything at all.

At the same moment that there was a knock on the door of the cell-like room Tommy and Rebecca were in, Murphy was patting the well-muscled rump of a black Marine veteran named Sam, who had been a member of the Delta Force, as Sam scurried onto one of my wife's jets. At the same moment that there was a knock on the door, Carolyn was piloting her own helicopter from her mansion in Virginia to the headquarters of her company outside of Baltimore, while two lawyers talked to her through her headset about a two-hundred-million-dollar takeover offer her company was going to initiate within the next twenty-four hours. At the same moment that there was a knock on the door, the Judge had just jumped out of the unmarked car that met his plane at the airport and brought him the short distance to the NSA HQ at Fort Meade, where two nervous analysts met him at the side door used by the dernza. Within half an hour the Judge had his driver take him back down the parkway to his favorite restaurant to get some breakfast. On the way he had the car stop at a pay phone, from which he called me.

At the same moment that there was a knock on the door, I was wandering out into my rose garden, examining the buds on my prize Mr. Lincoln rosebushes. The buds were as large and full as plums, ready to burst into four-inch blooms that are the stuff poetry is written about. I pulled a hose out of the greenhouse and dragged it the hundred feet out to the rosebushes, leaving streaks of mud across my jeans and bringing the morning's first sweat to my brow. I stopped to fish a leaf out of the blue water of the pool with a long net, watching the circles in the water expand with each drop that fell on its surface. I made a mental note to have the electric pool cover fixed so someone didn't fall in. I have a strange fear of water, convinced that my loved ones will drown and yet transfixed by its calm, serene smoothness. My fear is that the water is so inviting, so soft and surrounding, so quiet and cool. Designed to lull you into complacency and then swallow you when you are relaxed. Inviting you with your reflection and then turning unhuman, uncaring, when you were below that reflection.

As I pulled a few weeds around the pool, one of my wife's butlers, conveniently named James, came jogging out with a cordless telephone.

"It's the Judge, Mr. Steele," he said, gasping for breath.

"Thank you, James," I answered, taking the phone with a certain amount of glee, since I was standing outside my beautiful home on a beautiful day talking to my former boss who was undoubtedly going to ask for my help. "Yes, Judge," I said into the phone.

"This conversation did not take place" was the first thing he said.

"Well, hello to you too, Judge. I've been fine, thank you."

"Cut the bullshit, Steele," he blurted with a tired sigh. "We need to talk fast. Is this phone secure?"

"Nothing is completely secure," I said, just to anger him. "Nothing is ever really safe. This is a gray line, but I'm on a cordless phone, but the frequency is coded, so I have a relatively high level of confidence that we can speak safely."

"I don't like it," the Judge said. "But under the circumstances I've got to take the chance. Thanks for the plane. I've talked to Murphy, and he and a bunch of his Manhattan gun-toting fairies are on their way to Philadelphia."

"What is going on?" I asked, ignoring his slur at Murphy.

"I can't tell you any details, but I think we may have lost an agent, and I need an off-the-books mission to try to save her—or him, it. I'm calling you from a pay phone on the parkway. I believe we may have an internal problem. A big internal problem, so I don't want anyone to know what's going on before I figure out what's going on. And I mean anyone. That's why I called Murphy. The idiots may have kicked him out because he's a faggot, but I don't have to tell you that he's damn good. Tonight at dinner I'm going to ask you to come back and help out on a case—some case I'll make up. I want to be seen in public asking you to come back to handle something so that it won't raise too many eyebrows to have you around the HQ. What I really want is you around so you and your wife's company boys can handle this baby for me before it really blows up."

I looked at the perfect blue sky, decorated with soft, frosting-like clouds, my mind spinning with all the possibilities. An internal problem? That meant the Judge suspected that there was someone in the agency who had been helping Rebecca. That was why the Judge needed outside help that could not be traced inside. I knew that the Judge must be desperate if he was asking me to do such an outlandish thing—let alone ask me about it over the telephone. He was clearly stretching to justify his actions—he was the one who fired both Murphy and me, after all.

"Now here's what I need you to do," the Judge said.

"Wait a minute," I said. "I haven't said yes . . . yet."

"Hell, you sent the jet to get Murphy. That sounds like yes to me."

"That was Carolyn saying yes," I offered, dropping a handful of weeds at my feet. "That was her sending her plane because she wants in on the action."

"Good. I need her more than I need you. This thing is going to cost money. Real money. And I can't promise I can get Uncle Sam to repay the loan. This whole thing will have to stay off the books until we settle the internal problem. Does Carolyn have the cash? I mean, I heard about this SFS takeover this morning."

"That's insider information," I said, hoping that I angered him by reminding him of the idiotic conflict-of-interest charges that sent me into retirement. "Damn spies are an arbitrager's best friend, Judge. I believe Carolyn not only has the cash, the staff, and the hardware, she also has the interest. But you're going to have to let her play too. She'll want in on the action. She won't be content to sit behind a desk and cut the checks."

"Goddamn it," the Judge said, his southern drawl coming out. "This isn't the amateur hour. The last time she got involved, in that Mexico thing, we practically had an international incident. This is big, Steele. Really big and really dangerous."

"I'm just being honest with you, Judge," I said, walking back toward the house. "You know she's not an amateur. She's been involved before. She'll drive a hard bargain. But I'll let you talk to her. She's flying out of her office right now to pick up some other executives and then go up to Manhattan for a meeting. Write this number down: 202-789-4565. That's the mobile phone in the chopper. Call her in the next ten minutes, or it will be tough to get through that phalanx of secretaries, receptionists, and ass-kissers."

"You're going to let your wife do your bargaining?" he asked with a Texas twanging drawl as deep and long as the Rio Grande.

"Sexist pig," I said into the phone. "She's not just my wife, Judge, she's the owner of those jets and computers you want your hot little hands on and a woman who is piloting her own turbochopper to her own Fortune 500 company. Besides, she'll be getting ready to land, so you'll have her at a disadvantage. She'll say yes to whatever you want just to get you off the phone so she can negotiate the winds on the pad. I've calculated all this into my suggestion that you call her direct."

"I don't have time," he snapped.

"You're scared," I snapped back.

"Damn it. I'll take that for a yes. I'll call Carolyn, and I'll see both of you at dinner tonight. At eight. Put Murphy on Carolyn's payroll. Don't pay him and his gay goons too much. Keep them hungry, like you did when you were running a case for the organization. I told him three hundred thou max. I'll tell him to contact only you. I don't want him talking to me or anybody inside. I'll send a courier to your house right now with a summary of what you need. You talk only to me. If you have to talk to someone else here talk generally, without specifics, to John X and only John X. Do not let him know what you know or why you want to know it. And I expect you back in your office tomorrow—after we put on a good show tonight, in case anyone's watching."

"Got it."

"And," the Judge added, "I don't like it one bit that John called you up to cry about Paul. Paul's my number two, the DDNSA, and I won't have him bad-mouthed. It's my job to stand up for my people. What the hell are you doing listening to that bunch of cow turds anyway? What did he tell you?"

"Nothing you don't already know, I'm sure," I said, thinking that he was the one with cow turds close to his mouth. Stand up for his people, he said to the man he fired?

"I doubt that. He's being damn squirmy with me. We'll compare notes when we get together. See ya."

"Good-bye," I said, a split second after he hung up.

I stood next to the blue water of the long pool and watched the morning sun reflect off its calm surface into dancing crystals of light. There was another green oak leaf floating on the water's glassy surface, the anthropomorphic shape drifting toward the wide steps that went down into the pool. It was nearing the end of summer. We were coming out of the comforting water to the acrid reality of spy hunting. Coming out of the water, I thought, onto hard, dry land. Like fish into mammals, we were becoming hunters of the traitors.

At the same moment, hundreds of miles away, there was a second knock on the reinforced door of the small room in the lodge where Rebecca and Tommy had spent the night.

"Just a minute," Rebecca said, and pulled on a short robe while Tommy pulled the sheets up over himself. When Rebecca opened the door her father took one step inside and said to Rebecca, without looking at Tommy, "Time for a family meeting."

"We'll be there in two seconds," Rebecca sang.

"A *family* meeting, yes?" her father repeated.

"I want Tommy there," Rebecca said. "We're mar—" She stopped, not quite ready yet to tell her father that they were married. "I want him in every meeting. I take full responsibility. I want him to know what is going on."

No one said anything for a long while, the rain outside beginning to pour so hard that the belt picked it up.

"All right, Rebecca," her father mumbled very slowly. "You are the expert, yes? You are the recruiter. But I want Tommy to understand the consequences. He has met us at a turning point. This is no time for training, yes? We must be at our best."

"I am at my best," Rebecca said forcefully, "when I am with him."

"Meet in the conference room in fifteen minutes. We will have full status reports on all the brothers and sisters. You, Becky, need to tell us how much time we have. You must tell us who will get to you first," her father said sternly. "And, Tommy, welcome again to the family."

"Yes," Tommy said, impulsively standing up with the sheet wrapped around his torso. "I—well, I won't let you down. I've told Becky I'm here to stay. I'm with you."

"Good," he replied, touching the brush of his white moustache. "You know, I can't wait for all this to be over. To be normal again, yes? I wish, I crave, to be one of those retired gents at the country club with nothing more to worry about than whether I am losing my golf swing. I'm glad to follow this plan, Rebecca, but I want it to be over. Tommy, you must understand, we did not want it like this. The point was to stop everything and get on with our lives as common citizens. A safe, orderly move into the world of normal people, yes? I hope you'll understand."

The three of them stared at each other, not sure what to say.

"I'll see you in fifteen minutes," Doc concluded, and closed the door behind him.

Tommy jumped into the small shower and must have asked questions to Rebecca, whose voice as she dressed was barely audible over the noise of the pounding water. Only phrases and words are audible, even after the tape was put through ten different tests. More equipment has gone over this short segment in the past weeks than maybe any piece of tape has ever been subjected to. But still, we have only just a taste of what she said, and Tommy's subjective memory.

". . . twelve brothers and sisters . . . in Berlin right before the war . . . smuggled . . . my father came to the United States . . . Key West

. . . the color of eggplant . . . A bank, just like any other bank, but it . . . Yes, that's right. All in the business . . . Tommy, you have to just take my . . . a question of strategy and then . . ."

Then the shower stopped. Tommy dressed silently, the tape exploding with noise as he pulled the belt through his belt loops.

"I don't know what to say," Tommy offered. "I'm ready, I guess. Though I still don't understand what is going on."

"I know," Rebecca said, opening the door. "I'm not sure I do either. But you have to trust me. We're fighting for our lives. And we have risked our lives for a good cause. We have accomplished so much that I don't want to see the whole thing blow up right now. I asked you to come with me this week knowing that you could never go back. The plan was always that after our family reunion, after we got together with all of my father's brothers and sisters, we would have to go away for a while—maybe a long while. I wanted you to be with me. I couldn't imagine disappearing for a year and being without you. It was selfish of me, gambling that you would stay with me if I brought you to this family reunion. But I didn't plan on all this excitement. I thought I'd have the entire week to explain this all to you, slowly, carefully. Time to win you over so you understood what it is that I hope we can accomplish. That's why my family wasn't surprised when we told them about being engaged. They knew that we were all going to have to take an extended vacation after this, so they knew that I must be planning on staying with you. But come on, cowboy. This meeting will be an eye-opener."

They walked down the hallway without saying anything and stopped in front of the door to the communications room.

"Don't worry," Rebecca said, knocking on the thick steel door. "Just listen at first. Just do as you are told."

The door opened and they went in, the faint transmissions from Tommy's belt disappearing the moment the secure steel door shut behind them.

By the time these last intercepts had gone from Bobby to John X to Paul to the Judge's desk, the Judge had sealed off the transmission room and called the National Reconnaissance Office for a clear satellite code line for the transmissions. The Judge, Paul, Bobby, the techy who worked with the transmissions, and John X had been sealed in a control area in the basement of the agency, next to the acres of computers that were the brains of the organization. The Judge had issued strict orders that no one outside of the control room be told what was going on and that no one, but himself of course, could leave the room without the armed guard who sat by the door accompanying them. Food, toothbrushes, and white shirts were delivered, and the shifts began. Much to John X's relief, Bobby, who was the only one who could have told them about the bug in Tommy's belt, was off the first shift and was escorted home by an armed guard. The Judge had listened to thousands of feet of tape-recorded conversations between Tommy and Rebecca, and, unbeknownst to John X, he had heard several of the internal tapes that recorded John X's own calls.

The Judge sat down across a white Formica table from John X. Paul sat down next to the Judge and put a video recorder on the table between them and pushed the on button. The two wall-mounted peripheral cameras, present as a matter of agency policy when a hot project is on, were voice-activated and captured all of their faces. When I saw the three tapes weeks later, running all three of them simultaneously on three monitors so I could get a feel for the scene, I was struck not by what I saw but by the piano-wire-tight tension in the melody of their voices. They were all near the breaking point on day one of the project.

"Now, John," the Judge said slowly, rubbing his deep-set eyes. "Tell me how in God's name you got a bug into all these buildings at Rebecca's place."

"I'm sorry, sir," John X answered, his voice breaking from the lack of sleep and the tension in the room. "I don't think I should explain my sources at this point. I believe—"

"Goddamn it!" the Judge screamed. "You will tell me how the hell you got mikes in all these places, all these different rooms—hell, how you even knew where this goddamn place was—or I will fire your sorry ass this moment."

"I cannot," John X said quickly and quietly, his eyes never blinking, "compromise my source."

"You're fired," the Judge said. "Now, let's try to avoid putting you in prison for the rest of your goddamn life. I don't think I have to read you FISA or the Internal Security Act verse by verse, do I? Tell me where these tapes are coming from. How did you get a transmission source in each room? Who do you know who is on the inside of this family?"

John X stared at the two of them blankly, swallowing hard and struggling not to blink.

"You understand," Paul pointed out, "that you can be imprisoned for aiding and abetting treason? You understand that we may have to assume that you are part of Rebecca's plot here because you are refusing to cooperate? You understand that we are talking about some serious shit here?"

"Under FISA," John X said, "you have to be able to prove that I knowingly bugged an American citizen, in the United States, without his or her knowledge."

"Jesus!" the Judge shouted. "Who the hell cares? I'll get you behind bars no matter what the law says if you don't start cooperating."

John X looked from the Judge to Paul and then said, "Should I leave now, or would you like to have me arrested right here?"

"Damn it," the Judge said after a long pause. "We're not going to have you arrested. Just tell us what the hell is up so that we can evaluate this information."

"I'm not sure I understand your need to know my sources right now," John X said to the Judge. Paul opened his mouth to say something, but then paused as if he too was suddenly not sure why they did need to know the sources right now.

"I'm not sure," the Judge boomed, "that I understand your need to not tell us your sources right now."

"I believe," John X replied, "that Rebecca has help within the organization and that it would be better for all three of us if I did not reveal the method by which I received this information. I swear to you that I am not assisting Rebecca or her family in any way—hell, I'm the one who is blowing the whistle here. But I want to protect the integrity of my—my methods. When I was in the war, sir, when I was in military intelligence in Vietnam, I revealed a source, a method, too early, and friends of mine, very close friends, died."

"Bad analogy," the Judge snapped. "This ain't war, my friend, and this isn't slipshod military intelligence."

"Is there someone else in the family involved?" Paul asked. "Do we have an insider we can trust?"

"No," John X offered, his pale skin growing paler every minute under the bright lights.

"Damn, this is frustrating," the Judge growled, scratching his scalp and getting up to pace the small room. The Judge leaned against the bank of computers opposite the bank of six reel-to-reel recorders. I could see the concern in Paul's face that the Judge would treat the expensive equipment like a piece of barroom furniture, but Paul remained silent. "Okay, you may be right. From what we've heard, there may be an insider, somebody Rebecca thinks is double-crossing her. But so what? Why not talk to us? Are you going to help us or not?"

"Yes," John X said. "I'm going to do everything I can to get Rebecca back. You can continue to try to have the satellite transmissions traced if you want to and try to find the source, but—"

"I don't really give two shits where the damn bugs are," the Judge volunteered, waving his hands under the harsh fluorescent lights. "I frickin' know that they're in Rebecca's family house and that damn lodge. I just want to figure out how the hell they got there and how the hell you know about them."

"I suggest," John X said, "we spend our time worrying about how to get Rebecca out of there."

"You suggest, do you?" the Judge barked. "I can't trust you any more than I can spit on you! I think you're damn right. We do have a mole here, and I'm not so sure that it isn't you."

"That's my point," John X said, his voice cracking with each vowel. "As long as I'm the only one who knows where the bugs are and how the information is transmitted then the transmissions can't be stopped, even if there is an internal problem here. I think that is a safeguard that we should protect."

While John X and the deputy dernza argued for quick action, the Judge did not respond, listening while he drank gallons of coffee.

No one inside the agency knew what the men locked in the control room were up to, and two of the men inside the control room had no idea what the Judge was up to. The Judge confessed later to me that he did not know what Rebecca was up to or whether anyone else in the organization was helping her, assuming that she was up to something. The tapes the Judge had heard had him worried, he told me, but he was afraid to report up the ladder until he knew more of what was going on and if there was anyone else up the ladder who might be a suspect. He had to have Rebecca; then he would report.

The Judge was not a professional spy, but the Army and the back rooms of Texas politics had taught him a thing or two about keeping these things under control. I guessed he'd tell State and the White House when he was good and ready, and not before. He'd have his outside team—me, Carolyn, and Murphy's crew—come up with some information and he would appear brilliant in his guesses. Which is why part of him respected John X for refusing to let on how he broke open this case. John X was honest, he guessed, but a little too worried about covering his own butt.

Another worry the Judge had, I knew without asking, was whether his outside team was up to the job.

An hour and a half after the Judge hung up, the phone rang again. I was putting on a suit in order to go into town when James knocked on the door and said, "It's Mrs. Steele on the telephone, sir. She's in the helicopter again."

I picked up the phone with one leg in my pants. "Yes, darling," I said, expecting her to be livid that I had had the Judge call her.

"How quickly can you get over to the airstrip?" she asked, with the whirling sound of the big helicopter in the background.

"Twenty-five minutes if I risk wrecking the car," I suggested. "Why are you in the air?"

"We're in a hurry. I'll be there in twenty minutes," she said. "If you aren't at the company hangar by the time I'm there and Max rolls the Lear out onto the runway, I'm leaving without you."

"What are you talking about?" I asked, knowing perfectly well what she was talking about. She had obviously talked to the Judge and decided that she should get in on the action immediately. I knew that because she had asked Max, her favorite pilot and a former Air Force ace, to fly her. Max flew only when she was really in a hurry, because he was the only person who Carolyn admitted was a better pilot than she was. As I stood there with one leg in my pants, the thought crossed my mind that if Carolyn was ever going to leave me for someone it would be Max.

"I've talked to the Judge and I've talked to Murphy. Murphy and his boys have just landed outside Philadelphia. I'm going to get in on some of the action this time. You won't believe what he told me was going down."

"I knew it! He told you?" I shouted as I pulled on my trousers, the phone wedged against my sagging cheek.

"Hey, it's my plane. Of course he told me. He'd never guess that I'd show up. So get over to the hangar, honey, or you'll be left out of the fun."

"Carolyn," I said, trying to remain calm, "this is not fun. This is serious. You are not going anywhere. I am an analyst. My job is here running the mission. I do not go into the field. I do not stick my head into other people's jobs. This is too fast. Now go back to your company and do that takeover thing you were planning on and—"

"You've got eighteen minutes," she said, hitting the throttle on the chopper. "You're with me or you're not. But I'm on my way."

"Damn it!" I screamed as she hung up. Was she going through a midlife crisis late in life, or had I missed something in my analysis of her usually calm, rational thought processes? Her confidence had gone out of bounds. She was playing with government secrets and other people's lives as if they were a computer game in which the object was to see how much fun you could have in as little time as possible. She was trying to overcome the fear that her attempt to save Mike Carter had instilled in her. She could wipe out the past by future success. She would come out swinging, I knew, afraid to be timid. Carolyn would get her way—and I couldn't help but love her for it.

Theory number 349: Love isn't blind, it just makes you blind. Physical attraction is at the heart of most love, but it robs you of all peripheral vision. Love is focusing intently on one person, to the detriment of seeing everything else around you. People see all too clearly who they are going to fall in love with, but once in love they lose all sight of reality—since reality is not the object of focus, but the objective world peripherally around us.

The irony here, which I did not realize until weeks later, was how love or jealousy tied so much of this tale together. If not for John X's seemingly irrational jealousy, we would not have known about Rebecca's family. If not for Rebecca's love for Tommy, she never would have taken the risks that led us to her family. If not for my wife, then the Judge would not have asked me to come back to help on this little project. And if not for Carolyn's sudden lust for excitement, and my irrational love for her, which allowed me to put up with her absurd way of butting into things that she knew nothing about, we wouldn't have saved Tommy.

But there was no time to philosophize or curse. I grabbed my tie, and as I searched for shoes in the walk-in closet, I yelled at James to bring the car around and leave the engine running. The courier sent out by the Judge arrived just as I was running out the front door. I grabbed the packet he brought, threw it onto the passenger seat, and mapped out in my mind how to get to the airfield. I slid past the chain-link fence around the hangar just as they were pulling up the jet's steps.

I laid on the horn, grabbed the packet and my tie, and ran for the plane. I knew there was no stopping her, so once again I tried to slow her down, distance myself, back off from her wild proposition. As I ran toward the plane I thought, no, you're a big boy now. You're no coward. You can keep up with this woman. Ah, Carolyn, I thought as her manicured and bejeweled hand reached down the steps and grabbed my hand, with my rep tie in it, pulling me into the plane, I am glad we've met.

16.

SOMETIMES PEOPLE CONCENTRATE so much on achieving the best that they give up or ignore the very good. Voltaire said it more simply: "The best is the enemy of the good." Now he may have been talking about the moral inferiority of all people who have one talent that shines above everything else, but I believe it more likely that he was talking about people's inherent unwillingness to want to be good at anything unless they can be the very best. Why even bother trying if you're not going to be the best in the world? You professional spies, bureaucrats, and politicians probably understand this attitude better than most. That attitude keeps many very talented people from having, or using, the courage to do what they want to do. Instead, many talented people simply sit on their talents, admiring those they imagine to be better than they could ever hope to be.

Tommy was a frustrated architect because his good work was not, in his estimation, the best. Rebecca was a successful spy because she was goal-oriented—no one really cared how she accomplished her missions as long as she accomplished them. Her file reflects that her work was messy but she always got her man or her information or both. She lost battles but never wars.

At approximately 10:00 A.M., in a hard driving rain that turned the sky into late evening, my firsthand experience with war began. I was sitting in the back of one of my wife's jets, sipping an orange juice and reading the last page of the packet that the Judge had sent me, when the call came through from Murphy. The summaries of the tape-recorded conversations shocked me when I first read them, and I couldn't wait to hear the actual tapes. Max was flying the plane and Carolyn was in the copilot's seat, so the real copilot, dressed in a white jumpsuit with Carolyn's company logo sewn onto its breast, brought the mobile phone back to me.

"What the hell are you and Carolyn doing?" Murphy shouted above the static.

"Sightseeing," I said. "Carolyn had a sudden urge to see the Liberty Bell again, so we're off to Philly for a history lesson. In fact, I believe we are almost there."

"Look," Murphy said, "I'll send you postcards. Stay out of this. I just got the word that our friendly agent's family farm is in the process of being invaded by Colombians, and I don't mean coffee growers."

"Impossible," I said. "They couldn't get all the way to Pennsylvania without having Customs and DEA all over them. Unless they were already here. Maybe—Jesus, it's absurd. You've got to be kidding."

"Boss!" Murphy shouted, as if he were punching me. "It's your job to figure out how it happened. I'm just telling you what is happening—and believe you me, it's happening. I'm taking my boys in on the double right now. I rented two choppers and put them on your wife's bill."

"That's why it is going to be hard to keep her out of it."

"What?" Murphy shouted, his voice louder with each word. "I can't hear you. What did you say?"

"I said that you can't keep Carolyn out of your fun and games if she pays the bill. Besides, we'll just wait in Philly to pick up the pieces."

"Don't say that," Murphy said. "I don't want to come back in little bits. I like the way I'm organized right now, thank you."

"Is it that bad?" I asked, suddenly becoming truly worried.

"Steele," Murphy said, his voice garbled and distorted by the phone, "say a prayer for me. This one doesn't sound fun. Thank God I'm a loyal, patriotic, God-fearing, honest, helpful, trusty gay American. Otherwise, I'm not sure what the hell I'd be here for. I can't believe this is happening in Pennsylvania."

"Murphy, you've got to tell me what's going on. Have you been in contact with the Judge?"

"I'm not talking on this phone, pal," he said. "I'll tell you everything when I see you back at the hangar in Philly. I hope to have our lost friend with me then. If I get there on time."

"But is the Judge running this thing? Does he know what is going down?"

"I've talked to him once. He gave me a goal, no details. This one is on my own."

Good God, I said to myself. What had we gotten ourselves into?

I sat back heavily in the seat, and the open packet spilled its contents out across the carpet of the plane's floor. An eight-by-ten glossy photograph of Tommy stared up at me, and for the first time I stared back into his wide, trusting Hoosier eyes. I wonder what color they are, I asked myself as the plane streaked across the blue sky. I knew that Carolyn would insist on taking one of her company helicopters from Philly to the Pennsylvania woods to try to help Murphy. She would feel she owed him one.

When Tommy jogged out of the communications room with Rebecca's brothers when the alarm went off, the black box ticked back into action. A communications expert met the brothers in the hall and told them there was gunfire on the edge of perimeter three in the northwest and two large planes were coming in on the farm from the south. Orders were shouted over walkie-talkies and mobile phones. Men and women began to covertly fan out into different quadrants of the farm.

Rebecca's father spoke calmly to the men assembled around him in the hall, each of them offering suggestions or information only when he paused. "Whoever these guys are, they aren't that good. The skirmish in quadrant three must be a distraction. The airplanes have the men in them. Paratroopers, yes? I say plan two, agreed?"

"Yes," several of the brothers and Rebecca said.

"But that leaves no room to try to negotiate with them," Jan offered, dissent in his voice.

"You don't negotiate with two carrier planes full of armed men," Fritz said. "They want blood. They want blood now. These aren't Colombians here to make a point and then split."

"If they aren't part of the Medellín cartel, if they've been hired by somebody, we fight them now on our turf or we fight them later on their turf," Joe pointed out.

"Or both," Jan said.

"Remember, they may not want to fight a battle," Doc said, leaning against the rough concrete wall. "They may be mercenaries. Paid to do a job, yes? Although they do want to show off their equipment, they just want us. The family. This may be just a kidnap mission, nothing more. If things don't go well, each team is on its own. Split up, yes? No plans, just out and meet in Key West when it is safe. Meet at the boat."

"Okay," Fritz added. "I hate to do this, but I'm going to send the planes off with the kids now. You sure you don't want to go with them, Rebecca? We shouldn't risk you now that we are this close to the family reunion. You should go."

"No," she said quickly. "Let's just say I'm changing jobs and this is one I'd like to try out. Tommy and I are staying."

There was a long pause in the concrete hallway, the family silent together under the bare light bulbs that dangled over their heads.

"Let's go," Doc said, and they were off.

We later traced the flight paths of the three fat carrier planes and discovered that they came from an abandoned private corporate airstrip west of Wilkes-Barre. The parking lot next to the old hangars had tire marks from a rented bus on it, and inside the hangar, in a bathroom that had been used frequently even though the water was turned off, we found a Berlitz *How to Speak Spanish* book and a copy of *Soldier of Fortune* magazine with several help-wanted ads circled in the back. Afterward we found the bus fifty miles away, near the Ohio border, in the parking lot of a small-town airport that was completely vacant most of the time. The vinyl seats were stained with an amazing amount of blood, and there were four empty cartridges shoved in between the back and bottom of the third seat. The investigators found bits of brain matter in one of the dried pools of blood and determined that some of the passengers on this bus had to be dead. To this day we have no idea who these non-Spanish-speaking mercenaries, dressed in Colombian fatigues and armed with South American versions of heavy armament, really were. We all have a guess, because we know now who hired them, but their identities, like their operation, were cleaned up quickly and discreetly. Buried somewhere in an unmarked grave. It was as if they never existed. Maybe they all answered the advertisements in the back of *Soldier of Fortune* that were taken out by people who did not exist and who paid in cash. Maybe the ads were just a cover, and the men were recruited in person in South America and only the leaders of their little army needed the guide on how to speak Spanish. Even though we are the largest, richest intelligence operation in the world, we still have to admit we simply don't know who they were.

But to Rebecca's family, huddled between two Pennsylvania hills, they were Colombians out for revenge. They had to assume that the invaders were trained guerrilla fighters who would find the woods around the family home as easy to negotiate as the jungles of South America. Why they were here, and whom they answered to, were concerns they did not now have time to mull over. Now, Tommy explained to me later, they only had to worry about staying alive. If they lived, if they won, then they could chase down their true enemy, following the trail to the ends of the earth if they had to, in order to seek revenge. Right now they didn't care who was on the other side of the gun—they just had to avoid the bullets.

The fat planes, which had been rented the day before in Dayton, came zooming under the cloud cover and dropped poorly trained paratroopers into the fields around the family house like a dandelion spewing its lacy white seeds across a lawn. The slow planes made easy targets, but the family marksmen held back because the family was sending four planes full of wives and children up at the same time from the short runway tucked in the edge of the mountain. Instead, the family's men shot at the Colombians as they came down, well-aimed bullets shattering kneecaps, and then swept into the field to capture them. But when they got to the field all they found were a dozen old mannequins, dressed in fatigues and weighted down so that they would land right where they were pointed. This was exactly what the Colombians' strategists wanted—to pull all of the family's hired guns out onto the field and away from the lodge, while four dozen Colombian troops came up over the mountain and descended on the lodge.

Only the immediate family was left in the lodge: Doc, Jan, Fritz, Joe, Joe's wife, who refused to leave, Erik, Rebecca, and Tommy. Eleven lookouts were dug in within three hundred feet of the front door of the lodge.

"Jesus!" one of the lookouts shouted into his walkie-talkie, his voice echoing in the room in the lodge where Tommy sat loading a rifle. "They're here! They are—" and then his voice stopped in a barrage of automatic gunfire that made Tommy jump out of his chair.

He stood against the cool concrete wall and swallowed hard before he said a word to Rebecca, who flinched at the sound of gunfire but kept on loading weapons.

"This is a goddamn war," Tommy said. "I mean, this doesn't just happen. This doesn't just happen in the United States. Where are the cops? Where's the Army?"

Rebecca flipped her shorter amber hair out of her face and said, "They'll be here, if whoever is helping our Colombian friends hasn't paid them off. But by then it may be too late."

Later we discovered that three-fourths of the U.S. Attorney's office and all of the federal magistrates had been called to Washington to receive a first-ever award from the FBI for their regional management of secret information. They had been recommended for the award by the NSA public relations office. The local Bureau men went to Washington to see the awards ceremony. The county sheriff and two of his four deputies were called to the state capital by the local Secret Service group for regional training in counterfeit detection. The NSA had passed information on to the Secret Service that there might be an increase in counterfeiting in western Pennsylvania and suggested the training. Another of the deputies was called by Army intelligence and told to look for a series of files that they had to have immediately, which kept him in the office all day. Army intelligence got its information from the NSA. The other deputy was alerted by ATF, which had been alerted by the NSA, to the whereabouts of a still, which the deputy spent all day investigating, only to determine that no still ever existed.

In short, there was not a single law-enforcement officer on duty and available within a hundred miles of the family farm. They had all been steered out of the area by someone within the NSA.

Rebecca strapped a holster on over her dark green jumpsuit, then strapped a long carbon knife onto her left leg, pulled a flak jacket on, and heaved a heavy M-16 onto her shoulder. Tommy told me later how he stared at her, again mesmerized by her sudden transformation before his very eyes. "We can wait here for them, Tommy, or we can go out and meet them. The only way to get out of here may be to meet up with the others below and get on a copter that is supposed to come and get us. What do you want to do?"

He paused for a second, listening to men detail the size of the force that had come over the mountain and was now engaging the few lookouts who were placed around the lodge. The brothers ran up and down the hallway to the communications room. Doc stood in the middle of the communications room and shouted orders that could be heard down the hall in Rebecca's room.

"What do you want to do?" she asked again, as Fritz stuck his head in the room.

Tommy stared at the woman he had fallen in love with, now dressed in full combat gear. He told me later that he hardly recognized her, except for the fire in her eyes. The raw determination that shone like some secret hot stone in her pupils. "How did you know," he said, pushing a lock of her hair up under her helmet, "that I would stay with you? How did you know that when you told me we were going away for a year, just disappearing until we saw how things worked out, I wouldn't simply walk out on you? Just walk across that front field and keep on going back to my nice, normal life as an architect?"

"I didn't," she said, loading the last chamber of her rifle. "I didn't know. But I guessed that you love me enough that you'd find some way to stay. Some way to justify this whole thing in your mind so that you wouldn't leave."

"Is that what I've done?" he asked. "Justify the whole thing?"

"That's what we all do," she said, checking the safety on the gun with the passionless precision of an assassin. "That's life."

Tommy exhaled loudly, his breath almost speaking on the tape. I imagined he wondered what life was all about that moment, sitting on the floor with a rifle in his lap, listening to gunfire outside the concrete lodge.

"Stay or go?" she asked.

"I think," Tommy said slowly, "it makes sense to stay here. Stay here and wait."

"No," Fritz said quietly, coming back down the brightly lit hall. "They've already cut us off from our own men. We need to get out of here, split up, and get down onto the front field. We have to make a run through the woods and get to the house. They've got stuff that will punch a hole in these walls, and they plan on using it. The helicopters can't land up here. Somebody must have tipped them off on what our plan was, because they found the hole in it and exploited it for everything it's worth. We've got to get out of here before they get to the front door."

Rebecca took her brother Fritz's hand for a moment and said, "Okay. Good luck."

"See you in Key West," Fritz prayed, and kissed her hand and ran back down the hall. Rebecca watched him for a second and then turned to Tommy.

"Get a flak jacket on," Rebecca ordered, all romance out of her voice, and the sound of the calm, trained agent in charge surging into her throat. "You carry the backpack with the radio. Over your shoulders and through your belt. Let's go."

"But—" Tommy said.

"You've got to keep trusting me—us. If we say we've got to go, then you've got to go. Damn it, I love you. I trust you. You've got to trust me," Rebecca said.

Tommy undid his belt buckle to put on the backpack, and the microphone clicked off.

The tapes don't tell us what happened in the next thirty minutes, except for the sporadic sounds of running, machine guns raking the trees, and sudden blasts of what Tommy later said were bazookas aimed right at him. Tommy told me in great detail how the group of eight plunged out into the driving gray rain and split into four pairs of armed ghosts that disappeared into the trees south of the lodge to haunt and hunt their enemy. The undergrowth was heavy, so they moved slowly and quietly at first, wary of stumbling across a team of Colombians in the thick Pennsylvania woods. As Tommy and Rebecca eased into a small clearing by a stream, bullets flashed over their heads, and they hit the dirt, the hearing device in the belt blinking back on for a few minutes.

"Where are they?" Tommy gasped, rolling out of the heavy backpack. "Jesus, where are they?"

"Don't stand up," Rebecca whispered. "I think we're right on top of them."

"Great," he said, wiping the mud off his face with the back of his wet hand. "This is some way to spend a family reunion."

Tommy remembered how a smile broke through the tension on Rebecca's face, and she rolled toward him and planted a kiss on his dirty cheek. "My mother didn't want me to bring you," she whispered. "She said it was a mistake. That if you refused to go along with us, particularly to meet up with the rest of the family in Key West, then we would have to kidnap you or kill you. But I knew that you would go to the family reunion and that you would stay with me. I just knew it. I couldn't stand going away without you. I had to take the risk and bring you with me."

"Thanks," Tommy said. "Thanks a lot. I'd love to just lie here in the mud and chat, but we've got to go. We can't stop here."

"Throw something. Throw a rock as far to the left as you can. A big rock. Watch where the shots come from."

"You're bleeding," Tommy said. "Your arm is really bleeding."

"I'm okay. Throw the rock. Now."

Tommy grunted as he heaved a rock thirty feet to their side. The moment the rock hit the ground a stream of gunfire burst into the grove where it landed, decimating the trees and bushes like a tornado.

"Behind the big rocks," Rebecca said, pointing her cut arm. "Right over there. About two hundred feet." Another fusillade of bullets tore through the tree branches, tossing them like a giant green salad.

"Almost three hundred feet," Tommy said, listening carefully to the sound of gunfire, which was becoming more familiar every minute. He guessed that there were at least three Colombians on the crest of a small hill on the edge of the clearing. I asked him later why he sounded so sure—why was he so good at measuring distances by the sound of rifle fire? How could he know the number of gunmen from the sound and be so certain about it? "I just guessed," he told me.

On the tape he asked Rebecca, "Now what?"

"You stay here. I'm going after them."

"The hell you are," Tommy asserted, grabbing her bloodstained arm.

"I'm trained in this," Rebecca said calmly, her breathing steady and measured as if she was fighting to stay in control. "You stay right here and don't move. Throw a rock the same place every two minutes or so."

"Trained in what?" he asked, but she was gone before he could protest, leaving him flat on his stomach in a puddle in the cold rain, an Armalite AR-180, fully automatic, digging into his chest on one side and an old Winchester 70 supergrade hunting rifle, which he had found in the arms closet in the lodge, stuck up into his other armpit. He glanced at his watch in the rain and tried to listen to something other than his heavy breathing. After three minutes he threw another rock back into the woods, and plugged his ears with his fingers as the gunfire splintered the trees. Even with his fingers in his ears, he told me later, the sharp explosions of the bullets made his head spin with the vibrations. "The silence between shots was even worse," he told me. "It was like that feeling of pressure you feel in your ears when you are in a climbing airplane. You try to swallow, but all you're gulping is air."

When the gunfire stopped the waiting became torture. The gray rain did not let up, and the cold puddle grew around him. Fear began to creep back up Tommy's dry throat, and he stroked the dark wood of the Winchester rifle as if it were a friendly dog. He told me later that he knew he was beginning to lose all sense of what was expected, of what was normal, as he lay in the mud in battle fatigues with a rifle in his hand. He saw himself as a character in a movie, and any moment now the director would yell cut and he would be able to get up and get a Diet Coke and go to the bathroom. But the direction never came, and he simply lay in the mud, thinking of the taste of an ice-cold soft drink and beginning to wonder if he'd ever be able to relieve his full bladder.

After ten minutes he looked up over the top of the long grass he was lying in and saw Rebecca walk out of the trees near the spot where the bullets came from. A dark-skinned man followed her, a smile on his face as he strode ten feet behind her with an AK-47 pointed at her back. Tommy could not see her face, but he could see her body shudder with fear. He didn't care if they saw him now, so he kneeled in the grass and watched. He propped the old rifle up on one knee and scanned the edge of the woods with the muddy Burris scope. There were two men moving out from behind a rock pile toward Rebecca and her captor, their arms full of big, dark guns that he could not identify. He scanned back to the man behind Rebecca and saw that he had fallen farther behind her as they climbed a slight incline.

I will have one chance at each one, he told me he thought at that moment. One shot for each. Miss and I'm out. Miss and Rebecca is dead.

The rain swirled in front of the old scope, and his hands stuck to the dirty wood stock of the well-used rifle.

"Something just came over me, Steele," Tommy said to me in my study late that night. "It was like I was back at the state fair in the finals again. My blood pressure falling as everyone else's went up. I'd say a little prayer to my dad up in heaven and lower the rifle and pop one off for him. I never sweated it. I didn't circle the sight or coax the bull's-eye into view. Just lower. Sight. For you, Dad. Fire."

He set the glass on the carpet and put his head in his hands, not in remorse but in pain, and said, "But this time it was somebody's head I was aiming at. Not some two-cent piece of paper taped to a fence. Lower. Sight. Pray. Fire . . . and I blew the guy's head off. A perfect shot that looked like it caught him right, oh Jesus, right in the left eye.

I passed the scope over Rebecca as she dove into a tangle of bushes and followed the two others as they started to move. Lower. Sight. Pray. Fire . . . and I got the one in front flat in the chest. The third shot hit the third man in the right shoulder and spun him around. He dropped to one knee but did not let go of his rifle.

"And that is the last time I saw Becky," he said into the dying fire in the study's wide fireplace, his eyes slipping down the ornate carvings on the mantelpiece and settling on the red glow of the embers. "She made a dash into the woods and the guy got up to follow her. I shot again, knicking his left ear, and then as he lifted his rifle—God, what a strong son of a bitch—I shot him in the right hip. The rifle pumped hard, and he started to get up again, and I lowered, heard him scream something in what sounded like English in pain and anger, and the sound brought my sight to his throat and I fired. The last shot cut his damn neck practically in half, and then—then there was no more screaming."

He paused and touched his unshaven neck, his fingers delicately balanced on his drawn Adam's apple. "What could I do?" he said. "I mean, this wasn't something I knew anything about. I could shoot something all right, but survival is something I'm not sure I know anything about."

"But you survived," I said, dipping one finger into my scotch to twirl the tiny floating ice cubes, hoping to raise his level of confidence before I told him what he had to do.

"Luck, Steele. Dumb luck. I don't know a thing about it. It just held for me that day. The luck held. I don't know what I did."

What he did was charge the downed men with the Armalite in one hand and the Winchester in the other, the Armalite releasing a stream of bullets that raked the area and nearly knocked him over until he got the feel for it. He chewed up the wounded men like a food processor and ran screaming into the woods. His belt picked up his uncontrolled sobs as he stumbled through the woods looking for Rebecca, each breath a hack, gasp, and abbreviated wail. He stopped crying after fifteen minutes, and he reloaded both guns with barely a sound. "Rebecca," he whispered over and over on the tape as he began to regain his rhythm and take long quiet steps through the trees. "Becky. Rebecca? Becky?" Within the hour he was moving to the edge of the woods behind the house.

He ran right into the back of six Colombians retreating from the house, and without a word he let loose with the automatic at their backs, and when it finally spit the last of its rounds, he fell to the ground and shot the last two men with the old Winchester. Both of them screamed in English, and danced uncontrollably as they were hit by his raging gunfire, their bodies tugged like marionettes by the bursting strings of blood that shadowed his shots. He threw the Winchester aside when he was out and stood straight up with a nine-millimeter Luger in his hand and walked through the field to the house. When one of the downed Colombians moved, his mouth mumbling the rosary, he unloaded the Luger into the man's bleeding body and then strode on. Tommy's face was covered with mud, and tears streamed down his cheeks in an erosion of emotion. Sometime in the midst of all the shooting he had urinated on himself, but he didn't even recognize it over the mud and water he was covered with.

Like a zombie, he met up with a group of the stunned hunter friends of Rebecca's family who had been slowly stalking the six Colombians he had just eliminated. He never admitted it while he sat in my living room later, but the tape shows he mumbled incoherently when they slapped him on the back and pulled him into one of the barns.

"Jesus," one of the men said, the first voice in the jumble of words caught on the tape. "Good show, cowboy. But you didn't have to butcher them."

"What do you think you are? Rambo?"

"Where's Rebecca?" Tommy whispered drily, each syllable a near strained scream.

"That was a foolish display, cowboy. You're just damn lucky that you didn't miss. Otherwise, one of those South American boys would have gotten off a good one at you."

"Where the hell did you learn to shoot like that?"

"Becky. Where's Rebecca? Rebecca?"

"Was he in 'Nam? Shit, he's too young. Where the hell did he come from?"

"He's the boyfriend of the boss's daughter. That's who he is."

"Okay, that makes sense. NSA, huh, cowboy? That who you are?"

"Orders were to try to get them alive, cowboy. We need to try to figure out who these guys are."

"Screw orders. This boy's just done some good shooting. Now we just have to get out of here. A big chopper just dropped another half dozen men in the southeast quadrant. Let's move out and meet them on the field and then drop back while the firepower is still strong. If we wait for them here then we won't have anyplace to drop back to."

"Where's Rebecca?" Tommy asked again, with the sound of gunfire at his back.

"I don't know, cowboy," one of the men said. "You've had a little bit of a shock. You better stay right here and wait for us. Just sit down on that bale of straw. Okay. We'll find her. You comfortable? Just wait right here. Don't move until we come back."

"Where's Rebecca?" Tommy asked again, his voice dazed and mumbling on the tape.

17.

THE HALF DOZEN MEN who were dropped by the chopper in the southeast quadrant were Murphy and his handpicked agents. Like any good soldier, Murphy remembered, and reported later, all of their actions in great detail. He also had a slow-running cassette tape in the communications pack that one of his men carried that gives some flavor of what they experienced. While for great stretches of time all you can hear on the tape is the sound of the heavy breathing of men moving stealthily through the farm and the tortured drops of rain falling from the broad leaves of the trees, the sounds conjure up other senses. Listening to the action, I can smell the fear of these trained men. The odor of the kind of sweat that breaks out even in a cold rain.

At first I was confused by Murphy's description of what happened, but then Murphy drew a small map with two lines intersecting in the field in front of Rebecca's family house. "There were four quadrants," he explained. "The field of grass was in the center, the house was in the northwest, near the center. The lodge was in the northeast, near the edge of the circle. The woods ran from north to south on the east side. The planes came from the west. The Colombians came from the east through the woods toward the field, and from the northeast to the back of the lodge. The road ran from east to west on the south edge of the circle, and we came from the road in the southeast quadrant. Get it?"

"Sure," I said, hoping I'd understand as he explained to me what happened.

Murphy's men moved along the southern edge of the woods in their gray rain gear, visors pulled down on their bulletproof fiberglass helmets, which were wired for communications up to five hundred feet. Murphy had spared no expense. Each man was armed with a high-performance long-distance Uzi, a nine-millimeter, and a pump-action rifle slung across their backs with a night scope. In full flak jackets and abrasive stickum gloves, they were ready for action.

Murphy had waited at the airport for two hours, moving from my wife's jet to a turbojet helicopter rented with my wife's money. As the rain turned into a full-fledged storm he got the radar reading he was waiting for—four planes from three different directions, all converging on one area in rural Pennsylvania. The three green lines that showed their flight patterns all inched forward on the screen in the company hangar and then, just as they crossed, other lines appeared, going away from the spot, each representing another aircraft taking off. Murphy and the ragtag assemblage of gay pistoleros cheered as they saw the fireworks shoot out of the center of the screen.

"That's it," Murphy said. "X marks the spot. Saddle up, boys. It's time to ride. Let's take these choppers in and get our woman out. Everybody take one last long look at the photos. Memorize that face and find it."

They passed around several faxed copies of photographs of Rebecca and Tommy that had been taken secretly just days before when John X went through another of his jealous rages. Rebecca looked beautiful in each photo, but Murphy's men wanted to know who the hunk with her was.

"Who's the farm boy?" one of the men, wearing a baseball cap that said "Freddy," asked.

"He's nobody. Get the girl. We want her alive, and we want to get in and get out fast," Murphy ordered, fastening the stiff flak jacket. "Remember, the machinery is only for self-defense. Don't fire unless you have to, and stick together. We're not trying to win a war, we're trying to kidnap someone."

"What a distinction," one of the men snorted, putting on his ammo belt.

"It's the only one that counts today, my friend," Murphy said. "Find Rebecca and there's a five-thousand-dollar bonus in it for you."

"That's better than the farm boy," the man said with a smile.

They landed the chopper a half mile south of the farm, sending it back with orders to return when they called, and hiked into the woods in the pouring rain until they came to the edge of the field that made up the front yard of the farm. Two fresh corpses were propped up against a stump, bullet holes riddling their chests. They were both Colombian mercenaries, and the men searched them quickly, looking for clues to what was going on. They heard their first shots of the day as they were itemizing the urine-soaked contents of one of the men's wallets for their report. The seven of them hit the dirt, and Murphy pulled out a pair of high-power battery binoculars.

"On the far edge," he said quietly into his mouthpiece, the words clear in the hot helmets of each of the men and recorded on tape. "About six guys coming our way and, Jesus, they are getting hit from behind by some damn good shot. It's only one crazy guy. Man, look at that guy go. It's a slaughter."

"Let's get to the house," one of Murphy's men said. "That's where we'll find them."

"And get out of this frickin' rain."

"This is bullshit," another said. "Like a needle in a haystack. How the hell are we supposed to find her in the middle of a goddamn war?"

"Calm down," Murphy said. "Let's go north and get within scope range of the house, staying along the west edge of the woods. Sam, you watch the wood side with the infrared. If anything is giving off heat, I want to know about it. Freddy, you watch our backs. Both sides may be coming to this field, and I don't want to get caught between them."

They skirted the edge of the forest for twenty minutes before Sam picked up moving heat on the infrared sensor and told Murphy that there were men coming east out of the forest right toward them. Murphy paused for several seconds, thinking about what to do. Then Sam reported that there was another group coming down from the north and along the edge of the woods right in front of them.

"Go back," Murphy said loud and clear into his microphone, the words silent to the outside world. They slowly backed up fifty feet, each step planned and picked out to avoid noise, and saw a group of a dozen men coming from behind the house and zigzagging right across the rain-streaked field and heading in their direction.

"Shit," Murphy whispered, wiping the sweat off his forehead with the back of his already muddy hand. "We're right in the middle of it, friends. Get a dozen feet between us and hit the floor in a circle.

Freddy and Sam, you point into the woods, I'll take the front, Bill, you take the back. Keep down. Don't move, and don't fire until they are on top of us. If they walk right past us, that's peachy, baby. I don't want to fight either side if we don't have to."

Five Colombians were moving west out of the dark woods toward the field, every sense probably honed for any sound, smell, or sight. Doc, Fritz, and three of their hunter friends had come out of the woods north of the Colombians and were now moving south dangerously fast along the forest edge, away from the house to the main road, where in only twenty minutes a modified Cessna was supposed to land and take them out of the area. The eight hunters who had pushed the Colombians back into Tommy were now zigzagging east across the field after Jan had radioed in that there was a group of Colombians coming out of the woods toward the field. To the south, on the edge of the road, ten of the Colombians who had hiked in had waited for orders and, receiving none, had decided to move up along the edge of the forest toward the house, unknowingly following the footsteps of Murphy's men. Two hunters had been waiting behind them, knowing that they couldn't take on all twelve, and followed them now as they moved along the perimeter.

Murphy and his men lay on the wet ground in a circle right at the point where these groups would converge. The rain continued to roll off the thick leaves of the trees, which sheltered a buzz of mosquitoes and bees. There was the smell of something dead not far away in the woods, the heat pulling the odor of rot out into the cool rain.

Murphy heard a branch snap, and then a footfall on soggy leaves coming from the woods. "Wait," he whispered into the microphone, as if he were coaxing a horse from charging out of a gate. "Wait, boys. Here they come from the tree side."

"It sounds like they'll pass us from the north," another man mumbled, his voice choked with anticipation.

"Spanish. They're speaking Spanish."

"With a goddamn Brooklyn accent," Murphy whispered, hearing the stilted voices coming toward him. Murphy knew enough Spanish to know that these men sounded much the way he did when he tried to impress someone in a Mexican restaurant by ordering in Spanish.

"They're on your side, Murphy," Bill whispered into his microphone, the voice amplified in each earpiece.

Something moved on the edge of the tree line, and more than a dozen pairs of eyes stared at the shaking leaves of a small tree, waiting to see who would emerge. Then one of the men in the field let out a fusillade of bullets, the sound exploding into the silence. The moment the bullets stopped there was a sudden low moan as a massive Holstein milk cow stumbled out of the woods and into the field. Red patches of blood were scattered like ships on the black-and-white map of her hide as she mooed pleadingly. There was a questioning look of horror in the cow's wide, rolling eyes, which Murphy explained in great detail, as if to justify what happened later. The cow tossed her neck around aimlessly, fell to her knees, and then struggled to stand.

"Oh Jesus," Murphy said into his microphone, more upset by the death struggle of the poor Holstein than he was by the corpses they had seen by the road.

Another round of shots rang from the tree side, as if someone there wanted to put her out of her misery. The cow's haunches collapsed underneath her, and then, with a long last bellowing cry, she fell to her side and did not get up.

"Murphy," Freddy whispered as the sound of footsteps approached Murphy. "To your left. Watch to your left."

Murphy slowly pulled his pistol with a silencer level with his shoulder and stretched out one hand for balance so he could spring up. The lead Colombian stepped on Murphy's hand before he saw anything. The silencer popped, and the Colombian's head burst open like a melon, raining blood down on Murphy as the man's inert body swayed and fell forward with the whoosh of breaking branches. Mud splashed around the body, and red crept out, like ink being absorbed into a blotter.

The four other Colombians froze for a second, but then ran back along the edge of the trees to the north, where they met the sharp, loud cracks of Doc, Fritz, and two of the hunters peppering them with automatic weapons fire. The men coming from the middle of the field all stopped for a moment but then ran right for the action when Doc radioed a Mayday as the Colombians hunkered down behind fallen limbs and began to return fire.

"Let me hit them from behind, Murphy," one of his men said pleadingly, thrusting his hips into the wet ground. "Jesus, let's get them all."

"Don't move," Murphy ordered, desperately wanting to roll away from the bloody puddle he was lying in. A mosquito landed on the sliver of exposed neck between his flak jacket and helmet, and he longed to swat it, but held his immobile silence, feeling the bug draw blood out of his skin.

"Men coming up from the south," Freddy warned into his microphone. "Lots of them. Coming right our way."

As soon as the ten Colombians from the road heard the gunfire they moved quickly up toward it, a scout radioing back that there were men coming from the middle of the field toward them. Twenty feet from Murphy's circle of men the Colombians stopped and took up positions to fire at the hunters coming across the field. Two of the hunters fell in the first barrage from their right side, and the rest of them hit the ground and returned fire toward where the shots had come from. Within seconds, a full-scale battle was happening on either side of Murphy.

"Stay down!" he shouted above the torrent of automatic weapons fire. "Stay cool! Let them shoot each other up!"

"We can't stay here, Murphy!" one of the men screamed through the microphone in his helmet.

"Let's run for it! Into the woods!"

"Don't move!" Murphy ordered, gagging on the smell of the dead man's fluids oozing in front of him. "Wait it out. Let's see what happens."

"What is going to happen, Murphy, is that we are going to end up dead with no girl," Sam grunted.

"Man, the damn mosquitoes are eating me alive."

"Let's split, this place stinks—stinks like we shouldn't be here."

"Hang on," Murphy said, in as soothing a voice as he could muster as his sweat mixed with the rain and the bullets screamed over his head. "Wait it out."

The minutes ticked by slowly, the gunfire becoming more and more sporadic, which worried Murphy even more, since that meant the different groups might try to move, and would then stumble over them. Just as the guns went silent, a Cessna flew out of nowhere, thirty feet off the ground at one hundred fifty miles an hour, its side door open and a machine gun raking the woods where the second set of Colombians had taken position. As the Cessna circled, two choppers charged each other over the field, one of them showering the hunters in the middle of the field with gunfire. Murphy watched the acrobatics through his muddy binoculars. He was so caught up in the spectacular display of fighting that he didn't hear the Colombians running their way until they were within twenty feet.

"Hit them!" he screamed, pulling his Uzi up and firing it in one stroke, the first barrage strafing the knees of the lead man and sending the others scattering for cover. The north half of his circle was instantly engaged in a noisy firefight, and after five minutes Murphy knew that they were going to have to move or they would get bogged down, with fire from both sides.

"Got 'em! Got 'em! Ride 'em, cowboy!"

"Hey, hey, hey—scored at ten o'clock on the circle!"

Lightning etched across the slate sky, followed by the boom of moving thunder, which shook the sheet of rain. The bugs disappeared in the mayhem, but the smell of rot grew and blossomed in the puddles of water that gathered around them.

"Freddy's hit!" someone screamed.

"Let's get the hell outa here, Murphy!"

"Hold the circle!" Murphy yelled as he pulled the trigger and felt the gun buck into his shoulder. He knew that Freddy was on the south side, so now they were in the midst of the squeeze. He gunned down every moving thing, telling me later how he relished the sense of complete abandon. He wanted to reach out, he told me, and strangle each one of them. He explained how he imagined the feel of their wet skin in his powerful hands as he spun the gun around, aiming low to catch anyone crawling toward him.

"I'm all right," Freddy gasped between clenched-tight teeth. "Just the arm. Flesh wound. I'll shoot left-handed."

"It looks bad."

"This whole scene looks bad."

"Murphy, what the hell are you going to do?"

"Kill as many of the bastards as I can," Murphy said in a moment of weakness, his shoulder bucking up against the recoil of the shotgun as he sprayed a moving tree branch. Smoke spurted up out of the trees and the grass of the field exploded as if it were being plowed from underground as the dueling choppers sprayed the ground with machine-gun fire. Red flames of spurting guns stood out like fireflies in the gray rain. In the midst of the explosions all around him, the mobile telephone on Murphy's belt rang.

He grabbed it without letting his trigger finger off the Uzi and in a strangely calm voice, as if answering in the comfort of his own home, said, "Hello."

"Murphy?" came Carolyn's voice out of the black phone. "This is Carolyn."

"How nice of you to call," Murphy said, over the smashing cacophony of the battle around him.

"What?" Carolyn said, sitting in front of me in the pilot's seat of the big company chopper that had met us at the Philadelphia airport. Carolyn had radioed ahead, found out where Murphy was, and decided to fly a company helicopter out to help, all over my constant protests. I saw Mexico all over again, but found myself being nothing more than a passenger. But neither Carolyn nor I had any idea of what we were flying into.

We had left Max back at the airport with the Lear jet, since Carolyn was concerned about excess weight on the chopper. My knuckles were white as I gripped the padded bar above my head—the "Jesus Christ" bar, so named by Carolyn for my expression whenever she turned too fast and I reached for it. I watched her out of the corner of my eye, seeing the single bead of sweat that ran down her face. In the midst of the screaming engine noise and constant flickering lights all around us in the cockpit, I saw the face of that wooden mermaid in my mind, and I wanted to ask her, why are you doing this? What are you trying to prove?

"I can't hear you. Where are you?" Carolyn shouted.

"Where the hell are you?" Murphy shouted back, his voice screeching over the phone and through the helmets of his men.

"Who are you talking to?" Freddy asked, as he released a round of bullets at the sound of running feet.

"Put up a flare," Carolyn said. "We're coming in to help you."

"Jesus Christ, Carolyn!" I yelled up at her, my glasses bouncing against the lenses of the binoculars I was looking through. The farm was still several hundred feet below us and an eighth of a mile away. "It looks like a battlefield down there. Let's get the hell out of here. You are *not* going down there."

A bullet grazed the top of Murphy's helmet, snapping his head to one side and throwing the phone out of his hand. He shook his head, wiped his mouth with the back of his hand, and reached for the phone. The mud around the phone shot up like a geyser as bullets struck all around it, and for a moment he thought he had lost consciousness and was seeing some dream of the surface of Mars. Then he grabbed the phone and decided that they had to get out of there.

"I'm hit!" someone yelled as he put the phone to his mouth.

"Carolyn!" he shouted. "Where the hell are you?"

"I'm in a chopper above the fray," she said. "I'm getting close, so you've got to tell me where you are and what you want."

"I want out of here fast," Murphy ordered, blowing the mud and sweat out of his nostrils. "We'll take whatever ride we can get. We're bogged down in the middle of this shooting match, with both sides firing at us. Can you get that thing in here? You know there are two armed choppers dueling it out up there? And a crazy Cessna with a gunner shooting out of its windows?"

"I've got a read on all of them," Carolyn reported excitedly.

"Can you do this?" Murphy asked again.

"Do you have any choice?" Carolyn asked, aiming the chopper down while I hung on to the arm of my seat and said, "Damn!" over and over again.

"Watch for where the flare comes from," Murphy ordered. "Not where it goes. We'll stay on the edge of the trees until you're about twenty feet from the ground. Bring it down fast, but don't touch down. Do you read me?"

"Ten-four," Carolyn replied, sliding the revving engine up two notches.

"Don't touch down. Hover about three feet over the grass, and count the men who get on. We've got seven."

"We can hold seven and we have two," Carolyn said, a sudden bit of reason overtaking her.

"You're taking seven," Murphy ordered. "So you better have enough gas to get that baby off the ground."

"This is insane!" I shouted to Carolyn, my binoculars full of the smoke rising out of the woods and the fire in the field as the choppers chased each other and the Cessna around.

I tried to scream when Carolyn dropped the chopper out of the sky the moment the flare burst into the air from the edge of the woods. My tongue was lodged on the top of my mouth as Carolyn brought the big machine down through the circling helicopters, neither of which could figure out whether to fire on her because they couldn't tell which side she was on. She pulled up for a second as the Cessna charged the field, and as the ground rose up to meet us I saw Tommy.

He was running across the field toward the helicopter, a rifle swinging from his arms and his flak jacket open and spread out like wings. His mouth was open, shouting something, and the ground around him was erupting as bullets chased him through the grass.

On cue, when Carolyn's big turbojet copter hung for a second at twenty feet from the ground, swaying away from the sudden gunfire—more from Carolyn's unsteady hand than on purpose—Murphy and his men made a run from the forest. They circled and returned gunfire that was suddenly directed at them instead of the helicopter, and Carolyn brought the bird down to three feet right on top of them. They scattered, one knocked flat but unhurt by a bullet that his flak jacket caught, and then they hurled themselves, bloody, muddy, sweaty, and cursing, through the door I flung open.

Murphy pushed the wounded Freddy into the cramped back and was shouting, "Go! Go!" before he had swung both feet into the copter. Carolyn hit the throttle up full, and the copter sprang forward, but it could only edge up with all the weight. The men unloaded their backpacks, tossing them from both sides as the copter scooted across the field, trying to gain altitude.

"Get her up!" Murphy screamed at Carolyn as bullets exploded on the whirling blades and raked the tail section.

The copter touched down from the weight, the runners tangled in the grass, and the other two choppers rushed us from each side of the big clearing.

"Throw out your guns!" Murphy yelled, throwing his Uzi out the still open door. "Get rid of the weight! Ammo belts, radios, everything!" Metal flew around the copter as Carolyn got it five feet off the ground and it screamed away from the woods and toward the house and barns. Everyone threw off everything they had on them, and I kicked it out the door, where I hung on for dear life.

A helmet thrown from the chopper hit Tommy full in the chest as he got within a dozen feet of the helicopter. As he jumped back up our eyes met, and in a flash of inspiration I kneeled on the running board, my dress shoes slipping on the wet rubber, and held my hand out for him. He charged the copter as it started to lift off, and I grabbed his hand. He swung up on the left runner. His weight tilted the whole machine to the left, and the twenty-foot blades slanted toward the grass, but Carolyn turned it to the right, which threw Tommy in on top of the heap of men, and she hit the throttle again.

Murphy took Tommy's rifle and flung it out the open door and struggled to pull off the heavy backpack he had on.

"It's caught on your belt!" Murphy shouted as he was slammed against the side wall. "Take off your belt! Your belt!"

Tommy fell to his knees as the helicopter rolled to the left and ripped off his belt. Murphy threw the pack and the belt out the door and then tried to slam it closed in my face as I opened my mouth in shock, watching the belt bounce on the grass. The copter skipped up ten feet and dashed forward a hundred feet, the door sliding back and forth.

"Hang on!" Carolyn yelled as red tracer bullets shot in front of the windshield like schools of darting fish. "Here we go!"

The turbo kicked in, and within seconds the machine had got to forty feet and roared out of the field and over the first hill, skimming over the air wake of the Cessna as it turned and went back down like a hawk diving for prey.

"I need some help!" Carolyn screamed, her face stretched into that mermaid's screaming laugh, as the copter skimmed over treetops and veered away from the suddenly rising hills. Before anyone could move, another helicopter dodged our careening ship and went toward the field we had come from. I was stunned to see Carolyn's company logo on its side.

"Did you see that?" Carolyn shouted.

"Just fly this thing, darling! Fly!" I saw her pupils narrow and her shock turn into a smile. When she jammed open the throttle and pulled up on the stick, a sudden rush of confidence in her filled my soul. She pulled back a silver lock of hair and stuck it under her headset with a brash flick of her wrist.

Murphy slammed the door completely closed, the noise turning from a deafening whirl to a deadening vibrating hum. The sudden trapped smell of so many close and sweating bodies was overpowering, and I had to shake my head to keep from fainting. I realized then that I couldn't stand even the smell of war, let alone the dirt, blood, and pain. But I could see the relief on Murphy's mud-caked face, and that made everything all right again.

Tommy looked from one face to another in the jammed helicopter. Not finding anyone he recognized, he grabbed the shoulder of my suit and yelled over the strained whine of the overworked engine, "You have Rebecca?"

"No!" I yelled back, noticing that Murphy had his pistol aimed at Tommy's back.

"Where is she?" Tommy yelled, his eyes widening in desperation. "She said to look for this copter. A helicopter with the logo on it."

"What logo?" I asked.

"The blue C. The big C on the back of this thing. Where is she?"

Every plane, truck, boat, and rail car in Carolyn's shipping line empire had a big, bold blue capital *C* on it, for Consolidated Lines—or so thought the general public; I knew the *C* just stood for Carolyn, who was flicking toggle switches as if swatting bugs, trying to keep the bird in the air.

"You tell me," I said, slowly taking his hand off me as the floor of the helicopter dropped two feet below us and then came crashing up like a roller coaster ride. "Where is Rebecca Townsend?"

He looked again at the silent muddy faces of the men thrown together in a huddle in the back of the helicopter, with not enough room for them even to stand. They stared back, eating him with their squinting adrenaline-pinched eyes.

"Who the hell are you?" Tommy asked.

"Friends of Rebecca," I said. "We work with her."

"I know," he said. "At her business. The import-export shop. I've seen planes with this logo on them there before. She said a helicopter would come for us. So when I saw the logo, when I saw the big capital *C*, I thought this was it."

"It is," I lied, quickly and easily, suddenly realizing that finding Tommy really was the next best thing to finding Rebecca.

"But we couldn't find Rebecca," Murphy said, putting down his gun as the helicopter swayed to the right at a thirty-degree angle, throwing Tommy into my arms and then back out again.

"But we got farm boy!" Sam shouted from the heap of men.

"I'm getting some lift now!" Carolyn shouted. "We used up enough fuel that I can take us up a couple hundred feet, but I don't know if we'll make the airport."

"Just get us as close as you can, sugar," Murphy said with a lilt of laugh in his voice. "I know now that you can put this thing down anywhere, so just get us close. I don't want to have to walk too far."

Murphy slapped me on the back and said, "Hell of a woman, Steele. She's either so dumb she's smart or so reckless she's right on target. God knows why she married you."

"Just at the right place at the right time!" I shouted as the helicopter swung wildly to the left and climbed over a high hill.

"Where are we going?" Tommy asked me, wiping the dirt and sweat out of his dazed eyes again.

"To find Rebecca," I said, without thought or plan. He stared at me for a long time, his eyes studying the lines of my face and the sweat still dripping down through my thin hair. He measured my shallow, panting breaths with his dull eyes, and then, as the chopper bounced up and down and swayed right to left in wind like a ship in a storm, I saw him come back to full consciousness. His eyes brightened and he shook his head, tossing bits of grass and mud out of his hair.

"Okay," he said to me above the roar of the whirling blades.

"Okay," I said back, feeling as if I were walking out of water, pulling myself up out of the dangers of the lulling glassy pool and into the warmth of the light. I felt waves of exhaustion breaking over my head and a gush of fresh energy fill my lungs. I remember thinking suddenly, as I watched Carolyn confidently pilot the injured chopper, that maybe Carolyn and I might not only make Mike Carter's daughter's wedding, but live long enough to attend the christening of his first grandchild. Fear of failure, of drowning in indecision and despair, fell away. "Okay," I said again, confidence cloaking me like a giant white terry-cloth towel after a swim. "We'll find Rebecca."

THREE

THE QUESTIONING OF AUTHORITY

And they said to him, "What authority do you have for acting like this? Or who gave you authority to do these things?"

—Mark 11:27

18.

"WHO ARE YOU GUYS?" Tommy asked me as we jetted back down to Washington. "Why are you the ones she called to get us out of there?"

I paused for a moment and weighed the options. Theory number 321: Tell as much of the truth as you can when you are going to lie. It's a theory that is older than spycraft, and probably as old as man's imagination. Shading the truth is just another way of decorating our experience with our wishfulness, and spycraft is just that sort of style over substance that I am so good at. I decided to tell shades of the truth while Tommy might be grateful to us for saving his life.

"I'm with the National Security Agency. We're hired by the director of the NSA," I said, without pointing out that we weren't who Rebecca called to rescue her and Tommy. "As you know, Rebecca worked for us."

He paused, and then a flash of a moment later, while his eyes moved open into a look of shock and surprise, I noticed that his hands did not move. He was nearly totally insensate, shellshocked, or a damn cool liar.

"You're a spy?" he asked, proving that he was a liar. "She's a spy? Are you trying to tell me Rebecca is some sort of secret agent?" Of course, I knew he was lying, because of what John X had told me was on the tapes, but even if I had not known what he and Rebecca had talked about in the privacy of her bedroom, I would have known he wasn't telling the truth. When you're in this business long enough, you know what signs to look for in their faces, their hands, their legs. Even as he said it I knew there was something wrong with his sudden animation. His quiet hands suddenly came alive to help him speak. He crossed his legs while he was expressing surprise. His face reacted one beat too slow to my sentences, as if he had to decide how to react, rather than simply reacting. He was trying to protect what he knew about Rebecca to keep his options open.

"We'll talk about it," I offered tentatively, willing to let him go for a while. "But let me make this clear—we know you know. We know that you know that Rebecca works for us. So let's cut with the innocent schtick right now. We are going to my home, and we'll talk about it there."

"A safe house?" Tommy asked.

"More or less," I said, amused at his use of the terminology; he probably picked it up from Rebecca. "The neighborhood is certainly safe, and it is certainly a house."

This is where my report changes. You see, my fellow defenders of the faith, this is where I became immediately and intimately involved. Not just tapes or files or hunches. From here on out I don't have to apologize for my imagination or make excuses for what I choose to report on and what I don't. My daredevil wife, bored with her millions, stuck me right in the middle of the action, and with a creak and pop of my old bureaucratic bones I reacted the way I had been trained to react so many years ago. I took over the case and ran it. I was an analyst, but I was on the scene. I had in Murphy one of our former best field agents, and I had in my wife the very best operations manager we could ever get.

For the record, we made it to the airport with two minutes' worth of fuel left. After hiding the damaged helicopter in a Consolidated Lines hangar, we hustled our entire troop onto the same Lear jet that had brought Carolyn and me to Philly. Carolyn was happy to let Murphy and Freddy, dressed in a new compression bandage and drinking orange juice as if it was going out of style, help Max pilot the jet back to Virginia. She curled up in my arms and said, "I'm pooped."

Just as I turned to kiss her, Murphy told me the Judge was on the mobile phone.

"Murphy says that you have a different package than the one we wanted, but that this one is second best. He also says you and Carolyn bailed him and his freaks out of some hot cowshit. Now you tell me, what the hell were you doing there in the first place? Why is everybody involved with this mission frickin' freaking out? All I needed, really needed, was to pick up one of our own out of a hot spot."

"So nice to talk to you again," I said over the static on the encoded receiver. "Aren't we having dinner at eight tonight, and don't we say hello anymore?"

"What the hell is going on?" he shouted.

"Why don't I come into town early and we can have a cocktail and not talk about this over the phone? What do you say, old pal?"

"Screw you, partner. I'm at the pay phone, and I want an answer now."

"I'll be at the Hawk and Dove by seven," I stated firmly, trying not to move my arms so as not to wake Carolyn up. "Leave your Federal Protective guy behind. I'll have a car outside waiting for us. Tell your wife that we'll be a few minutes late to dinner. Carolyn will be on time, but let me warn you, she's had quite a day. A very expensive day, by the way. I'll save the receipts, and I'll keep our guests at my house until we can find a suitable place for them to stay."

"All right," the Judge mumbled, calming down and returning to his longhorn twang. "I'll see ya there. Tell me a story, Steele. You better tell me one hell of a whopper, because I got a tale that will turn your 'bacca juice green. And HQ is in the dark until we decide to let them know. This thing may go way up the line. To the top."

"Use those old college ties," I suggested. "Go around everybody else."

"Boola boola," he said. "Go, Bulldogs. And, Steele, the word is out on the street about Carolyn's little takeover. Three lawsuits have already been filed. The SEC and the New York State securities commissioner are investigating. The local politicians are crying foul. But, Steele, our stock, since I happen to own a few measly shares, went up three full points in very, very heavy trading. Maybe I can suck off a little of your fat moneybags."

"The insiders know she can pull it off," I said, gently kissing a strand of Carolyn's silver hair that was loose on my shoulder. "But what do you think of this operation we've just begun? What's the arbitrager's line on me?"

"Just get back," he snapped, hanging up.

I went to the rear of the plane, where Sam with his handgun sat next to a dozing Tommy Wood. I changed places with Sam, and as I sat down Tommy stirred and woke. He rubbed his face with his palm and stared at me for a second too long. While he was no longer shellshocked, he clearly was not at his best. I could read the stress on his face as if it were a bent board ready to break. He had been up too long and seen too much in too short a time. I had seen the same look on the faces of rookie combat troops right after their first firefight. A nervous, tense dance with everyone they spoke to, it came from being unable to find the words to express what they had just been through.

There is a Freudian theory there somewhere—that being able to describe and express what you have been through releases it from you, while being unable to explain what has happened adds to the tension. This theory, number 790, is clearly related to one of my mother's sayings about not bottling up your feelings or you'll explode, or don't screw up your face that way or it might freeze.

I paused to try to gauge how to enter into a conversation that I knew would take days to finish. The talk that I had listened to a hundred agents give to a thousand witnesses. The debriefing that happened before the witness even knew it had begun and was so wrapped up in by the time he realized what was going on that he continued because he had to, like a man gasping for air. Theory number 978: Beginning is everything for a sales pitch. Too much time is spent on the close of a deal. How the victim perceives you, your voice, your angle, your trustworthiness, makes more of a difference than anything you say later on. It is just that too many of those things are beyond our immediate control, so we tend to concentrate on the words that close the deal, that cinch it, that sew it up, that allegedly make up someone's mind, when we all know that someone is going to either buy or not buy from the moment they set eyes on you.

What I had to sell Tommy on was simple: I needed to know everything he knew, how he knew it, and where Rebecca might be. I had to convince him that I was on his side and that we had the same goals. I had to convince him that we could help each other or we could hurt each other—it was just a matter of choice. His choice. All I had to do was start right.

"I want to find Rebecca," I said, moving forward a pawn.

"Why?" Tommy asked.

"Because only she can tell me what I need to know."

"What do you need to know?" he asked again. "Who are you really?"

"Whether you believe it or not, I am a soon-to-be-rehired public servant. A federal government bureaucrat. To you, I am the United States Government. My job right now is to find and protect Rebecca. I know she is in danger, and I want your help."

"And why should I help you?"

"Because you, Tommy, are not only in love with Rebecca, you are engaged to be married to her. You've told her your deepest secrets, and she has told you . . . what? That is one of the questions I need to answer—what she has told you. You've got to find her because she's going to be your wife. I've got to find her because it's my job."

"What exactly is your job?" Tommy asked.

And so it began. Hours of conversation, broken that first night only by the three and a half hours I spent in Washington with the Judge. A match not so much between me and Tommy as between me and the midwestern logic, old-fashioned values, and Hoosier common sense that tempered his romanticism. On guard. Touché. May I have this dance. May I play you in chess. Your move. Tommy was perfect for the job we had wanted to recruit him for. He was as close to a natural as anyone I had met in a long time. He was inquisitive, stoic, quiet, and just charming enough to get more information out of whomever he was talking to than he gave in return. Rebecca had made a good choice in recruits.

He was a square dancer who cut corners. When he began the long slow project of trying to manipulate me while I was trying to manipulate him, I kept remembering my favorite square dancing call—allemande left. Whatever that means, it summed up his constant effort to deflect my boring into his soul and to turn every question into a question and every exploration into a mirror. Allemande left.

"Why were you there with Rebecca?" I asked.

"Because she asked me to come visit her parents," he answered. "Were you invited too?"

"Why this week?"

"One day, really. Less than a full day. But look, I really just want to find her. You've got to understand, I really need to find her."

By the time the plane touched down I had scared him enough, by showing that I knew so much about him, that he had stopped with the obvious attempts to get me to answer his questions. Carolyn drove the car back, and I rode in one of the two vans that drove us through the countryside to Carolyn's Cottonwood Manor, which was greeted by admiring whistles from our guests as the vans were ushered by the stone gatehouse and we rode up the half-mile-long drive to the house. Cottonwood Manor had been built at the turn of the century by an oil tycoon who wanted a place near Washington to entertain the congressmen he owned. It was a high-gabled Tudor monster that sat on a slight hill in the midst of seventy acres of grounds. Carolyn had bought it so that her first husband, the ambitious politician, could entertain the congressmen he hoped to own, but it was really much too ostentatious for her. She kept it because her second husband, the boring retired bureaucrat, liked to play the gentleman farmer. Fortunately, with forty rooms, we had plenty of bedrooms for eight unexpected house guests, and the loyal and well-paid staff had learned not to ask questions.

It was only when I finally got in the shower to wash off the accumulated grime of the day that I asked myself the question that kept popping into my mind over the next week. Why did he do it? I asked myself, meaning then only, why did he risk his life to try to save Rebecca, but meaning much more than that later.

It is simple enough to say that he did it, you did it, I did it, *for love.* But that doesn't really answer the question. There are as many types of love as there are people in love, so as an analyst I have some obligation to describe this love that they had. For, like Napoleon and Josephine, Tommy and Rebecca changed the world.

I know that is a mighty big claim, particularly since they were not monarchs but only pawns in a bigger game. But it is only a reflection of our times that the people who change the world are not those who are reputedly in charge, but those who get stuck at the wrong place at the wrong time. Those people who change the world now are not those who planned on changing the world, but those who were the straw that broke the camel's back. They changed the world the way a lottery winner becomes a millionaire—they had to buy the ticket and pick the numbers, but their labor did not produce their wealth. They did something to put themselves in a place where they could change the world, but even Rebecca had no idea how far she would go and how much they would succeed. Maybe Tommy and Rebecca were born to change the world, just as I believe they were both born to be spies.

I met the Judge at the worn wood bar of the Hawk and Dove, and he stood there silently while I finished my scotch. The moment his back hit the leather seats of the big dark car I had waiting outside, he said, "Oh my God, what the hell have we got ourselves into?"

"What's this 'we,' white man?" I grumbled. "Am I to assume that I'm hired again?"

"Yes, yes. We'll talk about that tonight," the Judge said, as close to all business as he ever got. "This is what I know. Same ground rules. This whole thing is off budget until we figure out what is going on. And by 'we' I mean you, me, Murphy, and, yes, your darling wife, Carolyn, who won't let us play with her toys unless we let her play too. Try to keep both Murphy and Carolyn on a need-to-know basis. But to you, I'm going to tell the whole thing—and then I want to know what Johnny boy told you when he called."

He started at the beginning, from when he got the phone call from John X, explaining and handing to me all the summaries of what John had done up to the phone call he made to me. The Judge then told me about all the transmissions from Rebecca's family farm. The last transmission that they had recorded, decoded, and transcribed was of Tommy quietly sobbing as he sat in the barn, repeating "I killed them. Shot them. I killed them," over and over again.

"The goddamn French have the jump on us," the Judge said, explaining that he had spoken briefly with the DST courier who had come over that morning from Paris with a diplomatic satchel that contained a file on Rebecca. The file said that a solid Polish source had linked her to the sale of NATO mobile missile route plans to the East Germans last Tuesday, and then, totally out of the blue, a relatively good Czech source had told the French that she was linked to the sale to Moscow of Pacific bomb site blueprints. While the French would normally hold this information for some later self-serving trade, it was just too much, too quickly for even them to hold.

The bottom line was that they didn't believe either story and thought that someone was trying to set her up. They asked if we had any reason to believe that someone would want to blackmail her, or simply ruin her career. The Judge had checked our intelligence on both the Polish and the Czech source and had found that both of them were certainly in a position to know. He was also shocked, he admitted, that the DST had either one as a source.

"I hate it when the French are ahead of us in this game," the Judge muttered. "I remember when the Berlin airlift was going on and I was a grunt trying to keep away frostbite on the damn line. I saw this French tank that had two engines, two drivers, and a windshield on both sides. Why? So it could go forward and backward. That, Steele, you son-of-a-bitch lover of their wine, women, and faggot poets, is the French. Ass backwards. Never heard of reverse."

"Anybody else you'd like to malign?" I asked, just to annoy him. "Any racist, sexist, stupid thing you'd like to get out of your system after a hard day at the office? Getting shot at just seems to take it all out of me, but you've been cooped up all day in a basement."

"Catholics!" the Judge snorted, ignoring my diatribe. "And I only hate Catholics because so damn many of them are French."

I waited to see if he was finished.

"And," he said, "that weak-brained John X is a Catholic. What did he tell you, anyway? How did he get inside so quickly, and without anybody knowing about it? How the hell did he get bugs all over the family farm without anybody in the whole damn organization knowing about it?"

"What makes you think nobody in the organization knows about it? Did you poll everyone?" I asked.

"Are you trying to tell me, you fat-assed old cowpoke, that you knew about this surveillance operation?"

"I knew," I said, "that John was spying on his old girlfriend, Rebecca. I did not know about any surveillance operation, or anything about Rebecca's family farm. John told me nothing more than he told you."

I'm not sure that I was even conscious of the lie when I said it. For reasons that I'm still not sure of, I decided to live up to my promise to John X and protect his future, even though he had ruined mine. Maybe because his report had been the grounds for my early retirement, I felt that chivalry required that I not do the same to him. I don't remember that I even considered whether it was wise not to tell the full and complete truth to the head of the agency, the president's friend and true spy chief. I just did it.

We sat in the palpable silence as the car moved slowly around the Jefferson Memorial, the vanilla dome lit by bright halogen spotlights so that it looked as if it had just landed on this spot, a spaceship from long ago. Washington at night always looked like a backdrop for a play to me. All the theatrical landmarks lit up brightly so they can't be missed. All the important places sitting in a row. All the history spelled out on bronze markers. Theory number 578: Tourists are the last unconscious actors in the plays of our lives. They follow a script set down in a thousand tourist guides and stand in line to play their parts. They wear identifiable clothes, and, like Kabuki players, they share only a dozen different gestures. They point. They raise their cameras. They pause in front of anything for sale. All of Washington was their stage, where they could dream of being senators or spies.

"I hate to can John X," the Judge sighed. "I checked his file this morning when he started giving me trouble. He has a nice wife. She's a little crazy, I'm told. Doesn't like the business. She was in the Peace Corps when John was in Vietnam. He's got one kid at Brown and another one who was picked up on a DWI charge about a week ago. Lots of debt. I had to force him to take a couple of days off—he was a mess over the kid. He's been a mess over Rebecca for a while, too. Those POWs are all like that. Way too intense for their own good. Wound up too tight."

We sat in silence for a tense moment, contemplating John X, his future, and the roller coaster he had shoved us on.

"This may be really big," the Judge said, breaking the tension and shifting his weight on the seat. He grimaced a moment in pain, rubbing his lower back, and then went on. "What Rebecca's dad told Tommy may well be true. We may have stumbled across some sort of damn Mafia family that makes its dough by selling information. I've got every computer in research whirling right now. We may have a leak in our operation that you could drive a herd of longhorns through. Who knows what Rebecca has culled from our files and shipped to her family to sell on the market?"

"It was pure dumb luck that we found the leak at all," I suggested. "Assuming that her father was telling the truth and that this whole thing isn't a gag."

"Who invents a cover that has them breaking federal law?" the Judge asked. "Why tell someone you are committing treason to hide what you are really doing? It has to be the truth."

"Too simple to be the complete truth."

"Now there's a Steele theory if I ever heard one," the Judge said, kicking the back of the seat in front of him with his long, bowed cowboy legs. "The truth is always complicated, the lies are always simple. How the hell can you prove that?"

I ignored him for a moment, trying to think through what Rebecca must be thinking right now. What was her strategy? How had she been trained? She was both the opponent and the target. She had to be out-thought.

"Will she come back to get Tommy?" I asked no one in particular.

The Judge laughed and said, "Steele, you're a genius and you don't even know it."

"How's that?"

"Johnny boy's favorite techy handed me this as I left to come here." The Judge laughed, holding up a Walkman-sized tape cassette player. "From the mysterious John X collection of tapes that come over the satellite. If I didn't know ol' John better, I'd swear he was on her side. Why in God's name won't he tell me how he got into the place to bug it? And bug it so well that apparently—yes, apparently—

her family never found the damn bugs? I never should have put John in charge of counterintelligence up on Mahogany Row. I should have left him counting missiles with the Army accountants."

"I'd agree with that observation," I said, remembering the zealousness that drove John X to question my loyalties.

The Judge smiled at me and said, "He's so damn paranoid he won't tell a soul how he rigged this whole business."

"He told me," I said loosely, trying to sound as though I wasn't being careful, "that it started with his plain old-fashioned American jealousy. I think he's being quiet about the whole thing because he had nothing to go on when he started this investigation. He just wanted to figure out what his former main squeeze was up to with her new boy."

"Too convenient," the Judge mumbled, and then tapped one finger against the cassette tape in his hand and snapped it into a small tape recorder. "It hasn't been transcribed yet. Listen closely, because it's hard as hell to catch everything with all the background noise."

He clicked the tape on, and a messy round of voices began talking.

"What happened?" an older male voice asked.

"Did they get her?" a young, deep male voice asked in response.

"Just him. Here's his belt and his backpack. Nobody saw which copter got him, but Becky has radioed in and he's not with her," a third male voice said slowly.

"Damn them," the older man said. "He's either dead or a hostage who is soon to be dead. The damn Colombians won't take long to tell us what they intend to do with him, if they figure out who he is. Maybe ransom. It's all money to them. All business. Anybody told Doc?"

"Not yet," the second, younger man answered. "Let's just hope the kid doesn't tell them he's Doc's future son-in-law. That's a death sentence."

"I don't think he even speaks Spanish," the older man said. "Get on the box and send a coded message to Doc from the hunters that the Colombians got the kid—what's his name?"

"I don't know," someone said.

"Tommy Wood," the young man said.

"Tell him the Colombians got the kid and ask him what we should do. Ask him if we should keep hunting. We better clear out of here in twenty minutes, so get to it."

"What about his stuff? Will Rebecca want it?"

"Leave it," the older man ordered. "I don't think we want to give her anything to remember this guy by."

The Judge clicked off the tape as we circled the wedding-cake-like White House and said, "Miracle of miracles, Steele, you made Yankee lemonade out of a Texas-sized lemon. We've got Tommy and they think the drug dealers have him. Now all we've got to do is convince Tommy to help us find Rebecca. We have to get him on our side. Let's make him the bait. How about we train him to—"

"Too dangerous and there's no time," I interrupted, thinking about the belt left behind. Would they find the hidden microphone, and if they did, would they jump to the conclusion that Tommy was a spy? "She'd figure it out. We couldn't keep him long enough to train him to be our agent, even if he agreed, and once we did Rebecca would see him as a double right away."

"Find some way to convince her that the Colombians do have him. Let her fight the Colombians to get him. If you think you can manage it. I could have someone else do the dirty work . . ."

"Judge," I said, watching the lights flicker far off on the Washington Memorial as our car drove around from the White House and back down the Mall, "look, we know she doesn't even think those attackers were Colombians, so why is she going to buy a story that they have Tommy?"

"First," he growled heatedly, "we know that she doesn't know for sure that these guys weren't Colombians. All the evidence she has tells her that this was an attack by some pissed-off drug dealers. Second, it doesn't really make any difference who those guys were, she just thinks that they have Tommy. All we've got to do is put Tommy in the hands of the Colombians who we know are pissed off at Rebecca's family, let Rebecca know in some subtle way that they have Tommy, and presto, she thinks they were definitely Colombian mercenaries and goes to get Tommy back from them. He's just bait. He doesn't have to be trained. Hell, put him through some showboat type of training so that he thinks we are training him, but he's just bait. You don't have to train a worm to be a worm. He'll know how to wiggle once we set the hook."

Again, the Judge's logic and strategy reminded me why he was head of the agency. He had covered all the loose ends. It was a long shot, but it made sense.

"What will you need?" the Judge asked.

"I'll let Murphy figure that out. I'm sure I can supply the immediate necessities. What I need is information. The more I know, the more I can get out of Tommy Wood, and the more I'll understand what the hell he is talking about. I need to get into the organization's files and root around. I need to listen to the tapes. I need complete access."

"Done," the Judge concluded. "I'll hire you back tonight, you bastard. That way you can root around without sending alarms off to our potential internal problem."

"Thank you," I said, so gratefully that he would know I was being insincere. "What makes you think that you might be followed? Why do we need a public show of me coming back?"

"My game left ball," he said, imitating Lyndon Johnson's Texas squeak. "It tells me things that I often just don't see. Intuition. I don't like the feel of this thing, so I'm playing it safe."

"You're sure you're not just keeping it off the books and keeping it quiet to save your own ass?"

He paused for a second and looked me in the eye, not surprised that I would speak so directly to him. He was a man who liked to be challenged. The inside of the car was dark when we stopped at a red light, and I had to guess what his face looked like when he spoke. "I told you I'd go directly to the president when the time was right."

"And when will that be?" I asked. "Or is that something your testicles will tell you about too?"

"Steele," he said with a deep breath. "It is so goddamn good to have you back. Why in the hell did I ever want you to leave? Other than the plain fact that I can't stand your filthy-rich guts."

"I haven't the slightest idea, Judge," I languidly answered. "Not the slightest idea."

"I just want you to know, Steele, that the moment this thing is over, assuming that we live through it, I'm firing you for hiring Murphy and that pack of queers and running this whole operation off budget, in direct violation of our agreement with the House Intelligence Committee's directive."

"Wait a minute," I said, too quickly. "You hired Murphy, and this whole thing is your idea, and you're—"

"I have a career in front of me," the Judge said, his twang clipped by the years at Yale. "I've already put an end to yours. Don't make it my word against yours—considering the black marks you already have against your name. Besides, you have money. You'll be okay.

Just don't piss off your wife and you'll be fine. From this moment on, this is your project. I'll tell everyone right now that you're just telling a story, just doing your usual analysis. But when it gets hot, I'll let them know that you ran this show. So, my friend, the buck stops here, right on the other side of you, and right before it gets to me. You're in charge. Welcome back."

"Well then," I said, with just a trace of a whistle, "I guess I better get busy."

The limousine sped through the growing darkness toward the restaurant where our wives waited for us. The asphalt streets still glimmered from the day's heat like a well-seasoned cast-iron skillet, and the faces of the citizens we were sworn to protect flashed by on the sidewalks that contained the asphalt heat wave. The Judge and I were silent, both weighing the consequences of our actions. The Judge did not want to leave in disgrace, and I did not want to leave at all. I wanted back into the game, and this was my ticket. Hold the ship together and produce some results and then I could retire with my reputation rehabilitated. But if I failed, I was truly at the Judge's mercy.

I pushed a button and rolled down my window, letting the hot night air stream into the car. With it came the summer voices of the neighborhoods we cruised by and the smells of exotic cooking. We were in a foreign land in our own capital, tourists in a stretch limousine, surrounded by an economically repressed melting pot that had bought so much of the American dream that it could not rebel against it.

Millionaires have a choice, I thought, looking out the tinted car window. Guilt or insensitivity. I decided to try to master being insensitive to my guilt. However, I knew I would fail.

19.

THE SECOND DISCIPLE'S CODE NAME was Jimmy. James, the son of Zebedee, had a daughter.

Jimmy was a young woman, no more than twenty, who crossed her long legs as she sat down on the circular steps near the center of Constitution Plaza in Santiago, Chile. It was the week before the traditional vacation period in Chile, but because of the unseasonably warm weather she could look up into the scaffolding of the skyscrapers being built around the plaza and see dozens of shirtless men welding and maneuvering giant pieces of steel. She straightened her American sunglasses on her pert nose and unconsciously pouted as she watched the workers.

The cacophony of Spanish voices and pigeon wings fluttering loudly around her masked the footsteps of the middle-aged man who walked up and sat down next to her. She turned her head and smiled at him, and they spoke softly in Spanish.

"So this is it." She sighed. "Will you miss me?"

"What were you looking at?" he asked, brushing a piece of lint off his dark suit. He watched her eyes as they went back up to the top of the skyscraper going up above the plaza.

"The men up there," she said. "Walking on those thin ribbons of steel. They must be crazy. Romantic, bare-chested, crazy Chileans, yes?"

"I'll get you one if you stay," the man suggested with a smile. "I'll get you your own workman. Big muscular guy, that will make you happy. Happy and scared at the same time. How about that?"

She shook her head, her short black hair swinging from side to side. "No, there will be blond boys where I am going. Blonds do not scare me."

The afternoon winter light turned pale orange and cast shadows from the government buildings that surrounded the plaza. Bureaucrats walked briskly past them, not even casting a glance in their direction. The cold light bleached all color from their drab clothes. The normal cold would return tomorrow.

"Will you come back?" he asked.

"If I make it?" she asked.

"You'll make it," he concluded, as if he were trying to convince her. "You have nine lives. Will you come back for some of them? Maybe life three or four?"

"Not until Pinochet is gone. Really gone. He killed my brother in '73. I was three. My father disappeared while looking for him a month later."

The man shook his head and then ran a callused hand through her hair. She quickly pulled away from him and turned to see if anyone had seen his foolish gesture.

"Why didn't you ever tell me about this?"

"You never asked," she said.

"Is that the reason you are doing this? Treason must always have a reason," the man asked. He answered his own question. "It is never really a crime of passion."

He let the word "passion" roll on his tongue, *passione, passione, amore*. "In the end treason is always contemplated. Thought through. Planned, even if it is planned badly. Is that why?"

"Maybe," the woman offered, a drop of sweat rolling to the top edge of her red lips. "Maybe not. The reason isn't important. Success is what is important. Getting through customs is important. I've never asked you why you are doing this."

"Oh," the man said. "It is also a . . . a . . . how do they say? . . . a family matter. Too complicated to explain. My family is always too complicated to explain. But I will miss you. I wish I was going with you."

"But your government," she said.

"I don't care anymore."

"Then your wife. Your daughter."

"I don't think about them when I am with you," he whispered, slipping her a round plastic tube no bigger than a lipstick. She put it in her pocket nonchalantly. "You brought excitement back into my life. That makes my family happy. Your, your travel makes my extended family happy."

"This," she said, gesturing to her pocket, "brought excitement into mine. This information will change the world."

"Such big ideas from such a little girl," he said, feeling the sweat seeping down his collar and behind his tie. He thought of the microfiche she now had and prayed silently that all would go well.

He knew that he had to let her go, but he couldn't take his eyes off her. She took off her sunglasses and looked into his tired eyes. She leaned toward him, and their lips brushed together, like a feather dusting off an old shelf. Then she sprang up as if she was late and walked off to the small car that was waiting to take her to the airport, where she had no problem flying to Dallas, where she would study art and make one delivery.

20.

REBECCA HAD AN EYE for recruits, and, as I've noted, Tommy would have been one of the best. A young man with an excellent academic background, a facility with languages, an architect's eye for detail, an understanding of firearms, no living immediate family, midwestern common sense, and the strength of a carpenter. Then she made him fall in love with her, put him through his paces in this little mock war on her family farm in Pennsylvania, and put him right in our laps. He was half trained when we got him.

While Tommy had been shocked by the battle on the farm, when it really counted he had performed, shooting men right in the face rather than backing down. A theory that I don't usually admit because I hate the truth of it is that a field agent cannot be trusted until he kills another human being. Once he has killed and lived through it, then he is ready for tough assignments. The agent is ready to make tough decisions. Ready to commit the ultimate act, either in self-defense or in furtherance of some abstract, bullshit bureaucratic goal. Either way, he has become the machine that we, as an organization, need to obtain our goals. That is a component no training program that I know of can provide, thank God. But the act of killing, in all its stark horror, sets the professionals apart from the amateurs.

"How do you feel about killing those men?" I asked Tommy, in what was my study now, late that night after we had talked for hours about what he had been through. Carolyn and I had come home from dinner with the Judge shortly before eleven that Tuesday night, and on the car phone on the way back to Virginia Murphy had briefed us both for half an hour about his discussion with Tommy. Murphy said that Tommy was bothered by two things: first, whether Rebecca was telling him the truth or was playing with him just as we alleged she was playing with us; and second, that he had killed several men that day.

I wanted right then and there to tell Murphy what the plan was and get him busy working out the details, but I held back on the car phone, afraid that I could not explain the details in a guarded, coded way.

"Keep him up," I told Murphy. "Keep him talking, and start feeding him booze. Set up your normal listening-post operation in the library, and get me a tape recorder for the study. The Judge gave me a couple of tapes he might like to hear. I think I'll entertain our catch with a few tapes before I go into the office in the morning."

"He'll try to lie to you," Murphy speculated. "He'll test you right out of the box."

"Good," I said, leaning back into the leather seat of the long limousine.

"I've got a whole communications room set up," Murphy said. "He seems to think that if we're right, if we're really who we say we are, that Re—that his love must be brainwashed or something. He refuses to even consider that she shipped out to the other side. He's a patriotic—and good-looking—kid."

"Keep your hands off him, Murphy," Carolyn said, looking up from her reading to talk into the speakerphone.

Tommy was honest with me, once I reminded him how much we knew. He had repeated what had happened, rarely venturing theories of his own. I had to reassure him a dozen times that our intelligence told us that Rebecca was safe and that her family, as far as we knew, had all escaped. By the time the Judge got a crew of Murphy's friends and former agents to the farm at dusk, every person, alive or dead, had disappeared. The communications room of the lodge had been blown up with plastic explosives. All their search had discovered were the casings of bullets all over the property and two Uzis propped against a tree in the middle of the woods. The Judge called off the search until the next morning, still hesitant to make a big deal about the operation for fear of drawing attention to it.

"Tommy?" I said. We sat in my study, the walls covered by dark wood shelves and thousands of books. In the center of the far side of the room, behind a grand piano, were tall narrow windows with beveled-edge glass that looked out over the front yard, which stretched green and rolling for miles. In the darkness the windows became mirrors, reflecting everything that went on in the room in a muted and slightly distorted way. Raindrops splattered occasionally against the glass.

"Tommy," I repeated when he did not answer. "What about killing those men?"

He stared into his drink, watching the melting ice cubes circle the rim of the glass, and then he closed his eyes and opened them to look at me.

"When you shoot a man," Tommy said, slipping deeper into the soft leather of the chair, his eyes closing for long periods of time as if he were searching, diving, for something deep within himself and then coming up for air to look at the world outside, "something happens to you, you know?"

"No," I answered honestly as I put my tired feet up on the antique coffee table and admired the shine on my English shoes. I was startled, shaken by the feeling that he had just read my thoughts. That he knew my game plan. My reaction was simple honesty. "I've never shot anyone."

"But you're a spy. A real spy. And you haven't shot anybody? Ever?"

"Never," I said, struggling to remember the last time I had a gun in my hand. I was not a professional agent, like Murphy, I told myself. I was only an analyst.

"Well, something happens to you. You lose it for a moment, and then your soul hardens to it, and that machine you have in your mind that produces justifications kicks on and you say things to yourself like if I hadn't killed him he would have killed me. If I hadn't lowered the gun and fired he would have killed Rebecca. The rain, the sweat in your eyes, the adrenaline rushing through your body like a hundred cups of coffee all make you want to puke. But instead of vomiting, you pull back in yourself and start to get angry. Mad at being placed in a situation where you had—where I had—to make a choice between one person's life and another's. Furious at making the series of mistakes that led up to having to decide whether to risk letting them capture Becky or risk trying to blow them away."

The drink in his hand tilted so far that it was about to spill into his lap. Then his eyes flickered open, and he pulled himself up in the chair, leveling off the glass.

"Did I make the right decision? I don't know. You tell me that she got away, that she's alive. You tell me I was lucky."

"She got away, Tommy," I repeated for the thirteenth time that evening. "You've got to trust our intelligence—"

"There's that word again. Trust. All I hear is either luck or trust. Trust me—you're lucky. That's all you spooks talk about. Everything is just a matter of luck, but if there's anything that can be predicted you know it and I have to trust you. Trust that you're right. Trust and luck."

"You weren't just lucky," I said, fastening my eyes on his weary face and drilling the words into him like a builder putting in the crucial piece that will hold the thing together. "You were good. Damn good. That's why you can go in there and get her out. That's why I think you can be trained to do this. Because you are good and lucky and because you trust no one."

He met my laser gaze and locked in on my tired eyes. He ran his big, tanned workman's hands through his sandy hair without a blink, the casual gesture distracting me and reminding me of his very real presence. I was trying to get him drunk and he was resisting unconsciously. He was trying to keep control of a situation that was so far from his control, was so far from anything he had ever experienced, that all he could do was let his mouth drop open and show his perfect corn-fed teeth. "You want me to be your agent."

"I want you to save Rebecca," I countered, filling his glass again. It took an amazing amount of good bourbon and exceptional scotch to bring this sweating farm boy down. "You love her. They trust you. You're good. You're lucky. You're all we've got. If you find Rebecca and decide her family are the good guys, then you join up with them and leave us behind. But without us you'll never find them. And they'll never find you. They're looking for you in the wrong place."

"You mean that I'm your man because my mind, or my soul, is hardened," he said with a slight slur, letting go of my gaze and staring up at the ceiling until his eyes closed again, probably seeing on his eyelids the burst of blood that filled his gunsight when his perfectly aimed bullet hit the unknown Colombian's smooth, boyish face. "You mean, Mr. Steele, that I've seen the worst and justified it all so you think you can talk me into anything."

"Stop the philosophical bullshit," I snapped, putting my scotch down hard on the table. "Tommy, Rebecca needs you and we need you. Rebecca won't find you as long as we keep you cooped up here. You've got to go out and find her. She's strayed from the path, but she won't necessarily be prosecuted if she comes back in to Headquarters. I'm sure she can explain everything. But we, I, they need to talk to her."

He stared at me and smiled. I knew he wasn't yet buying into the program.

"Look," I said, "our interests and your interests happen temporarily to be the same. Use us to get her back."

"If I find her, you just want to talk to her? You're not going to arrest her on the spot?" The image of handcuffing Rebecca and reading her her rights passed quickly through my mind. Inevitably, the game we were playing might lead to that, and all the publicity that would naturally follow. Arresting her would be very problematic, but trying her would be virtually impossible. She would inevitably try graymail on the NSA, insisting that she needed virtually every sensitive document in the agency's possession for her defense. The agency would never release the documents, so the charges would be dropped and she would go free. I decided not to let Tommy know yet that arresting and prosecuting her might be out of the question.

"First, you don't have to bring her in right away," I argued, laying out my case again. "Just find her, and I'll go wherever she is and talk to her about what is going on. I'm sure that she will be in some country that will not let us prosecute her, so she'll be safe, you'll be safe, and we will get to talk to her and try to straighten this whole thing out."

"And if she wants to come back to the States, to marry me, have a family, what then? What's the deal if I find her and bring her back?"

"I can't make that deal right now. The attorney general's office would have to get involved in that decision. But you can make that deal when you find her. You'll be in a better bargaining position. The longer it is before we find her, the less likely there will be a deal."

"But that's the deal you have to make," he said suddenly, surprising me. Before he finished talking I knew I had made a mistake in mentioning the attorney general's office. That mention had made him aware that there were deals the United States Government was able to make and was interested in making. I had showed my hand too early, and he rushed in to take advantage of my mistake. "I want it in writing. I always wanted her out of this business. I hardly believed her when she told me she worked for you guys. All she wanted was out. All she wanted was to be normal and to leave all this bullshit behind. New names. New home. New faces, if we want. I've read what you guys can do."

"All right," I said, leaning into him, sensing that he was close to taking the bait if I simply agreed to everything he demanded. What did I care whether I could deliver it? "You can start all over again."

"What about jobs?" he asked, making the mistake of beginning to negotiate his reward before he had decided what he wanted to do.

"She keeps all the cash, all four or five hundred thousand, and you get to be an architect wherever you want. New diploma. New certifications. We'll take care of it all."

"Convenient that I don't have any immediate family living," he suggested.

"That's one of the factors that we looked at in deciding to recruit you," I pointed out, playing the she-doesn't-really-love-you card. "This was business with Rebecca, you know. That's why Rebecca thought of you as a likely target. Rebecca knew you'd be a good agent, even if all you said you wanted to be was an architect. Now you've got to be a good agent to save her."

He paused, and I could see the wonder in his eyes that he didn't dare express—what if she was only playing with him in order to recruit him? But recruit him for what? Not the organization, when she seemed to be planning to leave. As a personal bodyguard? Not when it was so easy for her family to hire one. The simple answer, he must have decided, must be the right answer—she fell in love.

"Save her from what?" he asked.

"Well, for starters, how about the people shooting at her."

"I've done that once."

"It will happen again. People are out to get Rebecca and her family. We don't know why, but we know they want her and they want to stop her."

"The only people I've met who specifically want her, and not just her family," he said carefully, each word falling heavily out of his mouth, "are you guys."

"Save her from us, then," I offered. "The only way to do it is to find her."

He got up and paced the length of the long room, his neck still craned to watch the ceiling as he walked. "Let me get this straight. You train me. Then you send me out to find Rebecca. If I find her, all you want to do is talk to her, and I can either stay with her or you'll get me out. If you can."

"Basically," I said. "It might be easier than that. She might come looking for you."

"Okay. And if I say no, you lock me up and let Rebecca and her family think that this drug cartel has me stashed somewhere in South America."

"Exactly." I was pleased with the scene I had worked out.

"It's not really a choice at all!" Tommy exclaimed, stopping in the far corner of the room, in the shadow. "It's blackmail."

"Patriotism by another name."

"Can you do this deal tonight?" he asked.

"What do you mean?"

"Can you have the Justice Department, or whoever is responsible for these things, put this agreement in writing tonight?"

"It's the middle of the night. Nobody's awake, let alone at their office."

"Tomorrow morning then," he said.

"Before we leave this house," I countered. "I'll get it to you in writing before we begin the mission."

"By noon tomorrow. I don't talk, I don't help, unless you agree."

I stared at him as he stared at me. I wondered if I'd be able to get the Judge and the Justice Department to go along with this proposed deal at all, let alone sometime tomorrow. The only reason they would even consider it was the possibility, if not the probability, that they couldn't prosecute Rebecca successfully anyway. But if I didn't agree, he might not tell me what we needed to know.

"Agreed," I said. "Tomorrow by noon, in writing."

"Okay." He exhaled it, as if it were a pent-up breath and not a word. "Agreed."

The room was quiet for a while. We sipped our drinks and watched the rain slide down the length of the windows.

"You know," he said from the shadows, willing to turn his story in a different direction now that he believed, however warily, that he had a deal, "I remember her eyes most of all. I remember seeing them this morning—God, was it only this morning?"

"Yesterday morning now," I reminded him quietly, thinking of Carolyn in bed a floor above as I suppressed a yawn. "It's almost three."

"I remember seeing her eyes. She was in silhouette, and she turned to me. Her eyes so, so bright against the darkness. She asked me if I would stay with her. If I would follow her to the end of the world. We were in this little concrete room. I had to decide whether to be with her after all this craziness or get out, if I could."

He walked into the faint light from the two lamps still on and sat back down in the supple Danish leather chair.

"That's when I saw my mother's eyes in hers," he said. "That's when I remembered my mom. I remembered waking up in my bed in my room on the farm with my mother sitting next to where I lay, her palm on my forehead as if she was taking my temperature."

Then he told me the story of the night his father died, his hand reaching out to the light of the lamp when he described the light from the hall lying square and flat on the floor. I saw that square of light as he described it, and it hit me again how carefully he could remember details. Like any good spy, or so goes theory number 431, he was a diarist at heart, searching, analyzing, describing to get the truth just right, to pocket the memory just so. Leaving little vignettes everywhere he went.

"So I told Rebecca yes," he stated firmly. "Yes, I said. I will be with you. I will stay with you, forever and forever. I said just—what, sixteen hours ago?—that I would follow her to the ends of the earth. I said yes."

He looked at me as he said "yes," and without my asking he said, "Yes, Steele. I'll do it. Yes, I'm your man. Count me in. Yes. Yes. Yes."

I stood up and shook his hand. The deal was struck. Now we just had to carry it off.

"This is the right thing to do," I said. "Now let's go back and try to remember every detail. Faces. Names. Numbers. Everything about them. Details help."

"Look, I know you want me to be some kind of master spy, remembering names and numbers, but I don't. I can only tell you what . . . what I know. Which really isn't much."

I looked him in the eye again, measuring the depth of his deceit. "If you hold anything back it could kill you. It could kill Rebecca."

He measured me in turn again, his hand rubbing his jaw. How much could he trust me, he wanted to know. I had the answer. I pulled a cassette tape from the briefcase near my feet and popped the tape in my Walkman. I listened to it for two minutes while he asked me again and again what I was doing. I found what I was listening for, and I took off the headphones and played the tape for him with the volume turned up.

"Yes," Tommy's voice said from the tape recorder, the recording crackling with the transmission interference from the black box to the satellite. "Yes, Rebecca, I love you. I love you, damn it. I love you, and I will stay with you forever."

"Forever?" Rebecca asked on the tape, her crawling toward him on the bed echoing in the faint squeak of the springs.

"Forever," he said. "I'll marry you, and I'll stay with you and your crazy family until the end of time."

There was the sudden harsh sound of a knock on the door on the tape, and I shut it off. The click of the machine made Tommy jump.

"But—" Tommy began, searching for a way to protest or explain.

"Don't even ask," I said. "That little concrete room was bugged. The whole place was bugged. We heard most of what we need to know. But we've got to know as much as we can to make this thing work. If you hold out on us you could end up dead. Rebecca could end up dead."

He put his face in his hands and shook himself awake. "I didn't lie to you," he asserted.

"No, you didn't. But you haven't told me everything. You've forgotten some details. Not too much. But lesson one in being a spy—it's the details you can't forget. It's the details that can kill you. Don't pretend to know anything you don't know, and don't pretend with me that you don't know things that you do know. You'll hate to hear me say this, but we've got to trust each other."

"You know," he said sadly, his voice nearly breaking, "I really do love her. I don't know where the hell I fit into this little game. I don't know who's acting and who's telling the truth anymore. I don't know if she didn't just play me for a sucker, or if you're playing me for a sucker. But I do, Jesus, I really do love that woman. I've got to, got to find her."

He inhaled deeply, pulling himself together, and I said, "Let's start finding her. Tell me about her family. Tell me about Rebecca's family."

"Okay," he said, wiping his nose. "Listen to this."

21.

THAT NIGHT when the Judge and his wife, Helen, got home from having dinner with Carolyn and me, there was a message waiting on their machine from the secretary of state himself. The Judge rewound, but did not erase, the message, leaving it for me to listen to months later. His wife told me later that the Judge stepped back when he heard the secretary's New York accent, and bumped into the corner of his new kitchen cabinet. The secretary almost always had one of his many assistants call the Judge, even though professional courtesy would tell the man to call himself. As the Judge was rubbing his bumped backside, the secretary's recorded voice said, "Sorry to call you so late, Judge. Your assistant said you'd have on your beeper, but it must not be working. I need to talk to you on a safe line as soon as possiblc, and I need to see you in my office at eight-thirty sharp in the morning. My private line number is 639-3081, and it's double-checked. I'll be up until eleven-thirty. After that, don't worry about it."

It was twelve-thirty, so the Judge decided not to call. As he was walking up the stairs to bed, his private gray phone line rang. The two Federal Protective Service guards, twice the usual number assigned to the Judge, who sat in his living room would not answer the gray phone. He got back downstairs before the answering machine kicked in again, and he talked for twenty minutes to Paul, the deputy dernza, and to three of the European specialists on a conference call.

The European specialists told him there were impending riots in East Germany, Romania, Czechoslovakia, and Lithuania, all at the same time. The Stasi phone operator who was a mole for us at the East German secret police had sent out a distress signal, and when contacted she said the whole Stasi operation was in chaos. Part of the headquarters was literally on fire, the computer had been ransacked and tapes stolen, people had come off the streets and taken away boxes of files. Who knew if they were looters or foreign agents, she said. The rumor was that top Stasi agents were committing suicide. She expected Soviet tanks within hours, she said. That was the only way to avoid total anarchy. She kept repeating, "The delicate balance is up. Our side is coming down. The delicate balance is up."

"The scary thing is," Paul suggested, "that the Soviets are not moving. They seem terrified, or maybe preoccupied. We've got five different studies on force dispositions, but nobody agrees on where they invade and with what. Langley is all hot to figure out what the new resupply points would be—they think that's the secret. The White House is screaming for more assessments and scenarios, but I'm not sure anything we have is any use in this circumstance. There's no increase in communications traffic. There's no troop movement. There're no flybys. No nothing that we can tap into. You know, we always just assumed a rapid response at one target country. With no response, all the satellite countries seem to think they can get away with this. My guess is—"

"Don't guess," the Judge ordered.

West German intelligence had sent out a coded message calling for a NATO intelligence meeting in twenty-four hours in Bonn. No one could figure out why the Soviets had let things deteriorate as far as they had without acting. Finnish listening posts were reporting massive surges in communications and flights. As of yet there were no reported troop movements from the satellites. The English GCHQ were reported to be all over the situation, and the French were caught off guard. The Joint Chiefs of Staff were meeting at nine and wanted an NSA representative at the meeting. The White House office had called and asked what to say. The CIA had called and was contemplating putting into effect the "Coconut Telephone" plan, which had been worked out after Poland had come over across the line in order to warn European agents that their cover might be blown. The organization's European specialists were urging caution. Any wholesale communication could be a mistake at this point, they warned.

The Judge was silent for a long while, contemplating all the decisions that should be made right now. He kept hearing a woman's voice in his head, her German accent soft and full of tears, saying, "The delicate balance is up. Our side is coming down. The delicate balance is up." The whole thing, the Judge told his wife later when he went up to bed, was a teeter-totter with two sides of equal weight. If somebody slipped off, then both would be thrown off. If the Soviets didn't play their role, then God knew what would happen. The delicate balance was up.

"How's the pain?" Helen remembered asking him when she saw him grimace and take a pill from the container in his pocket. He shook his head without answering.

The Judge took a deep breath, said okay to himself, and started making the decisions and issuing the orders that would keep them busy enough for him to get some sleep.

"Oh, by the way," Paul, the deputy dernza, said, "the State Department was looking for you. Before this all broke. Did somebody there get in touch with you?"

"Before this broke?" the Judge asked. "You mean he—they weren't calling about all this cowshit?"

"I don't know what they were calling about," Paul protested. "One of the secretary of state's cretins called and said it was urgent, so I gave him your beeper number. But it was before we got the first call. Did somebody get ahold of you?"

"Yes," the Judge lied. "Somebody got ahold of me."

The delicate balance was up.

22.

THE RAIN HAD MOVED south and east from Philadelphia to Virginia before dawn on Wednesday morning, hitting the tall beveled-glass windows of the house's study with a sharp steel clash. Tommy stood at the windows and watched the rain. It was too dark to see out into the yard, so I knew he could be concentrating only on his own reflection or the slashes of silver rain. As Tommy's voice rose and fell, swinging from loud and emphatic to soft and questioning, I wondered which of the two he was staring at: the distorted reflection of his tired face or the clear image of the driving rain. As I watched him I was reminded of those metallic pictures of the Mother Mary that, if you turn them just right in the light, suddenly change into pictures of Jesus. When Tommy moved to the right he saw the linear rain; when he moved to the left he saw the lines on his face.

"They told me," he said to the glass, "two stories. First they told me that their family was in the information business. They called it the information business, but I assumed they were talking about spying. We were sitting at the kitchen table right after the first plane dumped a ton of red paint on the house, and Rebecca's father told me that they bought and sold information."

"We heard that part," I snapped, a little too hastily. "They sold information about some drug shipment to a rival drug cartel. They got the information from the DEA, and the result was that mini-war that we all got caught in today, or yesterday now."

"Did they?" Tommy asked. "Were they telling the truth? Did they steal information from some agency and—"

"We don't know," I said. "Yet. But we will."

"They said that the whole thing happened only after a relative squealed on them," Tommy offered. "That's a crucial point, but I'll get to that later. They said—"

"Did they tell you about any other information they bought or sold?" I asked.

"Just hold your horses, Steele. I'll get to that," he said, and paused to wipe the fog of his breath off the window. "In that same conversation Doc told me that he . . . that they . . . they sold the plans for . . . for some spy plane to the Russians."

"No he didn't," I interjected quickly. "That's not on the tape."

Tommy turned and looked at me with a smile and then turned back to the window. "You were all over that place, weren't you."

I was silent, smiling at his unknowing complicity. Without him we never would have gotten into their lair.

"Just testing," Tommy said, and turned back to the window.

"I thought I convinced you this wasn't a game?" I asked. "Lives are at stake here. Maybe Rebecca's life. Definitely your life."

"I'm convinced," he grumbled. "But if you want me to be your spy, your secret agent man, you can't expect me to be a sucker. Agents don't trust anybody, right? Now I know you're telling the truth about what you know."

"You let us worry about how you became an agent," I said, knowing we had no intention of making him into an agent. He was only bait, pure and simple. "You just tell me the truth and let us figure out what to do."

"Trust you?" he asked.

"Sure," I said. "You're lucky."

"Steele," he replied, smiling at my joke, "maybe I'm just too tired, but I think I might even end up liking you."

"Tommy," I said, raising my glass in a toast, "I don't care a rat's ass."

He laughed quietly at his own reflection and yawned for the first time in our marathon session. I could tell he was getting looser, more comfortable, and more willing to talk. I could feel it, as old recruiters must feel when they have the bait in the fish's mouth. All he had to do was bite down hard on the hook. He had already tasted it, told us that he was with us, but he still wasn't quite there yet. He wasn't quite on our side, I sensed.

"The next morning, yesterday morning, in the communications room things were going very fast," Tommy whispered, his voice barely audible on the tape that was recorded from the miniature microphone Murphy had installed in the lamp near the chair where Tommy hardly ever sat. "So I couldn't really ask questions. But what I understood from Rebecca's descriptions was that the family her dad was talking about wasn't just their immediate family. It was bigger. Aunts and uncles all over the world are all some sort of information brokers. Her dad's brothers and sisters were all in the business somehow, and all sold stuff to governments, to multinationals, and to each other. But get this—Rebecca says no one has ever said anything about them because they always work through intermediaries. Although I find this impossible to believe, Rebecca claims that because they work through intermediaries, no one in the family breaks the law."

"Shooting someone isn't breaking the law? Treason isn't breaking the law?" I asked. "Impossible."

"What's impossible?" he asked. "The whole story? Or just the part about not breaking any laws? Look, that is why I'm doing this, why I am going along with your plan—because I think that they have Rebecca brainwashed. She spouts all this nonsense and tells these stories without batting an eye. Something is definitely wrong."

"Tell me about the family," I offered again.

"She has only met a couple of her aunts, uncles, and cousins. Most of them she has never met. Their family name was Bundt."

"Bundt," I repeated, taking specific notes in my mind.

"Their family was in the banking business in Germany for generations, Rebecca told me. They still have a bank, or some relationship to a bank. A big one. I think she said it was the Bank of Commerce or something. Before the First World War, Rebecca's great-grandfather bought oil leases in America and munitions plants in Bavaria. They built the machines that ran the war and supplied the gas that ran the machines. He had six sons, and one went to America and invested the family's profits in the stock market. He was the oldest son, and his name was Rudolph—which is Rebecca's brother's middle name. All of them, all of her brothers, have the same middle name. Well, Rudolph was crazy, Fritz—Rebecca's brother Fritz—told me, but he was a genius at the stock market, so more and more of the family's money was sent to the United States."

He paused and shook his head as if he couldn't believe what he was saying. Then he inhaled loudly and set the glass down, making a gesture that he didn't want anything else to drink. While I wanted him to remember the small details, like that all of Rebecca's brothers had the same middle name, I wanted him to get to the point of the story they told him.

"Of course, the reason Rudolph was so good at the stock market game was that he had a band of thieves who stole information," Tommy said, the liquor making him sound arrogant. "He was an expert at insider trading before it was a crime. It was all just business. Rudolph loved New York and refused to go home to Germany, even to visit. His father begged him, so the story goes, but he refused. The family fortune grew and grew, but on Christmas Day in 1928 Great-grandpa's crazy gardener, who had been fired on Christmas Eve for stealing a goose off the family estate, murdered the entire family as they slept and then burned their mansion down. Rudolph got a telegram in New York telling him that his family was dead."

"Rebecca told you all of this?" I asked.

"There's even more," Tommy said. "It gets much better. Rudolph moved his family, consisting of an American Jewish wife from New Jersey and ten kids, to Switzerland, selling everything he had in the stock market six months before the crash. So he was sitting on all this cash in his own bank when everything collapsed. His bank buys everything it can as prices collapse. In the spring of 1929 he had his eleventh child, Rebecca's father, Doc."

"Lucky son of a bitch," I said.

"Rudolph's wife dies giving birth to their twelfth kid—who is stillborn. Rebecca, by the way, sees this twelfth child as a disguised murder of her grandmother by her grandfather Rudolph, who insisted on having sex even though a doctor warned them that another pregnancy would be dangerous. After her death Rudolph goes crazy. A complete raving millionaire loon. He locks his kids up behind the tall stone walls of a giant Swiss chalet and creates his own little world within its walls. Sometimes the children do not go outside the walls of the estate for years at a time. Everything is brought to them. They are the center of their own universe while World War Two roars on around them. But they know all about the world, because they have delivered to the estate hundreds, literally hundreds, of newspapers and thousands of magazines from all over the world. Under their father's guidance, the eleven children begin to keep a giant, elaborate cross-file containing all the tidbits that they found in the international press.

"The whole thing started innocently enough." Tommy sighed, closing his eyes to remember. "Rebecca said that they were just playing a game at first, but when their father saw the type of information that was generated, he got back in the real game and began to show them how to use the information. Just like he did on the stock market. How to buy and sell based on what you know and who you know. Elaborate filing and cross-filing systems to keep track of everything. Dozens of librarians hired to research everything. They use the bank as cover to run their intelligence operations. A bank, Rebecca told me, always needs to know information to make investment decisions. It was a perfect fit.

"Rudolph goes back into the munitions business and supplies Hitler and his cronies with whatever they need. But he funnels all the money back into Switzerland and just sits on it, becoming one of the richest men in the world. When the whole world blows up and the Second World War starts, the crazy Bundt family is sitting on vaults of Krugerrands. They've got money, power, and they are selling guns, bullets, bombs to both sides. They amass more and more wealth from behind their stone walls, becoming more and more eccentric with each deal. The Allies and the Axis send their spies to watch over the family that controls the companies that they depend on for their munitions, and the family befriends them, manipulates them, blackmails them, or kills them, depending on what the circumstances require. Nobody owns them, Rebecca said, and they own everybody.

"As the war is coming to an end, grandpa Rudolph sees that the munitions business is just not going to be what it was, so he sets up a trust fund for his eleven children that is specifically designed not to funnel them cash, but to funnel money to their businesses. The catch is that they must all go into the same business in different countries—which is, after all, the only business they know. Like old King Lear, he divided up the world and gave them different realms in which to operate, keeping them separate so they wouldn't compete with each other."

"Compete doing what?" I asked.

"Selling and trading information," Tommy said, turning to face me. "Buying and selling whatever is worth knowing. Trade secrets. Insider information. State secrets. Remember, this all starts before computers, long-distance phone lines—hell, even before television, let alone twenty-four-hour cable news. Simple information is still really valuable, back in those days, if you know it before anyone else does. If you find something out in Berlin and can get that information to Wall Street before anyone else knows it, there was, and is, money to be made. Now the catch is, according to Rebecca, that new communications technology has made the different arms of the family compete even though they are in different geographic areas. Which is, maybe, why they are fighting."

"Who's fighting?" I asked.

"Rebecca mentioned that the family was squabbling. She didn't say over what. I don't even know if there are eleven different families, or if all of the brothers and sisters are still alive. I just know that there was going to be a family reunion. A meeting to settle some things, and that after that meeting, Rebecca thought, everything would be different. They were going to travel by boat to get to this meeting, wherever it was. Rebecca told me that I didn't need to know any more than that. She told me that all of this information gave me enough to decide whether to be with the family or not."

The rain slowed to a drizzle. I picked up a pen and scribbled down a few notes that I would fax to John X at HQ before I went to sleep. I had to know more fast. John X could have someone work the night shift, even though it was now past four in the morning, and leave me info to work on when I got there later in the morning. The hard part would be giving him the information we needed checked out without letting him know that we had Tommy.

"In those weeks, or days—who knows how long we really have —you have to be trained," I lied, knowing that Tommy would be thrown to the wolves within days. "Trained to find out what is going on and get Rebecca out of it. Let's go to sleep now. You've got a big day in front of you tomorrow. Murphy will start the training."

"Do you think any of this she told me is true?" Tommy asked.

"I don't know," I said. "I'll know better tomorrow. I'll have our people do some research and see how much of the story checks out. I find it hard to believe, but I also can't figure out a motivation for Rebecca to lie to you."

Tommy winced and said, "It hurts to even hear you say that—that she might have lied to me. The hardest part of this whole thing is that it all could be some hoax. It's like finding out—hell, it *is* finding out that she was living some whole other life that I knew nothing about and then wondering if she was lying about how she felt about me. What was real and what was fake?"

"The only way to find out is to find her."

Tommy went to bed behind a locked door. Murphy stationed an armed guard in the hall outside Tommy's room and had two shifts of men patrolling the grounds. I wandered into the library, thirty feet away, where Murphy had been listening in on our conversation for hours.

"God, I thought you'd never quit," Murphy grunted from his seat behind a computer, his earphones hanging around his neck. "But it was very interesting listening. I'm doing a search right now of agency files for the Bundt family. We're going to need someone to go into the big Cray computer for the serious shit. Oh yeah, and here's a present for you."

He handed me a photocopy of a long letter written on Justice Department stationery that detailed an agreement between Tommy, Rebecca, and the United States Government to put Tommy and Rebecca in the federal witness protection program.

"What?" I asked. "Where did you get this?"

"I made it while you were in there chatting away," Murphy said. "Idle hands are the playthings of the devil, you know. I pulled up a piece of Justice Department stationery from the files, scanned the headings and logo, and then copied the language off of an agreement for the witness protection program in another case we had on file. Man, I love having access to NSA files again. Ain't computers great?"

"This looks . . . perfect," I acknowledged.

"Note the signature," Murphy said. "A perfect copy of the signature of one J. David Roth, head of the federal witness protection program. Not bad for fifteen till four in the morning."

"But what if Tommy really does find Rebecca and really does want into the program?"

"There's not much chance of that," Murphy argued, "but if they do, then we'll get it for them somehow. Hell, they'll get it because they had every reason to rely on the two of us—two ostensible representatives of the United States Government. It's just the two of us who'll go to jail. But I'll take the risk if you will."

"Let's go for it," I said. "We both know that we can't prosecute Rebecca without revealing documents that it would not be in the national interest to reveal—or so go some of the magic words—so why not give them our guarantee right up front."

Murphy smiled at me and reached out to shake my hand.

"But here's the deal," I said to him.

"Oh shit," he groaned, withdrawing his hand. "I knew this wasn't going to be simple. All right, lay it on me. I'm your loyal servant."

"Good," I said. "Because this mission is a definite go and you're not going to have a couple of weeks. Tommy is the bait. He's got to think we're training him to be our agent, or whatever bullshit name you want to give it. But he is really nothing more than a worm on a hook. We just have to put him in the right place and Rebecca will, hopefully, come to him. So you have two goals. First, convince Tommy we are training him for battle so he doesn't think we are just using him. Second, set him on the hook."

"They think he was being held by the Colombians, right? Isn't that good-enough cover?" Murphy asked.

"Yeah, but *thinking* he's being held by the Colombians is not good enough."

"I'll take care of it," Murphy said. "What if she and her family could rescue Tommy from the drug lord's very clutches? They'd believe his story then."

"Murphy," I said, "that's exactly what I had in mind. You need to get Tommy into the hands of one of the cartel families, and you have to do it fast. Use every contact you have, but remember, Rebecca will be watching for you. It has to look real good. It has to look like Tommy went straight from her family farm into the drug lord's clutches. This little stopover with us has to disappear. And, as if that's not enough, remember, we've got to keep this guy alive."

"Let me work on it. I have just the person in mind to help us. I'll talk to the Judge, if you don't mind. Let me see what I can do, and you can make a decision whether or not to go ahead. All right?"

"Good," I said, finally shaking his hand. "Give that agreement to him in the morning, that should start your day out right. Tell him I had the attorney general himself approve it in the middle of the night."

"Let's not go too far," Murphy suggested.

"We probably already did," I answered.

Murphy only grunted in response.

I had one more thing to do before I went to bed. I called HQ and woke up John X and gave him a list of things to check up on.

"Where did this come from?" John X asked, his voice tight and strained.

"I've kept my part of the bargain," I said. "Nobody knows about that certain garment of Tommy's. Now you've got to keep quiet about this information. I need to know as much about the Bundt family as possible, and the only other person who is allowed to see this info is the Judge. Got it? No questions asked."

"All right," he agreed tensely.

At five-thirty I slipped into bed beside a sleeping Carolyn. Carolyn had never lost the ability to surprise me. But I wondered as I fell asleep what it would feel like if the woman who lay next to me suddenly rolled over and said, "By the way, I'm not who you think I am and I've been faking my love for you in order to get what I want." Wasn't that what Tommy was afraid of? First there would be shock and then there would be anger, I thought, staring at the dark outline of her thin back. I'd better prepare Murphy for Tommy's anger to come, I thought as my eyes mercifully closed for a short two-hour nap, until it was time to get up and go into the office for the first time in a year.

Like a kid before his first day of school, I dreamed that everyone at work would be mean to me.

23.

THE THIRD DISCIPLE was code-named John. John drove a car.

It was a small dark car with East German plates, and it rammed through the chain-link fence at the end of a short runway fifty miles east of Berlin. The windshield shattered as a metal post hit it, and then the electrified top wires raked across the top of the car, sending off a fireworks display of sparks. The car careened onto the runway, followed by two flashing red lights and the blare of a siren coming down the curved gravel road that led to the airstrip. Somebody was in hot pursuit.

The car dragged a ten-foot section of chain-link fence behind it as it rushed after a small two-engine plane that was taxiing down the runway to the far end, where the strip ended in the darkness of the looming white pines. As the plane turned in the darkness, the driver of the badly damaged car flicked on its headlights, momentarily blinding the pilot and his passenger, and then turned them off, showing only the bouncing sparks from the metal fence hitting the asphalt. The pilot pushed the plane's engine to maximum power, but held the brakes. The plane could not take off because the car was driving straight for it. The plane tried to swing over to the side of the strip to avoid the car, and then pulled into the narrow grassy area between the asphalt and the towering trees.

The car skidded to a stop in front of the roaring propellers, and two men jumped out and ran for the plane. A sudden burst of automatic fire shot out of the plane's open passenger window and hit the first man full in the chest. He was flung backward in midair by the force of the blast. As his body folded in a heap, the other man ducked the propellers and slid under the belly of the plane. The plane began to move back onto the runway, but the window that had been slid open for the machine gun to fire through was suddenly full of the yellow-green smoke of a sulfur bomb. The plane veered across the runway, with the man spread-eagled on its axle struts, and crashed into the section of chain-link fence dragged onto the runway by the still running car.

The pilot and his passenger threw open the door to the plane and stumbled out in a cloud of smoke. As they stumbled across the dark runway, the man under the plane slid on an army-surplus gas mask and fired two neat shots, one in each of their upper backs. He jumped into the plane just as two cars with flashing red lights and screaming sirens jumped over the fence posts left strewn over the far end of the runway. He headed the plane down the runway at full throttle, not bothering even to shut the door or turn on the plane's lights. Side by side, the two cars roared down the runway from the other direction, racing toward the oncoming plane.

At the last moment one of the cars slowed down and the other veered to the right.

The plane zoomed three feet over the hoods of the cars, tilting up into the sky to make a smaller target for their burst of gunfire, and then leveled off for the short trip over the border. The East German air force scrambled immediately after they got the call that a high party member's plane had been stolen, but the thief took the little plane up to a commercial air lane and then dive-bombed it over the border, stalling the engine and making a dead-stick landing with wrecked landing gear on a little airstrip outside of Stuttgart.

By the time the police and two undercover agents of the West German intelligence service got to the sulfur-stained plane, the pilot was gone, leaving no fingerprints and no clues. Twelve hours later John made his delivery.

All three of the dead men left on the East German airstrip were senior Stasi officers. The newspapers reported that they died in a plane crash, which had become a comic euphemism in Stasi for shot while trying to defect. If you lost too much faith in the motherland and her chosen form of dictatorship you were bound to run into a plane crash. Plane crashes were everywhere. People had no idea how dangerous flying was. Like Chicken Little, planes could come crashing down from the sky at any time.

24.

WHEN I WALKED THROUGH THE main glass doors to HQ the next morning old Charles, the potbellied Federal Protective Service guard, not only greeted me with the warmth of a long-lost friend who gave lavish Christmas gifts to anyone who was in charge of parking but also told me to report to the Judge's office immediately. The guards in the reception area already had my temporary pass made up, and they gave me an envelope with a series of cipher lock numbers on it so I could get into the locked rooms where the Judge and John X were running the mission. Charles walked me through the newer guards and past the long mural painted on the wall of the long hall, of people eavesdropping and breaking codes.

"Something's up," Charles said with the knowing wink that I had grown to trust. We stopped in front of the giant stained-glass seal of the NSA at the end of the hall, and Charles gave me three minutes of who was sleeping with whom. Charles was the best agent the organization had, even though he had never done more than guard the front door. He saw. He listened. He noticed details. And, most important, he shared his gut-level instincts with a precious few of the old hands.

As I greeted him I thought that when I had time I should ask Charles about Rebecca and see what he thought. But now the Judge was waiting.

"You're late," the Judge said when I knocked on his door in the corner office on Mahogany Row. "Don't tell me what you got out of him yet. We've got something big brewing, and I want you in on it."

"But I thought I already had a project?" I asked, loosening my tie.

"Keep your tie up," the Judge said, loading papers into an old leather briefcase. "I'm afraid it might be the same project. One of the secretary of state's goons just called to tell me that my meeting with the secretary—that's right, with the secretary himself—would be half an hour late and—"

"Nice of them to call."

"They only did it because the last time I was there he made me wait forty-five minutes and I told that pinko New Yorker that in Texas gentlemen were on time, cowpokes were late, and whores gave you extra time. He tried to laugh it off, but I think Mr. Secretary got the point. But anyway, Steele, the point today is that the secretary has had delivered to him from some undisclosed source—read probably the fools over at Langley—a top-secret document that is a prospectus of sorts. A sales offer that details something so big, so mother-fricking important, that the SOS thinks we should offer to buy it right quick."

"What has that to do with my project?" I asked.

"We know that Rebecca's family is gathering in or near Key West, correct? Well, the secretary said the package is coming through Key West," the Judge said, stopping to look up and watch my face. "I want you to come with me. Surprise the old bugger with the two of us. I'm sure he'll have a whole phalanx of his goons there, anyway. The more the merrier."

"But I haven't even gotten to my office. I haven't even filled out my W-2 or signed up for my health insurance," I mockingly whined, making fun of my more bureaucratic colleagues while tightening my tie back up.

"I've talked to John X. He'll have your office set up next to the control room we've sequestered down in the basement for the project. All the info is kept there. He'll have all the clearance papers worked out by the time we get back, and the team for the project will meet for lunch off site to figure out how to proceed. John X is working through all the questions that you sent him earlier this morning. Let's go, partner. Now."

"Back in the saddle again," I said, striding down the hall, matching the Judge foot by foot. I was feeling confident, cocky, and ten years younger as I strode down the long hallway with the dernza, all of my old colleagues seeing me back at my post, next to the chief. Returned to my rightful place as chief strategist to the king, and loyal retainer in the games of court intrigue. But as we went down the elevator to the basement to jump into the waiting car, my mind suddenly filled with images of Tommy as he looked that morning when I left the house.

I had dropped the agreement with the Justice Department in front of him at the breakfast table, and I stared at him solemnly, wanting to make sure he felt some bond with me as we began our adventure. He looked at me for a moment like a scared deer, and I shared his fear in that second. We had both got ourselves into something that was much more dangerous than anything we had ever done before. This man was not a soldier, I reminded myself. Tommy Wood was a private citizen whom we were asking, blackmailing, into risking his life for our country and for his love.

Even in the hard, unforgiving morning light on the veranda, his exhausting, pleading eyes and loose, tired movements had a heroic quality to them. Theory number 798: All men who are about to go off and risk their lives look heroic to those who have some vague idea of what they are about to meet. We hope they have no idea what they are getting themselves into, because their ignorance makes them brave. They have a visible sureness, bred of innocence, that makes people salute them as if they were brand-new soldiers, and pray for their success.

I wanted to ask him at that moment whether he was sure he wanted to go through with this now that he had had a few hours to sleep on it, but I was afraid that his exhaustion might have also produced a wave of sanity and I could not afford for him to say no. He was our best, if not our only, shot at breaking inside Rebecca's family.

He would have to do, then, I thought as we sped into Washington. Tommy was all we had.

25.

THE SECRETARY KNEW ME BY NAME, because he knew that I was married to Carolyn, and, as was his political nature, he was much more attentive to me than he was to the Judge. We sat in his giant, sprawling office with three of his constantly moving young aides. We listened to his sonorous voice as he detailed the last three times he had seen Carolyn and how wonderful she had looked each time. What a lucky guy I was, he repeated while the smile solidified on the Judge's drawn face and the pimply aides fidgeted. To have Carolyn, her power, her prestige, her commitment to the community, her wonderful taste in art—

"And her money," I said.

"Yes," the secretary agreed, startled for a second before he realized that what I said could be read as a confident joke. "Very good, Steele. Very funny."

"I just saw a story about your wife on the wire," one of the pimply, bespectacled aides said to me as he reached to adjust his socks.

"Oh really," the Judge mumbled, looking at his watch. "About Carolyn?"

"They are burning her in effigy in the small town in Ohio where the company she is trying to take over is based. The SEC is investigating, and the target company has filed suit in federal court—the Northern District of Ohio. It looks very messy."

"Damn," I cursed. "She probably won't have dinner on the table when I get home."

No one laughed, but two of the aides squirmed in their antique Chippendale chairs, the old wood squeaking with their weight. The Judge and the snot-nosed aides launched into an animated conversation about the growing protests in East Germany, Czechoslovakia, and Romania. There were daring tales of stolen documents and late-night escape attempts over the Berlin Wall. Most of the information the secretary of state was getting was from television; the intelligence agencies, the aides were quick to point out, couldn't keep up with what was happening. It had ceased being a game of chess, in which each side calculated what the other's strategy might be, and become a wrestling match between deadly novices.

"The whole thing could explode at any moment," Jeff, the oldest of the aides, said. "I mean, this could degenerate into chaos one way or the other, if the Soviets don't come in or if they do come in. But everything we know tells us they will come in. The question is, why are they waiting?"

"The secretary is going to recommend to the Joint Chiefs of Staff that the military alert be shoved up a notch," another of the aides reported.

"Maybe," the secretary chipped in. "I'll have to see what they think when I get there. Defense tells me he wants me to recommend it so he doesn't have to take the heat from the prez for being trigger-happy."

"The charts are drawn up," another aide said. "Everything is ready. Langley has drawn flow charts for the different decision-making courses. I think we're ready for every, and I mean every, eventuality."

I remember wanting to reach out and slap him around, just to wake him up. No one was ever ready for everything.

"Here's the point," the secretary said, gesturing strongly with his finger and then sliding his hand to point to one of his aides. "Tim, tell them about it, about the main point."

What Tim had to say was a stunner. The day before, the U.S.

Government had been offered a complete list of locations, repair schedules, launch codes, and trajectories of all Soviet midrange missile launchers from the westernmost border to two hundred miles east of Moscow. In order to demonstrate the validity of the package that was for sale, the seller turned over a sample listing for a missile launcher on the Czech border. Coincidentally, or so the State Department hoped, the numbers for that specific launcher were ones that the CIA had already secretly obtained about two years ago from a top mole in the Soviet Union. The numbers matched.

Then, just to prove that it was not an elaborate KGB setup, the seller also turned over a schedule of launch codes, locations, and dates at those locations for one of our own secret mobile missile launchers that most members of Congress hadn't quite yet figured out existed. Defense would not confirm that the U.S. information was accurate, but it would admit that "We better get this shit, and get it quick."

"We believe both documents were completely accurate," Jeff concluded, wiping his nose, "and according to Langley specialists, almost beyond a doubt, authentic."

"The importance of this information, if verified, is obvious," Tim said. "If we know where virtually every Soviet missile silo is, and the launch codes that must be sent to put the birds in the air, then we can call their bluff at any time. In fact, Defense tells us that if the launch codes are verified we would be able to stop a launch through our own satellite technology. They send the codes up, our babies up there catch wind of them and send out a scattered code to the location of the launch that confuses both the computers and the men on the ground. These codes are made to withstand an electromagnetic pulse even from a nuke detonating in orbit."

"Scramblers," I suggested. "I've heard of them. They are like invisible Patriot missiles. If you know the entrance code to the incoming missile's on-board guidance system you can tell the damn thing to go somewhere else. You just have to have the code to get into the missile's mind. And nobody—I mean nobody—has those codes except for the guys at the top."

"Exactly," Jeff said excitedly as he stood up and began to pace the large room. "Or, since we also know the geographic location, we send scramblers on the same coded frequency even before they go up, reprogramming the launch-site computers to not accept the agreed-upon code. Now this won't do a thing to the missiles that are completely controlled by fiber optic hookups, but even some of those have backup satellite lines that we might be able to break into. We could at least disable a good third to a half of their missile forces."

"It would be a total wipeout!" Tim shouted, almost clapping his hands. The three aides were beside themselves with excitement.

"Or a stalemate," I said. "Didn't you say that your source also had some of our launch codes and locations?"

"That's the rub," the secretary of state commented. "That's the problem."

"He only had one set," Tim said. "And our deal would be to buy all the information he has, to keep it out of anyone else's hands."

"Who's the wise guy trying to sell it to you?" the Judge asked, rolling his eyes at the aides' naïveté.

The aides all looked at each other and then at the secretary, who nodded his head in approval.

They were dealing through a munitions dealer who had been a regular source for years. "He told us where to send the money if we wanted the information and what satellite frequency we would receive it on. The quantity of information is immense, so satellite makes sense, but unless they have their own broadcasting source we'll find out about it before they go up in the air with the transfer. And if they do have their own broadcasting source, supercomputers, satellite hookups, ground platforms, then we are talking about some damn rich people. If they have their own platform to broadcast from, our only chance of stopping them may be to send in the Air Force and blow the whole thing to pieces if we can lock on to the signal and find out where they are."

"If the signal isn't relayed through several satellites and other platforms," the Judge offered, showing off his SIGINT background. "Are you prepared to do this? Have you made arrangements with the Air Force?"

"Yeah," the oldest rat-faced aide said. "We set up a code-name task force in the target area that has the firepower to get the job done. It won't be pretty, but it will be quiet."

"What about the munitions dealer?" I asked, the HUMINT man to the end. Who cared about blowing up the platform where the information came from, I thought, if you could find and stop the people who pushed the buttons.

They had staked out the munitions dealer right away and caught him talking to an intermediary, one of the aides explained. "He's a stockbroker in Key West who has never had a brush with the law. He's completely clean, and therefore not a probable source for this kind of information. We guess that it must be coming out of Cuba to friends in Key West. That's our hottest theory right now."

"Here's the twist," the secretary of state said, getting up slowly to pour himself another cup of coffee. An aide brought the coffee to him before he was out of his chair. "Tell them the twist."

"Both the munitions dealer and our nice little stockbroker were found dead last night," Jeff said, sitting down. "Separate incidents. Both look like suicide, but I'd bet my salary that they are both homicide. We've got everybody on this. Key West has more intelligence officers and cops than tourists right now. Keeping it out of the papers may be a problem. Langley is running the show."

"Sounds like Langley has this whole thing under control," the Judge offered in his best imitation of civility. "What do you need from us?"

"What we need . . ." the secretary began. He gestured for his aides to finish his sentence.

"Is to know," Tim said, "why one of your section chiefs has had a dozen men on the prowl in Key West since about nine o'clock last night."

"Are you guys on to this deal?" Jeff asked. "I mean, did the NSA know about this whole thing? And if so, what do you know and why didn't we know it?"

The air conditioner went on in the high-ceilinged room, letting a squeaky fan cough cool air across us.

The Judge was silent for a moment, undoubtedly considering what to tell and whom to tell it to. While the Judge paused I smiled at the senile secretary, and, not surprisingly, he smiled back. I broadened my grin and nodded my head, as if the two of us were in some rich men's cahoots around all these social-climbing professionals, and the secretary nodded back and opened his mouth to show his teeth. I was just about ready to try a wink on the imbecile when the Judge made up his mind to tell them that something was up. It was better to risk giving away too much to these rats than it was to look dumb.

"We have an agent, deep undercover, working with a group of international information brokers," the Judge dissembled, not quite directly lying. "Nobody—and I mean nobody, fellas—knows about this mission. We have reason to believe that they or some part of their organization is based right now down on those islands. The problem is that if you get involved, that might jeopardize the whole thing. They may have a mole in one of our intelligence agencies."

"Which one?" Jeff asked.

"I don't know," the Judge said calmly.

"That is quite an accusation to make without substantiation," another of the rodent-faced aides squealed.

The Judge smiled at them all, catching their gaze one by one, and then said, "You're like a preacher caught in a whorehouse, claiming to convert souls with your pants down. I can't trust anyone. Not even any of you, until I know for sure. Someone is selling our goddamn launcher positions and launch codes and you haven't figured out that there is something wrong with our security? How the hell do you think they got them? From a damn Ouija board?"

They moved their bony asses around in their chairs, not knowing how to respond to such a direct insult.

"What do you want us to do?" the secretary asked me, ignoring the bureaucratically impolitic Judge.

"Buy the package," I said, to the surprise of the Judge, who thought he was doing the talking for HQ—which he was, for I was speaking for myself, Steele, citizen, spy, collector of obscure trivia, and defender of a faith I made up as I went along. "Verify the information. Send the money to wherever they told you to send it and get ready to receive whatever they send you. And stay out of our way. We can pull this thing off if we get your cooperation and your support. Since you have guys crawling all over Key West, keep them investigating. Keep them looking for where this information is coming from. But tell them to keep their hands off any NSA operatives they come across. We can do this thing if you play dumb and just buy the stuff. Then, even if our mission does not work, at least you have bought the goods that you need."

I finished my plea with my best country-club smile to the secretary, and before any of his aides had a chance to butt in he said, "Sure, Steele. That makes sense. I'll authorize buying the information. You run your operation, Langley runs ours. If you succeed we all win, if you don't then at least we'll have what we want."

"But—" Jeff started.

"Our operation is separate," I said. "We don't need to know anything about your investigation—except for one thing."

"And what is that?" the secretary asked.

"We only need to know if the information is accurate. As soon as you are dead-set sure that the goods you are buying are the real thing, then we need to know. It is crucial we know if you've got, or are going to get, solid info. And I can't tell you why."

"We believe it is good information," Tim asserted. "Langley has analyzed it. Defense has analyzed it. Everything points to it being the real McCoy."

"Just tell us when you know for sure," I said. "And I suggest that you bargain with them. Offer a lower price. Try to get them to throw in more information. Anything to make them think that you are not sure, not positive that the information they are peddling is legitimate. They are bound to give you more to show you its quality, and what they give you may be a clue as to where it is coming from. Share the clues with us and we'll try to find you the source."

"Excellent idea, Steele," the secretary admitted. "How long should we keep up this pretense?"

"Well," I said, "until you are sure that the launch codes, the locations, the schedules are correct."

The secretary placed his china coffee cup and saucer on the delicate side table by his chair and walked over to one of the tall windows near his desk. He stared out the window for a moment and then gestured for us to come over. The Judge and I both got up and went to where he stood, the bright morning light looking radiant after last night's rain. I noticed that the old air-conditioning system rattled loudly right under the window, so if the room was bugged this would be the toughest place to pick up and record any voices.

The thick bulletproof glass kept the sounds of the outside world from entering the office, and I couldn't help feeling that we were inside a hermetically sealed bubble. We watched the cars streaming by the exit to the bridge on the side of the compound of mismatched buildings that made up the State Department, all of them moving by quickly but silently. The aides gathered quietly on the other side of the room, whispering to each other.

"Gentlemen," the secretary of state said quietly, "you did not hear, you do not know, you will forget immediately what I am about to tell you." He paused and looked in my eyes, then in the Judge's eyes.

"Yes," the Judge answered. "I understand."

The secretary nodded and smiled. "The information is solid. Thirty-six hours ago the Defense Department, with the direct authorization of the president of the United States, took the codes and locations, stuck them all in some supercomputer—hell, I have no idea how it is done—and sent by satellite a coded command to the missile site on the Czech border. Those smart bastards in Defense shut the missile down, reprogrammed it so it would operate only on our commands, and then told the Soviets that we would do the same to every one of their babies if they invaded Czechoslovakia or East Germany."

"That's why the Soviets haven't moved yet," the Judge figured out. "They are trying to decide what their next move is. This is no invasion of Hungary. This is no just lock up the rabble-rousers, like in Poland. Do they try to reprogram everything? Do they have time? Do they send the missiles up before they lose complete control? Have they already lost control and are just waiting for NATO tanks to roll into East Germany? They don't know what's going on."

"Bingo," the secretary said. "So the info is good. That's why we have to get it, and get it quick. So whatever you are doing, proceed on the assumption that the info is good and that the Soviets think that we already have it."

"I understand." The Judge smiled. "That's why you need to be ready to blow these guys out of the sky if you think they are transferring important U.S. intelligence."

"Bingo," the secretary said again, like a skipping record.

"What if we find them and don't have time to disarm them? Can I give our men, our lead men, the code to send in the Air Force to bomb the platform if we find it?"

The secretary paused for a second and looked as if he were going to ask one of the aides to come join us by the window, but then he blurted out, "It's your buddy, Judge. Ol' Casey with the Black Wing Squadron out of Miami. Just call him up with the location. The code word is 'Conch Shell.'"

"So I have your authorization?" the Judge asked. "As a last resort? I have your approval to order a bombing run?"

"As a last resort," the secretary said.

The three of us looked at each other, measuring the distance to that last resort in our minds as a prisoner measures his cell in his mind.

Then the secretary walked back to where we had been sitting and quizzed his aides. "Do we have anything else for these gentlemen?"

The aides responded with dumbfounded silence.

"We'll talk tomorrow then?" the secretary asked the Judge.

The Judge nodded his approval, and after another five-minute speech about the wonders of Carolyn we left hurriedly and rushed out to the Judge's car.

"Damn," the Judge grunted the moment the car door was closed behind him. "This is crazy."

"Rebecca's family is in the middle of this somehow," I said. "We've just got to find out how. Maybe we should get to Defense and tell them what we know?"

"No," the Judge snapped. "Let's just stick to our plan. We don't have any hard information yet about Rebecca or her family. Let's keep this thing quiet—very quiet—until we have something to show for it."

"We've got to speed up our plans," I said as the Judge's car tore through the traffic.

"Let's not panic," the Judge suggested with a grimace as he readjusted how he was sitting. "Let's proceed at a comfortable pace. No stampedes to conclusions, pal. There are so many unknowns."

"That," I said, "is for damn sure." The Judge's driver swerved to miss a car that pulled into our lane, and horns sounded all around us. I pulled my seat belt on and got ready for a rough ride. But as I sat in the back of that speeding car, I had no idea how rough it was going to be.

"What the hell was all that Carolyn cowshit about?" the Judge asked. "I mean, I know all those guys love her, but wasn't that a little heavy?"

"Campaign debt, my friend," I said. "Carolyn's hosting a fundraiser to pay off some of his debt from when he last ran for the Senate, five years ago, and lost."

"Money talks," the Judge said wistfully, "bullshit walks."

26.

When we returned to HQ the Judge and I went straight to the situation room, where John X was working everyone on the project like a slave driver. John X was on the phone when we were cleared to enter the soundproof room after typing the correct numerical sequence in the cipher lock on the door. The first thing I noticed were the four empty coffee cups in front of him. He was rubbing his eyes and screaming at the research librarian on the phone that he needed the information not tomorrow, not in an hour, but right now.

"I wonder," the Judge whispered to me, "if he'd work that hard to find his wife and kids if they skipped town. This lady must have been damn good in bed."

"Okay, okay," John X said, slamming down the phone and turning to the Judge, his voice racing with sleepless speed like a runner going so fast he has lost all control. "Unfortunately, there seems to be something to this Bundt family story. I'd love to know where Steele here got this shit. All the details check out. Bundts were wealthy as all hell. Shadowy past. Munitions dealer to Hitler. On a list of the ten wealthiest people in the world in 1939. Eleven kids, all of them without U.S. records of any kind or any info on their locale. And get this, there's a note that there was an intelligence investigation in 1926 of Rudolph Bundt, then in 1937 of his munitions company. Hoover has files on the family throughout the war. There's a ton of stuff on Bundt's bank, and I think this family was running a full-fledged intelligence-gathering operation. A parallel agency that—"

"Slow down, John," the Judge suggested, leaning back in a cheap government chair. "You sound like a rattlesnake in a stampede. You need some sleep, son. Why don't you go home and see the wife and kids and come back later. Steele can handle this during the day on his four hours of sleep."

"Two," I noted.

"I'm okay," John X nearly shouted. "Really, I'm fine. All keyed up and ready to go. Don't worry about me. As I always say, I've been under fire in 'Nam and none of this is torture like old Charlie knew in the bush. Don't worry about me. I'll find Rebecca. I'll find her."

John X's eyes were bloodshot, and his speech was too precise for comfort. I knew we had to send him home soon.

"We'll find her together," the Judge said, repeating what I had told Tommy and leaning back so far in his chair that I thought he would fall over.

My mind whirled as I compared John X and Tommy and their fascination with Rebecca. They were both drawn to her like the proverbial moth to a flame—drawn to something that could burn them, mark them, kill them. Rebecca's success with men might have got her what she wanted, but it might also prove to be her undoing, I thought. These men were not willing to just let her slip away into the night, but were willing to stalk her, hunt her down—but then, rather than trying to capture her, they wanted to prove that she was somehow misguided or brainwashed. They wanted to find her to prove her innocence, rather than punish her for her sins. Why? Maybe because they were sins these men shared.

"This whole thing, this whole story," John X said, rubbing his eyes again. "This wild tale might be, Jesus, it might be true. Rebecca may not be playing games with us—I mean, she might have told her ex-boyfriend the truth about this even if she was lying about wanting to marry him. She might have been funneling information out of this place for as long as she has been here."

"Ex-boyfriend?" I asked.

"Probably ex–live person by now," John X said, "if the Colombian cartel does what it usually does with witnesses. I mean, she left him behind, after all."

"John," the Judge said, "she wanted to marry him. We have no evidence that this boyfriend is alive or dead—or that he is even with the cartel. All we know from the tapes is that some of the family's men think that the Colombians picked him up. Unless you know more than you're telling?"

"No," John X blurted out.

"Of course, there's some truth to the story," the Judge said. "The question is, how much truth? I know that's hard, but I think you are too close to this thing."

John X ignored him and went on talking. "All the details are checking out. His family, Rudolph Bundt's brothers and sisters, were murdered by some crazy gardener. And that's not common knowledge—I mean, you would have to have access to the mainframe computer word search of old German-language newspapers to even find—"

"Which Rebecca has access to," the Judge reminded us, closing his eyes and examining something inside his head. "This thing just doesn't smell true, smell real to me. Too much conspiracy to ring true. Maybe we should explore other avenues—"

"But if it's all true—" John X started, and then stopped to shake his head and yawn.

If it was all true, I remember thinking, then a million dreadful possibilities came to mind. A family enterprise dedicated to buying and selling secrets that had operated for nearly fifty years under the cover of a legitimate business without being caught, and had planted an agent, a family member, so high in our organization, was terrifying. The odds of the family's pulling off this business for fifty years without being exposed were near impossible, but stranger things had happened in the intelligence business in the last fifty years. Even now,

I could not have explained the Soviets' quiet, static tension while Bulgaria had riots in the streets to protest communism, but for what I had learned that morning from the secretary of state. And it was pure luck that I was even told about that. Luck that one hand of the United States Government had let another hand know what it believed it was doing. I knew that was the exception more than the rule. The Soviets' holding back could not be explained by this intelligence agency, I remember thinking, any more than what we knew about Rebecca's actions could be explained. Of the millions of communications that we were listening to, none gave any real evidence of understanding what was happening. Everyone was simply asking the same question we were asking: What is going on?

But if this was true, why would the family risk so openly, so blatantly, being found out about now? Or were we just suddenly lucky? Why would the family suddenly become so sloppy? Greed? Arrogance? Were they so successful that they couldn't imagine failing so they took risks they shouldn't have taken? Risks like telling Tommy the things they told him? Some part of my paranoid mind was worried that we were being set up. That our finding out about the eleven Bundt siblings was also some part of the family's plan. The Judge was right: There was simply too much complicated conspiracy theorizing going on to make me comfortable.

"Give us two weeks and we'll track down every brother and sister, living or dead," John X boasted. "We'll find out exactly what the family is doing. We'll find all of them. We'll find Rebecca."

Theory number 398: The desperate always become boastful. Their overconfidence and cheerleading are the last resort when effort and ingenuity fail. As I found out soon, John X was grasping at straws.

"We'll get them all," John X whispered, hugging himself. He shuddered as if he had caught a sudden cold, and his eyes wandered over to the large photographs of Rebecca tacked to the wall between maps and calendars. "All of them."

"I bet," the Judge offered, "we'll get some of them in Key West. When they try to hand over the Soviet info they stole."

"What?" John X asked quickly.

"That's what the grand ol' secretary of state wanted," the Judge said. "Somebody, at the same time and place that Rebecca's family is supposed to meet up in Key West, wants to sell the U.S. Government locations, launch codes, and maintenance schedules for nearly the whole goddamn Russian army. The sellers have disappeared, but if they show back up it could be our biggest jackpot, or the biggest hoax, in fifty years. For proof of authenticity the seller offered up a verified bit of info on our own location and maintenance schedules. It was good stuff."

John X turned pale and stumbled backward against the cement block wall. His eyes rolled back into his head for a split second, and the Judge fell out of his tilted chair reaching up to catch John X as he swayed. They both ended up in a pile on the floor.

"Jesus!" the Judge shouted. "You need sleep, man. Now get home this moment. That's an order."

"Maintenance logs and locations?" John X, the old missile-maintenance expert, asked, wiping the sweat off his brow as he sat on the floor. "Do you realize what we could do with those? That could end the whole thing. If we knew exactly where each of their intermediate missiles was and which ones worked and which ones didn't work they could—I mean, we could—"

"Knock it off," the Judge said, dusting off his pants. "Of course I know what that means. The cold war's over. We win. Now get out of here. Go home. Get some sleep."

"But Bobby's not back yet, so there's no one cleared who can handle the technical . . . I mean, this is important, you understand. This puts the whole thing in—in a new light," John X gasped.

The Judge launched into a long explanation of how he understood how vital this information could be to the United States or whoever else got it. John X turned white again as the Judge spoke, but the Judge was too busy listening to the sound of his own voice rattling off throw-weight differentials, perimeter-portal control monitoring, and tacit rainbows to notice that John X was on the verge of vomiting.

"Let's let this soldier go," I said to the Judge as he paused for breath in his lecture about the arcane details of maintenance logs and why they should always be kept top secret and separate and all repair crews should have high-level clearance and be rotated out of duty every six months. "Come on," I said to John X. "Do you want someone to drive you home?"

"No," he said, breathing heavily. "I'll drive carefully. There won't be anybody on the parkway this time of day. I'll be fine. Really. I'll do what I've got to do."

"What you have to do is sleep," I suggested. As John X stumbled out of the situation room, I caught my reflection in the back of the one-way mirror on the door as it slowly closed. I didn't look much better than John X.

I couldn't figure out then why we all put ourselves through this torture. What was so compulsively addictive about this business that we insisted on going on until it killed us? Why did something so crazy attract seemingly sane people like my wife? The joy of the hunt for information couldn't be it, nor the joy in manipulating people and events for your own ends. There must be more, I thought as the Judge began asking questions of the techy left in the room. Something intrinsic to the human psyche that seeks to solve mysteries. That loves to discover. That primordial urge to play hide-and-seek that is at the root of all our adult meanderings. While Hamlet's question might have been "to be or not to be," there was no question that he loved the search for his father's killer. The search itself became the reason to be. To discover became the reason to live. To search for the answer, regardless of the importance of the question, became the foundation of the searcher's sanity.

In the end, I did not then, and I do not now, have a theory about why we spies do what we do. But when I saw John X's addiction, I knew that spying was his life, and if he screwed it up he would die. If he did anything that set him and his team back, then he would see no reason to go on. He had screwed up with Rebecca, and he was out to make amends by finding her and proving his mettle as a spy. I did not know it then, as he left the room, but I sensed and rolled over in my mind that John X, unlike me, had everything on the line.

The next I heard of him was from the mouth of an aging Vietnamese madam who smoked Lucky Strikes and wore a phallus-shaped piece of onyx on a necklace that was nestled between the two sagging breasts that were revealed by a cheap low-cut dress. "John man had a bad day," she said with a French-Vietnamese accent.

"A very bad day," I said, watching her long white teeth in a blood-red, tight-lipped, knowing smile.

I spent most of that day buried in files, piecing together everything I have told you about Tommy and Rebecca. That first day back in the office I absorbed so much information that I thought my head would pop off if I listened to another tape or saw another video or read another file. John X had done a great job of putting together massive amounts of information, organizing what was crucial and what was not, in such a short time.

The Judge was pulled into several top-level meetings to assess what was going on in Eastern Europe, and while I was having lunch at my desk Murphy called to give me an update. He and his team had Tommy learning some self-defense martial arts, and the basics of how to take a computer apart and put it back together again.

"Is this phone secure?" Murphy asked.

"As secure as they get," I said.

"He's a natural," Murphy said. "He's got the eye for it, and the memory. I think we'll be able to pull this one off. He'll know enough about everything to do a passing imitation of James Bond. And about our little fishing expedition . . . ?"

"Where James Bond is the bait?" I asked.

"That's the one," Murphy said. "We're all set. Elaborate details are all worked out."

"All right," I remember saying, my mind wandering back to the bulging files on Rebecca and Tommy. On the covers of the files John X had written notes showing an intimate knowledge of Rebecca's file and her agency biography. It was hard to figure out from John X's scribbled notes what he was looking for, but I got the distinct impression that, whatever it was, he was close to finding it.

At 3:35 the Judge burst into my new/old office and shouted, "Grab your jacket! We're going downtown. We are in big, big trouble."

The rest of John X's day can easily be pieced together. He left the HQ without a wave to Charlie or the other guards, and drove into Washington to his bank. He had his safe deposit box opened and took out an unmarked, loaded service revolver, wrapped in a North Vietnamese flag, and his life insurance policy. He put the revolver and the flag in his briefcase and read the policy carefully in one of the little booths the bank provides for its customers. He underlined the provisions that detailed the exclusions for acts of war, and he noted in a margin that his insurance agent had assured him that there were no other exclusions. He put the policy back in the box, put the box away, and asked a bank clerk for pen and paper. He wrote a letter and addressed it to the Judge at HQ. He put a stamp on it and stared at it for a long time. He withdrew three thousand dollars in one-hundred-dollar bills from his family's savings account, forgot to get change for the pay phone, and dropped the letter to the Judge in the mailbox as he left the bank.

The bank's security cameras recorded his every move.

He stopped at a phone booth somewhere on the same street as the bank, and using his phone credit card, called a D.C. drug dealer whom he had known in Vietnam and had developed into an informant for the organization. After five or six more calls, probably to people his informant told him to call, he scribbled an address on the back of his hand and hailed a taxi. What John X wanted was not easy to find, but he knew the people who knew the people who could get you whatever you wanted if you had the money to pay for it.

Madam San's Oriental Massage Parlor was over a pawnshop. She had gotten a call, she told us later, from a friend who said that John X was a special guest and had money to spend. Madam San was fifty-six and tired of her business, so she was later very willing to talk. She named an outlandish price for what John X wanted, and he agreed to pay it. She said she would need about two hours to procure all the necessary elements, and he said that was fine. It was ten in the morning. John X disappeared for two hours and fifteen minutes.

That afternoon Madam San sat in a brightly lit police interrogation room and smiled at the Judge and me, frowning at the bevy of uniformed cops who crowded around us. The Judge had insisted that she be read her rights again and had ordered a soda for her, so she thought he must be on her side.

"You suits," she said, referring to the Judge and me. "You suits understand. These coppers don't. We have often 'Nam vets who want things. Things they remember. Good trade for us. And legal, yes? My brother-in-law says very legal. I really shouldn't talk without my brother-in-law."

"Is your brother-in-law a lawyer?" I asked.

"No," she said, smiling brightly. "He undertaker."

"Look," the Judge grumbled, turning to the oldest and least hulking of the policemen, "where the hell is that AUSA? I want this woman granted immunity and I want her talking now. Do you understand? I need a prosecutor and I need some action right now."

"I'll go call him again," I said, getting up as the Judge continued yelling. Apparently I was going to have to use Carolyn's name to get the government moving.

As the Judge yelled, the door swung open and an Assistant United States Attorney for the District of Columbia, dressed impeccably just in case there were TV cameras available for him to give a statement to, strode into the room in a wave of expensive cologne. Within twenty minutes Madam San had immunity and was sitting upstairs in a comfortable office with a court reporter, telling her sordid tale.

John X had paid twenty-five hundred dollars for a dark room with a Thai stick burning in it and a dirty mattress on the floor. He covered the mattress with the torn red flag he brought with him. Madam San had found the youngest female Vietnamese prostitute in Washington, where there were many, and had her waiting in the room when John X arrived. John X had also requested, and Madam San had delivered, a Vietnamese teenage boy and a black teenage weightlifter.

I was at first repulsed and overcome by a sense of moral outrage that one of our own had stooped this low, but I lost my judgmental rage as Madam San described the pathetic reenactment of something he must have seen or participated in when he was in Vietnam. He had lost all hope, and there was only one thing he had left to do. One wrong to right. One high to relive.

Madam San described in painful detail how John X gave the boys orders to hold the girl down. After the two boys had done every act imaginable to the young woman, John X told her to ask, to beg, for more. Then Madam San heard John X order them to talk to him in Vietnamese.

I wonder still sometimes, late at night, when I remember Madam San's clipped English words that so vividly described this scene, what went on in John X's head during those few minutes of intense sensual reaction. When every sense was so assaulted, so overcome by the tidal wave of the fulfillment of fantasy and the gritty rope-tight tension of reality, what did he think? Was it all worthwhile? Was this the summation of his life? Was this the last thing he wanted to accomplish? Did the image of his children, in Little League outfits or new Easter suits, flash before his eyes?

I doubt it. Or at least I hope not. The only explanation for his behavior is that he was lost in replaying some scene that he was in in Saigon, or some other nameless city in that country too hot for civilization as we know it. The only way I can justify his actions are as those of a man who had decided that he could not live with himself because he had failed the country he had sworn to protect. Failed it not for money or fame or promotion, but for sex with a woman he then believed was a foreign agent. He, too, did it for love.

Madam San told us that John X pulled the gun out of his briefcase. "He called them names," Madam San said finally, breaking into a sweat herself as she talked to us. "Names that were not their names. He called the girl Blossom. He yelled at the boy, who he called Charlie, for raping her. He said Charlie gonna die for raping his girl. Charlie gonna die."

When the police got there the two boys had left but the crack-dazed girl still sat on the bed, wrapped in the dirty flag, John X's dried blood on her neck and in her hair. John X's body lay on the floor, his eyes staring straight into the lens of the Polaroid the homicide detectives used when they got to the scene. They found his National Security Agency ID in his wallet and called HQ. "In the middle of it all," the young woman said with a shiver, "when he was shouting and stuff, he just put the gun in his mouth and, you know, just did it. He just did it."

Since he paid cash, I guessed that he must have stopped at his bank, and the personnel people at HQ got us the name and number of the bank in five minutes. While Madam San was telling her story the FBI reviewed the bank's surveillance video tapes, found John X on them, and got a postal inspector to open the mailbox twenty minutes before the evening mail was to be picked up. They fingerprinted the letter in a van as they drove down to the police station and then reluctantly handed it over to the Judge to open. He read it quickly and said, "Oh God," then handed it to me. I read it slowly, still sitting in the room with Madam San, who was busy perfecting her rouge. It was written quickly but without mistakes, the last written words of a man who had analyzed and organized information for a living.

Dear Judge,

I'm not sure how to tell this all to you, so I guess I'll skip all the details and get to the point. You know I was involved with Rebecca. I was sleeping with her—or had been sleeping with her—off and on for the past six or seven years. No big deal. It happens all the time, right? But I've got to admit, I went too far. Rebecca needed some info for a project she was working on and I got it for her. Then there was another project. Then another.

No big deal. No information she probably shouldn't have had. Hell, she had Top Secret clearance, right? But she just didn't want to go through all the red tape. She didn't want to hassle with the bureaucracy. I understood that, hell we all hate the bureaucrats we are afraid of becoming ourself, so I helped her. Got her stuff. Put her in touch with people, or pretended I needed the information for my own research. I've been kicking myself about it since I found out that she may have jumped ship. But today I found out—what? How to describe it? I want this to sound important, dramatic, worth giving up your life for, but when I write it out it just sounds stupid. So unbelievably stupid.

I was the research assistant on the Mike Mechanic project. Defense brought me in without you even knowing about it. They needed an analyst with missile background, which I had from 'Nam, and they wanted as few people in on the project as possible. I had been military intelligence so the brass thought I'd be okay. The project was to catalogue the mechanical schedule for maintenance and replacement computer parts, and the location so you could find the damn things to fix them, for every B, E, and H class nuclear missile on the continent. In other words, one damn list of the whole fucking ball game.

It was stupid, but the cost cutters needed efficiency reports, so Langley and military intelligence thought this was the way to do it, as long as there was only one list and only a small group of people knew that the damn list existed. It was coded with a Byeman clearance for those who were on the mechanical support end, and for people who had designed and built the system, a Tango Kilo clearance for people who needed to know about the targets. Nobody who had TK had Byeman, so that the system could never be totally compromised.

It just so happens Rebecca had TK clearance. You can guess the rest. I'm not sure I can bring myself to explain all the justifications, all the reasoning, the foolish thoughts I used to justify my actions. But I gave the Byeman computer code to her so she could scan the thing. Just scan it to look for one location she needed, that was all. She was to use her own password and make no copies. The password she made up was "Key West," and seven weeks later I got a call that somewhere a break in the system had occurred and I was instructed to destroy all records and told that my password would be eliminated. Happens all the time, right? There's some glitch so they clear the system. I didn't think a thing of it until today, when you told me that she, or her family, had something to sell in Key West.

Rebecca won't be in Key West is my guess, Judge. My guess is that she is on her pretty little way to Moscow. Probably telling Gorby the story of the dumb hick who helped her get what she needed. I have no idea how she got a copy with the access I gave her, and I don't know anything about launch codes, but one thing I have learned this week is not to underestimate her. She's got it, Judge. Somehow I know it.

So what's left for me? Nobody is going to believe that I didn't help her steal it. Hell, I did help her steal it. All for a touch of that red hair. Damn. Damn. Damn.

It doesn't matter if you believe me or not. It doesn't matter if you think I'm some part of the setup or not. I don't give a damn anymore. I'm tired of the whole damn thing. The whole two lives. Three lives. Four lives. Hell, I've lost track of how many I've been leading. My job. My supposed job that even my mother thinks I have. The Mike Mechanic job that even my boss doesn't know I have. My wife wants a divorce because I'm never home. My mistress runs off with a new college kid. My oldest kid is picked up for drunk driving. I'm broke. And all I have are the memories of things that I could have done right. Things I could have stopped, but instead let go on and joined in.

I joined in this crime, all right. I joined in on helping Rebecca rip off my country when I could have stopped it if I had just thought for one second. I could have stopped these guys from raping a Vietnamese chick years ago, but instead I just joined in. I followed the gang leader and had the time of my life. Hell, I still remember it twenty years later like it was yesterday. And Rebecca reminded me of it too. The forbidden thrill. That's what you crave when you become a bureaucrat. The forbidden, illegal, immoral thrill.

I could have stopped it, Judge. But I was enjoying it all too much. Rebecca beat me, or maybe I beat myself. But I know she has it. The most important bits of information the goddamn government probably has. And she probably has it all in one nice, neat little package, gift-wrapped by stupid me. Unconscious coconspirator. It has a nice ring to it, doesn't it? Unconscious coconspirator. A nice put-him-in-jail-for-life ring to it.

I'm sorry. Tell everyone I'm sorry. Really, really sorry.

An agent to the end, he signed the letter with his code name: "Blue Marlin Double O."

Blue Marlin Double O, diving deep and going out to sea. Rushing into the dark, cool depths of oblivion. There ought to be a memorial for men like John X. Men who misjudge the severity of their deeds, and punish themselves harder than any of us would punish them. But men who believe they have done wrong will always find a way to punish themselves. That's my theory, articulated on the late afternoon of a fellow agent's death. Theory number what I do not know. That's my answer to the question that nobody asked. He did it because he had to.

27.

THE FOURTH DISCIPLE was code-named Andrew.

It was near midnight on the far eastern Mediterranean coast where the tall Israeli resort hotels stood sentinel along the wide white sand beach. They stood there silently, three-fourths empty since the terrorism escalated a decade ago, on the beautiful beach that curved around the blue of the sea like a woman's pale thigh wrapped around a wavy sheet. It created a romantic scene, but for the rows of concertina wire that separated the hotels from the sea and the guard towers that separated the resorts from the well-paved roads that came from the cities invisible beyond the deserted desert horizon.

The three branches of Israeli intelligence—the Mossad, which handled the external spying; the Shin Bet, which handled domestic security; and the Aman, which handled military intelligence—had been on alert every day for the last seven years. But they had beefed up their patrols along this section of coastline after a Mossad agent had disappeared at the Gush Katrif hotel five days ago. The Shin Bet and the Mossad had searched the hotel and found nothing. Two days ago a high-powered launch had tried to land a group of a dozen alleged Palestinian terrorists a mile north of this section of beach, but the Aman had got wind of their plan to move down the beach and bomb the hotels and had a group of Israeli sharpshooters waiting for them when they stepped onto the sand.

Five minutes after midnight a woman wearing a full, flowing silk bathrobe wandered down from the Gush Katrif's big fenced-in pool and stood staring out over the barbed wire at the dark sea. One of the tower guards noted her presence and radioed for a guard with a leashed German shepherd to walk her way and gently warn her of the dangers of being that close to the wire late at night. When the guard got to the spot where she was reported to be, he couldn't find anything, so he wandered off to check the perimeter of the walled resort.

The woman's long silk robe was wadded up in a tight ball at the base of a small palm two feet from where the guard and dog stood.

In a skin-tight French bathing suit that showed off her muscular curves, she slipped under the first strands of wire and slithered along the sand, dragging a rubber waterproof satchel, to the gate that had been left open for her. In a pile of sand outside the gate was buried a plastic bag with a radio, wire clippers, and a high-powered pistol with a silencer. She pushed the transmit button of the radio four times without saying anything. She pressed the radio against her ear and heard four short bursts of static in return. She crawled the forty feet to the next set of concertina wire and snipped a hole big enough for her to struggle through, tearing her bathing suit in two places. The silver wire gleamed in the moonlight, which cast a ghostly glow on the deserted hills of white sand. The sea rolled a night yawn as the wind picked up and threw it against the land.

Once she was through the wire she darted between the tall piles of sand, stopping every twenty feet to look around and listen for any suspicious sounds. As she neared the beach she counted the sand piles that stretched away from a mound of rocks that was once the end of the resort's section of beach. She went straight to the ninth sand pile and dug with her hands until she pulled out a wet suit, a mask, and flippers. She hurriedly put them on, silently cursing the painful scraping of the sand that got inside the suit. When she was dressed, the mask on her head, flippers in one hand and the rubber satchel strapped to her back, she pushed the send signal on the radio six times. After ten seconds the radio answered with three short bursts of static.

She buried the radio and the pistol in the sand and stared out into the dark rough water. She could see the faint lights of the patrol boats that slowly coasted up and down the beach, flicking on their bright halogen lights every five minutes to scan the area. There were barracuda and jellyfish in the water, and long strands of seaweed that could tangle your legs and drag you down. If you didn't swim hard and strong the waves would knock you into the razor-sharp coral and you would look as though you had been run over by a boat propeller.

After she had counted to one hundred she took one last, long, deep breath of the tart sea air and dashed to the cold black water. As soon as it reached her knees she lay down in it and, keeping her face and mask half submerged, crawled out to deeper water. The sealed rubber satchel acted like a life vest and kept her on top of the tall waves, but the undertow was strong and pulled her out and under unless she fought hard to stay on top of the rolling waves. Forty feet from shore the hand she reached out in front of her to stroke felt something slick and slimy, like ice-cold flesh. She flinched in the water, filling her mask with fog and her lungs with salt water. She dog-paddled backward and waited for something to attack her, and when it did not she cleared her mask and resumed moving straight out from the beach. Her left knee hit a tall ridge of coral, and she felt the cut in her knee and then the sting of salt water in it.

Two hundred feet from shore she began to swim in a large circle, riding the wide gullies of the rolling waves, waiting for someone to find her in the black sea on a dark night. After ten minutes she got tired and began to measure whether she had enough strength to get back to the beach. She told herself she could do one more large circle, and as she came around and was facing the beach again she saw the water part in a straight line behind the jet tow.

A man whose name she did not know was dressed in a full wet suit and moving through the waves quickly, his arms reaching down and holding on to the handlebars of a turbo-engine jet tow that rode one foot below the water and could pull two people at fifteen miles an hour. He almost ran right into her, halting at the last minute and then pulling her over to the jet tow.

They whispered a few words in English, and then he strapped a long snorkel onto her mask and they both grabbed the jet tow and let it pull them across the surface of the sea, the water parting away from their twin wakes. Four hundred feet out a searchlight suddenly shot in their direction, missing them by twenty feet. The man cut the engine on the tow, and they both settled on its underwater deck, only the tips of their snorkels peeking out above the waves.

The patrol boat passed by them quietly, its bright searchlight flashing on one more time as they scanned the beach, and when she came up to the surface she could hear the soldiers on board laughing at some joke she would never know.

He started the jet tow and pushed it up to high speed. She clung to the rings on the machine's back as the waves hit her hard in the mask and filled her snorkel with salt water. Then suddenly they saw a searchlight blink on, flooding a square in front of them with light. He cut the engine, but they still coasted toward the patch of light, both of them pulling up on the jet tow to slow it down. They spilled into the light, amid the shouts of the soldiers on the boat, who must have heard their engine start back up, and he gunned the jet tow back in the other direction, nearly jerking her arms out of their sockets. The searchlight dashed across the waves, jerking from black spot to black spot looking for them, but he serpentined the jet tow out of the searchlight's reach.

Then they saw the patrol boat right in front of them, the light behind them corralling them into gunshot of the boat. She braced herself for the inevitable shots, but he reached down and flipped up a panel on the jet tow. She watched the low-wattage light blink on the panel and his black-gloved hands push a red button three times.

She knew that he was calling for help, since they must be close to the boat that was going to pick them up, but she didn't see how that would get them out of this trap. He pulled the jet tow up near the surface of the water, slowing it down and exposing them as they crawled toward the patrol boat.

He pushed the mouthpiece of the snorkel out of his mouth and told her to let go of the jet tow's handlebars. She pushed the cold rubber of her snorkel out of her mouth and asked, "What are you going to do?" "Blow it out of the water," he said. He aimed the jet tow at the midsection of the looming patrol boat and flipped all the switches on the panel. The jet tow raced to its full speed, holding a straight course like a torpedo searching for its target.

By the time the sailors on board saw the jet tow streaking across the water in their direction, they were able to get off one round of machine-gun fire before it hit the side of their ship and exploded, blowing the midsection of the patrol boat out of the water and into two flaming parts. She watched with horror as the halves of the boat rose up to meet each other like an opening drawbridge and then collapsed into the flame-covered sea. The sailors were catapulted out into the water, and bits of fiery metal and bloody flesh rained down on the two of them as they dived under the water to avoid the falling objects.

A small boat edged between the burning pieces of the patrol boat that floated around them like icebergs of fire, two men leaning over its low bow and staring into the water. The flames were reflected and multiplied on the surface of the oily sea, so there was an unearthly look to the two swimmers as they made their way to the boat in their black wet suits, masks, and snorkels. They were hauled over its side, and the small boat roared off into the sea, disappearing into the darkness as dozens of patrol boats burst onto the scene and fighter helicopters hovered above, scattering the water and coating the bobbing boats with their bright white moving lights.

When they found the bathrobe the next morning, the fingerprint experts at the Shin Bet lab found two of the female Mossad agent's fingerprints on the inner edge of the pocket lining. After the two sailors who survived the explosion of the patrol boat described what the jet tow looked and sounded like, they knew that she had got away. Andrew had got away with her satchel of stolen gifts.

When the three intelligence chiefs met that morning in the opulent secret offices of the Mossad, which in an act of paranoid machismo the Likud Shin Bet had bugged after the Jonathan Pollard affair, the head of Aman argued that they should call the Israeli defense minister immediately, the tape Shin Bet later sent us showed. The Likud Shin Bet chief thought they should go directly to the prime minister; the political split between Labor and Likud had given the defense minister post to Labor and the prime minister to Likud. The director of Mossad was quiet while the other two hurled insults at each other, and then with one swift kick he knocked over the antique coffee table between them, spewing hot coffee across the Persian rug and shattering the delicate porcelain cups against the far wall. The two men sat stunned for a second and watched a tear roll down the scarred face of the ageless director of Mossad.

"I must resign," he offered, his voice choking. "I have failed my country. I have failed my family."

"No, Yair, you exaggerate," the Shin Bet chief said quickly, reaching to pick up a coffee cup.

"I wish," the director of Mossad and decorated hero of four wars said. "But you have to understand that Andrew has everything. Our missile locations. Our intelligence on Libya, Iraq, Iran, Syria. She knows how Gadhafi folds his damn underwear. She knows your private phone number. She could call the phone by Ariel Sharon's bed, if she wanted to, and tell him exactly where each nuclear missile is located today. She has everything and . . . and I am, what? I am nothing."

"It's worse than that," the head of Aman suggested, refusing to comfort the old man. "There was a communication this morning from one of our friends in Iran. He says the word is out that the Soviets have been offered a package that contains all of the American nuclear launch codes."

"Impossible," the Shin Bet chief said. "There is no way . . . it is not possible to have that information in one place."

"It's possible," the distraught director said. The three men looked at each other closely, communicating without words.

"Did we have it?" the Shin Bet chief asked quietly, either unaware or forgetting that the room was bugged.

"Maybe," the director admitted.

"Oh God," the Shin Bet chief said. "Oh my God."

"Is it possible that Andrew had access or could have had access to that information?" the head of Aman asked.

"Maybe," the director said again, putting his face in his hands.

"I don't believe it," the Shin Bet chief said. "It can't be for sale. She would never sell it."

"It is for sale, transferred by satellite. That is why the Soviets are waiting on moving in Eastern Europe. If they move after they have the American information then the Americans will have to back down."

"We'll catch her," the Shin Bet chief nearly shouted, visibly shaken.

"No you won't," the director said, standing up. "You go tell whoever you want. I will call the Americans. They must know."

"That's absurd," the head of Aman said. "Sit down. We'll tell our own people first. All of them. Then we'll figure out what to do. This may avert an escalation in East Germany. Plus, my friend, the Americans must not know we have this information."

"I'm going to call the Americans so they can join the search," the director of Mossad stated, as calmly as he could. "I'll let my friends know and—"

The head of Aman slipped his revolver out of his jacket and aimed it at his friend of thirty years. "Sit down," he ordered. "You are overcome with emotion. This is a crisis, and we must keep our heads cool. What we do now may determine the future of our country."

The two old warriors stared at each other as the grandfather clock behind them loudly ticked away the seconds. "There would be an inquiry if you shoot me," the director of Mossad said, without taking his eyes off the gun.

"There would be an inquiry if you call," the head of Aman suggested.

The director of Mossad sighed heavily, his breath puffing like the muffled blast of a silencer, and sat back down. They talked for an hour, and when the director went down the hall to the restroom he slid into an associate's office, locked the door behind him, and tried to call the Judge.

28.

I WENT BACK to HQ after our two-hour session with Madam San and went straight to John X's office, while the Judge drove out to Alexandria to tell John's wife what had happened. He called on his car phone to tell me that after he spoke to John's wife he was going straight to Langley to find out what he could about the Mike the Mechanic project.

"If what he wrote in that letter is true," I said, speaking into the receiver that John had spoken into for years—the phone he had used to call Rebecca, to call his wife, to do the business that led to his death—"then I think you ought to demand a meeting of the CIA, Military Intelligence, us, and maybe even State first thing tomorrow."

"Are you sure we want to do that?" the Judge asked. "Can we trust them? If she really has got the dope on this project she didn't do it alone. She must have had inside help. Let's stick to our plan."

"We've got to talk to someone. We need more help. This is too big to run off the books."

"Why?" the Judge asked. "If it's a question of money, don't worry about it. I'll get Carolyn reimbursed. If it's a question of statutory authority, break the law. These are special circumstances. The whole damn world is in an uproar. This stuff could be the straw that breaks the camel's back."

"We can't just shoot from the hip," I said slowly, not sure how he felt. "We can't just play cowboys and Indians with something this big. We need some authority. This is a government, not a rodeo."

"I'll get it, then," he said. "I'll get it from the top. And if I can't, then you or Carolyn probably can. Remember those old-school ties."

"He'd want to keep plausible deniability. The president would have to stop the project if we told him about it. And I don't even know how I'd explain it to him at this point. I'm not even sure what we're looking for."

"It's a ball buster," the Judge said. "It's the ultimate metaphysical spy problem—someone is guilty of something, we just don't know what yet."

His last sentence sent me reeling for a moment. Someone was definitely guilty of something, we just didn't know what yet. She might be selling state secrets. She might be trying to corrupt a new recruit. She might be on her way to Moscow. Whatever it was, she was up to no good. With his usual Texas twang and knack for shoveling off the unnecessary crap, the Judge had got it right again.

Someone is guilty of *something*, we just don't know *what* yet.

"This thing still stinks," the Judge complained. "There is something rotten here, and I'm going to find it. So we'd better play this close to the vest. Let's keep the letter and the reason for John's quick exit to ourselves, and let's still keep the bait-and-catch plan to ourselves. We can't hide John's death, but we need to keep the details quiet. I know we've got a damn mole somewhere, and I'm gonna find him."

After the Judge hung up he called Paul, the deputy dernza, and told him that I was now going to head up the project. He told Paul that he would not be needed any longer on the project; in fact, the Judge might close it down, not because of John X's death, but because of what he had learned from the secretary of state. Paul told me later he didn't buy the story, but he knew enough to not ask any questions.

I did realize on the way to John X's office that, other than the Judge and I, John X had been the only person in the organization who might have even guessed that we had Tommy. John X was also the only person who had known about Tommy's bugged belt I thought. I guessed that some techy had designed and outfitted it, but it was not likely that the techy would know for whom it was intended, or whether it had worked. Now, I believed, only I knew, and I planned to keep it that way.

The Judge sent two young agents to John X's office to help me investigate, but I couldn't tell them what I was looking for, so they mostly sat in the corners and read through unmarked files and told me what was in them. They thought I wasn't telling them what I was looking for because it was too secret, but the truth was that I didn't know. I was just trying to understand what had happened.

There was nothing in any of his files about our picking up Tommy at the farm. For all anyone knew, Tommy was dead, with Rebecca, or in the hands of the Colombians. There was no evidence in John X's office that Tommy was training at my wife's house. There was no evidence of the belt or the black box.

I was ashamed that only hours after a man committed suicide I was looking for evidence that he had lied to me, that he had set us up with his suicide note and actually killed himself for some other reason. I was looking for something that would explain why he did it that was different from what he told us. Even in committing the ultimate act John X had not freed himself of our suspicions; rather, he had fed them. The psychological weaknesses that led him to kill himself might have led him to misperceive or misconstrue Rebecca's actions. His weakness for Rebecca might have led him to lie to us even with his death.

Then I noticed his old, bulky briefcase, wedged between his desk and the wall. I opened it nonchalantly while the two men went through files. Its contents set me to thinking about the nature of our business. How suspicious we must always be. How we must be willing to take risks, if only to protect ourselves.

When your life is devoted to creating fictions and unraveling fictions, there is no baseline for what you assume to be true. Everything must be examined. Everything must be assumed to be false until it is proven true. This is the downside analysis that an intelligence officer must play with every day. Take nothing for granted. Take no prisoners of society's assumptions. Be no prisoner of the assumed reality.

It was not clear that John X had remembered those axioms of spycraft. His emotions got the best of him, just as they occasionally do to us all, and he made intellectual jumps of faith that led him to conclusions that might not have been true. He jumped to the conclusion that Rebecca had the top-secret information that he knew existed. He jumped to the conclusion that she was going to take it to the Soviets. Neither of which we knew to be true. He had breached the rule of need-to-know, allowing a Tango Kilo–cleared woman to use his Byeman code, and, ironically, it was that code that led to his exit. Bye man. Bye, John X.

But I had to admit, I thought as I ruffled through old dusty files, sitting at the desk chair where he had sat for years, staring out the window at the park he had looked at for years, and listening to the tick-tock of the old clock on his bookcase that he had listened to for years, that his hunches about Rebecca had been correct so far. He had done things that he should not have done, and they had paid off. He must have felt that he was enough attuned to Rebecca that he knew that this was what she had done and would do. He must have been confident enough that the crime had been committed to pass judgment on himself and inflict the punishment he thought appropriate. He must have decided that he could rely on his emotions more than on his logical, intellectual capabilities—that he had figured out the answer to the code to life.

I had thought that too, as I've told you. I had broken the rules to get closer to the woman I loved. But in the end I married the woman my emotions riveted me on, and recognized that the encrypted message of the meaning of the strange twists that fate makes in our lives was beyond my ability to break. I lucked out and got what I really wanted, and she got what she really wanted, without understanding why we were so fortunate. I remember that I breathed in heavily, thinking of John X and Rebecca and me and Carolyn. I saw the two young agents look up from their reading and study my tired, reddened cheeks.

"You better get home and get some sleep," one of them said to me, with the same cadence in his voice the Judge had used when he told John X to go home.

"Yes," I said, thinking of my home, my wife, my warm and generous life. I would go home and she would be there, tired from a hard day but gracious, caring, and tough where I am weak. I would kiss her and not think of shooting myself for all my sins. I would kiss her and forget about all the mistakes I had made, all the time I had lost, all the opportunities I had missed. I would live another long day, and strive not for the intensity of passion that John X had wanted at the end, but for the strength and continuity of understanding that old love brings when it does not end.

So many of you, my fellow spies, sinned for and with Rebecca, but you survived. So many of you made mistakes but prospered. Maybe John X, in his warped messianic way, believed he was dying for all of us. Maybe John X thought he had to do this because of all the information you fed Rebecca over those years. Maybe John X didn't think at all. Maybe John X just felt, and feeling too strongly drove him to want to be numb. To crave not feeling anymore.

"Yes," I said again to the staring organization boys, my eyes wandering out the window to the park. Had the two of them, Rebecca and John X, met there, under the towering leafy umbrellas of the red maples, on a park bench where they wouldn't be overheard? Had they met there to exchange, not words of treason, but words of love? It did not matter, I thought, leaving John X's favorite leather chair with his old briefcase in my hand. They were one and the same—words of love, words of treason. They were both a betrayal that John X could not in the end live with or without. He knew someone was guilty, and he guessed who and of what. I would have to do the same.

"Yes, it's time to go home," I mumbled, getting up and walking out the door with the battered briefcase. "I'll see you guys tomorrow."

In the bag were a spare black metal box, an antenna, and a rolled-up leather belt.

FOUR

THE DENIAL FORETOLD

"You will all lose faith, for the scripture says: I shall strike the shepherd and the sheep will be scattered, however after my resurrection I shall go before you to Galilee." Peter said, "Even if all lose faith, I will not."

—Mark 14:26

29.

THE FIFTH DISCIPLE was code-named Philip.

The air hung heavily over the slowly swirling dust on the dirt road that weaved around and over the hills of northern Transylvania. There was little traffic on the road: two canvas-covered Gypsy wagons going in opposite directions, each pulled by a stocky horse with tufts of dirty hair hanging over its heavy hooves. The wagons were painted with sun-bleached pale colors from another, happier and freer time, and the canvas tops had the look of an old master never quite finished, but rolled up and stored in the hayloft of some decaying barn.

The road was a strip of patched macadam that bisected the valley laced with cattle pasture and then climbed slowly through giant, ancient trees to the Hungarian border, only a mile away. As the two wagons drew abreast, the driver heading toward the border lifted his hat and waved, while his passenger, sitting next to him, talked on, oblivious to their beautiful surroundings. The second driver had stretched out and gone to sleep while his horses plodded on home the way they had gone for all their lives, the reins clasped loosely in his folded hands, which sat like hood ornaments on his ample paunch.

When the two wagons had passed each other, the canvas back of the sleeping man's wagon was drawn open, and a young man clutching a metal suitcase with a tape recorder in it and carrying a machine gun in his other hand climbed out and silently ran up to the other wagon and climbed into its closed back. The two men in front went on talking, their voices low and relaxed in the reddening evening light. Both were dressed in heavy burlap and cotton clothes that looked as if they had been sewn by hand by a farm wife who was farsighted and worked only at night, but they spoke in hushed accented English.

"You see," the passenger said after the boy in the back silently turned on the tape recorder, so that they could add blackmail to their arsenal of persuasive tools, "computers will never think, because the laws of nature do not allow it."

"Doesn't that depend on how you define 'think'?" the driver asked, slapping the reins on the horses' rumps and looking at his watch.

"Maybe thinking is more than consciousness," the passenger replied, as if admitting something. "But it must start there. And if you start with consciousness then you begin with something that computers can never obtain. The human mind can reach insights that are forever inaccessible to computers, because the human mind does not depend on algorithms or any other set of rules to solve problems. Gödel showed that much, you have to admit. In any mathematical system there must be certain propositions that are obviously true but that can never be proved within the four walls of the mathematical system. Am I making any sense to you?"

"Yes," the driver said. "My father was a physicist and talked at the dinner table about fractal geometry, quantum physics—and baseball."

"I would like to see a baseball game," the passenger said with a smile. "Now there is a game of rules. A game of numbers and their calculations. Humans imitating computers, yes? Pretending that they can make digital calculations out of the pure talent of some boy swinging a bat at the precise right time and precise right speed that can only come from intuitive feel."

The driver pulled the reins to the left and took the horses off the road and down a dirt path into the heavy woods at the edge of the pastureland. They were immediately enveloped by the overhanging branches, as if they were lumbering down a tunnel toward some other world.

"Where are we going?" the passenger asked, cleaning his round eyeglasses with a monogrammed handkerchief he had pulled out from under the rough peasant clothes that he obviously was not used to wearing. "Is this where we meet our contact?"

"Professor," the driver said, turning and pulling open the canvas flap behind them to show the young man with his machine gun pointed at them, "we are going to America."

"What?" he asked, quickly putting on his glasses. He looked from the boy to his friend driving the wagon, and a wave of recognition washed over his eyes. "I was supposed to be paid. I risked my life to get you that information, and you promised to pay me another installment. My family, my wife is counting on that money. I demand to be paid."

"I thank you," the driver said, pulling out a pistol and holding on to it loosely as he spoke. "We thank you, for all your help. We could not have done it without you. But we can't leave you here and risk that you might talk. Many people would be in danger. Our family might be hurt. So we have only two choices: kill you or take you with us. Frankly, killing you would be much easier. We could leave you here with a bullet in your head, and they wouldn't find you for weeks, maybe months. But I have arranged for you to go with me. You can help explain the information. You can put it all back together again, since I know that you scrambled it."

The professor looked at the man who sat right next to him and had just offered to kill him. He breathed heavily and said, "You're right. It is scrambled, just in case you tried to pull a trick like this. You can't kill me, and I refuse to go with you. I have a wife and two sons. This is my adopted country, and I plan on staying here."

"But we can kill you," the driver reminded him, clutching the pistol firmly. "Someone in the West will be sophisticated enough to figure out the scramble program. It might take them time, which we would rather not spend, but they would figure it out. And if we let you go you just might go and tell on us to your friends in management of the organization. A sudden wave of patriotism might sweep over you, and then where are we? In jail. In our coffins. No, Professor, you are going with us or we are going to kill you."

As he spoke his last sentence the wagon pulled into a grassy clearing where a dozen armed men stood around a small black plane. Some of the men were pulling off the wings leafy branches that had been propped against it to hide it from the air, and others were peering at maps and punching a calculator. They all stopped for a moment when the wagon pulled in, and then they hurriedly went back to work.

"Your choice," the driver said. "I promise you we will try to get your wife and children out. If you don't go then they will never get out. And if the West gets this information they will have all the bargaining chips. They will be able to ask for anything they want. I promise you that they will ask for your family."

"There must be some other way," the professor suggested.

"There isn't," the driver said.

The professor's hand trembled, and a tear came to his eye as he looked down at his lap. "You have an expression," he offered. " 'When you play with fire, you get burned.' I guess I made my choice long ago, when I agreed to help you. You know I didn't do it for the money. A man like me doesn't sell himself so cheaply. I did it for . . . for what? For the right of it. For the correctness of your cause. I made my choice, and I must sacrifice either my life or my family."

He paused and looked back at the young blond man he had never met who sat behind him with his finger on the trigger of the bulky black gun. "What is your name?" he asked the boy in the deep accented tones of their native language.

The teenager looked at the driver, who nodded, and he said quietly, "Turin."

"Would you shoot me, Turin?" the professor asked. "Would you kill me? Shoot me in the back if I tried to jump from this seat?"

The boy did not answer, his eyes moving from the driver to the professor with the quickness of a young fox.

"I see that you would," the professor said. "I can see it in the new steel in your eyes, my son. New steel. Still hot from the forge. You love your country and hate your government. I see it. It is the ones like you, like my own son, who will change this place soon. Ones like you are growing in numbers. The inevitable product of this society. A master race, yes? We created them, and they discovered they didn't like their masters."

The professor turned back to the driver and said in English, his voice calm and quiet, as if he were giving a funeral oration, "I am afraid to die. I am a coward, so I will go with you and let your people pretend I am a hero. A brave man who risked his life for your democracy. Your McDonald's and Pepsi. I will leave my family that I love, that I live for, for your television and designer jeans."

The driver patted the professor on the knee, and they stared at each other for a long time, measuring each other's fortitude and willingness to keep his word. The driver liked what he saw and said, "Good. But you must be brave to get out of here. Getting out of here is the hard part. This plane goes up like a rocket, but it flies forward more like an ostrich. She's not fast, but she's hard to detect."

The other men strapped the driver and the professor into the small black bird, which was an experimental version of a stealth Osprey that had disposable rocket launchers mounted under two turboprop jet propellers. The stolen plane had been dropped by a rented cargo plane, and it had virtually glided the four hundred miles from the Austrian-Hungarian border the night before, eluding radar by flying so low that its fat belly brushed the tops of the fir trees. Its pilot had landed it on the road at night, the lights of a dozen kerosene lanterns his only guide, and they had dragged it into this clearing and hidden it carefully from the search planes they knew would come. It was impossible to go all the way across Hungary without being picked up, but once over it was easy to hide the plane as long as you were hiding it in a place where it could not take off. When the search planes did not find anything they went back to their bases and waited for future meaningless and always pointless searches for spy planes they did not really believe existed, but rather were just the fiction of the Communist party bosses, who wanted to keep them on their toes.

The pilot gave the driver, who was now the bird's pilot, some last-minute instructions. As a bright red sunset stroked the hills around them awake, the rocket launchers burst into flame and shot the fat little plane straight up five hundred feet, with enough velocity that the professor knocked his head on the cockpit cover, which gave him a stinging headache for the next three hours of tense flying, over and around the mountains that formed the Iron Curtain. They trimmed treetops and veered around the stiff faces of the growing peaks, but even with the driver's expert flying and the sophisticated antiradar equipment on the stolen plane, they were picked up seventy miles from the border, and Hungarian Tiger jets scrambled on the ground to get up to meet them.

Austrian defense air traffic control saw the Hungarian movement and radioed the American Air Force base on the German border, which had two F-16s in the air within minutes after the Hungarian Tigers cut through the clouds. The games had begun.

The driver saw the Tigers go up on the Osprey's radar-detection scanner, and he went down fifty feet, until he was creating a wind that could be felt by the farmhouses he shot past. He just had to evade them for twenty minutes, he thought. Maybe only fifteen and they would be over the border. Then he cursed as he saw the F-16s dash toward the border, because he would have to evade them too, in their own stolen aircraft, once he got across.

A Tiger sneaked up on his back, and the driver heard the accented voices commanding him over every clear line to identify himself in every language that was in their manual. He took a gamble and answered in Hungarian, telling them he was a pleasure craft that was lost and could they escort him to the nearest civilian landing field.

The Tigers switched frequencies and he followed them, listening to them argue about whether to believe him and whether his shape conformed to anything they had ever seen before. They decided to set him down on their own airstrip, and switched frequencies and told him to turn around. The three Tigers were surrounding him now, so he went up a hundred feet and began a sweeping turn to head back toward their base. Then he told them he couldn't see where they were and dove the Osprey straight down to twenty feet above the foothills in a spiraling turn and went back toward the border. The Tigers lost him for nearly two minutes, and by the time they found him he was within twenty miles of the border and the two F-16s were asking the Tigers in their polite but overbearing accents what the hell was going on.

The Hungarian Tiger captain told the lead F-16 that one of the U.S. spy planes had gotten lost, and the driver of the Osprey immediately shot back on the open radio channel, telling them in fake accented English that he was a Hungarian civilian plane looking for someplace to land. The lead F-16 picked up a missile lock from one of the Tigers and scoldingly asked the Tiger captain if they were going to shoot down one of their own civilian planes. The Tiger captain pouted for a second and then in thick Hungarian ordered the Tigers to pull up, just seconds from the border. The F-16s dashed in tight to see what the hell was skimming into their territory at forty feet above the ground.

The driver expertly shot the Osprey straight up and under the F-16s, whose pilots then screamed skyward, thinking that they were being set up for an attack. He dropped the Osprey back down, falling like a brick, and ran straight up the border between the towering snowcapped mountain peaks. The F-16s asked for identification on the open channel, and the Osprey driver repeated, "I don't understand. I don't speak English," over and over again through his clenched teeth as he maneuvered between the sheer faces of rock and the iced-over peaks like a pinball bouncing from side to side.

"Goddamn, that's an Osprey!" one of the F-16s shouted over the open channel. "That's one of our own, Captain! That's the stolen plane!"

"Osprey, tip your wings if you read us," the F-16 leader ordered calmly as he put his jet into a turning nosedive.

The driver tipped his wings one way and then the other as he followed the terrain of the border north in the light of the moon.

"Follow us back to the base, Osprey," the F-16 leader said. "The game's up. We've got you. Let's put this baby down for the night."

"Ten-four," the driver replied in perfect English, watching the two F-16s back off his tail and head up and away. "I'll follow you." In the split second that they were heading up he dropped the Osprey down the side of a mountain and aimed for a small blinking red light that marked the end of a private runway that had been abandoned decades before.

He landed the plane on only three hundred feet, burying it in a group of trees at twenty miles an hour with brakes that were on fire. The driver and the professor jumped out and were pulled into a waiting van, which sped away while a dozen men covered the plane with cut pine branches on the dark runway.

"Welcome to Austria," the driver said to the professor in the back of the dark van.

"When do we see the baseball?" the professor asked. "When?"

30.

AS I WAS WALKING toward the double glass doors of HQ at Gatehouse 1 with John X's bulky briefcase in my hand, I saw the car that was waiting to take me home sitting in the turnaround off Savage Road. But then, just feet from the door, Charlie the guard stopped me. He waved to me from across the room with a scowl on his face, and I stopped and contemplated the distance between me and him, and me and the waiting car. He pointed at me and waved me over to him again, and I wondered if he knew that I had John X's briefcase. Had he seen John X walk out these doors for many years with the same beat-up leather satchel? Were his powers of observation so good that he knew the briefcase wasn't mine? For all the fabled security at Fort Meade, it was virtually unheard of to stop and search the briefcases of senior civilians or any military personnel. For years I could have walked out of the building with almost anything I wanted. Rebecca had probably done so for years, but now, the one time I didn't want to get caught, old Charlie was standing up behind his desk, his standard-issue blue shirt ready to burst its buttons, gesturing me to come talk to him. I could simply keep walking, I thought, my car speeding away from him.

But I decided to bluff my way through.

"Yes, Charlie," I said, changing the briefcase to the hand away from him.

"Hey, somebody's on the Judge's red line. Operator told him the Judge wasn't here and he said he wanted to talk to you. Guy with a funny accent. He's in a hurry, so you better step into the booth."

Two old wooden phone booths in the building's lobby were still outfitted with what looked like normal pay phones, but it was common knowledge among the Security employees that not only were these phones tapped, but you could have inner-office calls forwarded to them if you didn't want to go into the offices above for some reason. Many an agent wanted to stop off and pick something up and not be seen by the people in his or her group.

"Hello," I said into the receiver.

"This is Yarif," the long-distance voice growled on the phone. "Yarif Nir. It has been a long time, Steele. I thought you were gone."

My mind whirled with some way to figure out if this really was Yarif Nir, the famed director of the Mossad, whom I once worked with fifteen years ago.

"I don't have much time," he said, not waiting for me to answer. "Is your instep healed? Do you still swim?"

I sighed with relief. I had limped around with him and the Judge for two days after hitting the bottom of my foot on the last rung of a swimming pool ladder at the hotel where we were staying. He had been kind enough to tell everyone it was a war injury and not a silly swimming pool accident.

"My old war injury is cured," I told him so he would know that he was talking to me.

"Good," he said, and then launched into telling me that a top Mossad agent had disappeared with a cache of military secrets that could put the defense of his country at tremendous risk and he needed our help. The politicians, he said with some disgust, would not tell us immediately, or seek outside help, because the Mossad agent also took files that contained secrets they had obtained by spying. I learned only later that they were secrets they had obtained by spying on their own allies. Military secrets about the U.S., English, French, Japanese, and Germans. Important secrets, he said.

She must be found, he said desperately. He would send out by top-secret fax details on her and those who might have assisted her in her departure. His own life might be in danger, as was the identity of every one of his agents, so our agency must act immediately. Time was of the essence, he said, revealing his American legal education. Act now.

"I must go," he said. "Please have the Judge contact me on routine business."

"Tell me one thing," I asked, taking another risk. "Does the name Bundt ring a bell?"

There was silence on the other end of the line.

"Do they want to sell information and transfer it by satellite?" I asked the silence.

"Do you like to swim?" he asked.

"Yes," I said, knowing the simple code, designed not for encrypting a message, but so that a bureaucrat could not be quoted. I was answering my own question. "Have you ever heard of missile locations or maintenance schedules being for sale?"

"Where do you live?" he asked. "What country?"

United States, I thought. The agent must have stolen launch codes for U.S. rockets. Yarif was all but admitting that his country had stolen top-secret American information and one of his agents had taken off with it.

"One more thing," he said. "Check how you make your mortgage payments. That is the family bank."

Mortgage payments? I thought. I did not have a mortgage. Carolyn's house had no mortgage. The NSA's office, of course, had no mortgage.

"But," I said, "she had—"

"God help us," he interrupted me quietly. "You know enough to help us. Steele, my friend, I knew I could count on you. Remember, this conversation did not take place."

And then he was gone. The conversation was perfectly timed so that no agency, no matter how good, could trace an international call that quickly.

I stood by the agency's front door with the receiver in my hand, listening to the buzz of the dial tone. I was not yet quite willing to believe what I had just heard. Not only was the United States in a position to buy top-secret Soviet codes, the Soviets now had access to top-secret U.S. codes. John X had been right about Rebecca's infiltration of the Mike the Mechanic project.

Not surprisingly, I have a theory about the Mossad and the Israeli military, which I remember thinking about as I waved good-bye to Charlie and settled into the back of the dark car Carolyn had sent to pick me up. They were masters of getting to their goal, of accomplishing their mission, but the pressure of constant war, and the seed of revenge that ate at the pit of their stomachs, made them set up ridiculous goals and virtually criminal missions. They were like sharpshooters who, after winning every prize at shooting targets, decide that shooting people would be a lot more challenging.

But then I remembered standing next to Yarif on the side of a mountain while he pointed out the villages that were no longer there—victims of the terrorist attacks staged by their neighbors. No matter what I thought of their methods, as a professional I knew that they were our only true friends in the Middle East, and for me that was enough. They had fought almost daily for principles that we only talk about fighting for, and their patriotism was admirable. I could not help but think that if we Americans had half the patriotism, half the sense of identity tied to place and philosophy, we would be a better, stronger country.

Theory number 762: Professionalism and expertise cloud judgment, which is the realm of the generalist. That is why corn-fed politicians should pass the laws and Ivy League pimps should administer them. The Israelis, I thought sleepily, might have lost the distinction. The Mossad had done what the Judge and I were doing—running a mission with a loose and changing goal and without the supervision or authority of the people we were sworn to protect. I was guilty of the very crime I was accusing them of as I nestled into the back seat of my chauffeured car. Who was I to criticize?

Within moments of climbing into that lush back seat and saying a few polite words to the driver, I was sliding into the sleep I needed so badly. The hum of the car's engine and the gentle rolling of the long suspension as I was whisked out of the noise of the city lulled me into dreams. But Yarif's last suggestion nagged at me and kept me up even though I had had only two hours of sleep the night before.

Mortgage payments? What could he mean? I thought back to our last meeting and to the details he seemed to remember. I had hurt my ankle. We went swimming. We talked about war injuries. We talked about speeding the pace of the United States' foreign aid package to Israel.

Yes, I thought, proud of my ability to still search my own mind and find the nugget of importance in that crowded attic of remembered slights and irrelevant statistics. Yarif had called the cash transfers and loan guarantees the best thing for the United States since the mortgage-interest deduction. You are buying a peaceful home, he had said. Making payments for manufactured housing that will ensure peace.

I took the car phone off its rocker and plugged the modem of my laptop computer into it. I dialed into a general government information service to find out how the United States made transfers of foreign aid to Israel. I could find nothing at first, until I found a General Accounting Office report detailing possible abuse in foreign aid transfers. Nothing in that report rang any bells in my mind, but on a hunch I did a NEXIS search of newspapers and magazines on the day that the General Accounting Office study was announced.

There it was, one line in a *Wall Street Journal* article that I pulled up as the car sped toward home: "The G.A.O. report casts doubt on the ability of the Washington-based Bank of International Commerce to continue as the sole transfer bank for foreign aid payments." Then I searched for any article that contained the name Bank of International Commerce and the word Bundt within one hundred words of each other.

There were two references. The first was to a chocolate Bundt cake that was served to a local bank vice-president on his fortieth birthday. The article was about how different companies go about celebrating birthdays at work. The second story, from the *Los Angeles Times,* contained one sentence that made my head reel: "Many of the largest financial institutions in the world began as small, local banks. For example, the Bank of North America began as a two-teller operation owned by two brothers in the wilds of California and the Bank of International Commerce began as an investment house for a single individual, Georg Rudolph Bundt, in Germany."

"Oh, my dear friend Yarif," I said out loud. "You are one smart son of a bitch." I ran Tommy's story of the Bundt family over and over in my mind and began to realize how many pieces of the puzzle were falling in place. As I closed my eyes and began to plan what to do next, sleep crept up on me again. This time I could not fight it off.

I dreamed that I met Rebecca on a beach and she took my hand and walked with me along the shore. I dreamed the ocean waves burst on the sand with such force that the sound was deafening, and the cool spray made the hot breeze moist, alive, and enveloping. John X and Carolyn were there, and then Tommy and Madam San's young Vietnamese girl came out of the jungle to join us.

Then more people came out of the jungle, one by one, and stopped on the edge of the ocean and took their clothes off, leaving them on the sand in soft piles. First an old man took off his suit and shoes and waded into the water with us. Then a young man flexed his muscles and rolled into the surf. Then a young woman slipped out of a thin sundress, letting it fall around her white ankles, and scampered into the spray. Then another, and another, and another joined our group on the edge of the vast dark body of water. Dozens of unprotected, fragile human bodies on the edge of this immense, dark, powerful olive-colored sea that moved like the limbs of a forest in the wind. All of us living life on the edge—on the edge of drowning in the immense deep green sea.

I woke up with a start as a police car with siren blaring raced past us on the parkway, and in those first few moments of stupor I figured out what was going on. It didn't suddenly hit me like a stroke of genius, but crawled up on me out of my sleep and dreams into my foggy eyes, sticky with exhaustion and shock, like a reptile crawling out of the muck onto a dank beach. The idea came out of that dark sea, through the soft, vulnerable bodies, and stared me in the face. It was the face of a forced laugh, like the laughing mermaid from Mexico.

The car hit a series of stiff bumps, and as I bounced around in the back seat I reviewed all the facts as I knew them, as a good analyst should, and whistled quietly. I reached for the car phone, but then realized that I wasn't sure whom to call. Then, as quickly as the idea came to me, it settled into my memory, resting and ready to spring, and let me go back to sleep.

31.

BOBBY THE TECHY lived with his young wife and three children in a suburb of Ellicott City, north of Fort Meade in Howard County, Maryland. The exterior of their house was virtually identical to that of every third house in their late-seventies subdivision—aluminum siding surrounding a short saltbox-shaped structure with brick accents around the front door and the chimney that clung to the side of the box. The only difference was the large satellite dish in the back yard, ostensibly to get cable television, and the several small antennas that sprouted from the chimney. Bobby's wife, Jill, told the neighbors that her husband was "into shortwave radio stuff, you know?"

All they knew, they said behind her back, and then later to our agents, was that her husband, whom they called "the hermit," was hardly ever around and when his car was home he never came outside. Jill mowed the grass and took out the garbage, even when she was pregnant, which the neighbors noted was just about all the time. But then again, another neighbor volunteered, Jill was so young—"A child bride, you know what I mean? Certainly not old enough to be married and have three little ones"—that she could probably handle the chores better than they could.

The short asphalt driveway was cracked, and several neighbors had noticed the plain blue Chevrolet that was parked behind Bobby's Toyota. The car belonged to the tall, gangly Federal Protective Service officer the Judge had sent home with Bobby to guard him while he took a few hours off to rest and see his family. Bobby thought the guard was an unnecessary, and a paranoid move on the Judge's part, but it did make him feel important. This was the first time he had ever been guarded by the Federal Protective guys, and his involvement in whatever was going on with John X and the dernza seemed to him too small to justify the caution. The neighbors theorized that it was her father come up from Kentucky to take her back home, or some college friend of the hermit's who had come to live with them because he did not have a job. They knew the hermit worked for the Department of Defense, and the retired burr-haired Marine who lived across the street with his blue-haired wife complained bitterly about the hermit's long hair, untrimmed hedges, and Japanese car.

Jill was a seventeen-year-old high school junior who worked weekends as a waitress at a local college hangout in Rochester, New York, when Bobby was a senior majoring in electrical engineering and making the perfect recording of a Grateful Dead concert. He was quiet and shy, but there was something about his eyes that led her to say yes when he asked her out. She had dyed her hair blond that fall, and wore garish red lipstick and stiletto heels on their first date. He bought her natural Indian cotton blouses and flat sandals for Christmas. She remembered that Christmas Eve was the first time she saw him naked, scared by how reed-thin he was, and how he always sweated. In the middle of winter he was always hot and always wandering around his dorm room with nothing on but a tattered pair of gym shorts. But she began to become addicted to the feel of his warmth and the sweet, buttery smell of his sweat. She had always felt inadequate as a student, so she began to cut more and more classes to play with him between his classes. He was a serious student, but she was his first girlfriend, and he had never been truly loved, let alone idolized. He began to realize that to her nothing was important but his touch.

By the time he graduated that spring she was pregnant. Her stepfather was livid, and there seemed no choice but to follow him to graduate school at MIT. While everyone pitied her, she admitted in Bobby's family interviews several years later, when he was being recruited by the NSA, that she had never been happier. She hardly noticed that they didn't have any money, and time flew by. Bobby junior arrived one month after her eighteenth birthday, at the beginning of the second semester of his doctoral program in artificial intelligence. Her doctor talked to her about birth control, but she knew there was really no point to all the hassle, since she'd never remember to take the pills or want to interrupt the forward momentum of his passion.

Bobby brought home prizes for projects that she did not understand, and sometimes she would type his papers late into the night while he worked on another project. Her back would hurt when she laid a sleeping child on her lap and bent over the baby to reach the keyboard of the computer that Bobby had built himself, but he would sneak up behind her and kiss her neck, making the pain evolve into pleasure. When he finished his dissertation project, graduating with honors and seven different prizes, she was a twenty-two-year-old high school dropout who was pregnant with their third child. Bobby moved them from their small apartment with bars on the windows in Boston to a rented house with a yard and an apple tree in a sleepy little town in Maryland.

The children loved the apple tree, and she moved into the new rhythm of Bobby being gone all day, and sometimes late into the night. After their third child was born Bobby got promoted to work as a technical adviser to the director's personal staff, and she saw him less and less. They were able to buy a bigger house on his new salary, but the walls of the rooms began to seem closer to her every day. When Bobby was home he retreated to a locked room he had built in the basement, which he called his workroom. The children were not allowed in the room, which took up half the basement, and she had been in it only two or three times in the two years they had lived in the house. Bobby had covered the walls and ceiling with remnants of olive green shag carpet and painted the concrete floor black. The workbenches he built across one wall were full of electrical testing equipment and parts of computer systems. Another wall was covered with radio transmitting equipment and several computer terminals.

Even though Bobby got one of the largest raises in the agency, he gave Jill less and less money each month as he bought more and more equipment that he could not borrow from the agency. He began to ignore the children and spend hours staring at the computer screens in the locked room, trying to figure out some puzzle of communications design. Jill began to realize that she had married a mad inventor, just like in the movies, and that his compulsive desire to build a better mousetrap was keeping the kids from getting new shoes. She felt the bitterness hardening in her, and she began to think about her own future.

That was the start of her unhappiness, she told us much later. If only she had not started to consider what she should do for herself then she would not have become so unhappy. She admitted she wouldn't have been particularly happy, but the comatose state she had been in for six years had at least been comforting, if not entirely human. She imagined that she was no different from most women in the fifties and sixties, who found themselves becoming nothing more than an extension of their husbands, but the realization that she was in a common, if somewhat antique, trap did not give her any idea of how to spring the door to her jail. Fortunately, Jill met another woman, ten years older than she, who moved into the neighborhood, and she finally felt she had someone she could talk to. Samantha's husband was a salesman who was gone for long periods at a time, and she was an elementary school teacher who was having trouble finding a job. There was something in Samantha's past that always kept her from getting hired, but Jill was happy to have her around. They complained about their husbands together, went to K Mart to try on bikinis, and dreamed of having the money to buy whatever they wanted. Samantha did not have any children, but she adored Jill's three kids, and talked to her more and more about what she was going to do with her future. While the children ran naked through the sprinkler, which sprayed the satellite dish with every revolution, they would lie in the back yard in their bikini bottoms in the early-summer heat, Samantha having talked Jill into having the courage to go topless behind the tall fence, and discuss what Jill should do to escape her unhappiness. When Jill became resigned to her life Samantha would get angry, rubbing the suntan lotion hard onto Jill's back and thighs. Samantha would tell her that she was young and beautiful and could do whatever she wanted.

On weekends Bobby would spend more than twenty-four hours at a stretch in his basement workshop, eating out of the refrigerator he had installed and using the bathroom that was adjacent to the room. He would come out on Sunday morning, squinting into the light and the noise of the children playing, his face hollow and unshaven, his T-shirt stained with sweat and food, and play with the children in a daze. He would wrestle with them and hold them, but he seemed unable to understand their questions, as if he did not know their coded, mumbled kidspeak. She would try to talk to him, but only after several cups of coffee could he respond coherently. He wouldn't tell her what he was working on, but he insisted that she had to be more patient, that he was going to make them famous and rich. She had believed him for a long time, but then she began to realize that she didn't care whether he was famous or rich, she simply wanted him back. If she couldn't have him back, then she didn't want him at all.

But she couldn't leave. She had little money, no education, and, with three children under five years old, no way to work. She was unhappy, but sometimes when he came home early and sat on the couch reading stories to the children in front of the fireplace, she loved him in spite of herself. On those nights when he was all there, the old Bobby, they connected on some spiritual level that she had read about in a magazine at the grocery store. But then he would be gone again: at work for days straight, or hidden down in his basement room connecting wires together and programming software for hours at a time. Samantha told her that enough was enough, she had to take a stand and make him change, but she didn't know where to begin. What words would she use? How would she make him understand? Wouldn't he simply apologize again, point out that she just didn't understand his work, and then scoop up one of the kids and go off being the perfect dad? And what had he done wrong, after all? He hadn't run off with another woman. He was promoted every year. He was the smartest person she had ever met. He was wonderful with the children. He didn't drink or smoke, and he had never raised his voice to her, let alone hit her, as she had seen men do on the soap operas. What exactly was wrong?

"What's wrong," Samantha told her, touching her hair and brushing her face with the back of her hand, "is that he never takes you out, he has no friends, he never even talks to anyone else in the neighborhood, he refuses to visit your family, and he spends all of your money on computer games he plays in the basement." "They're not games," Jill protested as Samantha began massaging her shoulders, "and it's his money, after all." No, Samantha pointed out, it was their money, both of theirs, and she should have just as much say in how it got spent, even if he did have some fancy degree from MTI or MIT, whatever it was called. He didn't pay any attention to her, he didn't buy her things, he didn't treat her the way a woman ought to be treated.

Then Samantha leaned over and kissed Jill's lips, changing Jill's life forever.

When Bobby came home from the situation room that John X had set up at HQ, near lunchtime on that August Wednesday, after being gone for two days straight, he was not surprised to find Samantha sitting in the kitchen feeding his youngest son tiny spoonfuls of unidentifiable mush. Samantha had been around all the time this summer, and while Jill had seemed to grow farther away from him, she clearly wasn't as unhappy as she had been during the winter. She left him alone to work on the projects he had in process in the basement, including the miniature bug in the belt that he had shown to John X. Now that John X was actually using the bugged belt, he was going to try to get the agency to pay the bill for the work, daydreaming of how the extra money would make Jill happy.

"Hi," he said to Samantha, who did not answer but merely pointed to the tall Federal Protective guard who followed him into the house. "This is Greg," he explained to Samantha and Jill, who had appeared from the kitchen, still wearing her nightgown. "Greg is going to be staying here with us for a while."

"What?" Jill asked. "Why is he going to be here? You aren't in trouble, are you?"

"I knew this would happen," Samantha said. "I knew there was something weird going on here."

"There is nothing weird going on here," Bobby replied, trying to keep his voice calm. "I'm working on an important project for the

Department of Defense, so they decided to furnish a little bit of security, that's all. Greg, this is my wife, Jill, and her friend Samantha. Samantha lives down the block."

"Hi," Greg said with a small wave, and then his voice turned serious as he addressed Samantha first. "I'd appreciate it if you wouldn't tell anyone, particularly other neighbors, about my being here. I wouldn't want to raise any fears."

"Well, you've already done that," Jill snapped. "What is this all about, Bobby?"

"I told you," he said. "Absolutely nothing. Everybody is safe and sound. It's just my hyperparanoid boss trying to make me feel important. It's all exaggerated. Now, Samantha, if you wouldn't mind leaving us here, I think—"

"She's not leaving," Jill said quickly, afraid of being alone with these two suddenly strange men. "I want you to stay, Sam."

"Sure," Samantha agreed, snapping her gum. "Whatever you want."

"Look," Bobby said, "everything is okay, honey. Let's offer Greg here something to drink and put him in front of the television. Can we turn up the air conditioning in here? It's damn hot. Greg, we've got cable TV here, and maybe a few old magazines. You're going to have to put up with the kids wanting to watch *Star Trek* later on, but, at least until nap time is over, you've got the couch to yourself. I'm going to go down to the basement and do a little work and then get some sleep."

"The basement?" Greg asked.

"My computer is down there," Bobby explained, and then, realizing why Greg was asking, he added, "No windows, no doors. Nobody can get down there without walking right in front of you here by the television. Perfectly safe."

"I don't like the sound of this at all," Jill said. "What am I supposed to tell the kids? I don't want to scare them, I—"

"Just tell them," Bobby interrupted, going down the stairs, "that Greg is a friend of Daddy's who is going to stay for dinner. They'll love him. I hear he's great with kids."

As soon as Bobby turned the corner in the stairs to the basement and was out of sight of Jill, he stopped and exhaled deeply, seeing stars when he squinted his eyes closed in the dark. He tried to shake the tiredness and tension out of his head and focus on what he had to accomplish. While he had given John X two of the belts and black boxes, he had another, identical bug in a drawer in his workshop. He was going to examine it under a microscope to see how it could continue to short out and if there was some way to stop the interruption in transmission. Even though his whole body craved sleep, he knew that for John X's sake he had to at least make an effort to figure out what was going wrong with his little invention. Besides, if it didn't work properly he could kiss any extra money from the NSA good-bye.

He unlocked the door to his dark room, only the green light of a computer terminal flickering across the floor, and clicked on the small light by the door.

Rebecca was sitting on a stool in a corner, a glossy black Luger pointed right at his head.

"Shut the door behind you and I won't shoot," she said, her eyes burning in the half-light that twinkled in her hair. He paused for a moment, not sure what to do or how to alert Greg upstairs that she was here. The door on its spring swung closed behind him. He slowly put onc hand up and twisted the lock closed.

"Now, Bobby," she said softly, her voice purring and liquid like an oiled machine, "slowly put your hands on your head and walk to the chair I've put out for you." He followed her instructions, sitting in his desk chair, which she had moved to the center of the room. "Now I don't want you to get any funny ideas about what you can or can't do, all right? This is my radio, and I want you to understand that there are a dozen men listening and waiting to crawl all over this place if you make one wrong move." She pushed the button on the walkie-talkie, and a second later a deep male voice said out of the tiny speaker on the radio, "Tigerpaw? Is everything okay?"

"Ten-four," Rebecca reported. "Everything is fine."

They exchanged glances, Bobby as nervous as Rebecca was calm. Out of the corner of his eye Bobby saw that the video camera hidden behind the mirror on the bathroom wall was on, a small red light shining behind the bulb that hung from the ceiling, triggered when Rebecca came into the room without punching in the cipher code on the pad hidden under the phone by the light switch. Everything that happened was being recorded, so if she did kill him the NSA could at least figure out what had happened. He told me later that in the midst of his fear he wondered what the videotape would show she had done before he came into the room.

"Are you armed?" she asked.

"No," he said softly, his voice breaking.

"Good," she said. "Let's show me that you aren't. Please take off your shirt very slowly." He hesitated, and she said, "I promise you, if you do exactly as I say nothing will happen to you or your family—or that goon you brought home to protect you."

"How did you—"

"Just follow directions," she interrupted, gesturing slightly with the gun. "Take off your shirt, and then your shoes and socks. I want to see your sides and your ankles, pal."

When he finished she stood up and took two steps toward him, her body tense and ready to spring in the black leotard top and patched jeans she had on. "Okay. Now I'm going to handcuff you to this chair. Put your arms up on the armrests. That's right. Perfect. If you move I will push the button on the radio and shooting will begin. Shooting that would probably wake your kids up from their nap. So don't move, Daddy, okay?"

"Yes," he answered hoarsely, afraid even to blink as she quickly wrapped the plastic cuffs around the arms of the chair. Then she backed up and sat down again, lowering the gun but still keeping it in her hands.

"Quite a place you've got down here," Rebecca said, admiring the equipment near her on the wall. "You've got some expensive goodies. Maybe too expensive for your salary? Maybe you've got somebody paying you on the side, Bobby? Huh?"

"I refuse," he said tensely, "to be accused of treason by you of all people."

"Good point," she agreed, with a laugh that was warm and full of human feeling. She pulled a tissue out of her tight jeans pocket and wiped her nose. "Maybe a bit simplistic, but a good point. Unfortunately for you, it also tells me that you know something about me. Not an agent, are you, Bobby? An agent wouldn't make such a simple mistake. Just a commo-tech. Just a geek. But I bet you're honest. Now tell me where Tommy Wood is, will you?"

The request confused him for a second. Hadn't she got the report that the Colombians had picked up Tommy? He couldn't admit to having heard her family's men talking about Tommy, but there must have been a mix-up in communication. "I don't know," he said simply and honestly, and then added, "what you're talking about."

"Bobby," she sighed. "I know you are part of the team that poor John X put together to track me. You've been seen going in and out of the situation room that John X set up. Johnny even sent a guard home with you, little good that he did. You were involved in getting transmissions off the satellite that came from my family home. In fact, Bobby, you even listened to those transmissions which led the Judge to report that Tommy was kidnapped on my family's farm by a group of South American drug runners. So now all you have to tell me is if that is true, and if so, what you know about it. Is that so hard?"

"How'd you get in here?" Bobby asked.

"How'd you find my dad's house?" Rebecca asked in return.

They stared at each other for a long time, and Bobby reported later that he was overwhelmed again by her beauty. She stared at him without blinking, not glancing at his thin naked chest, somehow undressing him further with her penetrating look. He felt hypnotized by her stare, her high cheekbones, and her sparkling, fiery hair.

"I got in here rather easily," Rebecca said, breaking off her stare. "Because Samantha is a friend of the family."

"What?" he almost shouted, feeling the plastic handcuffs cut his skin when he tried to raise his arms, forgetting that his hands were cuffed to the chair. "No, no," he said. "That's impossible. She lives down the street. Her husband is a salesman who—"

"Can be bought," Rebecca said, finishing his sentence. "As can Samantha. Just a coincidence, but once we found out about it we took advantage of it. Who knows when it might be useful? Although I admit no one ever dreamed that it would be so useful so soon. Samantha has been paid to get close to your wife and find out about you. Very close to your wife, in this case."

"What?" he asked, not understanding her meaning. "Why?"

"Because you're talented. You're a loner. You've got massive debts, probably to pay for all these toys down here, and an unhappy wife. A wife who might leave you, taking your children, unless she is convinced by my friend Samantha to stay here with you. It's a perfect recipe for an approach by us. Our goal was to recruit you."

"First of all," Bobby said, "who is us? Second, how do you know I've got debts? Third, my wife is very happy, thank you. So if you'd just leave us alone . . ."

Rebecca picked up a brown envelope on the worktable and walked over to him. She pulled out a dozen photographs and laid them in a stack on his lap. The first one had the grainy look of a telephoto lens and showed Jill kissing Samantha, whose hand was wrapped around the back of Jill's neck, in Samantha's car in the parking lot of the local grocery store. He could see the faint outline of the children in the back seat—without their car seats, he noted. The second photograph also was grainy, and was partly obstructed by what looked like a closeup of a maple leaf. It showed Jill and Samantha in the doorway that led out to their fenced back yard, both of them wearing only the bottoms of their swimsuits; Samantha's hands were on Jill. Their four-year-old son was standing ten feet away, playing in his round blue plastic pool. The third photograph showed Jill and Samantha completely naked in a strange bedroom; he assumed it was Samantha's because of the photograph of her on the bedside table.

He stared at the photographs in his lap as Rebecca shuffled through them, each more graphic than the last. His left knee began to shake uncontrollably, and he again tried to move his hands, to brush away a tear.

"I'm sorry," Rebecca said. "She wasn't hired to do this. She was hired just to find out as much about you as possible. This relationship would not have furthered our ultimate goal of recruiting you. We told her not to, but it apparently just happened. I'm really sorry, but I've got to show you these so that you'll help me. I'll have Samantha break it off and move away. You can start over with Jill. You don't have to ever let her know you know. Samantha thinks all Jill wants is more attention from you. She says Jill loves you but you just ignore her."

"And if I don't help you?" he said angrily, gritting his teeth and spitting out the words.

"Oh, Bobby," Rebecca began, putting the photographs back in the envelope and sitting down. "What a mixed-up world this is. I'm sitting in a basement torturing you because I want to find the man I love. I'm willing to do anything—anything—to find him and get him back. If I thought it would guarantee his safe return, I think I might be willing to kill you right here with my bare hands—that's the truth. That's how I feel right now. My back is to the wall. For reasons I can't tell you, I've got to find him very quickly, and I'm not sure where to begin. That is why you've got to help me."

Bobby exhaled loudly and shook his head again, straining at the handcuffs. "Pardon me," he said quietly, "if I don't feel much like helping you solve your problem. Pardon me if I don't see the humor in the irony here."

She got up out of the chair and began to pace the room, circling behind him into the dark shadows. "I'm not sure," she offered, standing behind him, "if it's irony or paradox. Irony or paradox, that is the question about what we do. You know, I'm just plain sick of the paradox. I'm getting out of the agency because I just can't square what I do with what I believe anymore. Do you know what I mean?"

"No," Bobby said quietly, afraid of what she might do when she was behind him. It would be simple to lower a rope around his neck and choke him to death. Or maybe simply a blow to the head with a blunt object.

"I've come to the conclusion," she theorized, walking in front of him, "and I know it's not an original conclusion, but I've finally come to believe it myself, that secrecy is not only impossible in but anathema to democracy. We all grow up here in America expecting openness in government, you know. We expect to know about all the factors that go into a decision that our leaders make. Hell, the right of privacy is in the Constitution. Maybe not completely spelled out, but it's there. So how can each one of us have a constitutional right to privacy and then you and I work for an agency that spies, that eavesdrops on everybody? Sure, we're supposed to only be doing it on those lousy foreigners who don't have our cool constitutional rights, but you and I both know that's a joke. We hear both sides of the conversation, after all. We get transcripts from the English, after all. We're always finding some reason that the Constitution is a troublesome old scrap of paper in the way of our pursuit of our goal."

"The Constitution also prohibits treason," Bobby snapped. He guessed that she was giving him this speech so he would feel comfortable with her and willing to talk.

She smiled at him and crouched down to look him in the eye. "I didn't know you had this in you, Bobby," she said. "You're always so damn quiet around the ninth floor when I visit."

"This isn't the ninth floor," Bobby pointed out, his voice rising with each word. "This is my house. My house, where I have a right of privacy, which you have obviously broken every goddamn way I can think of."

"You see," she said, remaining crouched so she could look him directly in the eye, "I truly don't believe I'm committing treason, and I believe that when you learn what I have done, assuming that you're a good boy and are still alive, you'll agree with me that I've done the right thing. I've acted out of moral principle. But I can assume from your comments that you have been listening to John X and the Judge and that you have some idea of what is going on. And I believe that you actually agree with me. I believe you too think that what we do, what the agency does, is heretical to our country. The only power it gives us is the power to blackmail, like I now have over you, since I don't believe you'd like the Judge to see these photos of your wife. I don't think that would be good for career advancement, or for getting the security clearance to continue working on the projects you are interested in. So I think you will help me find Tommy. Right?"

He watched her breasts heave underneath her leotard with every breath, and he wondered, he told me later, how he was going to go on with Jill after knowing this. Had it really been his fault, he asked himself, or was Jill just seduced by a professional, hired and trained by Rebecca's family? Maybe if he got copies of the photographs, he thought as Rebecca stared at him, he could threaten to expose Jill if she didn't let him keep the kids and— Then he realized that he was no better than Rebecca, planning on how he could blackmail his wife to keep his family. Were they—he, Rebecca, John X, the Judge—all the same, he told me later he asked himself.

"Bobby," Rebecca said very softly, her eyes boring into him, "I need your help. I need to find him. I've got the Judge trying to find me, get me. My old friend now hunting me down. I need your help."

It struck him then, he told me later, that he had nothing to lose by helping Rebecca. She would undoubtedly find out from someone else everything that he could tell her, except maybe about the belt. In fact, he wondered if she already knew more than he could tell her that was important.

If she knew that Tommy was in the hands of the Colombians, he couldn't shed any real light on why or where he was, other than what she probably had already figured out. He could try to save his life, and maybe his wife and family, if he tried to cooperate—at least in a limited fashion. Besides, he told me weeks later, when he handed me his resignation, he thought she was right. Nothing good was going to come from all this technology turned and twisted for unspoken purposes. No one was going to be safer or smarter or fairer in the future because of anything he did. All his work at the NSA had led to was heartache.

He tried to shake out of his head the images of Jill and Samantha.

The sight of Samantha kissing Jill's soft cheek would not go away when he closed his eyes. This tragedy wasn't caused by Rebecca, he told himself, it was caused by the whole system, the whole intelligence world that he had fallen into. He had to get out while he was still half sane.

"How can I help you?" he asked when he opened his eyes. "I propose a simple deal. An accommodation. I live. My family lives. Samantha is gone. You are gone. You agree and I'll help you."

Rebecca did not move or exhale, on the camera seemingly afraid of breaking the spell if she spoke.

"Who knows about Tommy and me?" she finally asked quietly.

"Me, John X, Paul White, and the Judge," he answered, not knowing that John X was dead. "Oh, and old man Steele."

"Steele?" she asked loudly. "So he is involved. Why?"

"I don't know," Bobby said. "John X, or maybe it was the Judge, got him involved, for reasons that no one ever told me. You know, old analysts never die, they just become consultants."

"The Judge got Steele involved?" she asked again. "You think the Judge called Steele in? Yes, that would make sense. Keep it off the books. Hire some more help from the outside."

"Maybe it was John X," he suggested. "I really don't know. All I know is that he all of a sudden showed up at HQ and was given access to the situation room and copies of files, a stack about a foot tall."

"So that's the team I'm up against," she said.

Bobby watched her think, her eyes moving quickly over some scene in her head. He wondered if she was judging the capabilities of each of her foes, measuring them in her mind. "Steele," she said, as if she understood what Bobby was thinking. "He's the one to worry about. Anybody but Steele."

"He's big-time," Bobby said. "I've heard stories about him. A legend, practically."

"How did you bug my family's house?" she asked suddenly, untwisting her legs.

Bobby paused for just long enough to realize what she had said. Somehow, he told me later, she knew about her family's home being bugged, and that revelation changed his mind about her again. The only way she could know about that was to have someone on the inside who was feeding her information, because there were no bugs to be found.

"John X handled all that," he said, slowly and carefully. He realized that he was risking his life by lying, but no matter what he thought about the NSA, when the time actually came he could not bring himself to be disloyal. Maybe his patriotism was just habit, he told me later. But he could not reveal the one true secret he knew. "They were already there before he pulled me in. My job was to pull the transmissions out of the air from the birds they were sent up to and make something understandable from the encrypted audio. I don't know anything about placement."

"But you must have some guesses about the bugs," she said. "What kind were they?"

"I don't know," he said, and then realized he would have to give her more if he wanted her to believe him. "But I can tell from the transmissions that they were small and weak. There must have been some sort of booster box that was positioned nearby that shot them off a series of platforms, probably Keyhole satellites. I'd bet there were twenty mikes—maybe more that didn't work, since with something that small the odds of picking up all the transmissions are also very small. John X was really just plain lucky that he got anything that could be amplified enough to hear at all. Plain old-fashioned luck."

"Why did Johnny bug my dad's place?" she asked.

"Rebecca," he said incredulously, "everybody knew that John X had something for you real bad. He had you followed for weeks. He had all your telephone calls recorded since this Tommy person came into the picture. I think he was just jealous and just wanted to snoop on you."

"The Judge didn't order him to do it?" she asked.

"You know I wouldn't know if he did," Bobby said. "But I don't think so. Everything about the whole scene led me to believe that John X was acting on his own, and I think he was way out on a limb."

"What do you know about Tommy?" she asked quickly.

"The last transmission that I knew about before I left to come home," he said, "was one between some men, speaking English, who I guess were guys hired by your father, telling each other that Tommy was picked up by the Colombians."

"Nothing from DEA or the Bureau?" she asked. "Or from G Group? You would think that they would pick up some calls from those South American bastards boasting about their capture."

"Nothing before I left," he said honestly.

"What are the Judge's plans now? How is he trying to find me? Is he trying to find Tommy? How far has this thing gone up the ladder? Has he told anyone at State, for example?"

"Again," he suggested honestly, "you know that they would never let me in on that kind of info. I don't need to know that, and I don't want to know it. I do know that the Judge and Steele went over to the State Department this morning. What for, I don't know. I know that they want to find you and are combing the damn world for hints about where you might be. But I guess that this has not gone up the ladder much at all. There is no hint of State or Langley or anybody else trying to coordinate what they are doing with us. So I'd bet that the Judge is playing this one close to the vest. He's probably afraid that they'd have his hide if one of his top agents was going over to the other side."

She smiled, obviously pleased that her disappearance had not triggered an investigation by the State Department or the CIA. She gestured as if she was talking to herself, maybe congratulating herself, and then turned and said, "Is that what you think I'm doing? A mole for the Soviets?"

"Rebecca," Bobby said seriously, "I don't think anyone really knows what you are doing. At least nobody has told me. All I know is that John X thinks that you are target number one, enemy uno, and that we ought to unleash the whole damn arsenal to get you. The Judge is the one who is holding him back, probably trying to figure the whole thing out before he gets the boys in blue involved. That's what makes me think that he is terrified that you are going to be a major-league embarrassment to him."

"You don't like the Judge?" she asked, with a smile that was captured on the videotape and would melt any man's heart.

"Rebecca, I don't like bureaucrats. I don't like politicians. I don't like self-promoters and back-slappers. I don't like anybody who's my boss. So of course I don't like the Judge. Hell, I don't like any of them. I don't like you. All any of you has brought me is pain. I want to just be a scientist, okay? A researcher. Is that some kind of crime? Is that so horrible that you've got to entrap my wife and ruin my life? Is that so goddamn wrong that I end up handcuffed to a chair with somebody pointing a gun at me? What the hell did I do to deserve all this?"

Rebecca sighed and stood up, pulling her hair back again. "Bobby," she said softly, "all you did was get in the way."

"Get in the way?" he asked. "Get in the way of what?"

"Of things bigger than the both of us. People's plans that have become part of history. Events that are spinning out on their own once they've been started."

He strained at his handcuffs, his face red with the anger he had worked up on his lack of sleep and fear that his life was forever changed. "Nothing is bigger than individual people," he concluded. "Nothing."

Rebecca paced the room, laying a hand on the black bag that she had brought in with her, and then moving toward him quickly. "That's true," she said, close to his face. "I agree with you completely. But both you and I have got involved with an organization that is based on the opposite principle. Some Jeremy Bentham principle of sacrificing individuals for the common good of the whole. That's what this is all about. That's what I'm trying to stop."

Just then there was a beep on her walkie-talkie, and a male voice said, "Tigerpaw, this is the Den. Do you read me, Tigerpaw?"

Rebecca picked up the walkie-talkie and spoke back to the voice. "This is Tigerpaw. I read you, Den. What's up?"

"We've got a phone call upstairs that's come in from NSA to the guard, Greg. Seems that some of your friends want Bobby back at HQ early. I suggest we go in, pick up our guests, and move on. Do you agree, Tigerpaw?"

"Agreed," she said. "Let's do it."

Like a gentle summer breeze, Rebecca's four brothers and two sisters-in-law silently descended on the small tract house from every door and window. Greg was disarmed within five seconds of their arrival, and Samantha helped load Jill and the children into the U-Haul truck that had pulled up in front of the house. There was a knock on the basement room door, and Rebecca opened it when her brother Erik asked for Tigerpaw. Erik and Joe unclipped the cuffs on Bobby's hands without saying a word.

"What happens now?" Bobby asked Rebecca, fear gripping his voice.

"We are going to put you and your family up in a nice house not too far from here until this whole thing blows over. No one is going to get hurt as long as everyone follows directions. I promise you that.

You have been very helpful, Bobby, and some day you will know that you did the right thing."

"What about Samantha?" he asked, his voice showing his doubt that he would ever understand Rebecca. He was standing like a prisoner between two tall men with obviously fake beards on below their baseball caps, which said "U-Haul" on them.

"She disappears," Rebecca said. "Gone forever."

"Who will explain this to Jill?" he asked.

"What do you want me to do?"

"You tell her," Bobby said, his voice shallow with the bargain he was striking. "Show her the pictures. But don't tell her that I know. Tell her that you will show them to me if she doesn't cooperate."

"Can you live with the secret? Both of you?" Rebecca asked.

"We've got to try, don't we?" Bobby asked. "I just want to try to keep my family together."

Rebecca touched his arm. "I'll take care of it. I'll try to make this work."

"Thank you," he said, wondering, he told me later, how this would look on the videotape. Would the agency think he had sold out to her to keep his family together? Would they protest that he had blackmailed his wife to keep his family together? But then he realized, he told me later, that he simply didn't care what we thought. Just like Rebecca, he felt he had done the right thing.

The brothers took Bobby and his family to a secluded cabin in the West Virginia woods and kept them under very close guard for eight days. When he did not show up for work the first night, Paul, the deputy dernza, called his home. When there was no answer Paul sent a team of Federal Protective boys out to the house, and when they reported in that the entire family was gone without a trace Paul tried to call the Judge, but by then the Judge was in the middle of our scheme and never even mentioned it to me. It wasn't until I returned to the agency, five days later, that anything was done to search for him and his family.

In the middle of the night on the eighth day, while Bobby slept with Jill curled in his arms and his children spread out around them in sleeping bags on the floor, the guards simply disappeared, leaving no evidence that they had ever existed. Bobby and Jill, with their children in their arms, walked the seven miles to an interstate and hitchhiked to the next rest stop, where Bobby called Fort Meade collect. He asked first for the Judge, then for Paul, and then finally for the only person who was there at the time who understood what had happened—me. Bobby resigned that day, and as far as I know is living with his ever growing family somewhere outside of Seattle, where he works for one of our major suppliers. Jill is going back to school, and every year they send me a Christmas card with a photograph of their happy brood.

When Paul sent a group of agents to Bobby's house when he didn't show up for work, they found Rebecca's black bag in the basement room, but didn't find the video camera until later that afternoon. By the time Paul had seen the tape, I was nearly a thousand miles away, and the Judge did not report to me what it showed because by then I knew much more about Rebecca than he did.

Rebecca's black leather bag contained a change of clothes, two boxes of ammunition, a pair of black gloves, and a paperback book. Rebecca had read the book while she waited for Bobby to return, sitting in the basement room, unaware of the silent video camera recording her every move. We tore the book up looking for some evidence that it was in code or contained hidden information, but after days of analysis our technical department came to the conclusion that it was simply a recent best-seller that she had with her to pass the time.

The only thing interesting about the book was the bookmark in it. On a three-by-five index card was a poem scribbled in Rebecca's handwriting. Several words were crossed out, and one sentence was written over a doodle that the techies say was nothing more than a doodle. A poem written for Tommy? For herself? Or just to pass the time?

> If you would choose me, instantaneously
> I would be standing before your eyes—
> naked and hungry as a she-wolf.
> The night would explode
> with our passionate feasting.
> Until then, I shall hang my hunger
> deep in my heart, far away
> from anyone's curious, tourist eyes—
> lest I am found alone,
> naked at the feasting table.

32.

CAROLYN'S HOUSE was ablaze with lights when I woke up again in the back seat of the car, the driver politely telling me that I was home. Murphy's boys were busy trying to convince Tommy that he was more than simply a decoy by teaching him all the tricks of the trade they had picked up after being agents and mercenaries for years: martial arts, memory techniques, ballistics, and computer use. Tommy sat eating dinner while he was lectured by one of Murphy's gang on the key phrases he had to know in four different languages. When Tommy saw me he managed a weak wave, and I saw my own exhaustion in his eyes. I left the briefcase in the dining room and went to hang up my coat.

"The Judge called," Carolyn said after kissing me hello. "He'll be here in half an hour. He has okayed the plan or mission, whatever you call it, that Murphy has been working on all day. He wants a jet that can take you to the Bahamas tomorrow morning. The only catch is that the Judge wants you and Tommy to go alone, which has angered Murphy."

"What?" I asked incredulously, wondering if my tired mind was playing tricks on me.

"He told me, without laughing, that the plan was to do it just like we freed Mike Carter," she said nonchalantly. "The same basic plan. But this time, we provide the victim."

She stopped and looked closely at my face, talking to me with her large blue eyes. Each eye looked like a miniature world from far away—the blue sea surrounding the dark land of pupil. I knew she knew that John X was dead. I guessed that the Judge had told her enough of the details for her to understand what had happened. I could also sense that her coolness was an attempt to compensate for the hot emotions she knew I must be feeling.

I kissed her and inhaled the delicate perfume that was dabbed behind her ears and stroked the gray-blond hair that fell gently to her shoulders. Her skin was still soft, although it had become slacker and drier with age, but money had bought her the finest creams and the best exercise specialists. "I love you, Mr. Steele," she said.

She had lost one husband, and I could see in her eyes that something told her she might lose another, and yet she was the one who pushed me on, willing me to take risks to get the job done. Theory number 679: It is the very romantics who are most willing to risk their own lives who are most concerned and conservative about risking the lives of their loved ones. It is as if they hear all the warnings they receive all their lives, telling them not to do things, and rather than following those warnings, they store them up to regurgitate back to the people they care about.

Carolyn and I had a quick dinner in the kitchen, neither of us saying much. Her takeover attempt was going well, but there was trouble with a corporate bond rating. She had canceled all of our social engagements for the next three weeks and told her senior staff that she would be on vacation for most of the month. Carolyn, in her brassy, confident way, was on a roll.

She told me about the evening news and the videos of riots in the streets of East Berlin and Hungary. There was more talk of the Soviets invading. Everyone had a finger on the trigger, she said. Lithuania was considering declaring itself independent of the Soviet Union, and there were the largest uprisings in the communist bloc countries in twenty or more years.

"Intelligence people must be going out of their minds," she said. "Your organization must be so busy."

I didn't say it, but it struck me that while I had been back on the job only one day, and I had spent most of that day outside the office, it had not seemed particularly busy to me. When I had walked past A Group in the DDO, which was responsible for the Soviet Union and the Eastern bloc, they did not seem particularly hectic. There were none of the signs of crisis, no people running into rooms that they did not have clearance for, the alarms over the doors going off to alert people that the coded badge the person entering had on was not on the approval list for that door's individual access computer. I didn't see any carts with covered food plates being wheeled in so people didn't have to leave their stations to eat, or the telltale arrival of more military brass in the areas usually run by civilians.

The events in Eastern Europe were running ahead of intelligence networks, and the press knew more about what was really going on than we did. Maybe we should have been busy trying to figure out what was going on, but we didn't have time to read all of the newspaper accounts, let alone contact all our sources. I was buried in this case, but the East European specialists in A Group were sitting on their hands, waiting for what they believed to be the inevitable Soviet reaction. Their greatest hope was that we wouldn't get dragged in. They hoped that the Soviets wouldn't do anything without notifying us first so we wouldn't put the whole Air Force in the air and send the subs diving. The only question they were asked to answer by the White House, and could not answer, was why the Soviets hadn't done anything yet.

Unfortunately for me, I believed I knew.

The Judge was ashen when he arrived at the door, and asked for a drink before we made the long walk to the study. I poured Glenlivet, and we sat and stared at the honey-blond liquor for a long while without talking.

"Okay," I began tensely. "What the hell is going on? Why move up the plan? Hell, why make a plan without consulting with me? What's the rush?"

"First," he said, "the plan I presume you are talking about was your idea, remember. You're the one who sent Murphy off to set it up. Second, what John X told us in his letter has checked out so far. Therefore, it is my judgment that we need to move fast. We need to get Tommy into the hands of Colombians so that Rebecca can try to get him and we can get Rebecca."

"But this is dangerous. Really dangerous."

"Goddamn it," the Judge interjected. "I know that—but that is the only thing we know. The whole thing is spinning out of control, and nobody knows cowshit. We've got to find Rebecca and find out what's going on. This is as neat and trim as it gets—using the very people she pissed off to get to her. She'll believe it because all the evidence points to them kidnapping Tommy on the farm."

"Why just Tommy and me going down there?" I asked, knowing the answer but wanting to hear the sounds of the Judge's reassuring voice say the words.

"If I was trying to sneak up on someone, make a delivery, and get out of there, I wouldn't ride in with the whole posse," the Judge said. "The more people who fly in, the more noticeable you'll be."

I didn't respond, knowing that he was probably right, and reluctant to admit that my urge to take Murphy and his armed men might originate in fear more than anything else. I was vain enough, I have to admit, that it didn't strike me as unusual that the Judge didn't suggest having just Murphy place Tommy in the hands of the Colombians. Murphy was the trained, experienced field agent, after all.

I was just a desk jockey, likely to screw up a delicate, complicated, and somewhat impromptu transaction. But the Judge's prejudices always led him to think the worst of Murphy, regardless of the facts.

He told me about the second call from Paris, telling us that they not only had an agent on the run but they believed Iraq and Iran had each lost one. The Pacific Rim specialists in B Group had heard rumors of a Chinese agent showing up in Tokyo, but had not yet been able to substantiate the story. The intelligence community was going wild with stories of agents going over to the other side, and NSA was hearing the flak on encoded messages sent between embassies and their home countries all over the globe.

"Something bigger than Texas is going down," the Judge said.

"I think I've figured it out," I said softly, the strained sound of my voice surprising me. Until the words came out of my mouth I wasn't confident that I had any idea of what was going on.

"Tell me," he said, not surprised, but sounding like a man who would not put up a fight.

"No, you tell me about Mike the Mechanic first."

He spoke slowly, explaining how the program had started and then how it had finished. All the pieces fit, and there was a very good possibility, but not a probability, that Rebecca had enough of the files to disable three-fourths of the country's nuclear arsenal. If the Soviets did invade Czechoslovakia, Hungary, or East Germany, they might have enough information on us to make any threat of retaliation meaningless. "If those tanks start rolling toward Berlin," he said wearily, "they might just not stop until they get to Paris."

"Well," I continued, "let me put some icing on that cake. Our friend Yarif from the Mossad called today for you, but since you were out, I talked to him. He confirmed our worst nightmare. Someone is offering to sell the Soviets the same type of information that we are being offered. They aren't stalling in East Germany because we cracked the code on one of *their* missiles, they're stalling in hopes of having the dope on virtually all *our* missiles."

"Mother of Jesus," the Judge said. "Tell me what he said."

I repeated my conversation with Yarif, and the Judge shook his head and stared into his scotch. Our only hope, the Judge pondered, was to try to get the Soviet information first, before they got ours, and hope that it was accurate.

"It will be accurate," I stated flatly. "That is crucial to their plan."

"Whose plan?" he asked, sliding down into the leather chair.

"The family Bundt."

"Hit me," the Judge said, pulling himself back up into his chair. "Tell me the story now, Steele. Give me your grandiloquent theory on what the hell is going on."

"I'll spare you all the disclaimers," I said, standing up and going to the same window Tommy had stood at the night before, and I watched my reflection in the glass the same way he had watched his. "It is probably all bullshit and my usual romanticism, but here goes. The Bundt family, through a dozen shell companies, owns a bank. A big bank. The Business Bank of International Commerce."

"Holy shit," the Judge said. "That's our bank. I mean, that's where the agency banks."

"Exactly," I pointed out. "Long ago it was called the Bundt Bank of International Commerce. The BBIC. Then the name was changed, but the initials remained the same. While the NSA uses a thousand different banks, the BBIC is our house bank."

"They have always, as I've been involved, underbid everyone else for our work," the Judge said. "Plus, they set up the secret transfer system. They are big and they've got the right connections to get the job done."

"That's right," I said. "For example, the BBIC owns a bank in Israel, the National Bank of Commerce."

"Which is where the Mossad banks," the Judge remembered. "And why it is so easy for us to make payments. The same is true of the Deutsche Bank of Commerce. Easy to make payments to our agents through a double set of books."

"And so on and so forth," I said. "The First French Bank of Commerce. The Bank of Credit and Commerce in Turkey. The Commercial Bank of New Delhi in India. It was all very convenient for all of our payments and transfers to agents in the field. It was also very convenient for the family Bundt. They did exactly what we do when we investigate—they followed the money. They had access to our top-secret banking records—they were the ones, their experts at their bank, who set up the secret banking systems that allowed us to transfer cash without anyone knowing about it—so they could follow the trail to our agents. Plus, they could tell where hot information was just by knowing how much money we were willing to pay for it."

"But why?" the Judge asked.

"Why the bank? Or why did they decide to trade on our information? Who knows really if the bank came first or the addiction to collecting information came first. You know the info that John X put together. You know what Tommy told us. This has been going on for a long, long time. Information is money. They were capitalists, that's all."

I ran my finger around the ring left on the bird's-eye maple table by my wet glass and wondered how the Judge would react to this information.

"So Rebecca's father tells Tommy that his family, the Bundt family, buys, sells, and trades information for a living. We've got him saying that on tape from the bugs that John X got into their house."

"But," the Judge objected, "that info is suspect, because we don't know how John X got bugs into their house. Hell, for all we know the whole scene in their kitchen where Rebecca's Nazi-speaking daddy tells Tommy about the business could have been a setup. Playacting for the microphones they know are there."

"Too attenuated," I said, slipping into my role as a professional analyst. "They could not predict how Tommy would react. If it was a setup, then the whole attack on the farm, the plane dropping the red paint, it all would have to have been a setup, and that's just too much to believe. Those guys were shooting real bullets at Murphy and company. Hell, they were shooting real bullets at me! No, I discount the possibility of it being a setup to almost zero. The Bundt family did not know they were being listened to, and they had no idea that we would pick up Tommy and he would explain the rest to us."

"All right, moneybags," the Judge relented. "So Rebecca's family really is in the treason business big time. What is the next dot in this connect-the-dots thing you do?"

"Suddenly, information that is crucial to the very survival of countries all around the globe gets stolen. Soviet info is offered to be sold to us. The Israelis lose an agent with U.S. info. We get these reports from all around the world that key players in intelligence operations are defecting, disappearing, dying. All of it at the same time."

"For some reason," the Judge said, as if involuntarily dragged into my train of thought, "the Bundt family is calling in all their chips."

"Getting all the information, the most important information, they can get all at one time."

"They'll make a fortune," the Judge said.

"But that's what doesn't make sense," I offered. "Why risk everything? Why be so desperate that you take everything you can get all at one time, risking exposing your entire operation? This will bring down the family. This will put their bank out of business and spark a dozen investigations. When they've got such a good thing going, probably making a fortune while at the same time guarding their confidentiality, why take the kind of chances they are taking?"

"They are crazy?" the Judge asked. "They are nuts. Just like all of the spies who go over to the other side. They are unbalanced, psychos. Delusions of grandeur."

"But this is a business," I said, pacing the room, lost in thought. "There are hundreds, maybe thousands of people involved. A profitable, successful business doesn't just go nuts. A business doesn't suddenly slip into insanity. They've operated for fifty years in a slow, stable way, and then all of a sudden they risk putting themselves out of business."

"Everybody makes mistakes," the Judge said, crossing and uncrossing his legs nervously. "Look at GM or Ford or Chrysler. Hell, they all made a series of incredibly stupid decisions."

"It's as if," I pondered, ignoring the Judge, "they want to put themselves out of business. As if, in their usual calculating, silent way, they have intentionally decided to do themselves in. To put themselves out of business. But why?"

"Maybe they just got tired of all the lying," the Judge said. "Maybe some sense of decency, patriotism, whatever, came over them."

"As an analyst, I have to ask, what would be worth putting themselves out of business? I rule out money. They've got all the money in the world, and they could get much more over the long haul by continuing to do exactly what they have been doing. In fact, that is why I think the whole sale of Soviet missile info in Key West may be a ruse. The fact of the matter is that the Bundt family would be stupid beyond belief to take that kind of risk for any amount of money. Plus, putting the Soviets out of business eliminates one of their largest customers. You see, they've made money on the cold war. They lose everything if the cold war stops."

"Jesus, Steele, maybe they want us to just blow the hell out of each other," the Judge suggested, gesturing with his glass of scotch. "Maybe they want to start World War Three."

"I've considered and rejected that theory," I said matter-of-factly. "This is too complicated a way to start a war. Besides, how could they get the hundreds of people involved all around the globe to go along with it? No, the fact that there are so many people involved—people in France, in Japan, in Peru—means that the reason has to be easy to understand, and probably even admirable."

"Admirable?" the Judge scoffed. "What the hell could be an admirable reason?"

I turned quickly and walked right to the Judge's chair, leaning over him as I spoke quietly. "Let me tell you a secret about the very rich," I said. "And these people, the Bundts and their friends, must be very, very rich. The very rich will still do things simply to make more money—hell, you can never have too much money—but they won't risk their very capability to make money just for money. No, the very rich become communists, or terrorists or religious nuts, because they believe in causes. They are motivated, just like other people, by a need to make the world a better place. It's just that they don't have to worry about feeding their kids or making mortgage payments, so they can take their need to save the world to extremes. They can become rescuers of the world full time."

"Save the world," the Judge said quietly and flatly, without looking up at me. My words seemed to have put him in a trance, as if he recognized something in them that I had not yet seen. "They want to save the world."

I leaned over even closer to him, my mouth close to his giant, weathered ear. "World peace," I whispered.

The Judge exhaled slowly, and then he uttered a short little laugh. "You think," he said, turning to me and staring me right in the eyes, "that they are purposefully trying to end the cold war—hell, all wars—by . . . by . . . by what?"

"What do they have?" I said. "That is what I've been asking myself. What is the one thing they have that no one else has as much of? Not money. There is always somebody richer. Not power. Governments have more power. The answer is information. Military intelligence."

I walked back to the dark windows, afraid for some reason to look at the Judge as I explained what I thought was going on. "The family decides to put themselves out of business, or at least out of the treason business. They decide to risk everything to obtain the one thing that is death to their business, and ours—world peace. Sure, everybody wants peace, just like they want to find a cure for cancer. But this family actually comes up with a plan to get it. This family of twelve has the wherewithal, the resources, the connections, and the plain old-fashioned gumption, to try to pull it off. They can do it because they have the information—the information that each country, that each enemy needs to know to defeat the other.

"The likelihood of success is remote," I continued, watching my lined face in the window and wondering if I sounded at least half sane. My voice was harsh and weak. "The likelihood that some members of their family might die trying is great. But after making billions constructing the weapons of war for generations, and then billions more trading on the information that both sides want to know about each other, they decide, with unbelievable bravado, to try to bring the world's warring enemies' fast race to self-destruction to a grinding halt. Then their luck improves and world events start to turn their way. They realize that the Soviets are in a dangerous situation, in which the use of force against their own people is almost inevitable. So they move up their plans and try to strike while the iron is hot. While the world is already in economic and social turmoil they know they will have even more of an effect."

I stopped for a moment, afraid to look at the Judge.

"So here is what they do," I said, racing now to my conclusion. "They convince—no they don't have to convince anyone, because the cause is so just, so good. They coordinate each branch of the family to find some way to steal their country's top secrets, and they disappear, taking risks as they never have before, because the goal is now not money or power, but peace. But they do not plan to sell these secrets. Nor do they plan to trade. They plan to give them to each country's enemies in order to ensure peace. Everyone knows everything, so no one can move. Check. Checkmate."

"It would—" the Judge sputtered. "It would start a goddamn war."

"Again, I've been thinking of that—how to transfer the information without starting a war," I said. "I can think of only one way—you transfer it all at one time on one day. They will effectively end global military competition, at least on a nuclear level, by telling the other side everything they need to know to beat their opponents at the same time their opponents are finding out everything they need to know to beat them. Iran to Iraq and back. Israel to the Arab countries and back. The Chinese to the Taiwanese and the Japanese and back. The Indians to the Pakistanis and back. North Korea to South Korea and back. Every ancient hostility that you can think of they will try to end by making each side's military plans and military potential known."

The Judge did not move or say a thing, so I went on. "All of this is, of course, possible because of technology. The technology has caught up with us, to the point where information is more powerful than our bombs. Our bombs are dependent on the information that can be stored on one shiny little disk. Our weapons are so smart that they can almost be reasoned with, talked out of exploding, told to shut down, scolded into backing off.

"All of this hinges," I went on, turning away from the window and pacing back toward the Judge, "on the big transaction. The center-court game. The Soviets get our locations, launch codes, entrance codes, satellite-hookup codes, targets, and maintenance schedule, and we get theirs at the exact same time. The ultimate disarmament plan. Without that trade, the rest of it isn't worth a hill of beans."

"Rebecca goes to Moscow," the Judge said very softly, his words no more than a whisper against the sound of the wind picking up outside the old house, "and a Soviet agent comes to Washington."

"No," I said. "That's the beauty of the whole plan. It's all done by satellite. We are talking about massive amounts of information that has to be transferred simultaneously, so there is virtually no other way to do it. The only trick is that the receiving party has to know it is coming, to have their reception dishes turned the right way and on the right frequency. That is why they have to set up these charades of offering to sell the information to the different parties. They have to have all of us with our satellite dishes ready to receive something."

"Let's assume this cock-and-bull story is true," the Judge said, taking a drink of his scotch. I noticed that his hand was shaking as he brought the glass up to his mouth. "Won't we be able to tell the location of the broadcasting source when we begin to receive the satellite transmission? Can't we just blow it up as soon as it starts?"

"Maybe," I said. "That's probably a risk they are willing to take. They can probably do the whole thing in twenty minutes, and if they are smart—and believe me, I think they are brilliant—they will transmit from a mobile station. Like a truck or a train. And they may transmit different info from different places, so that if you blow up a transmission source you are only stopping information that would go to you, and not the dirt on your country that would go to your enemy. So you'd be hurting only yourself if you attacked the transmission point after the transmission began. You have to stop them before they begin. Plus, just to complicate things, they could do satellite-to-satellite transfers before they send it down to a base station."

"This is way too much guessing, Steele," the Judge said, spilling his last swig of scotch. He reached down and furiously dabbed at the wet spot on the Oriental rug with a cocktail napkin. As he came back up he hit his head on the edge of the side table and scowled. "But while you are reading minds, where do you think they will transmit from?"

"One location will be near Key West," I proposed. "That's where we'll have dishes turned to, because of the deal they've offered Langley through the stockbroker. They lure Langley and the State Department down there with a fake offer to sell and then presto, surprise, they hand over the whole damn thing for free."

"What do we do?" the Judge asked, his voice quiet but as tense as a high-pitched piano wire.

"There are bound to be mistakes when you try to pull off a project this big. Like the Colombians deciding to try to wipe you out right in the middle of it all. Like falling in love right when you are about to take the biggest gamble of your career as a double agent. In the midst of all of these unexpected problems they forgot to be more careful with Tommy, and because they weren't careful we got a toehold in on their plans. Without Tommy we never would have looked where we looked and found what we found."

"But we did, goddamn it," the Judge said. "Maybe not 'we,' maybe only John X, and I'm beginning to agree that his whole motive, his only motive, was jealousy. Rebecca's new love. Whatever the reason, the question now is, can we take advantage of it?"

"If we can get the Soviets' secrets and catch Rebecca before she gets ours to the Soviets, then we win the whole ball game. Every other power in the world will be effectively neutered. We will dominate for decades. It's hard to say this without a cynical smile, but if we pull this off the world will be ours."

"The world will be ours," the Judge repeated. "Funny how the whole business comes down to the same bullshit that Hollywood puts out. When we reach our ultimate potential, when we damn well figure out a way to put an end to the bloody arms race, the only language we have to explain it all is a bunch of melodramatic jingoist jargon."

"You don't sound convinced," I said.

"Convinced of what?" the Judge asked, looking up at me. "Convinced of the justice of our cause? Convinced that we can pull it off?"

"No," I said. "Convinced that it is worth trying to pull off."

"Not my job, partner. My job is to get the job done, not worry about whether it is worth doing."

"But there isn't anyone else to make the decision," I argued, surprised at his morose, bureaucratic turn. "Just you and me. Nobody to consult, to question, to turn to. We are doing much more than carrying out policy objectives that have been sent down from above. It's just you and me. On the spot, pal. If I'm right, then you and I are about to decide whether to scuttle the cold war."

"Maybe we need to go higher up," the Judge said softly, his voice telling me that he didn't want to or think we should.

I thought of the gray-faced men who would sit around the room deciding what to do. I could hear their verbal scuffling to protect their turf and their inherent mistrust of something bigger, grander, more lasting than they were. The secretary of state with his minions and tortured political ambitions. The generals all worried about accusations of interservice rivalry. The White House aides with the silent stares that were permanently pasted on their faces from always trying to pretend they knew more than anyone else in the room. The president's chief of staff, who was really nothing more than the chief pollster for the country.

I looked again at my own reflection in the tall, narrow windows, wondering who I was to judge so many good people so harshly. But then again, I thought, secure in my knowledge that my observations were right, there was something very big at stake here. Something called national security, which was all tangled up with ideas of patriotism, democracy, and the simplistic, intrinsic belief, which if I was honest with myself I had to admit I shared, that our vision of freedom was what the world needed to be a better place.

"But you know what they'd say," the Judge said, as if reading my mind. "They'd say, well, friend, we'll have to study that. Buddy, we need more time. Partner, we need more info, more background, more evidence. Naw, it would never get by a summary judgment argument in my court, let alone theirs."

Right then I remembered the little stream that ran through our front yard when I was growing up. My grandfather told me for years that the stream went all the way to the Mississippi, but I never believed him. When my father and mother brought me home the morning of grandpa's funeral, I tramped down to the stream in my best clothes and began to follow it. I was afraid of the water, even though it was no more than a foot deep in our front yard, but I knew that it got deeper, darker, faster as it went south. It went into a small creek, where I saw a turtle, then into a larger ditch that was surrounded by burrs that clung to my clothes like parasites, then to a river that was named after a saint I now can't remember. But I knew from the books my grandfather had read me that that river, seemingly as wide as an ocean, flowed into the Mississippi.

In that moment of realization years ago, as I stood on the banks of the swollen river in my tattered Sunday-best clothes, I began to believe in people, in history, in books, and in what I was told. For cynicism, theory number 345 says, does not develop with age; it is something that you are born with, grow out of, and then return to on your downward slope to your second childhood. The true cynics are newborns and the near-death, for they know the harsh reality of life in a way that the rest of us can only guess at.

"We've got to go forward," I said, pacing across the room and remembering the river that seemed so wide that it had no other bank. "We've got to take the gamble. We've got to do it. If we don't do it then we'll regret it. We won't be able to look our children in the eye, because we will have skipped a chance to save their future."

"But you don't have any children," the Judge said with a snort.

"If we pull this thing off I'll get some," I said, sitting back down. "I'll adopt half the western world and raise them here in this big house and know that the world is a little less dangerous because of what we tried to do." I stopped pacing to catch my breath. "You know," I said, "while I am talking about peace I sound like some crazed general planning how to win the cold war."

"But the facts are inescapable," the Judge mumbled. "That is, if you are right about what is going on, then we have a chance to win the absurd game we have been playing since the end of World War Two."

The Judge was silent while I thought about what we had gotten ourselves into. Patriotism was at the heart of everything we were doing, after all. It was the lame justification for the actions we took. Now that we were so close to the most patriotic win of all, we hesitated, we faltered, letting our own misgivings about a world dominated by one country, even if it was the United States, get in the way.

The Judge walked to the tall windows and looked at his reflection in the dark glass, just as I had done and Tommy had done the day before. Our indecision and self-consciousness seemed to be measured by our habitual watching of our own actions, spying on ourselves, as it were. But then, as the Judge examined his reflection, I saw him slide his service revolver out of the shoulder holster under his suit jacket. He stroked the polished handle, and I saw his eyes in the reflection in the window. They were looking straight at me, measuring the distance between us.

"Judge?" I asked, my eyes riveted on the well-oiled gleam of the pistol's barrel.

"The damn thing hurts my shoulder in that new holster," he said, sliding it back into the leather. "I've got to get it broken in. Particularly since it looks like you and me are a two-man posse, partner."

He gestured to the bottle of scotch, and I poured us both another. He raised his glass and said, "To our children."

"To our children," I agreed.

"I'd get a son if I were you," the Judge said. "I mean, as long as you're being a rich son of a bitch and buying human beings from some poor adoption agency, I'd buy a son. Fate gave me three daughters, and I love them, but I'm enough of a sexist to still want a son around. So as long as you're buying up everything I wish I had, why don't you buy that son I never had?"

"Just fate," I said to his hard words. "You got children, I got money. The scam is to make opportunities for love out of both of them."

The Judge snorted and smiled at that.

"The same game plan still holds," I said. "Tommy is our bait. She'll come back to get him and we'll get her. We'll let all the intelligence forces try to catch someone trying to pass this information to the Soviets and we'll just fish for Rebecca. The governments have the resources to throw a broad net; we've just got to go fishing with the bait that will attract the fish most likely to be the prize. If she's passed it on to someone else, the best way to find that person is to find her."

"What do we tell Tommy?" the Judge asked.

"Nothing more than we already have. All he has to do is find her and try to talk her into coming back in. If this plan that you and Murphy have cooked up works, she'll come to him. He'll just sit in a Colombian drug lord's private jail until she and her family break him out. Unbeknownst to him, we'll be following him. He'll be like a homing device. Wherever Rebecca is, he'll be, and we'll be able to track him—I'll see to that."

For a moment, glancing toward the dining room, where I had left John X's briefcase, I almost boasted that I would bet my life that Tommy would not get away from me, but caution held me back.

"Then the only training Tommy needs," the Judge said, "is how to be bait. So let's move. Let's go tomorrow."

"Well," I said, "we don't know yet whether he's really with us, whether he'll even go along with this plan."

"Let's say you're right about all of this," the Judge said. "Let's say that the family is up to something big. Don't we know enough to lead us to believe that, whatever it is, it is going on right now? Even this very minute? Doesn't that argue for moving fast? That's why I think you and Tommy ought to get on a plane as soon as possible, tomorrow morning, fly to the Bahamas to a place Murphy has set up as a transfer point, and get Tommy into the hands of the Colombians."

I walked back to the bar and stared at the many bottles of colored liquor without touching any of them. They were lined up neatly, their exotic, colorful labels shouting of old mysteries and colonial splendor. I found it awkward playing the part of the patriotic hawk, willing to risk anything for my country, conniving to keep information from my government. It just really wasn't my style. Yet my time away from the spy business had refreshed my memory of what this was all about—finding out information that would keep us from shooting at each other, or at least allow us to be prepared when they decided to try to shoot. What this was all about, I reminded myself, shaking off my sophistication and battle-weary mentality, was our children: the generations that followed us. We had to have some sense of ethical responsibility for them, whoever they were.

"When did we first meet?" I asked, planning on giving him a big patriotic speech about the importance of doing what our country asked us to do.

The Judge looked up at me and smiled. "The day I took the oath of office, seven years ago. At the damn stupid thing that Kingston put together for the career officers to meet the new director."

He looked at me, and I shook my head no, and this time he laughed. His laugh wiped my speech out of my mind.

"That's right, that's right," he said. "You interviewed my friends when I was appointed to the bench. How the hell could I forget?

Some Yankee Bureau man come down to Texas to check out an Army J Corps lawyer who happened to get a friend elected to the United States Senate. You had no idea I was in Army intelligence. The senator who was promoting me thought that might not sit well with people, so they sold me just as a hard-core J Corps lawyer."

"I was supposed to interview your friends," I said, running my hands gently over the smooth bottles as if they were women's shoulders. "Routine part of the ol' federal vetting. I didn't plan on running into you."

"You walked into Billy's old barbershop and asked for Hank Wilcox," the Judge said. "Not too many men would put their barber down as a reference, now, are there?"

"I remember Hank saying 'That's me,' and he just went on cutting hair while I asked him questions about you. He laughed before he gave every answer, which I thought was a little strange, but he never said a word about whose hair he was cutting."

"You never would have known that was me in the chair," the Judge said, "if I hadn't chipped in and started to praise myself as the most honest, straight-shooting man in the whole state of Texas, and Hank laughed so hard he fell down and hit his head on the edge of his sink."

"I remember you standing up and stretching out one of those big hands of yours and introducing yourself. I had no idea what to say, so I said, 'Nice to meet you,' and left town."

"The amazing thing," the Judge said, slapping the side of his leg and shaking his head, "was that they went ahead and appointed me anyway."

"You would have got that appointment if you had been a communist wife beater," I said. "It was absurd to send a runt like me down there when you already had enough clearances to know things we'd never let a federal judge know. But I guess they wanted to put on a show. Treat you like everybody else. Ignore those stars on your shoulder, since it was a civilian job, after all."

"I presume so," the Judge said with a soft, final chuckle. I looked him in the eye and told him with my glance that he and I knew each other better than we pretended, and well enough to know when it was the other's sincere, deep conviction that something had to be done and had to be done now. His dark eyes, surrounded by tanned and wrinkled skin—eyes that had seen many things and lived many lives—smiled back at me with a glimmer of soul revealed. I saw it for a split second, that dash of friendship that went beyond professional respect, and then it was gone. He snorted a quick breath that I knew meant yes, I recognize, I understand, I concur. We have to do what we have to do.

"I presume," the Judge said, "that you recommend we continue to not tell anyone about Tommy?"

"No one. Every damn agency in the U.S. Government is going to be so busy trying to track Rebecca down, if my theory is true, that they won't have time to mess with us. We tell them enough to start the search for her and maybe somebody will be lucky enough to catch her, but I doubt it. All they will do is scare her into our net. All of their action will make her move up her plans and take risks she wasn't expecting to take. And to get her, we need her to make some mistakes. We can go to the Joint Chiefs tomorrow morning. But tell them nothing about Tommy. You'll invoke section nine of the Code and get a meeting of all the intelligence heads and the JCS at ten tomorrow. You can call on the way home, or from here."

"Now wait one cotton-picking minute," the Judge said. "I said I'd go along with your story here, not tell it to anyone else. I thought we were talking about going it alone. If something goes wrong then I'll report to the Joint Chiefs, but we still have to operate as if Rebecca has a mole on the inside. If we tell the whole damn network, which is exactly what we'll be doing if we go to the Joint Chiefs, then she's bound to find out. We've got to do this one on our own."

"But they've got the resources to help by—"

"But you've laid it all out yourself. We've got surprise. We've got the bait," the Judge said. "Plus, I refuse to endorse your theories about what's going on here by taking them to the Joint Chiefs. I'm not saying that you're wrong, Steele. I'm just saying I need more proof before I go blabbing to that back-stabbing cabal of bureaucratic bozos."

I exhaled deeply, aware that I had made the argument for going it alone.

"I'll agree on two conditions," the Judge stated, all traces of friendship gone. "One, that we tell nobody, that we go it alone. Two, that the mission starts immediately. That you're on your way to the Bahamas tomorrow to give Tommy to the Colombians."

I shook the sleep out of my eyes and suppressed a yawn. "Okay," I found myself saying, without really thinking. "Agreed, let's go do it."

"I'm going home," the Judge said. "You've got work to do."

"Why don't you just stay here?" I asked. "We've got plenty of room. Call Helen and tell her you don't want to do the hour drive."

"I may not get to see her much after tonight, Steele," the Judge said. "So I'd better go home for a while."

We shook hands solemnly, and he folded his long body uncomfortably into the back seat of the waiting car. I went to work.

33.

THE SIXTH DISCIPLE was code-named Bartholomew.

The late-night international telephone operator at the small transfer station on the south side of Bombay thought she heard glass breaking as she plugged in one of the ancient cords to connect a line from a downtown tourist hotel to the satellite broadcast line that would send the caller's words up out of the atmosphere and back down again to the London number she had just casually dialed. She listened to the first seconds of the caller's conversation, heard the sounds of a homesick young traveler asking her parents for money, and went on to the next call. She thought she heard glass breaking again, the sharp screech of rigid fragments hitting metal, but then again, it was hard to hear anything with her large operator's headphones on.

It was two minutes until four in the morning in Bombay.

The tape that played constantly in the next room, recording every conversation any of the three operators had with anyone who needed their assistance to call from the southeast quadrant of Bombay to anywhere else in the world, recorded the whirl of the long white fan blades that moved the hot air of India through the row of wood slats that opened up to the outside. Only the employees' break room had windows, and the sole operator who remained at her switchboard later said she thought that maybe her partner, who had gotten up to get a soda, had dropped the thin glass soda bottle, shattering it on the concrete floor.

But as she was picking at her unpainted fingernails and waiting for the next late-night call to come in, a man's gloved hands reached around her, pulled a black hood over her eyes, and tied it around her long, straight black hair. He pressed the cool end of a snub-nosed revolver against her ocher neck and said, "Act perfectly normal or I will kill you."

She swallowed hard, feeling the rim of the gun's end, and asked, "What do you want?"

"Quiet," he said, in what was to her ear, which was trained to listen to the lulling theatrics of the Queen's English, an obviously fake Scottish accent of someone trying to disguise his voice. "Do what we say, or both you and your mate here will find yourself sleeping on the bottom of the river with all the other corpses."

Just then a call came through, and she tried to figure out what to do. She could hear the sounds of someone else coming into the room and opening what sounded like boxes, cases, or luggage.

"Answer the call," the man with the gun to her throat said. "Perfectly normal."

She took the call and made the connection, feeling across the board for the right slots. She had made so many connections that her fingers could do the work without her eyes. For a moment she thought of breaking into the call and screaming, but the sharp metallic sting of the cold revolver kept her from saying anything out of the ordinary.

The Bombay security force would determine later that two men broke into the transfer station and knocked out one operator in the break room; then, while one man held a gun to the neck of the other operator, the second man set up a small but powerful computer and modem. The second man must have known something about the telephone station, the operator told the security men later, because he quickly and silently connected the modem directly to her phone board and within two minutes said the only word he uttered during the break-in.

"Ready."

The other man spoke directly into her ear in his fake accent, the tape picking up his voice clearly. "I will dial the number. You connect it to this line and then wait."

In the next long, silent five minutes the trespassers sent millions of bits of top-secret military information over long-distance phone lines to a number that could not be traced because the call was made directly from the transfer station. They left no fingerprints, and did not harm the operator, who was instructed to continue to answer the phones normally while they waited in the next room. After five minutes of answering calls and hearing nothing she pulled off the hood and crept into the hallway to see if they were around. Finding only her coworker moaning on the floor, she hurriedly called the police.

After hearing her story the Bombay police called the security agency, which came over too quickly for the police to believe that this was a routine case. The police did not know that the director of the Indian Security and Intelligence Agency was at just that moment contemplating whether he should call London and let them know that there might have been a break in the Indian government's top-secret computer files. When he heard from his agents who went to interview the telephone operator, he decided he should alert the new prime minister. Even though the caste-sensitive director of security did not trust the new man, the prime minister should hear the telephone operator's story and know what had been stolen. The future of the country was at stake.

"There was one strange thing," the young telephone operator told the security men as she stroked her long black hair as if looking for something in its glossy forest. "Before they left, one of them kissed me. Here on the cheek. Very softly. Brushed my face. Just a perfect kiss."

34.

"DO YOU trust him?" Murphy asked quickly, turning to me and setting his drink down on the heavy mahogany table. Murphy was alone in what Carolyn called the music room, his feet up on an ottoman and a drink in his hand, watching the television without any sound. "I mean, Tommy is just too good. Where does a kid from Indiana already know all this martial arts shit? Why are we so lucky to be handed him on a silver platter at the scene of that—that battle, just so we could conveniently get him to go back into the family for us? Why are we so lucky that he agreed with you, that he believes in you, that he believes that the only way to save his lovely Rebecca is to turn on her? Doesn't this make you a bit nervous, boss? Don't you get this feeling that the whole damn thing is just a bit too gift-wrapped?"

"First, for the last time, would you stop calling me boss? Second, how could anyone, no matter how much they knew about the organization, have anticipated our decisions and our strategy?" I asked in my own defense, not willing yet to admit that I shared some of Murphy's concern.

"But that is just the point," Murphy said. "Rebecca did know the organization. Rebecca knows you and me and everyone else involved."

I spoke carefully now, with the studied deliberateness of a man who is used to having his words recorded. "Murphy, there are details, important details of the plans and arrangements, that no one inside the organization knows—things you, Carolyn, and even the Judge do not know."

Murphy stared at me for a long time, measuring my words against the look on my face. "What are you telling me?" he asked. "Are you telling me that we are even more on our own than you let on? That even the Judge doesn't know the full scoop?"

"He knows enough," I said, seeing the rolled-up leather belt in my mind. "Enough to bail us out if the time comes when we need it. I take full responsibility. It's my head, my career, and my money on the line."

Murphy stood up slowly and walked over to where I sat. He stood in front of me and put out his hand to shake. "All right, you son of a bitch," he said. "Once again you've done the right thing. I want us to be out on our own without somebody back at the organization to screw things up. The less they know the better."

"Good," I said, shaking his hand. "Because they don't know a damn thing worth knowing."

"One thing I know," Murphy said, "is that you're not the man to lead this mission."

"What?" I said, stunned by his directness.

"You're a desk jockey, and you know it. I'm a field guy, and you know it. You need me to be there. You need as much firepower as you can load on a plane to be with you when you are flying down south to deal with those people. Hell, these are my contacts. I set this trade up—admittedly, not for tomorrow, but it is my mission. Why the hell the Judge doesn't want me to go is crap. You and pretty boy Tommy are walking into a scene that's way too complicated for just the two of you."

"Murphy," I said, speaking with the fever of a new convert, "rule number one billion, remember? Don't trust anybody. If the organization thinks we need a week to put together the transfer, then do it in one day. If the Judge thinks that just Tommy and I are flying down to the Bahamas to make the transfer, then bring an entire army. How's that?"

I knew that Murphy was right and the Judge was wrong. I could not go on the trip by myself, and therefore I would have to risk being more obvious, making more noise, as the Judge had called it, by bringing a whole planeful of men.

"You are crazy," Murphy said. "I get to go?"

"Everybody goes," I said, letting the words sweep out of my mouth in my exhaustion. "We fill the plane. You are second in command. Carolyn goes, because she wouldn't have it any other way. Freddy, Sammy, the whole crew, armed." What I didn't say was that I believed we needed everyone because we might end up chasing after Tommy as soon as he was picked up by Rebecca, because we would have the black box that would pick up the location of Tommy's belt.

"You are really crazy," Murphy said.

"I know. But you taught me how to make crazy work for you. You're the pro."

Murphy let out a howl of laughter and slapped me on the shoulder so hard that I nearly fell out of the chair. "All right!" he shouted. "We all go, and we go tomorrow, but you've got to promise me one thing."

"What?"

"You let me test Tommy to make sure he isn't just bullshitting us."

"Sure," I said, my fatigue leading me to rely on Murphy's instincts and not just my own. When I was tired I had a habit of agreeing with everyone. "Let's go through the logistics, all right?"

"Okay. Let me report this to you, boss, since, according to the Judge, it is your plan. If it works he takes the credit. If it flops you get the blame. We need to get the fabulous Tommy into the hands of the same arm of the drug cartel that attacked Rebecca's clan. Because that's where Rebecca already thinks he is. And we not only have to get him to them, we have to make them think that they need to keep him alive and protect him from being kidnapped by American gringo security operatives, like none other than Rebecca. After all, they have to put up a good fight or Rebecca is never going to believe it—and if the whole thing is a fake then Rebecca will find out through one of her many sources. Tommy really does have to be kidnapped by the cartel so that Rebecca can really save him, now that he knows our tune."

"With luck," I mumbled, "no one gets killed."

"Luck is with me, you old geezer. For example, the United States Government just happens to have in its custody one little sucker named Miguel Raphael Escabedo, who just happens to be the first-born son of the number one finance man of the Medellín cartel."

"So?" I said, rubbing my tired eyes.

"So," Murphy said, pausing for effect. He shook his head at my slow-wittedness, as if my inability to guess his plan showed once again how unfit I was to run a mission in the field. "The kid is all macho hidden-homo spit-in-your-face courage, but for some reason his family wants him back. If one of their friends suggested that the best way to get him back is to take someone who is important to the gringos and then offer a trade, they might try it. After all, in the two weeks we have had little Miguel, and have not turned him over to Justice to do their legal thing with him, they have tried everything. Now someone close to them suggests a kidnap target, and then a trade."

"In other words," I said, "Tommy really does get kidnapped by a Colombian drug cartel, and we guarantee his safety by making him the ransom for this Miguel guy?"

"You're learning," Murphy said. "In ten years or so you might be a decent agent. Of course, you'll be using a walker by then, but it's never too late. The key, Steele, is having someone the Colombians trust. That is where my friend Jacob comes in. Jacob of the Bahamas. Jacob the pirate. Jacob the big fat two-timer with sand between his giant toes. He suggests the deal. He arranges the deal. Tommy is kidnapped on his island while visiting with a northern spy chief. It's all very, very cozy.

"But," Murphy said in almost a whisper, "we've got to be sure, damn sure, that Tommy really is singing our tune. So that's where my little idea comes in that is outside of the plan. We've got to test him, you see? We've got to make sure that the first time he's pressured he doesn't spill the beans and tell whoever is putting a gun to his head that he is now a semitrained United States agent who has been convinced to help us find his ol' lover baby."

"This," I said exhaling, "is the part I'm worried about."

"The test?" Murphy asked. "You've got to be kidding. This whole plan is so out of line, so full of potential pitfalls, that testing Tommy is a cakewalk in comparison. At least we're in control when it comes to this test. The Judge himself recommended the woman who will run the test operation. The test is a piece of cake compared to the rest of the plan. Once Tommy is in the hands of the Colombians we'll be lucky if we ever see him again."

"But—" I began.

"No buts about it," Murphy said. "We stage a kidnapping the moment we set foot on the island. Tommy is whisked away on a boat, raced around the islands all afternoon, and then brought to a safe house that is, unbeknownst to him, only four hundred feet off the beach of my friend Jacob's island fortress. The safe house is equipped with cameras so we can watch how Tommy handles himself under interrogation. We see if he breaks."

"And if he does?" I asked.

"Then we scrap the Judge's plan, get back in the plane, and come home. The sign of a good mission plan, mister sit-on-your-ass-all-day-at-HQ, is that it is in stages and you can back out after any stage that does not work. That's how you stay alive out there. You know your alternatives. You know how to get out. Unless you're an atrophied analyst on the ninth floor who—"

"Go to hell," I replied with a smile.

"I've got a round-trip ticket," Murphy said. "I'm bringing back information for the agency. I'm going to try to find a mole in hell to feed us regular reports of what all our former friends are doing down there."

"With your luck," I said, "all you would find in hell is moles."

The plan was simple and straightforward. We would have a mock trial to see how Tommy did, and even if the Colombians' spies saw the mock trial they would only think that someone else was trying to get Tommy so he must be valuable. I simply nodded yes to Murphy and shook his hand.

"Let's get to it," I said. "We've got to burn up some phone lines and make some arrangements. I brought home two phone scramblers and decoder manuals."

"There's only one way to get that done," Murphy said. "Get Carolyn on it. We need to pull out the big guns to get this done. She must have access to secure phone lines through her companies or her lawyers or something. If not, she'll know how to get it done."

"By the way, did you give our boy back his belt?"

"Sure. It was nice of you to clean off the mud."

"Details," I said. "It's always important to pay attention to details."

"Yes," I said, heading for the stairs.

When I tiptoed into our bedroom and softly kissed Carolyn's forehead she reached up and pulled me down beside her and kissed me back.

"What's up?" she said, reading my mind in the dark.

"I've decided to talk you into adopting a child," I whispered.

There was a long silence in the big dark room, the breeze waving a heavy tree limb across the window, the shadow looking like a giant finger beckoning us to come out into the dark world beyond our tight stone house. "You have, have you?" she asked. "And why is that?"

"I don't really know," I said, running my hand through her tangled hair. "But I think it has something to do with my megalomaniacal ideas about saving the world, creating peace in our time, and having an unnatural desire to wake up at three A.M. every night to change a stinking diaper."

"That makes perfect sense," she said without laughing, the perfect straight man. "Completely understandable. Should I get up out of bed right now and call some adoption agency, or do you think you can hold off until morning?"

"No, I think we better get on it right now. Let's go pick one out after midnight. It's the best time. You can see which ones are sleeping and which ones aren't. We definitely want a sleeper."

"Okay," she agreed, getting up out of the bed. "Let's do it."

"Great," I said. "But since you're up, there are a few little matters that we ought to tend to first."

"Such as?" she asked.

"Such as making the world safe for democracy. Such as finishing the plans you started and arranging to go to the Bahamas tomorrow morning. We need secure phone lines, a jet, twenty thousand dollars cash, maybe a boat, and your wonderful organizational skills."

"I've got the plane, the cash, and the flight plan already worked out. I just have to figure out the timing with Murphy."

"Let's do it," I said.

She walked across the dark room in the bathrobe she had thrown loosely around herself and took my hand. "Okay," she said. "Let's do it. All of it. Save the world first. Get the baby second."

"Priorities, priorities," I sighed as I kissed her. "They make the world go round."

We worked into early in the morning until the arrangements were finalized. Then I read files until I fell asleep over them and went to bed, fitting into the curve of Carolyn's warm back. I did not dream as I slept in the comfort of my own bed. I did not ask myself why I was hellbent on stopping Rebecca's family from achieving the holy grail of world peace, as they saw it. I did not realize until much later that the Judge and I never discussed just letting Rebecca's family carry out their plan, but only discussed world peace as the product of American dominance. So I suppose, in some myopic way, I committed the ultimate patriotic act. The Judge's reasons were known, as always, only by himself.

I woke before the sun was up and lay in bed staring at the ceiling of the tall room. I realized then that violating a dozen federal laws in the space of a few days, to say nothing of lying to the entire United States military establishment, had come so easily to me that I had never stopped to think of the consequences. I did not have to fear poverty or hunger, or even pain, but a loss of the freedom I so much enjoyed. If all the eggs the Judge and I were breaking did not make a decent omelette, then I was cooked. I'd lose everything.

And that is the lesson, fellow spies and political hacks. Even the old hands get caught up in the action and forget about themselves and the consequences of their actions. When I suddenly realized that I could go to jail—real, cold, metal-barred jail—I turned as white as Murphy's linen pants and closed my eyes tight with the intellectual pain of being such a damned amateur. I, like Rebecca, might be able to keep them from prosecuting me by graymailing them, but they might take the risk of at least indicting me to bring shame on me and keep me from becoming a high-priced consultant to one of their suppliers. I did not think of turning back, of marching right back into the situation room and telling them what I had cooked up. That was out of the question. But I suddenly thought of being cold at night. Of hating the food. Of missing my wife.

I glanced over at her—yes, I remember every detail so, so well—and touched her gentle cheek with my glance. Watching her eyes move under her eyelids, I closed my eyes to memorize her face and the movements of her lips, as if that memory, that image burned into my enfeebled brain, was a handle to hold on to in case the bottom fell out. As if somehow I might lose her in the islands that lay in front of us this day.

All I had feared was the end that John X had met—but death was easier to accept than the accusation of treason and a life behind bars. Death is essentially incomprehensible to all of us, and therefore, my theory number 432 goes, never feared as much as the punishments inflicted on the living. And if I had the choice between death and imprisonment if this scheme did not work out, which would I choose? I asked myself this question, but I knew the answer. I was a coward, I knew, remembering the look on Carolyn's face that night so many years ago when she danced me out onto the veranda and asked me to take her right then and there. I would take the certain punishment rather than the uncertain death.

Was I beginning to go crazy, suddenly thinking of death and imprisonment? Were the tension and tiredness catching up with me? The answer was clearly yes, and those of you who have been in the field doing actual operations will recognize in me that stage every agent goes through after days of tightrope walking. A loss of confidence. A weakening of certainty. A questioning of the mission. A reevaluation of the risks involved. I was going through the usual emotions like a training coach putting marks on a checklist.

But the Judge would be proud, I thought. Proud because even an old horse like me could recognize and therefore handle my own emotions. Yes, I thought, settling my stomach and trying to conjure up a pretty picture of just myself and Carolyn walking hand in hand on a beach. I should go back to sleep, I told myself. But I realized there was only one thing I could do, and I couldn't remember how long it had been since I had done it. I prayed.

35.

As Carolyn and Freddy dropped the jet down from the clouds and the frying-egg islands, with white sand surrounding yolk-yellow palm trees, came into view, it struck me that treason and tans go together like hand and glove.

Islands ringed with beaches, and dotted with tall royal palms that begin to yellow in the dry heat of August, are a magnet to spies and their prey. Long, warm days, stretched even longer by salt breezes that carry the languid, hypnotic scent of sensuous native flowers, attract those who commit treason and those who seek to catch them. The purveyors of information who commit bloodless, intellectual crimes, either for money, or if they have money then for ideology, all congregate along the equator like fat settling around a wealthy man's waistline, enjoying the nonjudgmental life of the tropics.

My theory, number 871, is that they are attracted not by the beauty of a tropical island, but rather the lack of enforced laws and the lax rules of behavior. The spies and the spy catchers are accepted in the islands because they have money, and money buys love in the tropics as no place else. In the tropics it can buy true, lasting friendships and true, lasting love, because in the tropics money buys time and the small creature comforts that promote civilized discourse among the giant red flowers and bronzed island girls. Rum drinks on a wide whitewashed veranda as the sun sets on a calm sea have a way of solidifying relationships and making even the mundane sighs and the momentary shared experiences lushly romantic. Not having to really work for a living gives the spies, and their prey, time to cultivate the finer, lasting things in life.

Our new friend Jacob Clark, the part-time DEA agent and full-time refueling king, was busy cultivating all kinds of friends on the small Bahamian island where he pretended to be a rich American with a controlling interest in a small fleet of fast planes. He was to meet our plane with a prearranged artificial kidnapping when we landed on an airstrip that he had installed next to his remodeled nineteenth-century plantation. The sprawling white stucco house sat on top of a gentle hill that looked out on the airstrip on one side and the glassy blue bay on the other. The property was on the end of the ten-mile-square island and was surrounded by water on three sides. The fourth side had a ten-foot-tall brick-and-stucco wall that separated Jacob's compound from the lazy city that spread out on the bay side of the island, tucked into the side of the hill and protected from the daily beating of the salt wind and ocean spray.

The thick underbrush, twisted and gnarled by the constant sea wind, had formed an almost impenetrable thicket across the land side of the plantation, and the array of sophisticated electronic devices that were littered through the jungle added to the fortress's strength. The ocean beat on twenty-foot-high sheer cliffs that were broken up only twice on the mile-long ocean side, and Jacob had built tall, strong gates with gunsights that aimed down the century-old stone piers at those two places. English cannons, forged before the war of 1776, lay in the sand by the new gates, reminders that these had always been crucial points to protect against pirates and the Englishman's enemies.

The bay side was beautiful but problematic. The narrow sand beaches widened a hundred feet at low tide, and the land gently rolled down to meet the beach in several places. In the shade of the palms Jacob had built a dozen small stone houses, each a sentinel post for the weak bay side, which was the beautiful, soft underbelly of the beast. Large binoculars with night scopes were mounted on rotating pedestals in the wide-open front of the houses. Below the stone wall that ran across the front were waterproof metal boxes that contained well-cleaned automatic machine guns mounted on spring-loaded stands that would pop up when unlocked. On a long shelf above the open front of the houses were Israeli bazookas that could blow a twenty-ton ship out of the water from a thousand feet away.

Jacob wanted to feel safe. Unfortunately, each new piece of equipment just reminded him of what he didn't have. Each new piece of equipment led him to take risks to get another new piece of equipment, until he was caught in a circle of consumer spending, just like most Americans back home.

For a substantial fee, Jacob allowed his private airfield to be used by drug planes making final refueling stops before going up the eastern coast of the United States or over to Europe, and the DEA ignored, or managed to botch, its investigations of his little filling station in return for the information he fed them. It was a profitable deal for everyone involved.

A large mirror next to the landing strip flashed Morse code up at our circling jet, and seconds later a lilting voice came over the radio, telling us that we could land. The voice suggested a speed and a declining altitude that my wife said was nearly impossible, but seconds later, our seat belts cutting into our chests, Freddy had landed the plane on the short strip with a dozen feet to spare.

While the jet turned and taxied back up the runway, Freddy called Tommy up into the cockpit to show him how to land a plane. One of Murphy's men shut the cockpit door and nodded to Murphy.

"Okay," Murphy said, "let's make this easy. As soon as you hear a shot, hit the dirt, and stay down until I tell you to get up. Jacob's fake kidnappers will keep all of us at gunpoint but will take Tommy, Steele, and me into the jungle by the side of the strip. They will separate us and take Tommy. Steele and I will come jogging back to the plane. They may shoot over our heads a couple of times, so don't panic and just stay calm. The code for trouble is 'blackbird.' The okay, clear code is 'soda fountain,' okay? If anybody shouts 'blackbird,' everybody go for cover and get ready to fire. Everyone takes one walkie-talkie and one gun, nothing more. Got it?"

"Got it," Carolyn said. Murphy nodded to his man at the cockpit door, who opened it, and Tommy came out.

"Okay," Murphy said. "Welcome to paradise. Let's all get comfortable before we continue Tommy's training."

Murphy was the first one out the door, his automatic pistol tucked into his unsnapped holster. We waited for him to call for us, and when he did, Carolyn, Tommy, and I walked out into the bright sunlight glaring off the strip and found ourselves surrounded by heavily armed young men. Jacob stepped forward from the crowd and hugged Murphy, and within seconds he was kissing Carolyn and shaking my hand all the way up to my shoulder.

He was a giant of a man, three hundred pounds of sweating, rotund black flesh dressed in a white cotton tent of clothes that billowed around him in the warm tropical breeze. He immediately gave us assurances that he would do whatever we asked of him and suggested that he give us a tour of his island retreat.

Freddy began talking to the man who ran the airstrip, about refueling and where to store the jet, while Murphy's men stood around uncomfortably eyeing the semiautomatic weapons of their hosts. Just as I was beginning to relax in the perfect weather, a burst of automatic weapons fire flew over our heads.

Everyone hit the pavement except for Tommy, who paused to stare at the crowd of armed men who came running across the pavement at us, and then fell gracefully on his stomach next to me.

"Let's fan out!" he shouted into my ear. "We've got to move or they'll take us!"

"No," I said, because I didn't know what else to say. "Stay calm."

"Murphy!" Tommy shouted. "Go for the plane. I'll cover you. Run for it!"

Murphy's words were drowned out by the sound of Jacob's men returning the gunfire, their aim, of course, just slightly too high to hit anyone. Tommy jumped up and ran low and diagonally out of the line of their shots and toward the jet. It suddenly hit me that he might mess this whole show up by being so damn brave and resourceful, but the attacking group wrestled him to the ground just as one of his hands touched the stairs to the jet. Tommy whirled and smashed his heel in the first man's eye, shoving it up and out of its socket, and then swung the wheeled stairs in the path of the half dozen others who attacked him.

The next man who got to him swung his rifle butt at Tommy's back, but Tommy swung down and out of the way, catching the rifle in his hands and shoving it up into the jaw of the attacker. He reached for the rifle's trigger, but the next man kicked the gun out of his reach. Tommy dodged his two swings and then ran around the back of the still-hot jet and grabbed the hose of the fuel truck that had pulled up to the plane. He twisted open the nozzle, and jet fuel shot out of the hose in a twenty-foot arc, just waiting for a spark to become a giant flamethrower. As the remaining men surrounded him he sprayed the high-pressure fuel at them, the wet stream evaporating as it hit the hot pavement, leaving only a ghostly hiss of danger.

He screamed, "Don't shoot at it, or you will all blow up! This will explode!"

The dozen men warily surrounded him as he whirled around with the spraying hose, and then one of them pulled me up from the ground and marched me over to Tommy, pushing his pistol against the side of my head.

"Drop it!" the man shouted above the sound of the gushing hose. "Or he gets it. Drop it or I shoot!"

I was too stunned to react at first. All I could imagine was the warm end of the gun barrel that knocked against my scalp with each step. If he tripped, I thought, or was stung by an errant mosquito, my head would be blown away. That was when the feel of having a gun to your head was burned into my memory. The cocking of the gun sounded like the crunching jaws of a giant fish. Every other sound was dull and muffled, as if I were underwater. All I could think of was, what next? Will I hear it, or will it just happen before I can recognize a sound or sense the heat?

My eyes met Tommy's, and I cursed Murphy and his goddamn ideas under my breath. All this for nothing, I thought, not able to ignore the gun that might accidentally go off at any moment.

I could see Tommy waiting, balancing his options, wondering whether I could grab the gun out of the man's hands and save the day. With the heat of the pistol searing my head, I watched his eyes dart around him, his now-trained mind grasping for some way out of this predicament. Please, I thought. Make this easy. Give up just this once. Live to fight another day. This is just a dress rehearsal.

I watched his eyes examine the different competing interests, comparing his options. Then I saw him decide. Tommy turned the nozzle off and dropped the hose. He was immediately surrounded by the black troops dressed in jungle camouflage, and his hands were cuffed behind his back.

"I'm sorry," he said to me as they dragged him away. Sorry for what? I thought. For not getting me killed?

"What is this all about?" I demanded, my voice actually breaking from true fear that somehow something had gone wrong. But none of the men answered me. They silently led Murphy, me, and Tommy into the jungle that bordered the airstrip and then separated us. I tried to talk to the two men who marched me toward the sea, telling them that I was in on the secret so they need not march so fast, but they refused to say a word.

After ten minutes of struggling through the thick undergrowth, my pants torn and sunglasses lost, one of them looked at his black watch and nodded to the other. They unlocked my handcuffs and then suddenly they were gone, leaving me in a real, pulsating, alive jungle.

I stumbled in the vines, watching for the animals that made the sounds that surrounded me, and then heard the shouts of the men back at the airstrip. I followed the sound until I found the clean black asphalt edge that was carved like a river in the middle of the sea-green jungle.

Carolyn ran up to me, followed by the bouncing fat of Jacob. Their clothes were covered with the black tinge of the asphalt they had been lying on.

"Are you all right?" Carolyn asked.

"Yes," I said. "But did it work? Did they take Tommy?"

"Yes," Jacob answered, breathing hard from his short run. "But one of my men died. Murdered. The one he kicked in the head. Where the hell, my new friend, did he learn to do that?"

As if on cue, Murphy stumbled out of the jungle, his gun in one hand and a three-foot-long snake in the other. The green viper writhed in his hard grasp, and Murphy, covered with mud, smiled demonically.

"Look what I found," Murphy said. "Deadly. One drop of venom and you're gone." He held the snake right behind its cocked jaws and then threw it in the air like a lasso. It arced up twenty feet like a piece of rope, and two shots from Murphy's pistol tore it into little pieces before it hit the asphalt.

I put my head in my hands in disgust at Murphy's bravado. It was the kind of thing that got him thrown out of the organization. Losing a foreign asset just for a test. Showing off like a high school quarterback who just got his first touchdown. We should have known that when attacked Tommy would use some of the skills we had taught him.

Murphy smiled and lied, "I taught him, Jacob. I taught him how to do quite a few things."

"What now?" I remember asking, trying to avoid looking at the crowd of men who had gathered around their fallen comrade, silently mourning and recognizing what kind of life they had chosen. Although I knew that the word "chosen" was a misnomer to these men, who really had no choice but to take any job that was offered to them.

"We wait," Murphy said. "There won't be anything to see for several hours. They have to drive him around the island a dozen times in three different boats and then march him through two miles of jungle. He'll be blindfolded the whole time and, hopefully, all the while believe that he has been kidnapped."

"I'd say your student did pretty well," I said quietly to Murphy, with a gesture to where the dead man lay. "I'm glad I'm not lying there with him. Did they have to use me as their bait? I really don't like having a gun put to my head. It's bad for my heart, Murphy."

"It won't happen again," Murphy said, as if talking to a scolding schoolteacher. "Let's all go relax before the show begins."

"I don't want any more screwups," I said to Murphy as I looked around for Carolyn. "This is the worst beginning to a mission I've ever heard of. Are we incompetent or just plain stupid? Jesus, what the hell have we got ourselves into? I want Tommy back here tonight, all in one piece and ready for tomorrow."

"Don't worry. He'll be ready to be kidnapped for real tomorrow. He'll know all about being kidnapped. He'll be an expert victim."

As Murphy talked I saw Carolyn walking toward the group of men who were putting the body of the dead man on a canvas stretcher. They stood around the body, touching each other's shoulders or stooping to pick up the weathered stretcher, all looking down at the dead man's open eyes, staring straight up. The dark-skinned men parted as the blond lady dressed in white walked slowly toward the dead man, her eyes riveted on him, ignoring all the men who moved out of her way. Four men held the corners of the stretcher, and she stood before them, examining the bloody face and bruised black body. I saw one of the de facto pallbearers flinch as Carolyn's pale, thin hand, lined with lavender veins, reached out and touched the dead man's arm.

She squeezed his lifeless bicep and then took his big, rough hand in her small white palm. She held it for a moment and then walked away, never making eye contact with the crowd of black soldiers, who watched her every move.

She came and stood by me, touching the spot where the gun had scraped my forehead, taking my arm and then my sweating hand. Her fingers trembled in my clutch. I wondered if she was thinking of Mike Carter, or maybe another brown-skinned man she had left on the ground in that valley where the little town by the river grew laughing mermaids. The threat in the abstract had once again become real.

"Are you all right, ma'am?" Jacob asked, coming up to where Carolyn, Murphy, and I stood. We all looked at Carolyn as if she were a seer—the only one who grasped the sudden tragedy, who would interpret for us.

"Yes," she said. "I'm fine. Let's get on with it. I presume we have some work to do."

Carolyn didn't fool me. I knew the cool confidence in her voice was a well-practiced act to cover up emotional turbulence. She had been shocked by the sudden, unexpected sight of death. To walk out of a plane into such a beautiful, living, growing place and suddenly be confronted with such brutality would be shocking to anyone.

"Unfortunately," Murphy said to Carolyn and Jacob, "we have the worst kind of work. We have to simply wait."

"Come then," Jacob said in his rhythmic voice, which swung from word to word, sounding like a practiced hotel keeper who was trying to get his guest to not notice some unpleasantness—like death—in the lobby. "Come up to my house and relax. Have some refreshment and a bath. Rest for tomorrow. Let me have a meal prepared and your beds turned down. You must taste my island hospitality before you leave. You should enjoy this brief respite in your travels."

Jacob ushered us up a palm-lined path to his plantation home, which sat on the hill like part of a lost movie set.

It was expensive when people got killed, Jacob explained as we sat on his wide veranda listening to the wind scratch through the palm trees. The relatives had to be paid. The man had to be buried. The local officials had to be bribed—and would anyone like another drink?

Murphy said yes.

"Quite a mess, really," Jacob said, folding his giant body into a handmade wicker chair that was as wide as he was. A servant came out with a cane tray bearing a second round of tropical rum drinks, which Jacob called widow makers. "It upsets me greatly, but I've planned for all of it," Jacob said. "My friends, don't worry a bit. It will all be taken care of. I have made the contact this morning with the Escabedo family. They know you are dropping off the American for safekeeping here, and for one hundred thousand American dollars in cash I have agreed to let them kidnap him tomorrow at noon—and not one minute sooner or later."

"Why would they believe you?" Carolyn asked, stirring her drink but not tasting it.

"Why wouldn't they?" Jacob responded, with a smile as wide as his belly. "I have never led them astray. Whatever my motives—and motives really don't matter, do they—I have delivered what I have promised. You have to understand, that out here a man's reputation is built slowly, over time. The drug cartels have dealt with me for years. They know that I know that if I betray them they can eliminate me and my family with a snap of their very, very big fingers. I am protected from the casual thief and the vagaries of politics, revolutions, and unstable governments by my little army here. But no one can protect themselves from the cartel families. Not even governments can protect themselves from their power. You must deal with them in order to do business here."

"But you are going to betray them?" Carolyn asked, the businesswoman in her fascinated by this arrangement.

"Not in the least," Jacob said. "I will deliver one valuable American citizen, just as I promised. Again, I cannot and do not guarantee the consequences of the delivery, and I was not asked, or paid for, information about the delivery. In fact, Mrs. Steele, as your husband has made sure of, I have no idea why this American is valuable to my cartel friends, or even who he is. All I know that my cartel friends don't know"—and he leaned forward and whispered—"and that my people here do not know yet, is that you would *like* him to be kidnapped."

Jacob smiled and threw his drink back into the vast open expanse of his mouth. "All in all," he said, "a most fortuitous set of circumstances that I can help both of my friends at the same time."

A silence fell among us as the breeze brought the smell of salt and the sound of screeching birds. I thought of the black box that John X had left me, now deep in a black leather bag in my room in Jacob's fortress. John X's death was on the surface bad for our investigation, and yet it had made possible my ability to keep secret our means of following Tommy. I had no idea then what Bobby the techy knew, or where he was. It wasn't until much later that I realized how close we came to losing our one advantage, surprise.

But John X's death had thrown me into the middle of this thickening paternalistic plot to deceive our government for its own good, and that might be very bad and very expensive, in all senses of the word, for me.

The birds screeched again, and the salt-air breeze that swept past us on the veranda was tinged with the smell of rotting flesh that is always present in the jungle. I watched the slowly moving fronds of the palms and wondered what was out there in the shadows in the middle of the day.

Maybe Jacob, the fat island king, was right. Death is bad for business, even if you are in the business of killing.

36.

THE SEVENTH DISCIPLE was code-named Matthew.

The tourists were lined up outside the Munich Hofbräuhaus at Am Platzl 9, but the regular Bavarians who knew the words to all the oompah-band songs slipped in through the back door, where the staff, dressed in lederhosen or dirndls, came and went in three seven-hour shifts.

Matthew slipped in through the back with the regulars slightly after 6:00 P.M. and waited a moment in the dark-paneled hallway so that his eyes could adjust to the darkness. When he had caught his breath and could see the detail in the antlers that lined the hall and were used as coat hooks, he swung open the door to the main room. The sudden sound of a brass band and more than a thousand revelers made him pause for a second, and then he dived into the crowd, knowing that he was finally safe in their numbers. No one would try to get him here, among a thousand tourists.

He scanned the long tables, looking for the face that he had memorized from a photograph only hours before. It was a typical Munich face: ruddy, slightly overweight, full of good cheer and with sparkling eyes. There were a hundred similar faces in the beer hall, but as he walked among the drinkers he couldn't find the one he was looking for. He pulled back his long hair and wondered if the locals could tell that he was an American just by looking at him. He had long brown hair that was too clean for him to be a European, and his casual clothes were still too tailored for him to be a German. He hoped that his deep tan and long hair made him look ten years younger than his thirty-five years, but he was sure that he was obvious to the trained eye. Fortunately, there were only two sets of trained eyes among the early revelers.

He stopped at a bar and ordered a liter of Helles just so he would not be so obvious as he walked among the tables. The beer was crisp, with a smooth aftertaste, and he sipped it slowly because he had to remain alert. Far to the south side of the massive hall the true regulars had the Stammtisch section, where their reserved tables had engraved wood markers and metal bells for calling the waitresses. He scanned the faces in that section but knew that it was unlikely that he would find his man there. No, he told himself, his man would be buried in the midst of the tourists, slowly sipping as they drunkenly threw beers down their throats around him.

"Prosit!" dozens of people around him yelled, toasting their own good fortune at being in such a warm place drinking such cool, fresh beer.

He moved into the center of the main hall, bumping elbows with hundreds of people and searching their faces for the man he had come to see.

"Good beer?" an accented voice asked behind him. He turned and looked down at the face he had been looking for, a jovial-looking man who was sitting at a table.

"I'm from Chicago," Matthew said.

"Ja," the man said. "The Magnificent Mile is very long."

Matthew smiled at the code and answered in turn, "If only the Cubs could hit that far."

The man nodded and gestured for Matthew to sit next to him on the bench. Matthew squeezed in at the crowded table and was introduced to a dozen visitors from Japan his man had just become fast friends with, as he explained to them in Japanese how the beer was made.

"I know seven languages," the man said to Matthew. "But fortunately my new Japanese friends here have about a toddler's understanding of English."

"Good," Matthew said. "Do you have something for me?"

"Not for you," the man said, slapping Matthew on the back. "But for the cause. For the effort. For the world, yes?"

"Yes," Matthew said, looking around him as casually as he could. "I think we should make this quick."

"Why?" the man asked. "You're not being followed, I hope."

"Not that I know of, but there's no reason to take any chances."

"Relax," the man said. "Look like you're just another tourist having a good time. I want to savor this moment. This is important to me. This is the conclusion, the grand finale to a career, young man. Professor. Government service. Political figure. You are witnessing the most important moment in West German intelligence since the Wall went up. I hope you appreciate your little place in history."

"I do," Matthew said. "But I'd like to keep it as short as possible, so if you don't mind, I'd like to just take that little gift from you and go on about my business."

The man reached under the table and pushed his hand into Matthew's pants pocket, leaving a microcassette wrapped in a pack of chewing gum. The man left his palm on the inside of Matthew's thigh and squeezed gently. Matthew shot him a startled look, and the man said, "Now if they are watching us they will think I was trying to pick you up and you left quickly in disgust. Now go."

Matthew stood up, leaving his beer behind, and walked to the nearest fire exit, which opened into an alley that he had checked out earlier. As he opened the door he saw two men get up from a table near the door, each with a hand in one pocket of his jacket. As Matthew stepped into the hot summer air he felt a hand slam him up against the stucco wall of the outside of the beer hall, and felt the edge of an ancient beam cut into his cheek.

"I hate it when you do that," he said to the man who was reaching for his arm. Matthew suddenly pushed himself off the wall, propelling both men backward and onto the ground as he swung around and pulled the silenced Luger from under his jacket.

"Police!" one of the men screamed in English, lying on the ground.

"Right" was all that Matthew said as he squeezed the trigger the first time, with both hands on the gun to steady his shot as he unloaded a full clip into the two men. Their bodies danced with the shock of each quickly delivered bullet, and then in five seconds they were quiet. A line of blood ran out of the mouth of one of the men. The other had a red spot the size of a quarter in the middle of his forehead.

Matthew slapped another clip into the Luger as an unmarked car sped into the alley and stopped fifty feet away, both doors swinging open and pistols appearing from behind them. He moved back into a shallow doorway, concentrating on getting out rather than listening to anything they shouted. He fired one shot into the lock on the door and then hurled his weight against it. The door crashed open into a dark hallway, and he took the stairs up three at a time. He passed up the first door on the first landing and slammed into the door on the second landing, which opened onto another hallway. He left that door open, knowing that half of the men chasing him would be forced to follow the route down that hall, and went on up the next flight of stairs. He opened the door on the third landing and softly closed it behind him, hearing the men coming up the stairs two flights below him. He opened a window and went out onto a fire escape, carefully shutting the window behind him.

Matthew leaped from the fire escape to the next building, threw his leg through a shut window, and then stepped into a family's neat apartment. He brushed the glass off his jeans as two children watched him from the couch in front of the television, while their mother screamed.

"Sorry," he apologized, and then walked out the front door of the apartment and down the hall, took the elevator down to the basement garage, and waited only a few minutes for another resident to come to the garage. As the middle-aged woman opened the door to a late-model Mercedes he gently put his gun to her head and gestured for her to move over to the passenger seat. She began to yell, so he was forced to hit her once with the end of the gun, and then, in stunned silence, she got into the car. He quickly drove out of the underground garage, but took a moderate pace as soon as he was on the Munich streets. He noticed that the woman was trembling so much that she had bit her lip, and he tried to reassure her by turning on the radio.

The sounds of Wagner filled the leather-clad interior, and he smiled as he turned onto the Autobahn. The deep sounds of cellos swept over him, and he blinked twice at the sound of the timpani. He had made it, he told himself, imagining the report they would file on his escapade. The rest would be easy. Drop the woman off before he got to the checkpoint. Leave the car a mile from where they would be waiting to pick him up. Take a nice leisurely stroll through the woods to where the plane was to land. He'd be in a sunny clime, wearing a swimsuit, before the sun rose again in Munich.

"This is good," he told the woman sitting next to him as she began to cry. "Very good. Don't worry. You will be safe. Everybody will be safe."

37.

WHILE TOMMY was tied up and waiting to be interrogated, Murphy and gang settled onto the house's many porches to drink the local beer and nap away the time. Carolyn and I decided to take a shower and a walk on the beach now that we suddenly had nothing to do.

Carolyn was so used to having a phone by her side, even when we were on vacation at one of her summer or winter homes, that the sudden quiet of an island room made her nervous. She paced the length of the ash floors, twisting the white lace drapes around her arm as she stopped at the flung-open French doors to stare over the treetops to the plane of blue sea beyond.

She stopped suddenly, standing in her long ivory slip by the tall windows that let the warm afternoon light in through the cotton lace. A wisp of silver hair fell across the furrows on her brow, like sterling lying across linen. She looked at me and said, "Be careful, okay?"

"Okay," I agreed.

She looked as if she did not believe me, and in her eyes there was a lesson—a theory of sorts—that you can love someone and yet not trust their judgment. That the love and passion you have for someone, even when it is weathered by years and other loves, is something different from and alien to trust, dependence, and a willingness to follow. Theory number 342: No emotional reaction you have to anyone is one hundred percent. You love those you hate and you hate those you love, which is important when you are in the business of guessing and manipulating human behavior. The essence of good spying is understanding the complexity and serendipity of human relationships.

"You don't believe me," I whispered to her. A strand of hair fell over her eyes. "You don't believe I'll be careful."

"I believe," she said, pushing the hair out of her face, "that you will do whatever you can to accomplish your mission, your goal here, whatever the danger to you."

"That's my job."

"But you will also do everything you can to keep me out of danger," she offered. "Which is why I plan to stick close to your side. I'm here to protect you, not just to have some excitement."

"Good idea," I said, "but it won't work. This is not a chivalrous group. They won't stop to help a lady in distress." I walked to her and held her in my arms, feeling the sweat on her forehead as she pressed it into my shoulder.

We dressed and wandered out to the beach to see the ocean, ever conscious of the watchful eyes of Jacob's guards following our every move. The ocean lapped and pulled gently at the wide expanse of white sand beach, like a lover pulling at a tangled white sheet. The afternoon sun glanced off the water and shot back up into the sky, illuminating the undersides of the clouds tumbling over the island. For a moment I felt we were on vacation.

We held hands and talked about Murphy and his men and what our next move should be. Theories popped into my mind so quickly that I didn't even see the boat until Carolyn touched my sleeve and said, "Honey, what—"

The sound of machine-gun fire burst over our heads, coming from the guard tower behind us and directed at a black cigarette boat that was racing straight toward us on the beach. I pulled Carolyn down onto the sand, but she had the presence of mind to shout at me, "No! We have to run! They aren't going to be able to stop him! They can't stop the boat!"

We ran toward the sound of the bullets, hoping the guards were firing far above our heads. I saw the sand begin to dance around us like small geysers erupting, and I knew that the boat was firing at us. I tackled Carolyn, putting my body between her and the ocean. Then, seeing a depression in front of a sand dune a few feet away, I hugged her and rolled us together into it. The dune behind us sputtered and sprayed sand as it was hit.

The sound of the gunfire inches above us was deafening, but I yelled in Carolyn's ear, "I'm okay! Are you okay? Are you okay?"

She pulled her face away, spit out sand, and said, "What a perfectly absurd question. I'm not hit, if that's what you mean, but I'm not exactly happy."

Sand whirled around us as the deep side of the dune was riddled with bullets, and then it stopped as suddenly as it had begun.

Within seconds I saw the black tips of Jacob's guard's machine guns sticking out from behind the dune behind us, and then the sudden flashes of orange as they shot back at the gunfire that was coming from the ocean. I couldn't see whether the boat had landed, and I didn't dare raise my head to look. After thirty seconds of rapid fire above us, two of Jacob's guards rolled over the top of the dune and into the small gully where we lay hugging each other.

"Are you all right, man?" one of them shouted at us. "We've pushed them back."

"He says he's okay," Carolyn grumbled, "but I'm pissed off."

The man stared incredulously at her, his mouth open with surprise. A few random shots were fired above us out at the ocean—futile, frustrated gestures.

"She's fine," I said, and rolled over to see the boat speeding away toward the horizon. "But what was that all about?"

We were surrounded now by a half dozen of Jacob's men, and a dozen more were running down the beach from both directions. "You tell us, man," said one of the men, who seemed to be in charge. "Somebody wanted to kill you and the missus?"

"No," Carolyn said, her old spunk returning. "Probably just him."

"Mr. Jacob," the man said, "will be most embarrassed that they almost got you."

"They wanted to kill us—the two of us in particular," I said. "That means they, whoever they are, know we're here."

"Was anyone hurt?" Carolyn asked, shaking the white sand out of her blouse, her eyes begging not to see another death.

"No reported injuries," the man said. "Now we must get you up to the big house. They might try again."

"What the hell is going on?" Murphy asked Carolyn and me when he and his private army met us on the front lawn of Jacob's house.

"You tell me," I suggested. "Somebody tried to shoot Carolyn and me on the beach."

Murphy and his men, Carolyn, and I all went onto the veranda. We stood in a small circle, Murphy's men holding drawn guns.

"Let's get Tommy and get out of here," I said.

"We can't get him," Murphy reported. "We're beyond the fail-safe time. Tommy's at the interrogation site, so our agents turned off the two-way communications until they start the interview, in about fifteen minutes. We've got to wait it out."

"What if whoever shot at us now has Tommy?" I asked. "Or are out to get him?"

"No better way to find out than go watch the television we set up to see the tube pictures."

I pondered our options for a second and realized that in this moment of indecision everyone was looking to me for guidance. "All right," I said. "Carolyn, you and Freddy take half the men and secure the plane. Make sure it is ready to take off immediately. We may have to get out of here fast. Murphy and I hope to watch Tommy's guest appearance in Murphy's torture chamber, then pick Tommy up and we'll all fly out of here."

"Why don't we just take a group of Jacob's guards and everyone else go with you?" Carolyn asked.

"We can't trust them," I said. "Jacob may be in on this deal—it has all the markings of an inside job. They knew exactly where we all were. They can help, but I want you with our men at all times and ready to fire at will in your own defense. Okay?"

Everyone nodded yes. We stood in the sea breeze in the near-sunset warmth of the afternoon, solemn in spite of the perfect surroundings. I broke the trance by kissing Carolyn and saying, "See ya on the plane."

Murphy, I, and four of the men went to the building where Jacob had set up the television and the communications system. The camera was hidden in a small hut on the island, and we watched as a fat woman painted her fingernails and a stick-thin guard sat on the windowsill with a shotgun lying across his lap.

"Who's the fat lady?" I asked.

"One of Jacob's best," he said.

"She's disgusting," I said, watching her paint her long nails and hold them up to her round face.

"Isn't she," Murphy concurred with pride. "Quite, really. But there's something earth mother about her that makes her right for the part. Have some ice for that drink there."

We waited half an hour, hearing updates from the landing strip that everything was fine there. The plane was ready to go and there was nothing out of the ordinary.

"Maybe we should wait this out," Murphy said. "Not bail out yet. I hate to abandon this operation when it seemed so good on paper. How else can we get Tommy into the hands of the Colombians?"

Just then there was a commotion on the television screen as Tommy, blindfolded, was led into the hut, his hands tied behind his back and each one held by a tall black man. The fat woman began talking almost immediately, directing the guards to tie his hands to two beams that ran overhead. Then one of the guards untied Tommy's blindfold and pressed a .38 against his temple.

"I'm—I'm an architect," Tommy said to the fat woman's lilting questions, punctuated by the snub-nosed revolver tapping his head.

We watched her interrogate Tommy, her questions full of speeches about the excesses and sins of the American intelligence agencies. The fat woman clearly hated the people who were paying her, and she was falling in love with her victim. All she knew was that she was supposed to get him to admit that he worked for the United States Government, and as long as she didn't cause any serious damage she could do whatever she wanted in order to get him to confess.

I was frustrated by the purposeless barbarity that drove us to test our own men in this way, and nearly had a heart attack when I thought she was going to cut Tommy's belt in the process of undressing him with her knife. But instead she simply unhooked the belt, pulling his pants down over his thighs.

"Look," Tommy said hoarsely, as if he could hear me thinking. "I'm just an architect. I'm not a spy."

"Let's send a boat over to pick him," I said to Murphy after the first hour. "This stupid thing looks like it's almost over, and what the hell, we're out of ice. I want to get out of here fast."

The fat woman grabbed Tommy's genitals, sending noticeable ripples of shock up his bare chest.

"Then tell me, honey," she demanded. "Tell me, Mr. Tommy Wood, American architect. How'd you end up in this predicament?"

"Because we put him there," Murphy said to the television set. "Gun to your head," she said to Tommy. "Ropes on your wrists. Hope in my hands. How'd you end up here?"

"Go get him," I said to one of the men by the door. "Get him now and go straight to the plane. We'll meet you there. He's passed his test. He's with us, Murphy. You've trained him well."

"I married," Tommy said softly on camera. "I married into trouble."

Murphy and I smiled at each other at the strange weight to Tommy's words. Not watching the small black-and-white screen for that second, we missed seeing the arm reach into the window where one of the guards sat watching the fat woman with his automatic rifle on his lap. I had turned away from the screen for a moment, asking myself a simple question: Tommy wasn't married yet, right? Maybe the simple exchange of vows at Rebecca's family lodge sufficed for a ceremony, but would he say he was married if he wasn't? But my thought was interrupted and then lost in the roller coaster of events that followed.

When I heard the scream and the sound of bullets I turned to the monitor in time to see the long black arm pulling away from the slash on the man's cut-open throat.

Suddenly the door to the small room we watched on the monitor was thrown open and rifles popped into every window. The tall black guards dropped their weapons and began to raise their hands, but a short white man walked into the room and, in full view of the hidden camera, shot both of them in the face, pumping their twisting bodies as they fell to the ground. Blood spurted out of the tangled mass of flesh that had been a face. The fat black woman stood there silently, as immobile as a mountain.

"Oh my God," I said, transfixed. For a moment I felt as if I were watching a movie, and then it hit me that this was real. Murphy was shouting orders at the men with us: calling the boat that was racing out to get Tommy, alerting the crew at the plane that we had an emergency, screaming at Jacob's guards to prepare for an attack. He stood in the middle of the room with a phone in one hand and the drink he had forgotten to put down in the other. The control room exploded with Murphy's precise orders.

In the midst of the whirl of bodies running and shouting around me I stood and watched the screen. Three men came into the hut and carefully untied Tommy, who looked at them in shock. Then I saw her, one second before someone found the hidden camera in the shack and shot it, shattering the lens and making the screen black. For one brief, immeasurable moment I caught part of Rebecca's profile as she walked into the room. Her short hair was slicked back tight against her severe face. She was wearing patched jeans and a polo shirt, covered by a bulletproof vest. There was a sleek gun in her hand, and her eyes were wide with hope.

"Jesus, there's a camera," the microphones picked up after the camera went dead. I rushed to the speaker by the tape recorder, glued to every word and static sound.

"Okay, keep calm."

"Tommy."

"Let's move it, folks. Let's get out of here *now*."

"Are you okay, honey? Tommy?"

"Yeah, I—I don't know what—"

"Out of here! Now! Watch the doors. Watch for cross-fire."

"Jesus, there's microphones, too!"

"Drug money buys you all the toys you want. Blast them."

"Come on, let's get out of here."

"Did they hurt you, love?" Rebecca's voice asked.

"Let's go, people! Now!"

"Blast the goddamn bug—"

"Who? I mean—I mean—God, I missed you," Tommy said, his voice breaking with confusion.

"The Colom—"

Then the sound of a gun, followed by the buzz and beep of radio static. Rebecca had come and got Tommy.

I threw open the door of the building we were in and ran as fast as an old man could run to the main building, one of Murphy's men trotting behind me, at Murphy's order. When I got to the room Jacob had put us in I threw open my suitcase and pulled out the black leather satchel with the black box. I unfolded and plugged in the parabolic antenna, the whip antenna, and the small earphone. I could hardly hear anything until I stepped out onto the porch off our bedroom, the late-afternoon sun warming my cold sweat. Then the static broke, and I heard Tommy's voice as if he were in the room.

". . . know what to say. But God, am I glad—shit, I'm ecstatic to see you. You tell me how you are. Where have you been? What is going on here?"

"Steele," Murphy said from the doorway, "what the hell are you doing? We've got to scramble. Let's get out of here!"

"Oh, love," Rebecca said. "I have missed you. I've got so much to tell you about. Don't even say it. I know I owe you an explanation—many, many explanations. But there'll be time for that later. Let me look at you. God, are you a feast for sore eyes!"

"What the hell—" Murphy said as he saw the device in my hands and then the earphone. I switched the dial on the side of the box, and the small red LED lights blinked out map coordinates that were shot down to the box from the satellite platform.

"My little surprise," I whispered to Murphy, instantly deciding to tell him about the bug. "It's in his belt. We can track him anywhere. Hear him five miles out, most places."

"Jesus, Steele, you never stop surprising me," Murphy said with a laugh. "Let's go get them. The mouse has taken the bait. Are those map coordinates? Let me see that thing."

"Not yet," I said to his first suggestion. "The mouse needs to go back to her den, where all the other mice are. They are going south now. We follow them to their home. Unless she knows all about us, which is a distinct possibility, considering where she found Tommy. Which is why we have to get out of here. We're sitting ducks."

"Yeah," Murphy said. "I've had my fill of surprises for the day. Let's get to the plane and move fast."

"Any sign of trouble?"

"The coast is clear, literally and figuratively," Murphy said to the men who had come in after him. "Steele, you keep listening while you walk to the plane, but walk fast and keep two guys with you. Everyone else, in the plane fast. Guns out and safeties off, everybody. I'll go ahead fast and make sure Carolyn's got everything ready to go. You come more carefully, Steele, I don't want that black box to get hurt. Let's go."

"Who are these guys?" Tommy said, his voice shaken and high in my ear.

"These are some of my friends," Rebecca answered. "New friends. But fast friends. They will be your friends too, soon."

"Soon?" Tommy asked.

"Soon as they get to know you," Rebecca said, over what sounded like the rough hum of a high-speed boat, her voice very close to Tommy's, their mouths probably inches from each other.

By the time an NSA team got to the island, two days later, it was empty. About half a mile offshore they found three boats full of dead Colombians, who probably had been waiting to come ashore to get their prize.

Much to my surprise, the fat woman was still alive. She had a head wound where a bullet had grazed her scalp, and two bullets in her lower abdomen, but she was alive. Too tough to die. Too full of island spirit and anti-Yankee venom to pass quietly out of the world.

"Jesus," she was reported to have said to the first man who entered the island hut, "could have got here a little sooner, couldn't ya? You'd think with the billions and zillions you got laying around up there in Wash-ing-ta-town you could get a damn bit faster boat. What did you do, row over? A woman's gotta bleed to death around here to get any attention. Is that it? Do we all have to bleed to death to get your attention?"

38.

THAT STARTED my life with the black box. It was glued to my side, my life only half lived through my own body, the other half lived through the sounds of Tommy's daily existence. It felt odd being so close to him—hearing him in the bathroom, hearing him talk to himself, hearing him gasp with pain. Tommy was in my brain, or at least in my left ear.

As I trotted to the jet between my two armed guards, Freddy and Sam, I heard Tommy ask, "Who was that woman? Who were those people who had me?"

There was a long pause, and then Rebecca said very carefully, each word slowly chosen, "We thought they were employees of a Colombian family. A drug cartel. So we thought."

Tommy paused, then rushed into the silence, filling it with words. "Yeah, I know that. But where did they come from? I mean, they didn't seem Colombian to me. And why was I given, or transferred, or sent to them? Why didn't I just stay with the Colombians?"

I stopped and held my hand for the guards to stop with me so I could listen carefully to Rebecca's response. Tommy was going for the story, trying to make lemonade out of lemons. The transmission was losing power, their voices growing weaker every second.

"I don't know," Rebecca said. "As you said, honey, we have much to talk about. But I want you to know that I know what you've been through has been hard. You weren't trained for this kind of thing. But you have to be honest with me. We've been watching out for you. I wanted to get you earlier, but my family made me wait. This was really the first opportunity."

"You knew the Colombians picked me up at your farm?" Tommy asked.

"No," Rebecca said simply, sending shock waves up my spine.

"Then how did you find out the Colombians got me?"

"Tommy," Rebecca said. "Tommy, Tommy, Tommy. This is a dangerous game you are playing."

My heart sped up, and I imagined how Rebecca would be smiling at him, her full lips slightly parted, her hand playing with a loose strand of hair. The static had increased so that their voices sounded as if they were speaking in a flock of squawking sea gulls.

"What do you mean?" Tommy asked quickly.

"I don't know what to say. I was afraid of this. I was afraid we'd have to talk about it right away."

"Talk about what?" Tommy wondered. "Look, I'm a little—hell, a lot—shook up. I don't know what the hell is going on. Don't expect me to make any sense."

"The Colombians did not pick you up," Rebecca said. "Some of my old friends picked you up."

"Your friends?" Tommy asked. "Friends like these new friends? Because if those people were your friends, I'm not sure I'm going to like these friends, and I'd sure like to meet your enemies."

"Oh, love, you'll get to meet those people too. You see, right now my friends are my enemies too," Rebecca said. "At least some of them. The friends of mine that you met, who picked you up, are about to meet an untimely death, unfortunately. I asked my family to spare them—begged, really—but business is business."

"Oh my God," I said. "Where's Murphy? Murphy!"

I ran toward the plane, the earphone dangling from my ear. I tripped over a tree root and fell to my knees, twisting my ankle in my attempt to protect the black box. I got up and began to run again, pain shooting up into my hip. I stopped and put the earphone back in, hoping that the box was okay.

". . . don't know what you're talking about, but you can't just—just blow people up. I mean, Rebecca, what I've—I mean, after what

I've just been through you begin to understand the value, the importance, the goddamn sanctity, of life."

Tommy's voice faded in and out as they moved farther out of range, the boat's engine noise interfering with the signal from his belt.

"Too late," Rebecca said. ". . . bad. Really too bad. I don't want you to think that . . ."

I started running again, gritting my teeth against the pain.

As I came through the palm trees I saw the jet sitting on the runway, the heat blasting out of its engines creating a wavy mirage of color over the black asphalt airstrip. Two of Murphy's men were climbing up the six steps to the door of the plane, while two more stood with their backs to it, their automatic rifles covering the surrounding trees. Then I saw Jacob running away from the plane with several of his men, his fat body moving faster than I would have thought possible. There was something strange about seeing him run. Something that set off an alarm bell in my head. He was coming toward me, but I knew he couldn't see me. Why was the fat man running?

The plane, I thought. Jesus, the plane. Carolyn was on the plane. About to meet an untimely end. Blow up.

"Carolyn!" I screamed as loud as I have ever yelled, my vocal cords ripping into the flesh of my throat, but the sound died over the roar of the jet. I imagined her in the pilot's seat, craning over a clipboard to make sure everything was ready for takeoff. I ran forward, the two guards at my side, and then I saw someone standing at the top of the stairs.

Standing tall and erect, a pistol in one hand. Maybe Murphy, maybe Jeff, maybe Stan. He saw me and waved me forward as if saying, come on, hurry up, come on.

I raised my arm and waved him toward me as I ran and ran and ran.

The blast of hot air knocked me back ten feet, throwing me face down in the dirt and saving me from the searing heat that followed the explosion a millisecond later, and from the shards of steel that swam through the air like black manta rays flung out of the ocean.

I hugged the black box and squeezed my eyes shut as the chunks of metal spun and fell all around me, thinking over and over of her name—Carolyn. Carolyn. Dear God, please forgive me for all my sins and spare my wife, my love, Carolyn.

Something heavy but soft hit my back and lay wet on my side. After the three seconds it took for the heat wave to pass, I raised myself up on one elbow and pushed the thing off me. It was the black-and-red charred mass of someone's leg with a leather boot still stuck on the foot, like a slab of meat in a holster. Nausea gripped me, but my anger fought it down and roared up through my bowels to my head and burst like a volcano of passion in my eyes.

The bastards killed her, I thought.

Emotions hit you like missiles at times like this, my friends. Logic and rationality are left behind, and the animal instincts take over. Survival. Revenge. The building blocks of all psychosis. I acted just as Tommy had in that Pennsylvania forest, without contemplation. I acted without thought. I pounded the hard dirt with my fist, mixing the sandy dust with the anonymous blood from the leg lying by my side. I was going to kill them. Kill them all. Twist the life out of them with my bare hands.

I looked around, tearing my eyes off the thirty-foot-high flames of the burning black hunk of the plane, and saw that both of the men guarding me were alive and transfixed by the leg. Then I saw Jacob.

Crawling away from me were the fat hulk of Jacob, his white jacket torn and covered with dirt, and two of his men. I placed the black box by the nearest tree and crawled toward him, not even thinking about standing up. The smell of burning gasoline scraped my nostrils. "Jacob!" I screamed as I crawled toward the fire.

He turned and looked at me, first in fear, but then as if he was captivated by my voice. I scrambled to him.

"What the hell happened?" he said to me with wide eyes. His fat body quivered uncontrollably, as if he was on the verge of going into shock. "What went wrong?"

"Give me your gun," I demanded, my eyes narrowing into focused lasers. My voice had never been more commanding, I thought as I heard myself give the order. It was as if it were someone else's voice, some person who was exploding out of my chest. "I need a gun."

He hesitated after he looked into my eyes, but then handed it over, pushing the big revolver's butt into my hand. "It's loaded," he said, unable to disobey. "What now?"

The smell of gasoline filled the air, and the sudden heat caused a strong wind off the airstrip. I weighed the gun in my hand for a second, and then with a snap of my wrist I raised it and put a bullet in the gun wrist of one of Jacob's men. The other fumbled with his rifle, and I shot at his leg and then rushed him, grabbing his rifle and pushing him forward. He fell in Jacob's lap, his deep red blood gushing from just below his knee all over Jacob's white suit. His leg kicked out over and over again in bloody rhythmic convulsions.

"Oh my God," Jacob said. "Oh God, oh God. You're crazy!"

I heard my men coming up behind me, and I shoved the pistol into one of Jacob's fat cheeks. "Why?" I asked. "This couldn't happen without your help. Why?"

"No," he mumbled. "No, no, no."

"Why!"

"I—I—I had," he stammered, his jaw immobile from the gun, "I had nothing to do with it."

I shoved the gun deeper into his cheek, feeling the jawbone jut out against the hot gun tip. Carolyn was too young. She had had so much to live for. I depended on her for so much. For life itself. "This is it. This is the end," I heard myself saying to him. "Why did you do it?"

"I didn't know they were going to do this. I didn't know," he mumbled. "They wanted you to think that the Colombians took your Mr. Tommy. They wanted to put a—to put a trace on your plane. They said they wanted to put a trace. That's all. A trace."

"Who?" I screamed in his face, my teeth gritted together so that I wouldn't bite him.

"Rebecca's friends. I knew Rebecca. From old times. They said—they said they were her friends."

"Who were they?"

"I don't know. I told you, I don't know," he said, gasping for breath, his chest heaving as if he were having a heart attack.

"Who told them we were here?"

"I don't know," he whimpered. "I didn't ask. Really. I'm on your side. Really. It must have come Stateside. That is all I know. I'm—"

"You're dead," I said, my finger itching on the trigger.

"No, no, no," he said, spittle spraying from his panicked mouth. I contemplated killing him—simply pulling the trigger to get my revenge—but a glimmer of humanity in his shiny sweat and wide stare caught my eye. Killing someone would be so easy. So quick. It was just like losing your balance as you walked a high wire—you swayed, tried to adjust for a moment, but then you fell, hurtling out of control. It would be so easy to pull the trigger and push this fat man off the wire. But my volcanic anger was settling into deepest sorrow, as the shield of hate split and began to drip my venom into my wounded heart with a rush of unbelievable pain. My throat opened to scream, but nothing came out. There were no words to describe the loss of the touch of her hand, the smell of her neck, the love in her eyes. There was no sound that could capture the rending of my heart. My eyes met Jacob's terrified gaze, and I saw nothing that reminded me of Carolyn, nothing that said that he was at fault, so I lowered the gun and pushed him away. His giant body fell over onto the ground like a tree, quietly quivering as he savored his sudden found life.

"Jesus Christ," I heard a voice behind me.

I whirled on them, but as I turned I saw that Freddy and Sam had their rifles up and pointed at me. They, I knew, were on my side. I lowered the gun.

"Carolyn," I said. "Carolyn . . ."

Then the tears came. Slowly sprouting and then blooming, like those time-lapse shots of roses growing and unfolding.

"Let's get some control here, okay?" Freddy said. "We may be up against a whole goddamn army. Let's get thinking here, okay?"

Sam pulled Jacob's limp hands behind his back and secured them with plastic clip handcuffs. Through my tears I saw him help both of Jacob's men quickly wrap their wounds, and then he handcuffed them, too.

"Carolyn," I said again, suddenly thinking of the brush of her kiss, the swirl of her long skirt. I don't think we've met, I said to myself. We had hardly met. Hardly begun a life together. "Is she—have you—"

"Give me the gun," Freddy suggested to me. "Or put it away. That's okay. Put it in your belt, man. That's fine. That's good."

I put the gun in my belt and crouched on all fours, my breath coming short and shallow. I squeezed my eyes closed and swore again, this time with more thought, that I would kill them, every last one who had taken Carolyn. I would find out who did this and track them down. I would use every tool, every dollar, every connection I had developed to make these people experience the horror I was beginning to feel.

Freddy pulled his walkie-talkie off his belt and leaned against a tree, his eyes jumping and scanning the scene like the eyes of a frightened doe. "Let's find out if we're all alone here," he said. I was silently thankful that Freddy and Sam were with me, their trained professionalism taking over in the midst of the crisis.

"Code Blue," he said into the microphone. "Anybody out there? Soda fountain, soda, soda, soda. SOS."

He held the walkie-talkie up to his ear and listened to the static and then shouted out Murphy's code again. "Soda fountain. Soda, soda, soda. Anybody out there?"

A woman's voice broke into the static, and with the first word I heard angels pulling my soul up from my gut and into my brain.

"Root beer float," I heard Carolyn's voice say over the scrambled static of the walkie-talkie. "Root beer float," she almost sobbed. "What happened? Who is this?"

"This is Freddy!" he shouted back. "We're at the airstrip. Somebody blew up the plane. Everybody on it is gone. Gone. There's nothing left and—"

I grabbed the walkie-talkie out of his hand, fumbling with the buttons. "Carolyn?" I shouted. "Carolyn!"

There was silence at the other end, and then her voice, strained with powerful control. "I don't think we've met."

"Carolyn," I said again, unable to respond.

"Steele, goddamn you! Don't scare me like that. I thought you were dead, goddamn you!"

"Carolyn," I whispered, cradling the walkie-talkie as if it were a baby, relief gushing over me like ocean waves, eroding the layers of hate and fear. My eyes opened and closed quickly as I said a little prayer of gratitude. If there was a God, he was fair and just and mine, I thought. All mine. My God. Mine. "Oh, honey, I love you."

"I love you too," she said, her voice breaking, but then pulling back into the stiff-backed tone of a soldier. "Where are you? We're in the big house. Just Murphy and me. We're not sure we should move."

"What the hell were you and Murphy doing up there?" I shouted.

"Steele," Murphy's voice said, booming out of the speaker, "we're having an affair. I've decided to go straight. She was looking for you, you idiot. And I was looking for her. Now get up here. We're surrounded by Jacob's boys. They're all milling around out here in the yard, trying to figure out what to do. They don't know we're up here, in the bedroom you were in, but any minute ol' Jacob's likely to show up and tell them to go hunting for us."

I looked over at Jacob lying on his side in the other man's pool of blood. The bodies of the two handcuffed young men by his mound of flesh were so small and thin in comparison that I laughed at the sight. I stopped my crazed laughing, aware that I would laugh at anything right now. The whole world was beautiful to me.

"No he won't," I said into the radio, realizing how valuable Jacob could be to us. "We've got Jacob. Murphy, just sit tight. We're coming up there."

"Be careful, boss," he said. "There's probably twenty of them milling around up here."

"We've got to come up," I answered tiredly, my very soul exhausted by the hurricane of rage had that raced through me. I exhaled slowly, feeling the weight of each breath. Carolyn, I thought, closing my eyes and seeing her face. My lucky Carolyn. "We'll radio you when we can see the house. Over and out."

"Walk like . . . like ghosts," Murphy said, trying to mask his sorrow. "That's what I always say to my boys."

Murphy's boys were all dead except for Freddy and Sam, who had stuck by my side. My joy at Carolyn's luck was tempered by these men's sacrifice.

I was in such a hurry to get up to see Carolyn that I almost forgot the black box. I put the earphone in and heard short bursts and pops of static. The map coordinates still shined brightly, so I knew that it was working but they were out of the five-mile range.

Theory number 497: Pain is a beacon to your consciousness. It draws attention to whatever part of your body needs attention, but then is lost in the rage of emotions that can hit you if someone has inflicted the pain. I had completely forgotten about my injured ankle in the excitement, until I calmed down and took that first step toward Jacob's house. The sudden realization that I would have to hobble struck me as almost funny after the ups and downs of the last twenty minutes.

But the pain in my ankle also woke me up to this: Jacob's confession that he had helped Rebecca's friends put a bomb on our plane had momentarily clouded the issue. Someone had to have told Rebecca that we were working with Jacob before "her friends" could corrupt him into helping her. The number of people who knew that we had contacted Jacob, assuming that our communications had been safe and not intercepted—a big assumption, considering Rebecca's knowledge of our communications system—was very small: me, the Judge, Murphy, and Carolyn. I believed that none of Murphy's men had known where we were going or why. Tommy had not been told, either. Bobby the techy had been sent home to rest before we had made the decision to go to the Bahamas.

All four who knew were beyond suspicion, I decided, so there must be a problem with our communications links. Somewhere, somehow, Rebecca had found out about our plans by intercepting our communications. Eavesdropping, as she was trained to do by the NSA, had to be the answer. Until I knew where the break in the chain of communication was, I had to be very careful. Walk like a ghost, I told myself as we weaved through the jungle—or become one.

Twenty minutes later Jacob walked slowly into the yard of his mansion with me at his side. He ordered the twenty men nervously pacing the courtyard to put their rifles in a pile. When several of the men protested he whispered the name of the Colombian family and gestured out at the jungle.

In three minutes the men were all lying on the ground with their hands cuffed behind them. Murphy and Carolyn came out of the house with their rifles up. I heard Murphy try to talk to me, but all I saw was Carolyn's quick strides.

"Miss me?" she asked.

"Not much," I lied.

"Good," she said, and kissed me. As she pulled away, I pulled her back and kissed her again, tasting the life in her mouth and the energy in her lips. She was very much alive. Very much. She stood next to me and slid under my arm, and I hugged her to me, believing that I could never let her go.

Murphy strolled among the prone men, counting on his fingers. For a moment I was worried that he would begin killing them, counting up the lives his team had lost and seeking revenge in equal numbers. Murphy had known his team well, and had loved them more, and differently, than any other commander I had ever met. I knew that he would not smile again for a long, long time. I wondered if he was thinking of his men by name, remembering each of them as he stared down at these unknowing accomplices in their murders.

I watched him carefully and slowly count the prisoners, terrified that I would be called on to stop him from doing something—that something deep inside me I wanted to do too. He looked up and saw me watching him, my eyes boring into that part of his soul that I had so recently come to grips with in mine when I thought Carolyn had been killed. He dropped his hands to his side, his rifle swinging by its strap, and unabashedly let a tear roll down his cheek. The late-afternoon sunlight, straight and Caribbean bright, reflected off the tear and glimmered like a diamond earring that had lost its way. I breathed in deeply, smelling the salty jungle air alive with sweat and blood and burning metal. Then I exhaled, pushing out the torn tension and last remnants of hormonal rage.

"Murphy," I said to his gaze.

"We're five short," he mumbled, wiping away the tear and walking to me. "Jacob had at least three more men than the two you left down by the plane. They may be out there. Waiting to take a potshot." I had underestimated Murphy. He was already in control.

Our plan had fallen apart—exploded in the flash of the plane shattering into a thousand parts. Somewhere we had gone wrong, and I couldn't help but think again and again about where. But I remembered the training our agents received: Let the analysts do the thinking after the mission is done; don't spin your wheels rethinking your actions in the middle of a mission. Just carry out the plan. Improvise to get over hurdles. Get to your goal. Get to your goal. Get to your goal.

"Let's get out of here," Carolyn suggested, flicking back a strand of her silver-blond hair.

"With what?" I asked, but really thinking, to where?

"Jacob's boat," Murphy said, leading us as a group away from the handcuffed guards. "Fast and fat, just like him. Where are our friends Tommy and Rebecca, by the way?"

"Last time I checked the box," I said, "they were still headed northwest. They must be in a hurry, because she isn't taking any obvious evasive action. Unless going in a straight line is evasive action among all these little islands."

"If she's in a hurry, then . . ." Murphy pondered.

"Then it must be time for the information trade," Carolyn said.

"Which means," I said, regretting each word, "that we have to follow them."

We all knew that we had no choice; the question was how to do it. Carolyn used Jacob's radio to send a message to her company to send her yacht in Key West in our direction at top speed and a helicopter immediately to an island Murphy picked off the map. Unfortunately, the communication had to be brief and cryptic, since it wasn't scrambled.

I shook my head again, trying to scare off the analyst in me and bring on the man in the field. Concentrate, I told myself. Weigh the options quickly and act. We were still in danger here on the island. We had been too damn lucky for our luck to last.

The five of us exchanged glances, bound together by the sudden tragedies around us. Every one of us had torn clothes and dirt-smudged faces, like a front-line brigade that had just come out of a firefight. The wind had picked up, bringing the strong jungle smell of rot and salt. The sun was moving lower in the late-afternoon sky. Night in the jungle or on the sea meant confusion, panic, and a chance of death. Time was running out.

FIVE

THE LAST SUPPER

"You are the men who have stood by me faithfully in my trials; and now I confer a kingdom on you, just as my Father conferred one on me: you will eat and drink at my table in my kingdom, and you will sit on thrones to judge the twelve tribes of Israel."

—Luke 22:28

39.

The ninth disciple's code name was James, son of Al.

James, as he thought of himself, doubted that the radar would be down on the autoroute de l'ouest, but even if he carefully measured his speed the trip from the outskirts of Paris to the small farmhouse near Les Eolides, southwest of the capital, would take only forty-five minutes to an hour. The eleventh disciple, Simon, who had flown in last week from South Africa, would be at the small house, cooking a perfect tenderloin and waiting for his arrival.

He pushed the accelerator down a touch on the rusty Peugeot as he thought of his cousin Simon basting the tender meat. It had been a long time since he had seen Simon, so this would be a very happy and a very good meal. James was bringing the wine and one computer tape, sewn into his jacket, Simon the meat and a compact disk from South Africa, and the tenth disciple, code-named Thaddaeus, would have a wonderful dessert and a floppy disk from Iran. It would be a wonderful little party, he thought.

James had calculated that the stop at the roadside gas station, where he would meet Thaddaeus and give Thad's friend the leather satchel containing ten million francs in exchange for the three floppy disks of information, would take no more than three minutes, unless something looked suspicious and he had to fill up the tank so that his stop would not seem out of place. Thad would get into James's Peugeot, and Thad's friend would drive away. The plan was very simple, as good ones always are. Therefore, he deduced in his logical way, he should have no problem being at the house for lunch at one.

James glanced at his bloodshot eyes in the rearview mirror and then scanned the highway behind him. He saw nothing out of the ordinary, and fiddled with the knob for the radio until he zeroed in on some American rock-and-roll, which he liked. He tapped his fingers on the steering wheel, smiling at the memory of skinny-dipping with Thad and Simon when they were just kids. He wondered what had happened to Simon's wife. He had heard that Thad had half a dozen kids squirreled away in Saudi Arabia.

He turned the radio up just before the autoroute went around a hill to the gas station where he was to pick up Thad. Before he even saw the petro station sign he saw the flames bursting ten meters into the air.

"Shit!" he said to the radio.

The station was engulfed in flames, as if a bomb had dropped on it, flames flowing in giant gasping waves out of the smashed plate glass windows and licking at the half dozen cars parked around the bright red gas pumps. People were running away from the building as fast as they could, carrying bags and children and looking over their shoulders at the volcanic eruptions of fire. A man with a video camcorder danced at the edge of the flames, trying to catch the spectacular blaze on film. The passing tourist would turn the tape over to a local television station later that afternoon, and French intelligence would have it by midnight. They sent a copy of the video to Langley two days later. Langley waited a week before realizing that it might be of value to the NSA.

The videotape shows that the autoroute was jammed with stopped cars and people running in all directions. James stopped his Peugeot on the grassy median and pulled a black pistol out of the glove compartment. He tucked the gun into his jacket pocket and ran toward the station. When he was within fifty meters of it a man in a uniform waved him down and shouted something that was incomprehensible to him above the roar of the flames, but the man's gestures clearly told him not to get any closer. When James kept running toward the inferno the uniformed attendant ran after him and, seeing his tweed jacket, yelled at him in English, since he had not responded to French.

"No closer!" the man shouted. "It was bombed! The gas tanks will go any minute! No closer!"

James ran faster, but the attendant caught up to him and threw him to the ground in front of the crowd of people thirty meters away. James rolled over and kicked the man in the groin and then rolled him behind a scrawny tree, where he chopped at his windpipe and snapped his neck. He knew he shouldn't have done it, but there was no choice. He had to get to the green Volvo parked by the outside pump.

He ran as fast as he could into the heat of the flames, covering his mouth and nose with his arm as he waded into the smoke outside the station. From five meters away he saw that there were two people in the Volvo, and he drew his gun just as an explosion rocked the station and sent chunks of metal siding flying into the sky. He dodged a strip of steel gutter that fell in front of him and ran toward the green car.

The man in the driver's seat was slumped over the steering wheel. When James touched the chrome door handle, he jumped back at the heat. He took a handkerchief from his pocket and pulled the door open, coughing from the smoke and having trouble catching his breath. The man fell out of the front seat, his dead eyes rolled up into his head.

"Shit," James muttered again, seeing that the dead man was his contact, Thad's friend. He reached over and shook Thad, who was slumped against the dash with blood dripping out of his mouth. James grabbed his wrist and felt a faint pulse. Thad was still alive.

The glove compartment had been forced open, the leather seats had been slashed, and the trunk and hood were open. He stepped over the dead man, reached under the steering wheel, and felt for the metal black box that had been specially attached. He touched its edges; it was hot. Whoever they were, they had not found it, but they had bombed the station to destroy the evidence of murder. He pushed at the tab on the edge of the box, so the cover would pop open and the computer disk would drop out, but it was stuck. Maybe they had found it, he thought, but had been unable to get it open.

He pulled his head out of the front of the Volvo and nearly doubled over, coughing from the smoke. He could see the whirling lights of the police cars and fire engines coming his way. He had to get out of there fast. He walked two steps away from the car and felt the ground sway up and away from him as an explosion ripped through one of the tanks on the far side of the station, throwing chunks of asphalt into the sky. He managed to dive back into the Volvo just as they began to rain back down. A half-ton chunk hit the back of the car, shutting the trunk lid permanently and shoving the front up in the air for a moment. James pulled himself up into the driver's seat, started the car, pushed Thad back into his seat, and put the Volvo in gear. "Thaddy," he said to his unconscious cousin, speaking English because Thad was uncomfortable with French, "we are going for a little ride. Just hang on, buddy. I'll get us to a hospital."

He floored the accelerator and pulled around the parked cars. Thad's body rolled over against the window.

By the time James was fifty meters away, racing toward the countryside on the grass median, he had the Volvo up to one hundred kilometers per hour. He pulled around the parked cars and slowed down as he merged into the traffic. The police were all speeding the other way, toward the giant flames and the rolling explosions that rocked the ground.

"You're going to be okay," he whispered, fumbling to feel Thad's pulse while his mind raced with plans on how to get to a hospital. He opened all the windows and gasped at the clean country air, his eyes moving constantly from the rearview mirror to the road ahead. Whoever had killed Thad's contact and ransacked the Volvo might still be around and would notice the soot-covered and bashed-in auto.

He made a quick turn onto a side road and spun the car around so that he was facing the autoroute and could see who might be following him. Thad's body rolled from one side of the car to the other, landing in James's lap. He pulled him up and saw Thad's eyes roll back in his head. He searched desperately for a pulse, but there was none to be found.

"Thaddy," he said, his eyes watering from the smoke and the shock. "Thaddaeus, pal. Come on. Come on. We were just so close, buddy. So damn close."

His cousin's body rolled into his lap again, a line of blood streaking James's jeans. The tenth disciple was dead.

James pushed him back into the passenger seat and pulled the seat belt around him so he wouldn't move. He wiped his eyes again and settled in to watch the cars that streamed past. He glanced over at his cousin briefly and noticed how much Thad had aged since he had last seen him. He was a middle-aged man now, with children, a business, a comfortable lifestyle. Was this really worth the risk? James asked himself, feeling the tension in his neck as he strained to look for followers. Was this worth losing lives for?

When nothing happened for five minutes he reached down and again tried to open the black metal box. It was still warm, but when he pried at the edge with his thumb it clicked open and a warm computer disk fell out of its insulated interior. He laid the disk in Thad's lap and glanced down at it as he drove, inspecting it for damage. Unlike Thad, the disk was untouched.

"You got it to me, Thaddy," James said to the corpse. "You made it, pal."

He would be only fifteen minutes late for lunch, he thought, tuning the Volvo's radio to the station he had been listening to in his Peugeot. The Rolling Stones banged out of the speakers, Mick Jagger's voice slightly melted with the burnt speaker cones. James sang along to the heavy beat, not really listening to the words, Thad's body bouncing with the potholes in the road.

40.

FIVE MINUTES from the island's shore, with the ocean spray streaking through my thin hair, I realized that Rebecca and Tommy had stopped. The red LED lights on the black box blinked the same coordinates over and over again, like a hypnotic set of seductive eyes, and I waited to see if they were just pausing in their escape. But as Murphy piloted Jacob's speeding cigar boat, with me, Carolyn, Sam, and Freddy in it, northwest through the calm sea for an hour, the map coordinates did not move.

"That belt could be on the bottom of the ocean," I said to Carolyn. "Maybe still around Tommy at the bottom of the ocean."

"I don't think so," Carolyn replied, emptying a bottle of sunblock onto her fair skin. "She didn't rescue him just to kill him."

"The box could be broken," I said. "It ran into some tough times when the plane blew up."

"I don't think so," Carolyn said again. "If it was working before, why would it suddenly be stuck? If it wasn't working it would be wildly off rather than right where they were when it stopped."

"They're there all right," Murphy asserted. "Just waiting for us idiots to try to sneak up on them."

"I don't understand the technology, but it could be like a clock," I said. "Just showing the time when it stopped, when it lost contact." If only we had Bobby the techy with us, or John X himself, to describe how this magic box worked, I thought, remembering my earliest lesson in the trade, that everyone needed to understand the basic ways the tools they relied on worked. Once again I had failed in my own eyes, I thought. So, more out of faith than anything else,

I put on the earphone and listened to the static. My unoccupied mind called up an image of the torn, bloody ligaments of the leg that fell on me when the plane exploded. My throat caught and I almost threw up, but the sudden sound of voices breaking through the static brought me back.

". . . do you think? Did you miss me, really? Damn, I sound like a mealy-mouthed schoolgirl, but . . ."

"I got it!" I cried, closing my eyes to concentrate, but the voices did not come back.

The sun was beginning to move lower toward the hazy line of the horizon. Evening began to settle on me like an old coat, and I accepted the tranquility of the cooling sea.

". . . permission to board? Why did we need permission to board from your dad? I don't—"

"Security, Tommy," Rebecca said. "You have to understand how . . . how sensitive this is. This gathering is . . ."

The voices disappeared in the static and engine growl. "Slow down!" I shouted to Murphy, and the boat rolled to a humming trolling speed across the water. "We're within listening distance," I said, feeling Carolyn's hands on my shoulders.

". . . all are gathering for the first time in—watch your head on the ladder—for the first time in twenty years, and I wanted you to be here. It's important to me that you are here. Even if you're not dressed for dinner. Here, I've got a couple of safety pins. We can at least keep your pants from falling off. We'll get you some new clothes on board. You're about my brother's size. Joe's size . . ."

"Damn," I whispered as the static etched into the voices. Could my speculation have been right? Was the entire family gathering out here in the ocean? "Move forward slowly and carefully, we're probably within four miles."

Ten minutes later the clouds broke above us and the last of the day's sunlight shined across the gentle waves. Suddenly the voices came back loud and clear.

"Got them," I said, raising my hand so that Murphy would stop the boat.

"What do we do now?" Sam asked.

"Listen," I answered, attaching the miniature tape recorder to the black box and praying that I had enough tapes to record everything we heard. "Listen and wait."

That tape is an amazing document, my dear friends. Only four people have ever heard the entire thing: me, the dernza, the secretary of state, and the president. The tape and the one transcript, with notes in the margin scribbled by the secretary of state to the president, are kept in the organization's vault, double-locked and secret-coded. It tells an incredible story, some of which you have already heard. From the scraps of voices the whole scheme became clear.

Tommy had married into trouble, and trouble was gathering four miles over the horizon. As I sat listening to their voices, Carolyn, Murphy, Sam, and Freddy stared at me, waiting for some gesture of surprise or expectation, but I was so entranced that I could only mumble comments at first, until I realized that the tape would pick up the details and all I needed right now were the basic facts we could act on. At first I was reluctant to repeat and comment on what they said, feeling as if it was breaking a confidence to publicly air their most private conversations. But soon all feeling was lost as I became captured by the sounds—guessing, reasoning, examining their meaning.

"God, you look good," Rebecca said, close to Tommy's ear.

"I look like I've been through a goddamn war," Tommy said. "You, on the other hand, are absolutely, positively, delectably beautiful."

There was the sound of a kiss, and then Rebecca said, "There are beds in our rooms below. Staterooms, they're called, my dear. Beds and showers and . . . and all my relatives watching my every move."

"That sounded good until you got to the end," Tommy said. "Very, very good. Particularly the shower part."

"You'd rather have a shower than me?" she asked teasingly.

"Tough choice," he answered. "Very, very tough choice. How about having one before the other? Is that an option?"

What became clear was that the Bundt family was gathering in the midst of the ocean, a sleek flotilla of expensive yachts anchored together. The eleven Bundt families, each the descendants of one of the eleven Bundt children, were having one last meeting. They had come from all over the world to gather in a large yacht anchored in the middle of the twelve other big boats and the dozens of small boats full of hired security guards that circled the ocean meeting.

This much of what I guessed was true—the family was gathering.

I was haunted with anticipation, waiting to see if the rest of my theorizing had even a smack of truth to it.

Rebecca took Tommy aboard the big boat, where he was frisked and given a room with a shower while Rebecca went forward to see her father in the captain's lounge. Fortunately, they didn't have any pants that would fit Tommy, so he put his torn pants and belt back on and toured the boat, asking Rebecca a thousand questions. The caravan of boats lifted anchor every other hour and moved a mile or two, on the principle that the move would mean added safety. Three of the boats had helicopters mounted on pads over their bridges, and one bridge was in constant communication with a four-man submarine that patrolled below the surface. None of the family members completely trusted the others, so each deck was filled with armed guards uneasily staring at each other through binoculars.

"They will have dinner tonight at six," Rebecca explained to Tommy, her mouth pressed against his neck. "Each family will be represented. Some of my aunts and uncles will be here. Some sent their sons and daughters—my cousins. I will be there also, but really only to explain the computers and transmitters the boat is equipped with and to load the information each family is bringing. I've asked to bring you. I want you to see them all, just once. Do you think California wines were a good choice? I picked a Heitz Martha's Vineyard '84 and a Beringer '82. Both are full-bodied Cabernets, but—"

"Why?" Tommy asked.

"Because this is such an American enterprise. Sure, these people have had wine from all over the world, but—"

"No," Tommy said. "I don't care about the damn wines. Why me? Why do you want me to be there?"

"Because . . . this is my family, you know? You will never see them again, so I want you to meet them. I want you to understand what they are all about and . . . and I just can't explain it. You have to see them. See how they interact. See this whole scene played out—to the end."

I pounded my fist on the side of the boat. "I was right!"

"Right about what?" Carolyn asked.

"They are getting together," I said, "to trade some kind of information."

"Look," Tommy began, his voice dropping to a whisper that the microphone barely picked up. "Is this dangerous? I mean, what is going on here with all the guns? Are they protecting themselves from somebody, or from each other? I mean, is there going to be some bloody shootout every time I'm with you?"

"No," she said firmly, anger tingeing her words. "This is the last time. No more of this. I promise. They don't trust each other, and we know—you know—that there are people trying to stop us. Each family is given as much time as they want today to send security people to the boat to check it out. Your cheek feels good now that you've shaved. Smooth and soft. Let's just go back to that room and—"

"Why?" Tommy asked. "Why don't they trust each other? Aren't they all family?"

Rebecca laughed and kissed him. "My family," she said. "My family has been in the espionage business so long they know they can't trust anyone. And they haven't gathered like this since Nixon was romancing Brezhnev. That was the first time this information exchange was suggested, apparently. By my Uncle Talmuz, the oldest son. He suggested it, but it took my brothers and me to put it all together. That's why I'm so happy. The boat is here. We're here. The computers are up and operational. And this whole thing is almost over. Once this is over, no more guns. No more secrets. No more danger. This is it."

"Why didn't they do this back then?" Tommy asked, kissing her back, his questions perfectly planned and perfectly natural, as if he knew that I was listening and checking up on his style.

"They couldn't figure out how to pull it off. The technology for the nearly instant, and nearly safe, transmission of this much information didn't exist then. We didn't have laser disk technology and compacted information. Now we can unload billions of bytes in minutes from the Cray mainframe on board, through the satellite network, to government offices all over the globe. They just have to know generally what they are getting, that's the only hard part. Once they know what it is we are sending—what format it is in, time sequence, compression codes, things like that—then they tune in to receive and it's . . . it's peace. Peace in our time, as they say in all those ineffectual political speeches. Technology has allowed us to do what hundreds of years of politics has not been able to do: communicate with our enemies with trust. And that will cause peace."

"Do you really believe that?" Tommy asked, as if he had read my mind. "Do you really think that is what is going to happen?"

"Yeah," Rebecca said. "Yes, I do. Or at least I think there is a good enough chance of it happening that it is worth the risks. Worth the lives. I've been in this business for a while, Tommy. I've seen how it works. Sure, every country will eventually develop a whole new set of secrets, but while they are busy doing that, if every country knows all the minute details of every other country's defenses and weapons systems, then no one can attack without suffering a devastating counterpunch. By the time they can reconfigure everything the world will be a different place. It is difficult to articulate what I'm talking about without sounding naïve, but the reality is naïve in its own way. The truth is simpler than we'd want it to be in our cynical, intellectual world. The truth is that Freedom, with a capital *F,* is ready to burst out all over the damn world, and this will release it from its bonds. This, Tommy, is what it's all about."

"I hope you're right. But how will all this work, and why are you telling me all this? Isn't knowing all this a . . . a . . . I don't know, a death sentence?" Tommy asked.

"Aren't we paranoid now. They have taught you well. It doesn't matter now. It's, what, five-thirty now. It will all go forward at eight-thirty exactly. Everyone will go on their boats back to wherever they came from, or maybe even somewhere different. Money lets you hide easily. And once it happens, we are all out of the information business. My father and mother will return to Pennsylvania after a while. Erik and his family are taking a sabbatical and then returning to Boston. Joe and Sandy are taking the kids on a trip around the world. Fritz is transferring to work with IBM in Australia. Jan is talking about selling his company and sailing around the world with the kids. My little sister Margert will finish at Brown, and she's talking about going to med school. I know one arm of the family is going to mine gold in Argentina. Everyone will disperse. Each of the twelve lines of the family will disappear back into the big old world, never to be heard from again. Poetic, isn't it, in its own weird sort of way?"

"Including you?" Tommy asked.

"Us," she answered. "You and me. We will go together."

"I see," Tommy said. "Now I know why I'm here."

"Yes," she said quietly. "That's why you're here. I want you with me. I want you with me and I have to leave tonight, right after I finish. They've given me the honor, and it really is an honor, of loading and sending the information tonight. Everybody else will go away for a little while, but then back to their normal lives, without the shadow of the family hanging around in the background. But I have to disappear. You know I can't go back as Rebecca Townsend, former agent of the NSA. No, I'm on the run for a while. Until they give up, forget, or decide that I'm really not a traitor after all. I have a boat waiting for us. I have some money. More than you would guess. I have an idea of where I want to go, and I want you to go with me. With the new me. New name. New job. New life. Oh, love, I don't care if you do think you're a spy now for the United States Government—hell, so am I. Or at least so was I. But after this there will be nothing to spy on. You won't have to save me, or whatever shipful of bull they sold you. It will be just you and me with a new life. You'll design buildings and I'll paint big, giant landscapes. Paintings that are bigger than life, of pastoral, country scenes. We'll build that house you designed—our house. The one on the hill that you told me about so many times. Maybe we'll have a baby, huh? Maybe we'll travel around the world and pick out someplace where we like the way the sun makes funny shadows on the walls and stay there the rest of our lives. Who knows? Who knows?"

I imagined them leaning on the wide white rail of the ship, staring out at the sunset. Their ruddy, sunburned faces reflected the first pink rays, and their eyes squinted out at the empty waterscape, focused on their thoughts. The wind tousled his hair and blew her yellow silk scarf as if it were a flag. There must have been a battle going on inside Tommy between what we told him to believe and the idealistic, romantic, quixotic world that Rebecca was asking him to travel into. We said that it was his patriotic duty to stop her treason, while she held out a vision of a world without war and full of beautiful landscapes and sunsets. He had a choice between the hard steel of our guns and our cold reality or the kinetic, flowing silk tapestry of her story of the future. Steel versus silk.

There was a long silence, and then Tommy breathed heavily. "I accept," Tommy said. "I think. I'm not sure if that's what I'm supposed to say, and I'm not sure what choice I have. You know I love you. And yes, I think you're slightly crazy and probably a danger to all of stinking mankind. But what's a lovesick guy to do? We are already really married. The official crap is the only part left to do. After all, I've already designed the house."

"But what?" she asked.

"What do you mean, but what?"

"There is something else. I can see it. I can hear it in your voice. There is some condition, some exception, some *but* to this."

"All right," he said. "On one condition: that you stop this nonsense about me being a—a—a spy, or whatever it is that you are talking about. I'm just an architect. I'm just me. Just me, thrown into this crazy world of yours."

"That's asking a lot," she replied. "Because I know what the truth is, and you're asking me to forget it. You're asking me to say it doesn't matter. I've done too much of that my whole life. The whole point of this new life is to stop making things up as I go along. To stop playing the clever spy with an agenda. To be honest, whatever that means, for a change. You've got to forget the garbage Steele filled you with. You've got to go back to being Tommy. Just Tommy."

I remember rustling in my seat on the boat as I listened to this, wondering how Rebecca knew so much about what we had said to Tommy. I was happy that Tommy was avoiding the issue of what he had agreed to do, or even that he had been held by anyone other than Colombians. She wasn't pushing him, but rather, like a good interrogator, giving him many opportunities to agree or reveal what he knew by the questions he asked. So far Tommy had refused even to get near the rope, let alone hang himself with it.

"Be honest? Like you were honest with me?" Tommy asked, filling the nervous silence. I wanted to take off my earphone and scream out loud, she knows, Rebecca knows, somehow she knows, but I was too transfixed by their conversation. "First I thought you ran an import-export shop. Not only were you a federal agent, you were a . . . a . . ."

"Go ahead and say it," she said. "Just get it all out. I was a traitor. A liar. A scoundrel and a thief. But that's all the past tense. I'm done with all that. This has all been a great adventure, but it's all over. Now I want to be Rebecca, landscape painter and mom extraordinaire. That's where I want to go. That's where I want to travel to now."

"But I'm not sure that's the Rebecca I fell in love with," Tommy suggested.

"Who was the Rebecca you fell in love with then? Don't you see, none of this makes any difference. You were in love with me when you thought I was just some working stiff living in New Haven. Then you were in love with me when you thought I was a spy. You stayed in love with me when you found out I was a traitor. So why not be in love with me when I'm an idealist, a revolutionary? Why not be in love with me when I've changed my name and am living in some exotic foreign country? It will be the same me, just different clothes. That's what being a spy is all about. It has always been the same me, just different clothes."

"I'll go with you," Tommy said in almost a whisper, followed by the sound of a kiss. "Déjà vu, you know? Here I am again, saying I will. I do. I will."

"She knows Tommy's been with us," I mumbled, my voice flat with shock.

"Are you sure?" Murphy asked. "You better be damn sure about that one, because that blows this whole thing wide open."

I gestured that I couldn't explain because I had to listen and then said, "It's blown. She knows."

"Holy mother shit!" Murphy shouted. "This is going to be fun, fun, fun."

"It begins at eight-thirty this evening," Rebecca told Tommy. "By nine o'clock sharp the world will have begun to change. The Greeks will know the location of every Turkish missile, and vice versa. The Israelis will know where every Syrian, Iraqi, Iranian, and Libyan missile is kept, and the code to defuse each smart bomb, and vice versa. The East Germans will know the West's secrets, and the West Germans will know every detail they ever wanted to know about the East. The North and South Koreans will know each other's military plans like the back of their own hands. Every Chinese secret will be common knowledge inside the governments of Taiwan and Japan. Most important, the Soviets and the United States, Tommy, these old foes, will be on the road to mutually assured survival. And, I'm happy to tell you, as an American, my guess is that the Soviet Union will simply disintegrate as soon as the U.S. has this information, because the U.S. can keep them from using force, and without force they will not be able to control their people."

"God, I was right," I said to Carolyn and Murphy as the boat gently rocked in the swell of the sea. I could feel tears welling up in my eyes in some strange mixture of pride and fear.

"This is unbelievable," Tommy said into the earphone in my ear. "It's nuts. How did you do this?"

"Each branch of my family gathered the most sensitive information on missiles, ships, troops, and defenses they could get their hands on, on every major power in the world. They've brought all that information in a prescribed computer format to this meeting, and at a prearranged time, when there is an open window on a satellite, I will transmit the information to dozens of waiting computers around the globe. In each country someone has posed as a seller of secrets and has prepared to deliver the promised goods by modem or satellite within the same hour on the same day—that way no one has the jump on anyone else. That way they are expecting something, and know the format it is coming in. They get the transmission, track its source, and find only an empty boat drifting in the sea."

"Man," Tommy mumbled. "It's gambling. It's terrifying."

"No," Rebecca said. "It's thrilling. I thought it couldn't be done, but the more you know about intelligence, the dumber it is. There's no mystery to all this information. There's no mystery to its power. Its value is only in the fact that the opposition doesn't have it. Let everyone have everything and there is no power."

"And no stability," Tommy said.

"Stability and the status quo have enslaved all of Eastern Europe and the Soviet Union. If we make things unstable, so be it. But we will make them unstable by weakening dictatorships."

"But I still don't—I mean, I know I keep saying this, but why won't everyone just think up new secrets, new locations for missiles, new battle plans? As soon as everyone knows what they need to know to shut down the offensive capability of each of these places, they will just move quickly to redo all of it."

"No," Rebecca said again. "We are going to be giving too much information. In a couple of hours these supercomputers are going to transmit Gorbachev's home phone number, the address of Mao's former mistress, and every code formula used by the Soviet military. The Soviets will know the access codes for every American military computer system and will be able to get even more information than we are sending them. They will be able to call the president's children directly on their private home phones. We will be sending so much information that is process-oriented that by the time they can reinvent not only whole new valuable secrets but whole new information systems, they will have gotten used to peace."

"Quite a gamble," Tommy suggested, repeating himself because he was so stunned. "High risks."

"And a big payoff," Rebecca said.

"But—" Tommy began.

"Tommy," she said, "you've just got to trust me on this one. You can't do anything. If you tried to stop it they'd kill you. You can't talk me out of it, because if I stopped now they'd kill me. So you must just stay with me and hope for the best."

"There's that word again," he said. "Trust. You've asked me to trust you before and you were lying to me."

"Not this time," she asserted, her voice getting louder and then moving away. "Now you are lying to me. You are simply refusing to discuss what you've agreed to and with whom. You know I know, but you won't talk about it. Look around you. Everything is exactly as I told you it would be."

"Our deal was," he said, "that you'd drop this nonsense. If I'm supposed to trust you, then you've got to trust me. Whatever you may think simply isn't true. I'm here with you. I'm sticking with you."

"I wish it were that simple," she said, her voice getting lower and tighter, like a cat ready to spring, as she sped through what she wanted to tell him. "But I know it isn't. I know because I've lived through the struggle myself. That struggle you go through inside yourself when you're not sure what's right. When you're not sure which side you're on. I've been there, Tommy. I know you can't get what they told you out of your head, even though everything around contradicts what you were told. Suddenly the supposed enemy is a real person with family and reasons for everything they do. People always have reasons, Tommy, no one tries to do things that are stupid or cruel just for the hell of it. People do what they think is right at the time and place they are faced with the decision."

"Rebecca," Tommy sighed. "For the last time, I don't know what the hell you are talking about. I don't really understand any of this. I feel like . . . like I'm trapped in some dream and there's a door there that just won't open."

I remember hearing those words and pulling out the earphone. In a near panic, I decided to contact the Judge. For some reason I was again reexamining our goals rather than just carrying them out. I tell you this so you know how natural it is for our men and women in the field to question what we analysts call their mission. It is almost impossible to stop analyzing why you are doing something before you do it. The *why*s crop up even more when there is no clear plan but only a goal in mind. If there is a clear plan, or so goes theory number 963, then you concentrate on the tasks prescribed by the plan and not the reason behind the goal.

Carolyn put on the earphone just in case we could pick up any of their conversations. Then I jockeyed with the radio on the boat for ten minutes before I got an operator who would transfer our signal to the telephone. I called the Judge's personal office number collect, and when he answered and heard my voice and code he had it transferred to yet another phone.

"Tex, you old cowboy!" I shouted at the microphone, trying to disguise what we were talking about as much as I could on an open radio band. "We need some help. Our red-headed friend is on to us."

"What makes you think so?" the Judge asked, a thin line of astonishment weaving into his voice.

"Trust me," I continued, hearing Tommy's voice in my own. "We've got a leak. But there's nothing either we or she can do about that now. My guess was right about what's up. It's crunch time, and her having advance knowledge isn't an issue anymore."

I explained the entire situation as best I could without being specific, yelling into the clumsy microphone and wondering at how strange it was to be standing on the rolling floor of a small boat in the ocean and discussing the dilemma of whether to risk world peace or world war.

"I can't do a thing on this one, partner," the Judge said, "unless I can evaluate your source. You gotta tell me how you got this stuff before I'm willing to take a gamble on my country's future, know what I mean?"

I knew that he was right. I was asking him to help make a series of major decisions without letting him know how high a level of confidence I had in our information.

So for the first time I told the Judge about the microphone in Tommy's belt buckle. He made me repeat what I had said, and then he laughed.

"You old rich dog." The Judge coughed. "You kept your best trick even from me."

"She makes the transfer at eight-thirty P.M. in whatever damn time zone we are in," I told him. "It takes about half an hour to make the transfer."

"Damn," he grunted. "We knew that, we just didn't know what she was sending us and from where. This afternoon while you were out being shot at we got the message that a package would be delivered to one of our computer lines that feed from the Pine Gap ground station in Australia. This must be it. Jesus, I'd love to see that stuff."

"I don't think we can take the risk," I said. "I believe we should try to go in and stop it before it gets to Merino." Merino was the code name for our giant ground station in Pine Gap, the most sophisticated intercept station in the world. I remember that it struck me as strange that the Judge didn't use the common code name.

"You'd be trapped, like a rat in a rodeo pen," the Judge said. "You'd never get out alive. Not a one of you. I can't let that happen. Let me just try to stop it with the military."

"What can they do?" I shouted back. "We've got to get in there and—"

"Bomb them," the Judge said calmly. "Just like we talked about. I've got the approval from the State Department. Terminate with extreme prejudice, you know. I could call up the Florida air station and have a squadron there in half an hour. My buddy the squadron leader could have a half dozen bombers lay down a carpet that would stop their transmissions right quick."

"Too many innocents," I responded, remembering how easy it had been to get approval from the secretary of state to kill people. "And, more important, we lose the opportunity to try to get what we want without giving anything up to the Soviets. We've got to go in and try to get the information we want and stop the rest."

There was a long pause on the Judge's end, as if I had just uttered some profanity that he had never heard before.

"Good insight, Steele. But you'll never get it done," the Judge said angrily. "All your goddamn money can't get this done for you, Steele. I don't know how the hell you got as far as you did, but don't try anymore. Let's stop gambling and put an end to this thing."

"We've got to try," I said. "And if we don't succeed by eight-thirty, then you have the Air Force drop enough metal on that area of the ocean that nothing gets transferred. It is just a question then of how much we win, since the ol' U.S. of A. wins either way. We can't take the risk, we can't upset the applecart. It's unbelievably naïve—it's damn insane—but we can stop it. Here are the map coordinates."

I gave him the numbers, and he was silent for a while.

"You're asking me to bomb these people?" he asked loudly.

"Yes," I said, thinking, but it was your idea, Judge. Why try to lay it off on me?

"Maybe even bomb you?"

"If you have to," I said. "We will obviously try to get off the boats and out of the way. But if we can't stop the transfer then you have to go ahead. Agreed?"

"What?"

"I said, do you agree? Do we have an agreement on the strategy?"

"What if there's a communications foul-up?" the Judge asked. "What if you get what you're looking for but you can't get ahold of me to stop?"

"Then we get off the boat with it and let you go to work. Just tell them to only hit the big boats. No lifeboats. As little collateral damage as possible. Give us a chance to swim away if we can."

"Crazy," the Judge concluded quickly.

"I agree with that!" I shouted into the microphone. "But do you agree with the strategy?"

"Yes," he mumbled, after thinking about it for a moment. "I don't see that we have any choice. But, Steele . . ."

"Yes."

"Go get on and off that boat, because I'm going to order up the best we can muster off the coast of Florida. They can be there in twenty minutes, and once I send them off I don't know if I can get them back."

"I understand," I said. "There's no going back."

"None," he agreed, either his voice breaking or the static on the line flickering up again. "You don't have much time. Then I'm going to rain down so much hot metal you'll think you're in a steel plant. Good luck, my friend. Keep your head above water."

"Thank you," I said, for things that I had not mentioned and might never get a chance to express. I thought how painful it must be for the Judge to agree to an order that might kill his friends. We would be long gone; he was the one who would have to struggle first with the decision whether to let the bombers fly and then later with whether he had done the right thing. "Thanks," I said again, meaning much more.

"My best, my very best to Carolyn," he said quietly.

"Yes," I answered. "I'll let her know. Over and out."

"Over and—Steele?"

"Yes?"

"Tell Murphy to keep his eyes open and his head down. And, Steele, be careful. I mean, really be careful this time."

"Yes," I repeated. "Over and out."

As I hung the radio up I turned to look into the four faces staring at me. Carolyn, with her silvery hair blowing in the wind. Murphy, his face lined by too much sun and too much tension. Freddy, with his lanky but muscular build and silent attachment to Murphy. And Sam, who wanted nothing more than to be back in the sky controlling a plane, where he was comfortable and everything was much less messy. I had just volunteered them for probable death. Sentenced them to risk their lives for their country without even being asked. But not a single one of them voiced a complaint.

"I don't think we'll get bombed," I offered.

"Why not?" Carolyn asked.

"Because Rebecca's information is too good," I said. "She must have an inside source. Again, she must have a telephone tap that we just can't figure out. And if she knows we've requested that her Dad's boat be bombed, she'll find some way either to not be on the boat or to get it moved or the order rescinded. If we stick close to her we'll be okay. That's why I told the Judge to go ahead. She'll know his plans before we will."

"Unless," Murphy countered. "Unless, unless, unless. Unless you're wrong and she doesn't have a source. Or it's too late for the source to get her this information. Unless she kills us herself. Unless we get killed just trying to get within a thousand feet of those boats. But for all of that, it's a great idea."

"We've got to try," I said, ignoring his pessimistic tone. "We're running out of time. We can't let this happen. All we do is float into their radar range and let them pick us up. Then we either talk them out of the transmission, scare them away by telling them that the Air Force is on its way, or—"

"Or die trying," Murphy said. It was clear now that my leadership was being directly challenged. Murphy knew that I was just a desk jockey, but I didn't want him reminding everyone else.

"No one has to go," I said, calm but angry, hoping this tactical retreat would force Murphy to go along. It worked.

"We're all going," Murphy said resignedly. "I just hate the idea of being taken prisoner—particularly if the plan is that the prisoner talks the jailer out of doing something. That plan stinks."

"What are our options?" I asked, my voice tinged with tension at being questioned. "We don't have any real weapons, just a couple of rifles and some explosives. There are only five of us. All we can do is show up and try to talk them out of beginning the transmission—or, as you point out, die trying. But my bet is that once those jets are in the air, the family will know about it, if not before. We'll tell them that they have to stop the transmission or they'll all die, and they'll decide to take their precious computer disks and get the hell out of the way. We may not win with that result, but that gives us another shot at them."

There was a short pause while the five of us all stared at each other. Then Carolyn said simply, "Let's do it." Murphy shook his head, but trained Jacob's speedboat back toward the yachts and gunned the engine.

The guests began coming to dinner promptly at seven. I remember listening with a sudden surge of wide-eyed wonder that I had been given the chance to overhear a group of people who seriously contemplated changing the course of world history. The NSA was founded by a bunch of eavesdroppers, and here I was listening real-time to the real thing, without translators or code breakers or computer jocks or even years or months or days or seconds interceding between me and what was going on. At that moment I craved seeing the action, smelling the perfumes and colognes of the people as they arrived. Suddenly sound was not enough, but it was all I had. My imagination would supply the rest.

Rebecca's father greeted the guests as they arrived, while Rebecca and Tommy stood in the background, talking to each other and to Rebecca's brothers. They commented on the appearances of aunts and uncles, nieces and nephews they hadn't seen in years, or ever met at all. The first guest was by far the oldest, Doc's oldest sister-in-law, Milda, who came with her grandson Luke, the son of Simon, who was from Argentina, and his two Japanese stepbrothers, although they had not been invited. Luke, now the first disciple, helped the old lady board the boat and was quiet while she kissed all of her relatives, examining each for a long time. Luke had brought the Pacific Rim disks from Japan, where the family's vast banking connections had helped him collect the information for weeks. Aunt Milda, whom I imagined smelling of dried flowers and old fur coats, was very proud of this teenager who had taken the code name of the first disciple. She seemed only to tolerate her two stepgrandsons, to whom she had barely been introduced.

Cousin Jimmy arrived next, in a tight mini-skirt that Jan couldn't help but comment on. She was the daughter of James, the son of Zebedee, who had died in a boating accident off the coast of Chile years ago. Her brothers had all left the family business to go abroad and lead normal lives, while she and her mother had run the growing banking company that financed much of Chile's debt. But until Rebecca led her away to meet more of her arriving relatives, she explained to Jan, who had a hundred questions, that she wasn't going back. She understood her brothers' urge to be free of the demands of the family, and now that the family's central goal was accomplished she planned on starting all over again in the United States.

Rebecca introduced Tommy to her Uncle John, whom she obviously knew well. John talked in a thick German accent about his escape from East Germany in a stolen Stasi plane, detailing each tense moment as if he were selling a movie script. But he thought it was all worth it. He for one would miss the challenges that the family had met, but he had known that this time would come; it was just a question of who and how and when. He was impressed with the computers that were set up on the boat. Impressed with the money that had been spent for this transmission.

John introduced Rebecca to his brother Philip.

"Rebecca, so nice to meet you," a French-accented voice said. "These code names are so silly, aren't they? But then, I have used it so long that it seems now like it is my name—which I suppose makes it my real name, for it never changes, while the name on my passport is like the seasons. So there, I am Philip, the fifth disciple, and it is very nice to meet you, Rebecca."

"It is nice to meet you," Rebecca said, as Jimmy walked back up to them. "This is Jimmy, the granddaughter of James, and this is my fiancé, Thomas Wood."

"Jimmy," Philip said. "I'm sure that you do not remember me—I believe you were two the last time I saw you. I brought you a wooden rocking horse with a red tail. You were probably two feet tall. My, you make me feel old."

"I still have that horse," Jimmy replied. "A little green rocking horse."

"Amazing the things we remember from childhood," another voice said; at first I thought it was Tommy's, but it was slightly deeper, older. "Children's memories can be so precise, and yet so selective, don't you think, Mr. Wood? I remember my uncle's farm I used to visit so clearly, and yet I can't tell you what my own family's home looked like until we moved when I was six or so."

"Thomas," Rebecca said familiarly to the deep, American voice, "this is Tommy Wood, my fi—"

"Mr. Wood," Thomas said, interrupting in the growing commotion, his flat, midwestern voice hard to distinguish from Tommy's. "Really, I am Rebecca's Uncle Thomas's nephew. Just standing in for the family today, you might say. I've heard so much about you. When I saw you standing there next to Rebecca I knew that it must be you. I was so glad to hear that you would be with us today."

"Oh," Tommy said, sounding confused. "You've heard about me? I've heard about you, at least about—"

"About me? But you don't—"

"About the family," Tommy interjected quickly—probably trying not to give the impression that Rebecca had told him anything important, I thought, trying to follow all the tense voices. The paranoia was palpable. "I have learned much about this family I am—am joining," Tommy said nervously.

"Yes," the nephew said slowly. "I'm sure that you are learning many interesting things. When this is all over, I'd love to talk to you again about your impressions. I've been to Indiana, and I know this might all be quite a . . . well, a shock. I wish you luck."

He'd been to Indiana? I remember noting to myself. How did Thomas, standing in for the eighth disciple, even know that Tommy was from Indiana? Obviously Tommy was well known in the family, and his presence on the boat, while seeming not more than a coincidence to me, considering what Tommy had been through, had been anticipated. My initial confidence that I had guessed right about what was going on began to fade into a quiet apprehension that something was wrong with the picture I had painted.

"Thank you," Tommy said. "I think that we've—" and then he

was interrupted by shouts of joy at the arrival of other brothers and sisters. Bartholomew was actually an older Indian woman, with a strange accent that cut short all her vowels, Matthew had come from Germany, and James, who described himself as the son of Alphaeus, was represented by his son Anthony, who had a Spanish accent and came with the daughter of Thaddaeus and the nephew of Simon the Zealot. In the midst of all the shouting and talking I learned that the family had been in constant communication over the past two years, arranging for the transfer of information that would take place today.

The last rays of daylight moved like burning orange waves over the ocean, showing the boats' silhouettes in the distance as the family began to assemble in the dining room. I pulled off the earphone, letting it settle around my neck, and looked through the binoculars that Murphy had handed me. Far off on the edge of the horizon I could make out several boats.

"This is it," Murphy said as he cut the engine, letting the boat drift toward the circle of yachts bouncing like little white plastic bleach bottles on the blue sea. "We should be within radar range, so any minute they will pick us up on their screens and come and get us. All we have to do is wait for them to get here. If we move too much they might fire on us, but if we just float they'll come investigate." Then he paused and smiled at me, adding, "I hope."

"I'm glad we are all here," Rebecca's father said out of the earphone wrapped around my neck, his ancient accent deeper and more German now, even though he had spent the last fifty years in America. I pulled the earphone on quickly, envisioning the wrinkled face and white moustache that Tommy had described. "It brings tears to my eyes to stand at the end of this table, like Papa did, and see my family again. Papa would have been proud. We have all carried on. Seven of us still alive. Four gone, but their families here. All families all represented here. All still collecting information. All still contributing. All part of the bank. All stockholders and depositors. All part, yes, still part of the family."

He said the word "family" as if it were a magical incantation that brought back ghosts and paid tribute to some lost civilization. Then he said again, "All part of the family."

"We are here because the family has done its business. We have come to a crossroads, and I believe there is but one way to go. We have disagreed. Some here today still do not support this action we are about to take. We understand their opinions. We respect their feelings and beliefs. But this decision has been made by a family council, and, having received the necessary eight votes, it has passed, and every member of the family has agreed to again abide by the decision of the family council."

He paused, I guessed to take a drink of water; his voice had grown weaker and older with each sentence. The microphone in the belt picked up Rebecca whispering in Tommy's ear: "Jesus, Dad looks old, doesn't he? We've got to make sure he takes a vacation. The strain of all of this has gotten to him."

"This meeting," he went on, "brings me both great joy and great sadness. It is a beginning and an ending. A beginning of a new life for each of the brothers and sisters here, and an ending of our life together. Although we have had few chances to see each other, to touch each other, the communication has been almost constant. For that I pray, and that I will miss, yes? For today is the end of the Bundt family. The Bundt name ends here today. No child shall have it, yes? No record shall show it. No mouth shall speak it. No member shall use it. This we have all sworn."

I remember closing my eyes as I listened to his accented voice. I remembered Tommy's description of Rebecca's father's disheveled brush of a moustache. His stroking the long hair as if remembering when it was thicker and shorter, groomed for someone who was part of commerce and not simply secure enough to not be concerned what other people thought. I imagined that his back was slightly bent from age and from the weight of carrying the family's mantle; he would talk with his aged hands, because the language was not his own, but what he had chosen to speak. Later, listening to this tape for the hundredth time, I noted that his voice was much older than the voice we had recorded talking to the real estate agent as he looked out over the NSA last spring. He had aged many years in those few months.

"But this is no last supper," he said, "even though we shall never dine again together. No one will die tomorrow, yes? There is no traitor among us. There is no savior among us, unless it is these silver laser disks. These pieces of silver, so unlike the thirty pieces that Judas received, will give this metal back its honor. Information is the savior of modern man, yes? No one of us is such a savior. We are but disciples, spreading the information, spreading the word, and the word is peace. The word is communication. The word is empathy. And through empathy, through communication, we can maybe, yes, just maybe bring peace to our world. And if this information, clad in silver, is not a savior, then it is at least a John the Baptist, telling of what may come if things, if things work out, yes? If our plan does not go astray."

Of course I had been right in my guesses, I remember telling myself as I listened to this old man's voice. I had guessed right because it was so simple. So unbelievable, and yet so obvious.

"I have thought much about this," the old man whispered, "as I traveled around the globe this past year photographing the satellite dishes that will receive the information we are sending tonight. I have seen these metal contraptions in a dozen countries—these giant mechanical ears—and I have thought about the power of the word. My camera has measured their angles, types, and directions, and I have measured our words. The words we send tonight to those receiving dishes are not words that you or I understand, yes? Rebecca tells me that the computer language is all numbers—but it is still communication, and that communication has the power of the word."

I made a mental note that if I ever returned I would turn the agency upside down, if necessary, to find any clue that Rebecca's father had been near the NSA.

"So I ask each of you to come forward, and as the oldest living brother, the one entrusted by our father to look after each of you and your families, I will take the disks and Rebecca will prepare for the transfer. It is with this gesture that we give away our family, our mission, our connection, yes? It is with this gesture that we say good-bye."

Rebecca whispered the name of the family each person represented as they walked, one at a time, to the front of the table where her father stood, taking the disks and solemnly shaking hands. The names came to my ears like a quiet wind passing through a century of tattered trees, toppled spires, leaning tombstones. Peter, James son of Zebedee, John brother of James and named after the sons of thunder, Andrew, Philip, Bartholomew, Matthew, Thomas, James the son of Alphaeus, Thaddaeus, and finally Simon the Zealot. Without saying a word they came up (Rebecca explaining that they were in order of birth), each holding a computer disk as if it were a jewel. "Look at their eyes," Rebecca whispered to Tommy. "God, this is amazing. So much history. So much emotion. So much . . . Jesus, so much family."

"Rebecca," her brother Erik suddenly said softly. "Come here. We may have a problem."

"What?" she asked. "I want to watch this."

"We've got somebody nearby. Luke noticed the intruder-alert alarm going off when he went out to have a smoke. Nothing big. Probably just a fishing boat. They're about a mile out. I've got the sub ready to pick them up soon, but what should we do—"

"They've got us!" I shouted as Murphy rushed to one side of the boat. "They've picked us up. They know we're here."

"Jesus!" Murphy shouted back. "Hold your fire!" I had been so busy listening that I hadn't even noticed the swirling of the water fifty feet from us as the submarine surfaced, machine guns trained on our boat. We had slowly worked our way to within a mile of the boats, and now, as the thirty-foot-long sub rose out of the water like a whale coming up for air, I heard speedboats racing across the waves toward us.

"No shooting," Rebecca said in my ear. "Take them quietly and quickly, and bring them back if they look suspicious. My guess is that they aren't fishermen."

"Why not just blow them out of the water?" the male voice that I knew was Luke's said, and I held my breath waiting to learn our fate.

"No," she said. "Keep everything quiet. No shootings. No killings. I don't want any of the other families knowing about it. Let's just get this over with and get out of here. Whoever they are, we'll handle them later, when it won't matter."

The black box was our most powerful weapon, but as the submarine came toward us I set the homing device on the box's side and slid the tape recorder over the rail of the boat. It would be weeks before they were retrieved.

"I'm dropping it overboard," I whispered to Murphy, who was busy wiring something to the ignition. "They won't kill us. They don't want to make any noise. They don't want the other families knowing there was even a disturbance. Pass it on. Play it cool."

"Sure," Murphy said, clearly not buying my direction. "But you don't mind if I've got a little plastic explosive wired up just in case, do you, boss?"

"Just play it cool," I said between clenched teeth, feeling my heart begin to race with fear.

And with that I dropped the box over the side, the small splash lost in the sound of the speedboats circling us.

We do things like that, those of us who have faith in finding things. We hide them away, like teenage emotions suppressed in our craving to be an adult, certain that we will be able to find them again when we need them. Dropping the black box and the tape recorder into the sea was a crazy action, but with probable death staring me in the face in the form of the black hulk of a submarine drifting toward our boat, it seemed perfectly logical. And if I hadn't dropped them over and if our men hadn't found both only two weeks later then no one would believe this story. But they were found, and thus, like it or not, the United States Government had to admit that I was not crazy. Or at least, regardless of my sanity, that I was not a liar. Not that I had told the truth, just that I had not lied.

41.

THE THREE SPEEDBOATS trolled around our boat, binoculars and machine guns trained on us. Without being asked, we held up our automatic rifles and several pistols and threw them overboard. Then a voice drifted our way from the deck of the submarine, asking if all our weapons were overboard. I nodded, and we all held up our hands in surrender.

All three boats charged us at once, and men jumped over to our boat so quickly that for a moment I thought they might capsize it. In seconds they had us all on the floor, and what seemed like a hundred rough hands frisked every inch of my body, giving me bruises that I would have for weeks. One of the men pulled me up to my knees, probably because I was the oldest, and asked, "Who are you?" in accented English.

I stared at him silently, refusing to answer. He hit my face with the back of his hand, the move sudden and powerful. It had been decades since I was last hit, and I'm not sure I was ever hit on the face, and the pain was shocking. My God, I said to myself as I fell over with the force, my eyes spinning as my head hit the floor. I can't take torture. I'm not prepared to handle torture.

Carolyn's gasp and the sounds of her struggle to move to my side brought me back to my senses. Make your brain work, I told myself.

"I'm not going to tell you," I said through the blood in my mouth. "But I will tell your commanding officer on the big boat."

He raised his hand to strike me again, but then decided to radio in what I had said. The appeal to his superior, done without insult to him, had reminded him that he should cover his ass before he began beating me up.

"How do you know there's a big boat?" he asked while he waited for the scrambling apparatus on his radio to make contact.

"I will talk to your commanding officer, or Rebecca Townsend, from the Bundt family, only. You must take me—take us—to her. You must take us to the Bundt boat."

The man was stunned into silence, shocked at the names I had rattled off.

"I don't know what you are talking about," he lied. "There is no such boat."

"Just radio it in," I said. "Let them know I asked to come to the Bundt boat to see Rebecca."

He turned away, and through the ringing in my ears I could hear him say, "This guy knows about the boats and says he wants to talk to Rebecca. Yes, he knows Becky is here." He spoke with a mixture of surprise and frustration. He described each of us, mentioning age, sex, size, and color of hair. Then, without a further word, they hustled Murphy, Freddy, and Sam into one of the speedboats and Carolyn and me into another. The man who had hit me climbed in after me.

"What's going on?" I asked, having appointed myself the spokesman. "Where are you taking us? Why different boats?"

The man who had hit me smiled as we began to drift away from Jacob's speedboat, and pondered whether to answer.

"The two of you," the man said cockily, his arms folded in front of him as he balanced his weight on the edge of the boat and pointed to Carolyn and me, "are going to see the wizard. You get to see the whole Emerald City, for some reason. Those three"—he jerked a thumb at the boat with Murphy, Freddy, and Sam—"get to stay with us. They apparently aren't worth anything. 'Disposable' was the word used." He stopped and smiled at his perceived wit and power, loving every moment our lives hung in his hands. "But you two get to go to the big boat. Maybe you'll get to live just a bit longer. Maybe." He laughed.

Murphy glanced at me across the water, and I could see him mouth the words "Damn it." He shook his head, as if exasperated by the situation I had got him into, and I marveled at his seeming lack of fear. I nodded to him, letting him know that he'd better try to save himself.

Murphy moved so fast I didn't even see the gun in his hand, or the quick kick to the guard who had held it a moment earlier. I just saw the bullets rip right through the man who had hit me, spraying us with his blood, the shot bursting out of his chest as if he had just exploded.

"Now!" Murphy screamed at Sam, and one second later Jacob's boat exploded, sending shards of metal and hunks of fiberglass into the air. Murphy sprayed the men on his boat with bullets as Freddy took the wheel and cranked the throttle. The explosion stunned everyone and sent the small speedboats flying across the water on the sudden waves. In the midst of the confusion Carolyn shoved one guard overboard after grabbing his gun. But another leveled his pistol at her forehead, and she dropped the gun as Sam, Freddy, and Murphy sped off in a hail of gunfire, the other boat in hot pursuit.

"Damn, damn, damn!" another of the men screamed. "You idiots! How the hell did you let that happen?"

Carolyn and I were shoved onto the floor of the speedboat with a man kneeling on both of us as we sped toward the flotilla. I knew that Murphy would be back to get us as soon as he saw an opportunity. The key for Carolyn and me, I thought as the bony knee cut into my sore back, was just to stay alive long enough to be there for that opportunity.

The submarine had obviously radioed in what had happened, because as we sped up to the boats there was commotion everywhere. The families were all rushing back to their boats, and everybody was pulling up anchor and preparing to disperse. There were shouts and screams, with guns drawn and mistrust blossoming, as boats narrowly missed each other in their attempts to turn around and pick up passengers.

For a moment I wondered if our plan had already worked. We had ruined their party, so they were going home without accomplishing their goal.

Later, when we heard the faint, gurgly transmission still picked up by the black box and its tape recorder for the ten minutes before the water broke through the metal casing fifty feet down on a coral outcropping, we learned that none of them were sure what the explosion had been and what was going on. Rebecca had simply interrupted the ceremony to tell them that there was an emergency and the plan to disperse had to be put into effect immediately. She would stay with the boat and carry out the transmission. Rebecca gave hurried kisses to her mother and father, and had to talk her brothers into leaving along with the other guests.

Then, as the rest of the family said their good-byes and gave short lectures on the value of the disks they were leaving behind, Rebecca ordered that the two oldest captured intruders be brought to the big transmission boat. Luke and his stepbrothers insisted on staying long enough to see who the intruders were. Rebecca tried to talk them into leaving, and Luke suggested that they simply take the intruders to their boat.

"I want them brought here, Luke," she said.

"But, Rebecca," a male voice responded, "you've got to do the transmission. Let us interrogate them on our boat, or your family's boat, while you get all this done."

"No," she demanded. "I want them here, Luke. Right here. I need to talk to them before we transmit."

"Why?" Tommy said. "Isn't that dangerous? Who knows who they are?"

"You do," she said—whirling to face him, I imagine. "You know who they are, and that's why I want them here. I want to know what they know before I start to transmit. For all I know, they've got you programmed to kill me the moment before I hit the button."

Luke turned to Tommy as Rebecca's voice stopped, the rustle of his nylon jogging suit telling his every move. Tommy told me later that he knew at that moment that the first disciple had decided to protect his cousin Rebecca.

"What?" Tommy said, stepping around Luke. "What the hell are you talking about?"

"Damn it!" she screamed at him. "I'm talking about Steele and Carolyn. You know what the hell I'm talking about. I want them here, right here in front of us, and I want to watch your eyes and see if you know them. I want to see if you're telling me the truth. I want to know—I want to know at least that, before I spend the rest of my life with you."

Then I imagine her whirling back to shout, "Bring them here right away! We're running out of time!"

"Yes," Luke responded, as if taking an order.

"Rebecca," Tommy said in a conciliatory voice. "Look, I don't know what you're thinking, but—"

"Don't bother," she barked. "I love you. For the first time in my life I'm really, really in love. And I don't plan on losing you, or even a part of you, to them, or to anyone. I will—will exorcise them, if I have to. I want us to be totally truthful. No stories. Everything frank, naked, plain. Everything just there for both of us to see. I know why you're doing what you're doing, and I know you won't stop until I force you to, because they taught you to preserve your options. Maybe it really isn't Steele and Carolyn after all, so don't admit it until you see him. Preserve your options. Maybe even then Steele won't admit to knowing you. Preserve your options. But I'll see it in your eyes. I've also been trained by those people, and I'll see it. In your eyes. In your movements. In your denial. So just don't say anything until they get here. Preserve your options. Just stay quiet."

"Look, is this a test or—" and then their voices were gone, the tape making contact with the salt water and slowing to a faint growl as the rolling points ground to a halt.

The man named Luke, young, tall, lanky, with a beak of a nose, met our boat as it pulled up to the side of the gleaming sky-blue yacht. He was wearing a neon-colored nylon warmup suit, and his two stepbrothers looked like identical Japanese twins behind their mirrored sunglasses. I thought it was strange that Luke refused to let any of the men in the boat come aboard but had them hand us over to his two stepbrothers. He said he didn't want many people around when it came time to transmit.

They brought Carolyn and me belowdeck to the long room full of computer equipment, where Rebecca sat in front of a screen entering last-minute codes. The green light of the monitor shined from the screen as if it were a window looking out on a tornado. The strange, powerful light made Rebecca's face look flat and tired, exaggerating the smudges of exhaustion under her eyes, and cast eerie shadows across the room to where Tommy stood in one corner, nervously flexing his hands. I tried not to look at him, not knowing whether he had told her that he knew us. I forced myself to keep all expression completely controlled.

Luke coughed, and Rebecca turned around in her chair and glanced at me and then at Tommy.

"Your friends are here," she said to Tommy. He shrugged his shoulders noncommittally, keeping his eyes moving across all of us: me, Carolyn, Luke, and the two armed stepbrothers, who stood at the door.

"You look hurt, Steele," Rebecca said, examining my jaw. "Did my cousins rough you up? I'm sorry if they did. You see, we weren't expecting you. You weren't on the guest list, even though Tommy has told me all about how much he enjoyed your company. You know, I don't think I've seen you since you retired. And you must be Carolyn. I don't think we've—"

"Yes," Carolyn interjected, breaking into Rebecca's monologue and asserting some sense of control. "Yes, I am Carolyn. You must be Rebecca."

"Yes," Rebecca said. "It's so nice to—"

"I understand that you used to work for me," Carolyn went on, as if she were engaged in pleasantries before a negotiating session that were in reality jousts to demonstrate her control. "I'm sorry I never got the chance to meet you." Carolyn was playing a dangerous game. "But I have heard so much about you," she said.

"And I've read much about you," Rebecca said quickly. "Corporate raider. Oppressor of native peoples. Raper of local economies. Under different circumstances I think I would have enjoyed talking to you, from what I have read. And of course Tommy has told me all about you."

Carolyn turned to Luke, who was standing beside her, and said, "Hello, Tommy. And how do you know about me? *Businessweek*? *Fortune*? Don't believe everything you've read, please."

Rebecca smirked. "Very good. Good try. But leave the bluffing to the professionals."

"Professional what?" Carolyn asked, obviously committed to die with dignity. "Exactly what are you a professional at, Rebecca?"

"Enough games," Rebecca said. "We don't have time for it. Steele, your only chance of surviving here is to tell the truth about Tommy. If you tell me that you trained Tommy, that you brainwashed Tommy, that you talked him into helping you find me, which he has obviously somehow helped you do, then I'll let you and Carolyn live. It's that simple. Cut-and-dried. Do you understand?"

"Do you understand this, my dear Rebecca," I said, following Carolyn's lead. "It is eight twenty-three by my watch. You have seven minutes before you are scheduled to start transmitting—don't ask me how I know—but at the exact moment you are scheduled to begin transmitting your precious information around the globe, the United States Air Force is going to bomb this boat out of the ocean. So it doesn't matter if you kill us now or just leave us on board. We are all going to die unless we get off this boat."

Eyes turned when I stopped talking, ricocheting from one person to the next. I saw Luke's eyes grow large and focus on Rebecca's face, then glance at the mirrored eyes of his stepbrothers. Rebecca looked at Tommy and then back at me, half of her face coated in the green glow of the monitor next to her, the other half gleaming with sweat in the warm yellow light from the dying sunset coming through a porthole. I watched the two halves of her face, seeing the struggle going on between them.

"You're lying," she said.

"No he's not," Tommy asserted. "It's all planned," he lied, not having any idea what had gone on since he had been kidnapped.

"What?" Rebecca asked, turning into the sunset. "What are you saying?"

"Honey," he answered, walking to her, "I love you. I want to spend the rest of my life with you. So here's the truth. Yes, I was picked up by Steele and Carolyn. Yes, I was trained to help find you. Yes, I was told, taught—I don't know, maybe brainwashed—to believe that I could save you. But now I really can. I've got an agreement, in writing, from the Justice Department. From the witness protection program. New lives. A new start. I arranged it all. Let's get out of here. Let's save what we have left."

She turned back into the glow of the monitor and looked at me, searching my eyes as if to say that we were the two professionals here and should therefore be communicating, and then turned back to Tommy, who took one of her limp hands. I have always wondered what she was thinking that moment after Tommy confirmed her worst fears and, unbeknownst to her, used his admission to gain her trust so that he could lie to her. What must he have been thinking as he quickly mixed the truth with what he thought was the big lie but was actually the truth?

"Here's the deal," I said, making it up as I went along and silently praising Murphy for his crash-course training of Tommy. "We all leave and I promise on behalf of the United States Government to back the agreement Tommy has negotiated. You've got total and complete immunity. Tommy has seen the papers. It is all guaranteed. You bring the disks and you trade them in for a new life with Tommy. New identities, new money, completely safe and completely free."

"And the information?" she asked without turning around, the voice coming from within her shadow.

"That's the ticket price," I said, hoping I wasn't bargaining for too much, since Tommy knew the agreement had no quid pro quo. I looked at Tommy as he stepped out of the shadows as if to say something, but then his mouth closed and he remained silent, letting me play my game. "The government gets the information," I said. "All of it. And you get your freedom and your life. If you don't agree, then you don't get your life and no one gets the information, because all these fancy computers will be blown sky high."

"And if you're lying?" she asked softly, not looking at me but turning her face into the last rays of sunset and staring at Tommy.

"You can't risk finding out," I replied. "And I'm not. I'm shaking every second you stall just because one of those pilots might have the wrong time on his Air Force–issue watch."

Everyone fell silent, and the stepbrothers rustled their feet, staring at Luke as if waiting for a command. I stared at Rebecca's back, boring my eyes into her soul and praying that she would listen to my reasoning and do as Tommy said. All that training in how to kill people, I thought, and Tommy had saved the day with wit and strategy. If we lived, I swore, I would have him decorated by the president himself.

"I talked to the Judge," I said, trying to impress her with specifics. "The Judge agreed to order the bombing. The Judge will make sure it happens."

"The Judge," she said wistfully, taking and then examining one of Tommy's hands, without looking at me. Then I think I heard her laugh, although I'm still not sure if it was a laugh or a sigh or some inarticulate acknowledgment of her own beautiful luck.

I saw her squeeze Tommy's hand and turn around with a smile on her face. "We'll wait," she said. "Let's let eight-thirty roll by, shall we? Wait and see."

I was stunned. I searched her face, and then quickly swung to Carolyn for guidance. Rebecca had just decided to gamble with our lives. After Tommy's brilliant move, we had been checked by her seeming irrationality. No one in the room knew what to say.

"No," Luke said, raising his sleek black Luger at Rebecca. "You told the family the transmission must take place at eight-thirty, and you must carry it out. You can't risk it. If you do not, then I will kill you and do it myself."

His stepbrothers raised their guns and pointed them at all of us, their young faces, half covered by the mirrored sunglasses, full of nervous fear. I exhaled loudly, shocked again.

"On whose authority?" Rebecca asked tersely.

"I am Simon's grandson," Luke replied in a stilted, formal tone. "These are the grandsons of Simon. The first disciple. The oldest brother. We are not guarding your prisoners, Rebecca, but guarding you. We were sent by our side of the family to make sure that you carry out the plan. You said the transmission must begin by eight-thirty, and so it must. We cannot risk that what the American says is true."

She stared at them all nervously fidgeting with their guns, judging their fortitude, and then said again, "We'll wait."

She had misjudged.

Out of the corner of my eye I saw Luke's trigger finger pull back, and I slammed my hand down on the gun as it went off, the bullet missing its target and grazing Rebecca's leg. As she fell she pulled out a gun and began firing. Tommy lunged at one of the stepbrothers, and Carolyn dropped behind a table, shoving a chair on casters out in front of me. Bullets scattered around the room, splintering the back of the chair, which I used as a shield as I charged Luke. Tommy's fingers dug into one stepbrother's throat, breaking his windpipe with a sickening noise, and then, with his gun in hand, he became the killing machine he had been on the farm. I grabbed the Luger from the floor and unloaded a chamber into the face of the shocked Luke. I will never forget his beautiful face, tanned, lean, the moment before I pulled the trigger. His eyes haunt me even now, so young and wide, full of determination to do as he had been ordered by his family. His father had died to make sure that this transmission went forward, and he died by my hand trying to live up to his father's expectations. That shot made me a professional, according to some unnumbered theory of mine. But I would never recite another theory in my entire life if I could bring back this poor, proud kid's life. If circumstances had been different, then, just as with fat Jacob back on the island, I could have found the courage and the common sense not to pull the trigger. But, I have told myself over and over, I had no choice. I had to kill the first disciple.

A moment after Luke's face exploded and his body was slammed back against the wall of the boat, Tommy riddled the other step-brother with bullets. Suddenly there was silence, and Tommy and I stood panting on opposite sides of the room. We stared at each other in unspoken acknowledgment of our partnership, and then I turned away and vomited, sickened by my own violence. Carolyn held my shoulders as I gasped for air, my sweat mixed with the blood that had spattered my face when I pumped the trigger.

Rebecca stood up and limped from computer to computer, surveying the damage from the bullets, red rivulets of blood streaming down her leg. Two of the video monitors were shattered, and tiny sparks flickered from a freestanding computer. "I think we can still do it," she said, transferring files. "Damn, this hurts. We've got until eight forty-five to make sure that everything can transmit."

"No we don't," I snapped, catching my breath and tasting my vomit in every word. "The goddamn Air Force really is going to start bombing this place in two minutes."

"No they're not," Rebecca said without looking at me, transferring her gun from one hand to the other as she pushed buttons on the wall of computers that helped operate the Cray supercomputer that was behind them. Her limping body was backlit by the green monitors and the flashes of white hot sparks. "They're not because—because the Judge is part of the family."

"What?" I asked, feeling the weight of the Luger still in my hand.

"You heard me," she said, turning around with the gun in her hand but not pointed at anyone. "The Judge, the very head of your precious little organization, is a, shall we say, an adopted part of the family. He is how we pulled this off. He is how we know all about your plan. He is my pipeline in and out of this mess."

"I don't believe it," Carolyn said. "That's not possible."

"How else did I know about Tommy?" Rebecca asked me, walking toward me and grimacing with pain. "Answer that, Steele. Who else knew but the Judge? I talked to Bobby the techy, but he hardly knew anything. Only Murphy and Carolyn, and both of them were with you. John X was dead. Only the Judge could tell me about your training sessions at your house. About the trip to Jacob's island. The Judge is the mole."

She stopped a few feet in front of me, her gun pointed at the ground, her eyes shooting at me. "Someday you'll have to tell me how you lucked into picking up Tommy, or how you even knew where the farm was. The Judge could never figure that out. He brought you back on the job because John X had told you so much and because he wanted some outside help to find me. For what is another story. He figured you'd screw it up and he could blame the failure of the investigation on someone outside of the agency, if anyone even had to know about it. He knew that your investigation would satisfy John X. John X's killing himself obviously was not foreseen. Had we known that John X was going to kill himself, the Judge wouldn't have had to bring you into the picture, unless it was just for sport. But he did. Figuring that between you, Carolyn, and Murphy you'd get yourself killed, or at least permanently lost. But you outsmarted us, Steele. In your own clumsy way, you, and Carolyn's money, got all the way here to see the big finale. I don't know how you did it, but I commend you for it. You turned Tommy—almost. And you got here. Damn good job."

I was too stunned to think, let alone say anything. Was she telling the truth? I looked down at my watch. I had ten seconds after eight-thirty, and no bombs. She might be telling the truth. It was hard to believe that the Air Force would let a second go by when so much information could be transmitted by computer so quickly. The Judge would have had them drop exactly at eight-thirty—and five seconds later the first explosions would rip apart the sea.

"One thing nobody knew, even my friend the Judge and my own family, is that I planned this so that I had an extra fifteen minutes. All the receiving satellite stations believe that it will take me fifteen minutes longer to transmit than is absolutely necessary. So even if we begin at eight forty-five, I can still finish the transmission before the satellites move," Rebecca said, more to herself than to us. "I knew there might be problems, so I gave myself fifteen extra—Jesus, my leg hurts!—fifteen extra minutes to handle any last-minute crisis." She was still moving from monitor to monitor, checking to make sure that everything was ready.

She tried to smile as she finished typing and walked toward me with the gun still in her hand. She held out her free hand to me.

"Now," she said, imitating the Judge's Texas twang, "give me your gun there, partner."

I walked toward her casually, tasting the vomit in my mouth. A rush of anger spit up from my bowels again, and I grabbed the wrist of her gun hand at the same time I shoved the Luger into her ear. With her weight on only one leg, she spun around in my arms, firing the gun into the ceiling, but I snapped her wrist back, and the gun fell as she cried out in pain. In one burst of fury at the Judge and Jacob and Luke and Rebecca, I slammed the metal of my gun into her flesh.

I had her, but what I didn't expect to see when I came out of the spin with my gun to her forehead and one of her arms pulled up behind her back was Tommy holding Carolyn with a gun to her head. Tommy and I stared at each other, our eyes meeting in a fierce embrace.

"Okay," I said, panting, my mind frantically searching the options I had in this Mexican standoff. "Let her go."

"After you," he offered, struggling to remain calm. I searched his face, striped with blood and dirt, for some touch of reason, and watched his muscular chest heave under his ripped shirt. Carolyn's eyes followed mine, beseeching, communicating something that I couldn't understand but I knew wasn't panic or fear.

"Tommy," I said, watching the clock tick by, "I thought we were on the same side here. I've promised you a new life. Listen—"

"Don't let her go!" Rebecca screamed, squirming. "Shoot her. He won't shoot me, Tommy. Do it, shoot!"

"Shut up!" Tommy yelled, suddenly soured by Rebecca's screaming. "Look," he panted, sweat pouring down his face. He spoke in short sentences that bolted out of him between deep gasps of air. "I'm only in this for you, Rebecca. I don't want to save the world. I just want to save you. I just want to build things and to live, to live with you. That's how they got me. They got me the same way they got you. Because we, Jesus Christ, because we love each other. That's why I'm here. That's why you brought me here, and they followed me somehow. That's why we risked all this. Why I risked coming here. Why you risked bringing me here."

He stopped, his arm still tight around Carolyn's neck, and I saw him search Rebecca's eyes. I felt her go limp in my arms.

"Okay," I said. "We release them at the same time and then lower the guns to the floor."

"The deal for immunity and new identity is still good?" he asked.

"Yes," I agreed. "As long as you don't transmit and we get the disks."

"You don't get the disks," Tommy said. "That was never part of the deal. The disks go overboard. Into the ocean. We tie them to an anchor. Carolyn lives. Rebecca lives. Rebecca and I get immunity and new lives. The disks are buried. That's the deal."

Now it was my turn to look into Carolyn's deep eyes, which were olive-colored in the light from the monitors. I couldn't chance her life on anything as small as national secrets, no matter what I had sworn to uphold. At that moment, as the words formed on my lips, I knew that I had left the service, left the organization, and now was bargaining on my own, for myself. The agency and the Judge had betrayed me. All I had left to believe in was Carolyn. I didn't care about anything other than getting us out of this alive.

"All right," I said. "Deal."

"How can I trust you?" Tommy asked.

"Trust," I repeated. "Your favorite word. I don't know. You've asked me that before, and I've never really had an answer. I guess you either know you can or you know you can't. Just a theory. But I think you know you can."

"Trust," he said, watching me like an animal in a zoo and then loosening his grip on Carolyn, who stood very still, unsure what was happening. "Can I trust you . . ."

"Yes, because I asked you to before and I did what I said I would do. Yes, because you know me as a man of his word. Yes, because . . . because that's all either of us has right now."

"All right," Tommy whispered, lifting his arm from Carolyn's neck.

I released Rebecca, and then we laid the guns on the floor very slowly, our eyes unblinking, as if we were in some ceremony—some Zen-like ritual of peace and understanding. We both stood up straight and backed away from our women and our guns. Then I blinked and breathed, again feeling some kinship with Tommy.

Rebecca reached down to the wound on her leg, her fingers touching the bloody gash, and then, without missing a beat, she grabbed the Luger from the floor and whirled around and jumped on my back, pressing the gun into my temple.

"Gotcha," she said.

"Goddamn it!" I screamed. "We had a deal, Tommy! We—"

"Don't move!" Carolyn shouted, aiming the gun she had picked up from the floor at Tommy's back. "Back up to this gun, Tommy, or I'll shoot. And if you move one inch, Rebecca, so help me God, I will blow away your boyfriend."

Rebecca laughed in disbelief, and Carolyn moved the gun an inch and blasted a hole in the floor three inches from Tommy's left leg, the shock of the bullet sending him sprawling. She had the gun to his head before Rebecca could exhale into my ear.

"Carolyn!" Rebecca shouted. "Jesus, if you touch that trigger one more time I'll take Steele's head off. My God, what the hell are you doing? Are you all right, Tommy? Tommy? Are you okay?" She was jabbing the gun into my head so hard she broke the skin, and still strangling me with her arm.

"Yeah," he grunted through clenched teeth. "Yeah. I think I twisted my ankle. Can we stop the theatrics and get out of here?"

"Okay," Carolyn gasped, her hands shaking and her voice cracking. "Now let's deal, Rebecca. You've got a choice, as I see it. Time is on my side. You can try to shoot your way out of this to get to your computers in two minutes or you can agree to give up. If we just sit here with guns to people's heads until after eight forty-five then I win. You've missed your damn transmission time. You won't be able to finish. Then there is no point in killing anyone, and you go to jail. Now if you agree to give up right now then both of these men live and you still get that immunity and that new life."

Rebecca began to shake, and I tensed, certain that a bullet would explode in my head at any moment. A desperate prayer ran through my mind, screaming for help, for miracles, for Carolyn to play her cards right.

"Don't you understand?" Rebecca explained through sudden tears. "This could save the world. This could mean—mean everything."

"The issue is," Carolyn said calmly, her voice becoming quieter and slower as Rebecca began to lose control, "will you sacrifice Tommy for that chance?" For a moment I could see the fear in Carolyn's eyes, but then she blinked and focused on the quivering Rebecca.

Rebecca stopped breathing, her body as rigid as a sword, and then she said, her voice desperate and disjointed with fear, "Yes. Oh my God. Yes. I must. You have to understand that I must. Please forgive me, Tommy. But I must."

I almost fainted when I heard those words. Maybe it was the stranglehold she had on my throat, or maybe it was the pronouncement of my imminent death. My eyes fastened on Carolyn, wondering how she could get out of this.

"Tommy, you wouldn't love me if I didn't do what I thought was right. I—"

"Rebecca, this is for real now," Carolyn whispered. "If you make the wrong choice there is no going back. No second—"

"Millions of people have sacrificed everything for peace," Rebecca sobbed. "Millions have died because of wars. I have to do this. I have to try this. I have to—"

Carolyn raised the gun so that it pointed directly into Tommy's ear, and Tommy said, "Rebecca—" at the same time I said, "Carolyn—"

A loud buzzer went off on the highest computer terminal, and the numbers *8:45* flashed on a screen. The hot end of the Luger dug into my temple, and Rebecca's arm tightened around my neck, cutting off more air. My eyes danced between Carolyn's face and the flashing numbers.

"Rebecca," Carolyn said in a slow monotone, "let's think this through. Let's—"

"This is it," Rebecca said in a steely voice, each word shot out with a spit of saliva. "Either let me push the button to start the transmission now or I kill Steele and fight my way to that button. Decide, Carolyn. Decide now."

Rebecca squeezed off my windpipe completely, and my eyes bugged out and went out of focus as I searched Carolyn's face for some hint of salvation. The room swirled around me, and right at that moment of impending death I remembered how the world looked when I was four or five and lay down on my back on the floor of a merry-go-round and watched the playground spin by me upside down. There was that same rush at seeing something remarkable for the first time—that startling realization of a new perspective. I heard the sounds of the playground screaming around me: mothers yelling, kids crying, toddlers issueing bursts of joy at their toys. Balloons went bobbing up into the air and then exploded into fireworks that showered sparks down into the night sky like phosphorescent weeping-willow limbs tossed by a breeze. The sounds of a parade came crashing around some corner of my mind, the band marching to a different drummer suddenly realized and released to echo off the tall buildings that rose up as I fell and fell and fell.

Then I could breathe, and Rebecca was running for the computer terminal and the gun was in Tommy's hands. Carolyn scrambled to me and sobbed just once as she hugged me. "I didn't know what to do," she cried. "I didn't want to risk losing you. I couldn't risk—not after this afternoon—I couldn't, I just couldn't."

I held her tightly as the computers began to buzz all around us, the transmission taking place as we sat on the floor holding each other, surrounded by dead bodies. "It's okay," I said over and over. "It's okay." I looked over at Tommy, who was watching us as he massaged his hurt leg. Our eyes met, and I saw the compassion in him again.

It was happening, I realized, as cogent thoughts began to creep back into my mind. We had not stopped the information transfer, which was now taking place all over the world. Rebecca had almost completed her mission and the mission of her family. As we sat on the floor of the yacht, slowly rocking in the evening air, the world was beginning to change. The seed of revolution was planted—or at least fertilized—right then and there.

And at what cost? Rebecca had been willing to risk everything—Carolyn had seen that in her face. She had been willing to kill what she loved. She had been willing to die herself to finish what she had started. To finish what she had believed in. All these bodies, I thought. Fragile, tragic, stupid in their lifelessness. Looking like nothing more than heaps of wet clothes. All these people caught up in this little drama. All unnecessarily wasted by our misguided strategies and missions.

Who was to blame? I asked myself as I sat there on the floor holding Carolyn and watching Rebecca dash from terminal to terminal, checking on the progress of her final act. No one and everyone, I supposed. All these people had died because of some abstract belief in peace, and yet those of us who knew peace's prosperity, knew freedom's joys and benefits, had not been willing to sacrifice for it. I was convinced at that moment that Rebecca might be starting World War III, but I was not willing to die, or see my wife die, to stop it. Yet this tall kid Luke and his young stepbrothers had been willing to risk their lives for the Platonic ideal that the family had set out to create. Jacob's soldiers. Murphy's men. All willing to risk their lives for something that they thought of as part of peace—money, duty, stability, anarchy. All willing to sacrifice for what they thought was right, or at least in their best interests.

All I knew that was right that moment was the feel of Carolyn in my arms, her heart beating and her arms holding me tight. That feeling was all that Tommy had wanted. He had wanted to save Rebecca, whatever that meant. He had seen the spark in her eyes, the romantic craziness of someone committed to a goal. And he had fallen in love with it and with her.

"I don't believe we've met," I whispered into Carolyn's ear, her graying hair tickling my lips.

"Yes," she whispered back. "I believe we have."

Her hug sent shivers up and down my spine, and I decided what to do.

"Tommy," I said, breathing hard as I squeezed Carolyn tight, conscious that our lives were still in danger, "the deal still stands. I promise you. You'll have no problem with the Justice Department. You lived up to your part of the bargain, and she did what she had to do."

Tommy exhaled and smiled, shaking his head at some thought. "I guess," he said, looking at his watch, "the Judge was with the family."

"Yes," I had to admit, tightening my hold on Carolyn. He would never let me live now that I knew. There was a showdown coming, I began to realize, my body too tired for another trip on the emotional roller coaster that I saw in front of me.

"Here it goes," Rebecca said, limping back to where Tommy lay with the rifle in his lap. It was dark outside now, and the portholes were small circular mirrors that reflected the lights of the computers. As long as they had the guns they were not afraid of us, but, strangely, I wasn't afraid of them either. "Beamed from satellite to satellite to ground stations all over the world. Twenty-one transmissions at one time." She kneeled and held Tommy in her arms, brushing the dirt off his cheek.

The four of us were silent for a while, sitting on the gently rocking floor, listening only to the sound of the computers whirling around us. I wondered whether they would try to kill us now, to cover their tracks completely, or if it was all over. The world beginning to change already without us.

"What now?" I asked. "How long does it take?"

"Probably about twenty-nine minutes," Rebecca said. "But don't bother trying anything. You can't stop it now. So there's no reason to try to kill me, my friend. You know, Steele, fifteen minutes ago you saved my life when my cousin over there tried to shoot me."

"Ten minutes ago I had a gun to your head," I replied.

"Five minutes ago I had a gun to your head," Rebecca said. "So I guess we're just about even."

"By some strange mathematical equation, I suppose you're right."

"The problem is," she said, "you know so much. It would be sloppy to leave you—"

Just then we heard the sound of an airplane engine coming on strong. It wasn't an Air Force jet, but the distinct loud whirl of a turboprop. "Oh my God!" I said, just before the first bomb exploded, missing the ship but hitting close enough to send the forty-ton boat rolling at a forty-five-degree angle. The computer equipment was bolted to the floor, but chairs and tables slammed against the far wall as the boat rolled back level.

"Let's get out of here!" I yelled, pulling Carolyn up from under a chair. "The Judge must have got his own ideas."

"That bastard!" Rebecca shouted, running to the computers to see if they were all still working. "He waited until he thought we would be done transmitting and then sent somebody in to make the evidence disappear. I'm the only one who really knows about him, and if he could get rid of me—" She stopped as we heard the sound of the plane circling and coming back. "And you," she said to me. "You, Steele. He's got both of us in one place. Just sitting ducks for—"

"Let's go!" I yelled, pushing a stunned Carolyn up the stairs to the hatch. "Let's get out, now!"

As she reached the darkness above deck, a bomb landed off the stern, blowing a hole in the boat and sending it reeling over on its side. At the same time, the sea around us began to explode into geysers as bombs fell. Carolyn was thrown against the rail, and then as the boat rolled a wave rushed over her and slammed her against a lifeboat. I stood in the lighted hatch as the boat lurched and rolled, terrified that she would be washed over the side.

When the boat righted itself, Carolyn was still standing by the lifeboat, her hands gripping the rail.

"Go get them!" she shouted at me. "I'll get the lifeboat down!"

I knew that it would take the turboprop at least twenty seconds to circle and make another run at us, so I turned and went back down the stairs. Tommy was trying to drag Rebecca across the room. The electronic equipment was sparking as the floor quickly filled with water. As I crossed the room the floor rose up in front of me, and the boat was sent scattering across the ocean again like a scurrying crab. I fell down hard. Then water burst through the floor, sending all of us swirling among the floating bodies and burning equipment.

I grabbed Tommy and Rebecca by the arm and pulled them to the stairs, where with superhuman effort Tommy pushed the now unconscious Rebecca up through the hatch. I pushed Tommy up, my hands covered with his blood, and pulled myself up out of the water just as it rushed to fill the room.

The boat was on fire in the back where the engine must have been, and it was sinking so fast that it rocked violently back and forth, the sheets of metal that made up its sides screeching like some giant dying animal as it was tortured and twisted. The three big round satellite dishes sitting high up on top of the boat were all on fire, like burning billboards lighting up the night sky. For a second I was transfixed by the sight of the slowly revolving white dishes burning around the edges, just like a movie closeup of a solar eclipse. Then a wave of water hit my face and I came back.

Strangely, whatever the plane was dropping, I realized, it was not powerful enough to sink the boat with one hit. Then I realized that the pilot obviously wanted to make sure the boat was in many pieces before it sank.

Carolyn climbed into the lifeboat. As Tommy and I lifted Rebecca into it there was a direct hit on the front of the yacht, and the shock waves sent all of us overboard, as if someone had just jumped off one end of a teeter-totter, slinging us through the air. Carolyn and Rebecca stayed in the lifeboat as it shot off the yacht like a missile, rocketing away from the explosion. I was in midair for a long time, and then I suddenly hit the water hard, feeling the sea being pushed away from me as I shot underwater.

The water seemed so heavy against my clothes and shoes.

I swam farther down at first, until I realized that the vague gray light in the other direction was the surface. As my lungs boiled, I realized all my nightmares had come true. You're going to drown, I told myself. This is it. This is the end that you knew would come, swallowed by the water that you knew someday would get you.

I pushed and scrambled, unable to get closer, and then suddenly I burst into the hard sea air, only to be hit by a wave when I tried to take my first breath. The salt water burned my nostrils as if it were kerosene, and my eyes refused to focus for a long time. I dogpaddled in circles until I finally got my bearings and scanned the horizon when I was pulled to the top of a wave.

The big boat was now, after repeated direct hits, just bits of wood and plastic burning on the dark surface, the firelight bright against the mottled twilight sky. But there, only a hundred feet away, was the white fiberglass lifeboat, with Carolyn standing upright, scanning the waves with a flashlight, searching for me.

"Turn off the light!" I shouted as I swam toward the boat, but of course she couldn't hear me. I was terrified that one of the pilots would see her light and make another round to finish us off. As I swam I realized that I couldn't move one arm at all, and my head was throbbing. The lifeboat, which had looked so close, was suddenly very far away, and I began to doubt that I could make it. What if I didn't drown, but simply ended up a vegetable, or, like Mike Carter, barely able to remember the date? What if, like Mike Carter, sitting in his office at Carolyn's company, I could barely recite my name? What if, what if, my brain kept asking as my body struggled with all its might. Everything was in hyperdrive, adrenaline spinning every sense out of control as I realized I was fighting for my life. But, having come this far, I told myself, you can't stop now. Not now. Not right now.

The beam from her flashlight hit my face, and I could hear Carolyn shouting at me, but I was blinded by the light. I struggled into it, flaying at the water until I struck something with my outstretched arm. Something soft that struck back. The vision of a shark flashed through my mind, but then suddenly I saw Tommy's head in the water and heard his voice.

"Steele!" he shouted between gasps of air. "This way, this—" A wave went over his head, and he did not come back up for a long time. When he did, I could tell that he was losing consciousness by the way his head rolled to one side and then the other. He had come back to get me and now was about to drown. He went under, and then his face burst back up out of the water, his mouth somewhere between a smile and a scream. Then it hit me that the face of the wooden mermaid that Carolyn and Murphy had brought back from Mexico, with the laugh that looked like a scream, was the face of someone breaking through the water into the air. The face of some-one, like Tommy, gasping for air, for life, and pushing through the weight of the water that contorted the face, pressing the cheeks and lips back, like the G force on a speeding pilot. Like a child bursting from the water of his womb into the cold, harsh air of the world.

If I live, I swore to myself, this will be the start of a new life. A life, I told myself as the waves hit my face, dedicated to something other than my chosen profession.

I shoved my body against Tommy and wrapped my hurt arm around his shoulder, but I knew I could not pull him very far. A wave washed over us, and he slipped out of my grasp. I cursed myself and imagined him dead, but then I went under and found him in the darkness and pulled him up, both of our faces breaking into the mermaid scream and my voice suddenly finding power in the air.

"Hey!" I shouted directly into his ear. "Hey! Wake up!"

I didn't even realize how absurd I must have sounded until Tommy told me later on in the boat how he was suddenly brought back to consciousness by someone shouting in his ear and telling him to wake up, as if he had just settled down to take an early-evening nap. But he did struggle back to consciousness, and we swam together for a minute until Carolyn could get the boat to us. With my last bit of strength I pulled myself and then Tommy into the boat. I rolled onto the cold fiberglass floor, unable to move.

Once we were all in the lifeboat, Carolyn took over, covering us with the aluminum blankets that were stored on the boat and squirting a bit of the precious water from the first aid kit into our mouths. My ebbing adrenaline kept me warm for the first hour, but then my wet clothes felt like ice around my quivering body. As I began to dry off I also began to feel the pain in my arm and from the cuts and bruises that covered my entire body. It was hard to focus on the questions Carolyn asked me as the sounds of the plane, still circling to make sure there was nothing left, kept creeping up on the corners of my mind. I grimaced with pain, not really caring if the airplane found our little boat or not. But, no matter how bad I felt, I knew that Tommy and Rebecca were worse. There were two deep gashes on his right arm from a piece of metal that had hit him in the explosion, and Rebecca had lost a tremendous amount of blood from the wound on her leg. Rebecca was still unconscious, and that first hour I was convinced that she would not live through the night on this boat that was hopping across the dark sea like a cork.

Then, just as quickly as it had come, the plane was gone, leaving us alone in our little lifeboat in the big sea. It was only us and the mermaids deep down in the sea who were left to battle. Only us and our fear.

The small fiberglass boat dipped down into the swells of the dark, rolling sea and then rode the waves up toward the bright stars until the water crested and fell back down again. After Tommy and Carolyn had dressed Rebecca's leg wound as best they could, we huddled together and stared up at the sky. Tommy's body shuddered against my shoulder every few minutes, his arms wrapped around the unconscious Rebecca, while Carolyn leaned into me as she pored over the map in the first aid kit, calmly holding the flashlight, which she turned off every three minutes to save its batteries. Everything seemed so quiet after the raging explosions of the bombs, the only noise the sound of the sea pushing the plastic walls of the deep little boat.

Tommy helped Carolyn try to navigate the boat by the stars, the two of them arguing across me about our probable location, but soon his pain got the better of him and he retreated under an aluminum blanket and tried to sleep. I think that I was in a mild state of shock, simply staring up into the navy-blue velvet sky at the pinpricks of starlight that pierced the fabric of the night. I remember hoping to see a falling star, imagining the stripe of color that would brush across the dark textured fabric of the sky, but stacks of gray clouds shouldered their way across my view. I silently cursed the clouds and then cursed the Judge. Over the years, he and I had talked and chewed on so many facets of life, luck, history, ruminating over our twisted fates like cows chewing their cud. We had argued about the existence of God, like two teenagers who had read their first book, and debated with equal fervency whether single malt or blended scotch really tasted better. We had discussed treason, our colleagues who for one reason or another had gone over to the other side, and the absurdity of thinking that you could get away with it. And yet never had I imagined that he was himself playing a role, lost in a double game.

At some point I must have fallen asleep, my last memory of Carolyn with a map and a compass spread out on the front of the boat, the flashlight between her teeth, trying to balance everything as waves hit the boat. I knew she was lost and that she had little hope of navigating the boat with just her compass and the stars, but I felt an overwhelming security just knowing that she was there, trying, giving it her all. Carolyn would never give up. She would never simply trust the sea to take us to land, or her boat that was looking for us right now. Seeing her poring over the map with a passionate intensity let me relax enough to wander off into sleep. This time I did not dream.

Carolyn woke me right after dawn had begun to crack across the hard shell of the night sky. "Honey," she said quickly and quietly, "I think I hear another boat."

"What?" I asked, unsure where I was.

"Shhh," she said. "Another boat. I hear an engine. Listen."

In the gray morning light, through the wafts of fog that rose off the gentle waves like rolls of English tweed, I could see nothing. But then, over the dull lapping of the sea against the side of the lifeboat, I heard the engine of a small boat not far away. One of Rebecca's family relatives? Colombians sent out by the Judge to finish the job? Everyone was our enemy now.

"I think we should signal it," Carolyn said. "I'm not sure Rebecca can make it much longer. She lost so much blood I had to give most of the water to her during the night."

"How long have—"

"Five hours," she answered. "We've had quite a night without you. I'm going to take the risk. Agreed?"

My brain was so foggy with pain and exhaustion that I nodded more in agreement that she should make the decision than in agreement with the decision.

"Tommy?" she said, as I raised my head to see him. He was sitting up with his back against the side of the boat, his face ashen white, but his eyes wide awake.

"Yes," he said. "I agree with you. I think we should use the flares."

Carolyn got out the flare gun and shot into the air. The flare burst bright red against the gray sky, and we watched it go up and up and then out. We then waited silently. When I had decided that the boat had not seen our flare, a voice suddenly shouted out through the fog.

"Identify yourself!" the voice shouted from not more than fifty feet away. They had obviously cut their engine and drifted to us.

I had heard that voice before, I thought.

"Murphy?" I shouted back, my voice breaking but strong.

"Hot damn!" was the response. "Is that you, Steele?"

The boat's engine roared to life, and then the boat was suddenly next to our lifeboat, Freddy at the wheel, Murphy and Sam standing with machine guns leveled at us. Always ready for a trap.

"Well now," Murphy said. "Small world after all, eh?"

I laughed. "Murphy, I've never been happier to see someone in my entire—well, at least since yesterday. God, do you guys look good."

"Can't say the same about you four," Sam said. "Let's get you out of that thing. Is she alive?"

"Yes," Tommy asserted, a statement more of wish than of certainty. "She needs water. Carolyn's been taking care of her all night. But she needs a doctor."

"This is your lucky day," Murphy said, helping Tommy into the boat. "Your yacht, Carolyn, the one you sent for yesterday, is sitting damn pretty about five miles from here. Just waiting to see what's happening. We found them just about the time of the bombing last night. I have to admit I thought you were all goners. We've been circling the wreckage all night looking for you. Hoping that maybe there was something to find."

"Always have faith," I told Murphy, giddy with life and sudden hope. "This is an example. Always have faith in people. People somehow, someway find a way to survive. That's my theory, that—"

"Enough philosophy, boss," Murphy said, trying to spare me from sounding completely stupid. "Let's get this girl to a doctor."

"No radio communication," I ordered, suddenly reminded that I was the boss. "I don't want the Judge and his friends to know that we're alive. I want the whole damn world to think we just disappeared. Went down with the boat. I want no communication from the yacht at all, except whatever is necessary just to remain inconspicuous."

"The Judge?" Murphy asked. "What—"

"You guessed it," Carolyn said. "My dear old friend was the mole. He was part of the family somehow. Bought and paid for, probably."

"He tried to cover up his role," Tommy said, wincing with pain as he moved. "He tried to kill us after he thought the transmission was finished, because we were the ones who either knew or could have found out. But only about half of the data was sent before the first bomb fell. God knows who got what and whether it was enough to make a difference. Who knows if she saved the world or just mixed it up."

"Now," I suggested, "we save ourselves. We aren't safe until we've got the Judge."

"Okay," Murphy said. "We're back in the game."

42.

It was the whitest thing I had ever seen.

Sitting silently on the rolling blue ocean, Carolyn's boat, modestly named *The Carolyn,* glimmered like an angel of mercy in the few rays of sun that broke through the gray morning mist. As we bounced on the waves toward the white yacht, a feeling of safety and security welled up inside me, and I covered my face with my hands so that no one would see the tear that came to my eyes. We had almost made it. Only the Judge stood between us and complete safety—for at any moment a bomber could slip out of the clouds and with a whistling sound of fear drop a half ton of steel on the glistening deck of Carolyn's beautiful ship.

Tommy and Rebecca were both rushed to a makeshift sick bay, where Tommy's cuts were sewn up by the medic on board and Rebecca was pumped full of plasma. Both were markedly better in two hours. Every member of the crew was informed that their lives were in danger, as was Carolyn's—which they were sworn by some law of the sea to protect, since she owned the boat—and that our only chance was to remain silent and anonymous as the big boat cruised at top speed to a helicopter that would take us to a waiting airplane in Miami.

The plan was simple: Evade everyone until we could talk to the secretary of state and have the Judge arrested. Several practical obstacles remained. In order to bring the boat into a harbor we would have to contact the Coast Guard or risk being intercepted by the DEA, either of which might have been notified by the Judge to watch for and intercept us. Secondly, we would have to find a way to simply drop in on the secretary of state without the Judge's finding out about our arrival. That meant we couldn't talk to aides, schedulers, or security guards.

But the hard part, we all knew without discussing it, would be the explaining. How do you convince the federal government that its top spy catcher is a spy? Normally I would go to the number two in the organization, Paul, but I wasn't sure that he could be trusted, and the person technically in charge of internal security on the ninth floor, John X, was dead.

When Rebecca came around that afternoon she assured us that the Judge was the lone mole in the NSA, as far as she knew, and this time I believed her. It would be too dangerous for there to be another, unless he or she had no knowledge of the others.

"What did the Judge get out of this?" I asked, leaning against the speeding ship's vibrating wall. "Why would he betray the organization and his country?"

"He didn't believe he was betraying them," she said, pulling her hair behind her and rubbing her tired-looking eyes. "And there was the one thing he was most jealous of in the organization, maybe in the world."

"What?"

"You," Rebecca answered, with a fairy's half smile. "You and your money. That's why he fired you the first time and why he convinced himself that you were a hopeless romantic who would screw up any investigation enough that—no."

Then she stopped and closed her eyes. "No, it's more complicated than that," she said. "I think he brought you back in because it made the whole thing more of a game. I told him not to, and he never really had a good explanation for why he did, except that it was always more fun deceiving you. He had this need to make a fool of you, to outsmart you, to make you spend your money while he collected mine. That dinner the night he recruited you back, he even gave me the bill for the family to pay, because he didn't think it was fair to make him pay for it. He was that convinced that you would screw it up. I gave him exactly one million dollars—the most I had ever paid anyone, either a member of the organization or the family. He loved the idea of having money, of being able to do some of the things that you and Carolyn do. He really had no concept how little one million dollars is. How he couldn't spend a month with the two of you and hang on to a penny of that million. But he was completely fascinated with your lifestyle. In retrospect, I should never have let him do it. It was just too complicated a scheme, but he had to improvise fast after you miraculously found Tommy—which you still haven't told me how you did."

"There's plenty of time for that later," I suggested, signifying that I had not yet decided whether she was foe or friend. I could feel the ice run through her veins when I gave the classic nonanswer. I knew that she knew that I didn't trust her yet, and that made her wonder if she could trust me. "But there is something I have to know now. We don't have much time. We'll be near enough to Miami for the helicopter to pick us up soon. But I have to know how. How did you approach him? How did you convince him to join you, to work with you?"

"I told you," she said. "The money—"

"It wasn't just the money," I said firmly. "As you said, it's more complicated than that. He is more complicated than that."

She paused before answering. "I did the one thing he hated most," she mused. "I outsmarted him. I got him in a corner where he had no choice."

"How?" I asked again. "Skip the details. Give me the bottom line."

"I told him about the family. But I told him that I had discovered them in my own investigation of the Bundt Bank. I convinced him that I had infiltrated an international conspiracy of a wealthy family that was trading and selling national secrets. He believed me because I had the evidence. I had information that I could have gotten only if it was true—because it was true."

"Why didn't he bring in the whole damn Army and arrest every member of the family?" I asked, the speed of my voice matching the charging boat.

"Because I also showed him, allegedly because of my infiltration of the family, that they had contacts in the CIA, military intelligence, the FBI, the State Department—again, because it was all true. He couldn't go to any other organization until we had found out everything we could about this family. The sweet part, the maneuver that he ultimately fell for, was I was able to convince him that in order to find out everything about them, we had to convince the family that the Judge himself was on the take. That the Judge had been bribed and would help them. He protested, but ultimately, when he realized that this could make him famous, he decided to take the risk. We opened a series of bank accounts in his name, with his identification numbers, his photograph, and his fingerprints, and had a million dollars deposited in the accounts."

"Did he believe in this?" I asked incredulously. "Or did he just want the money?"

"Who knows?" she said. "But he took it, and then we set up a meeting of the key figure in the family. The old man who ran things, I called him. The Judge would meet with him, now that the family's leader thought that the Judge had been bought—but at that meeting the Judge and I would arrest the man, this key player, and blow the lid off the whole family."

"This old man," I said. "Your father?"

She laughed. "Good guess. The Judge agreed to meet with my father at that restaurant right off the parkway between Fort Meade and Washington—where he has those private luncheons where he hires and fires people, you know the one?"

"Very well."

"The three of us met there, with a dozen federal agents surrounding the restaurant. Just as the Judge was ready to spring the trap on my father, my father said something like 'Mr. Dernza, you have a very simple business decision to make. We can call *The Washington Post* this afternoon and tell them that you have been bribed, giving them all the information about your Swiss bank accounts—which are full of money from the Medellín drug cartel, who would deny knowing anything about it, but who have conveniently, and unwittingly, left their fingerprints all over the transactions—or we can multiply the number in those accounts by ten and you can be a rich man.' "

"Why would he agree to that?" I asked.

"Because he thought he had no choice," she argued. "He turned to me, and I told him that I would back up the family's story. He was shocked—but not half as shocked as when I told him that I really was a member of the family, that all those people I exposed were really members of the family, and that this man was my father. I think he agreed to it all half out of the shock. He waved off the federal protective men and took the additional nine million dollars."

I heard the sound of the helicopter before I saw it, the piston-pumping whirl of the blades slicing the air as it came through the clouds toward us. We would be on our way to Miami and then Washington in minutes.

"But then he turned on you," I said.

"He thought he could erase his tracks. Eliminate the people he believed knew that he had taken the money. He would let the transmission go through, but then have someone bomb the plane. Not the Air Force, but some hired hit man."

"For money," I said. "All for money."

"No," Rebecca said, demonstrating her innate skill at understanding people. "Not just for the money, but for the pride, the competition, the preservation of his reputation. He knew he could probably never spend any of the money. He just didn't want to have to confess that he had been tricked, compromised by his own quixotic need to be a . . . well, a hero."

"The dream of every traitor is to be a hero," I offered.

A whisper of guilt sounded in my mind, because there was a hint that I had caused the Judge's treason. It hit me then, as I stood on the deck of the gentle iceberg of a speeding boat in the sudden wind of the descending helicopter, that this was what I had always feared. I had always wondered whether my good fortune led people to do more than just despise me, which I was arrogant enough to believe most of my fellow spies did, but to risk competing with me in the material world. My sudden wealth looked so easy, so comforting, that it might be worth a healthy bribe or two to have some of it. Had the Judge been hiding that much envy under all those barbs about my being a kept man? Could he have put his entire life at risk just for money?

Yes, I thought, seeing his tanned face and hearing his drawl in my mind. Yes, he could have. He was a true entrepreneur. He probably loved the risk. He probably loved the thrill of knowing that he was playing a game of many dimensions. I could see him now, sitting at his giant burled maple desk, his cowboy boots up on the edge, an unlit cigar rolling over his tongue, his eyes bright and pointed as he listened to a gaggle of young analysts spewing forth information about what had happened at around eight forty-five on that summer night. He would have listened intently, thrilled at knowing that he was involved in the perpetuation of the crime and the dozen secret plans to stop the crime and the public investigation of the crime and sitting on a hidden bank account that might be the only thing of value to come from the crime. If he couldn't get the public credit for stopping the crime, then he could at least get the satisfaction of being the recipient of some of the proceeds.

But no, I thought, he has convinced himself that he has brought peace to the world, or at least a new order, and covered his tracks while doing it. He would have his secret biography already written in his head: risked everything to bring peace to the world, forced to make difficult decision to kill his friends for the betterment of mankind, didn't do it for the money but the family would trust him only if they thought they controlled him by making him commit an illegal act. Now he could live out his life in anonymity, content with his soldiering.

He would have all his actions justified and his conscience would be clear, I thought as my blood pressure began to go up. He would be leaning back in his leather chair without a care in the world, not ever guessing that I was coming back to get him.

"I'm coming to get you, partner," I said out loud, not to Rebecca but to the water rippling around us from the gusts of wind swirling around the helicopter. My eyes were fastened on some unseen point where the sky met the sea. "You old cowboy, I'm coming."

43.

THE TWELFTH DISCIPLE was code-named Judas, but he was known within American intelligence circles simply as the Judge.

I am sure that the Judge loved his secret code name, just as I am sure that he loved being a traitor. I remember the two of us sitting in a fishing boat having long talks about a dozen different things—including whether the entire concept of treason had any meaning in a global, technologically sophisticated society in which everyone watched everyone else. We had both had a couple bottles of Stroh's and were tired of swatting the deer flies that hovered around the old aluminum fishing boat like a fog with noise, but we were feeling too good about each other to be too irritable. We spent most of the morning arguing the virtues of the designated hitter, and then the Judge complained that I was too lazy to be a good fisherman. Too rich and too lazy.

But somewhere in the midst of those conversations I remember a fleeting talk about committing treason. The Judge listed all the famous double agents: Kim Philby, Klaus Fuchs, Guy Burgess, Don Maclean, Joe Peterson, Bernon Mitchell, Ham Martin, Jack Dunlap, Victor Hamilton, Geoffrey Prime, Christopher Boyce. Their names fell casually out of his mouth like the lazy chirps of the birds that circled the lake, occasionally diving down to catch a fish, but usually settling for a snack of deer flies. "What made them do it?" he asked rhetorically. Each, he was sure, had his own peculiar reason. Each had his own mixed-up views that justified his actions. But were they all simply misled by their own visions, their own predispositions? He didn't think so, he told me as he cast his line out into the calm water. They all had something in common, he believed—they all believed they were smarter, more clever, than they really were.

"Cocky sons of bitches," he said as he again cast the shiny lure out onto the silent surface of the lake, letting it sink into the murky darkness for a few seconds before he started the jerky reel that brought it back to the boat. Outsmarting the enemy was too easy, he explained to me in so many words. All of them strove to do more than out-think their enemy—they strove to out-think their friends and employers. "I think," the Judge told me, after pausing when he thought he might have a bite on his line, "that they all just wanted to win the game." After a long draw on his beer, he continued. "Their shared delusion," I remember him saying, "was that they were better than their compatriots. Faster, smarter, more creative than the rest of us."

"But they weren't," I remember pointing out. "At least the ones who got caught." I explained to the Judge that I was convinced that every intelligence agency had been penetrated by double agents who had never been caught. Traitors the agency never knew about, and probably never even imagined existed. "It's just the less than brilliant ones, or the unlucky ones, that get caught," I remember saying to the Judge. "Like all those stars," I remember saying, pointing up into the bright blue morning sky hiding the stars like a veil. "There have to be millions of planets out there circling those millions of stars, and it's just not probable that there isn't one of those planets that can and does support life like ol' Mother Earth."

"A sobering thought," the Judge said, taking a swig of beer. Sobering that somewhere within the NSA—within "my agency," I believe he said—there was a mole. "A mole so clever that we won't ever even know that he exists, let alone how to catch him. Somebody just that much smarter than the rest of us."

"That's my guess," I remember saying, just as there was a hard strike on the fishing line in my hands, which I had been ignoring while the Judge worked so hard on his, constantly changing location, lure, depth, or distance to find those evasive fish. I spilled the remainder of my Stroh's as I hooked the fish deep and then fought a nearly two-pound bass into the net the Judge held out for me.

"You lucky son of a bitch," the Judge said. "Goddamn you, you are so filthy lucky. I can't believe it. What the hell did you do, pay that fish to jump on the hook while you leaned back over there filling yourself up with pee? You lucky son of a bitch."

The Judge believed he was that man. The one man smarter than the rest of us. The one man who saw the big picture, while the rest of us worshipped the small, false bureaucratic gods of order, precedent, loyalty, repetition, and forms in triplicate. The Judge loved the code name because he intended to take from everyone and give back just enough to feel virtuous about himself. He loved the code name because he could show his government that these people, the rest of us faithful bureaucrats, these so-called disciples of intelligence, had no connection to any true god.

"This is how I fooled them all" was the first line of the handwritten manuscript we found locked in his desk drawer.

> Irony, duplicity, frickin' fate are the ingredients of this soup. As fate would have it, I have accomplished everything I hoped to accomplish only to find out that I am dying of cancer. That is why I am writing this story down—risking that my own handwriting could be used against me if this letter was ever found—because I want at least the silent, professional admiration of my peers when I am gone. I want them to know that I was the master at this game. That I had no peer, no close competitor, no equal in deception or patriotism. I gave it all, not just for me, for my family, but for my country, only to have life pull a fast one on me in the moment of my glory. Prostate cancer—hell, I always knew my big balls would get me in trouble.

When I first read it, many weeks later, I wondered if he had been drinking when he wrote it, but then I realized he was simply drunk with his own perceived success. His boasts, his swoons, his exaggerated claims of sainthood and genius were the tip of the iceberg of his cold, twisted psyche, which had knotted itself beyond all recognition in the many different roles he had played.

> But I've even kept the cancer hidden from all of you so far, letting you believe that I am ready and able to be promoted, once again, at any time. The cancer is nothing more than an obstacle that adds to the fun of the chase. But let me spell out to you what I have accomplished.

First he explained discovering a hint of the family's complicated information business cartel through Rebecca. He described Rebecca's setup almost identically as she had described it, adding that he was blackmailed by the family.

"What could I do," the Judge wrote, "but accept?" He accepted without any intention of doing anything other than staying alive long enough to figure out a way out of this dilemma and have Rebecca arrested, he wrote. But when he got back to his office he realized how difficult it was going to be to explain how he had gotten so deep into this quagmire, and how he ended up with several million dollars in several Swiss bank accounts under his control. Even if the president believed him, he wrote, the Joint Chiefs of Staff would have his hide. The boys at Langley would laugh as they insisted on his retirement, without pension.

"If they found out, I was finished."

He realized, he wrote in a one-line paragraph, that he had ruined his career. But then, in a flash of brilliance, he decided that he could win both ways. He would play her along in order to find the location of every family member. Then he would be able to swoop in and take them all. He would become famous in intelligence circles, and just maybe he could keep the several million dollars and "live the life of Steele."

Seeing my name in the letter caught me off guard at first, but then I began to understand the many different roles I played in this story. I was not just someone who happened into this complex web of intrigue and conspiracy. I was part of the premise, the cause, the very foundation that the story was built on. I was part of the Judge's motivation, just as I had been part of John X's motivation. Rich man Steele, the bane of the hardworking intelligence officer who sacrifices so much for his country and gets back so little in return.

In order to bind him even more, the family had opened up lines of communication from the Judge to the Medellín family cartel so that there would be a record of his having a relationship with the people who were allegedly funneling money into his Swiss bank accounts. But the Judge did them one better: Under the cover of what the family had created, he really did begin to talk to the Medellín family, letting them know that they could be useful to the American government in its many interests in Central America. With Panama and Noriega. With the constant upheaval in Haiti. In settling the civil war in El Salvador. In helping infiltrate Cuban intelligence circles. He wanted open lines of communication so that they could better understand each other's interests, he wrote that he told the cartel, all the time planning that the cartel could be his allies in the ultimate showdown with Rebecca. Because he couldn't use organizations within the government to fight the family, he had to go outside. "And the family would never suspect a thing," he wrote, "because it was the family that was trying to create the appearance of contacts between me and these Medellín businesses."

You can almost read the chuckle in his stilted handwriting. The boast that he had fooled Rebecca and her family of trained, wealthy spies. The humor and irony in using the family's own cover, which was supposed to damage him, to create an alliance to use against them. "But why would the Medellín family help me with Rebecca's family?" he wrote in his letter, the words large and swirling as if they were wide-open eyes, rolling with laughter. Because they had made a mistake in their complex plans, he scribbled, a mistake that he was clever enough to discover.

When the Bundt bank purchased the information necessary to tie him to the Medellín cartel, they decided they could also make a profit off the deal by selling the information to a rival drug operation. The family covered its tracks masterfully, leaving hardly a trace that could ever prove that one of their banking companies had furnished the information.

> Now I had what I needed. I could tell the Medellín cartel who their true enemy was. I had opened up lines of communication with the cartel on the farce that the NSA could use their help in Central America. I proved my loyalty to the cartel by demonstrating to them that I was willing to reveal top-secret information about how the Bundt family had double-crossed them. I had gotten my chess pieces all in position. I just waited for Rebecca to make her next move.
>
> It wasn't as if I had a plan. I simply was trying to find ways to get myself out of the box Rebecca had got me into. I was just living by my wits, trying to construct as many tools to get back at Rebecca as I could without her realizing what I was doing. Helping her along toward her goal while secretly planning ways to stop her.

I imagine that he leaned back in his chair, as he always did, while he wrote this letter to himself—or was it to all of us?—and stared out the wide expanse of windows that met in the corner of his large office on Mahogany Row. The last few pages of his letter make it clear that once he had seen the damage reports from the planes hired by the Medellín family, he was confident that he had successfully double-crossed the Bundts. He had played a dangerous game, he knew, telling them just enough valuable information to get them to trust him, protecting Rebecca and then later getting her boyfriend back for her, but always planning to deny them in the end what they wanted most. He would deny them their transfer of American military secrets to the Soviet Union. He would pose as a protector, but in the end he would stop the transmission with all the forces he had at his disposal, and still not reveal his compromised position.

But what he hadn't counted on was the depths of John X's jealousy. He hadn't imagined that John X would break the family's story wide open, just because he couldn't stand the thought of Rebecca with someone else. Just another sign, the Judge wrote, of how off his rocker John X really was.

So when the Judge found out when the family reunion was, he let loose his first volley. He told the Medellín family that the Bundt family had sold the Medellín information to their competitors, and the Judge suggested where and when Rebecca's immediate family could be found all together in one place at one time—at their farm. He had hoped, he wrote, to direct the whole operation for the cartel, since he knew he could do a better job than anyone else in planning and executing an attack on the family. But the cartel shut him out, not about to let the head of an American intelligence operation plan an illegal foray into the United States to kidnap or kill their enemy.

"Of course," the Judge wrote, "they were incompetent." First, the Medellíns were steeped in tradition and symbolism. The cartel talked to so many people that Rebecca's family found out that the Medellíns knew about them and were planning an attack. That gave Rebecca's family time to prepare. When asked, the Judge reassured Rebecca that the NSA knew of no movement of Colombian terrorists into or around the country. The cartel was so stupid as to even do their traditional symbolic blood-on-the-doorframe warning the night before the attack, when they dropped the red paint on the family's house. Then, the Judge scribbled, the words short and angry, the cartel hired "a bunch of half-assed, gun-toting *Soldiers of Fortune* types to parachute in and try to kill off the family." If the Judge hadn't helped by getting every law-enforcement officer normally in the three-county area out of the way, the whole thing would have blown up in their faces.

I knew I was going to have to come up with another plan if there was going to be any chance of stopping Rebecca's family before the transmission. I knew that simply stopping Rebecca would not be enough. I had to find some way to get at the entire family, or at least enough of it to keep their plans from going forward. I needed to get to Doc and her brothers, at a minimum. Therefore, when John X and Paul called me up in the middle of that night and told me that they knew something was going on at Rebecca's family farm, I had to think fast.

It was a game of the possible, the potential, the practical solution to the problem at hand. I had to be clever enough to win with what I had at hand.

I can imagine him smiling again at this point, maybe fingering a good cigar and running a hand through his thinning hair. At this point in the telling of his story, he was once again the hero. The man on the edge, on the cusp, surviving by his wits alone. Woken up in the middle of the night by his own deputy to be told that somehow, unbeknownst to him, his agency was on the verge of discovering the entire conspiracy.

But we know what happened. He remained calm and cool, shut down Paul and John X's plans to immediately send agency personnel to the farm, and, with impeccable logic, called up Murphy and hired him to go in and kidnap Rebecca. If the cartel couldn't give him what he wanted, maybe Murphy could. If the cartel couldn't get Rebecca, then maybe Murphy could kidnap her, believing that he was helping the Judge grab back an agent who was going over to the other side.

But how to pay for Murphy's services, and how to cover in the office? Whom could he bring in to answer John X's questions and make John X believe that the Judge was acting to find the answers? Whom would John X, and anyone else who stumbled across what was going on inside the NSA, trust?

The person John X had called for advice, of course. Me.

That was a risk that was worth taking, the Judge wrote. To bring "rich old Steele" back in.

Steele would either look like a fool by finding nothing, or I'd be able to accuse him of running an entire operation off the books with his wife's money, which, considering his past, everyone would believe. His money would finally get him into real trouble, as it should have all along. God knows, his ethics were always questionable, and after he was let go over the whole Mike Carter Mexican affair, no one would question his ability to go out and do something on his own, without my knowledge or consent.

It was, the Judge said in so many words, almost too good to be true. The outside man the inside guys would trust and the outside world would suspect—and he would unwittingly pay for the Judge's backup plan with his wife's money.

The Judge had taken Rebecca's family money and not, in his mind, betrayed his country. He had befriended the Medellín cartel, used them to help him, and turned them over to the DEA. In the end, the cartel even supplied the plane to bomb Rebecca's family's boat. As a bonus, he had eliminated the members of the family who knew his true identity by bombing the boat with Rebecca and her father on it. He wished he had figured out a way to get the Soviet information without giving up U.S. information, but by the time Carolyn, Murphy, and I got so close, discovering the location and time of the transmission and, like dutiful agents, reporting it back to the Judge, there was no alternative but to blow us all out of the water. The Medellín cartel reported back, he wrote, that they bombed the boat exactly at eight twenty-nine, one minute before the transmission was to take place. For once, he wrote, they seemed to have pulled off a simple task.

Obviously, he didn't know that they had been late. When the Judge sat at his long square desk writing out the story of his ultimate success, he did not yet know that he had failed. As his pen glided over the paper, he had no idea that the transmission was partly successful. He probably smiled at himself as he wrote, pleased that he had pulled it off. There had been some tough times when he thought that I might have been close to breaking the case, but he had made it through on luck and ingenuity. He would have felt much easier if Carolyn hadn't gotten involved, "not only because my wife liked her so much but because her death might be noticed."

In fact, he explained, probably propping his feet up in comfortable pride, if it wasn't for Carolyn, Steele never would have even gotten close. "And, I'm sure," he pondered in his letter, "if I had only figured out the miniature microphone in Tommy Wood's belt, I could have kept this whole mess at the end from even happening." He would have even got the Soviet information.

For a moment, he wrote, his thoughts more disjointed as he began to wind down, "I thought I was going to have to shoot Steele in his own study when he told me he had figured out what the Bundt family was doing." But the Judge proudly recorded in his missive to posterity that he had kept his cool and thought of a strategy whereby he could have his cake and eat it too.

> Timing is everything. I was able to envision a scenario whereby my country would prosper and so would I. I considered holding the money in trust and then giving it back, but after thinking of the complexities of trying to give the money back if the whole thing fell apart, I decided that I would have to keep it. I could never convince the boys at Justice that I had taken the bribe money just so Rebecca and her family would believe that I was for real. I would never be able to convince a congressional oversight committee that I had to have the money placed in my wife's cousin's Swiss trust account so that I would be taken seriously by the family. I would never be able to convince anyone that ordering bombing runs by two-bit Colombian mafiosos on domestic boats was necessary to fulfill the goals of the mission. Therefore, I had to go it alone.
>
> But just as Rebecca could not have foreseen falling in love in the midst of the most important project in her life, I couldn't have foreseen that spot of blood in my piss that sent me to the doctor to see what was the matter. I waited until it was too late, avoiding the doctors here at the agency because I didn't want anyone here to think of me as anything other than infallible, but by the time I got to the G.P. in the sleepy town where I go fishing, he said the only hope was to cut me up, which would have taken me out of operation at the very time that I had to be here to stop Rebecca.
>
> She did kill me, in the end. Forced me to scramble around bringing Steele back and fighting off his attempts to figure out this whole mess instead of fighting the cancer. When I should have been undergoing chemotherapy, I was sitting down in that strategy room playing the game.
>
> But now that it's all over, that I've pulled off the greatest come-from-behind save in the history of the agency, I've got to admit the truth to myself. I feel terrible. I get dizzy easily. The old G.P. gives me six months at best. He tells me, sworn to secrecy as he is, that I'm committing suicide. Maybe that is so, but I've done it for a cause I believe in. The cause not of America, but of an American. I want to ride out into the sunset, the lone man on a good horse on a vast range that I own.

He left the letter in the secret drawer and went to his favorite restaurant for lunch. But something must have happened before he put it away. A phone call with a report on Soviet activity? A morning briefing memo that told him something was up in the world? We still do not know. All we know for certain is that at the bottom of the last page of the letter he left a quickly written postscript.

> P.S.: Just got the news. Seems some part of the transmission did go through, demonstrating that the damn Colombians screwed up yet again. A simple matter of timing. That was all. Crazy how it was almost perfect. But for a fluke in their timing, or maybe in her timing, I would have stopped the entire transmission. Now there are reports coming in from Pine Gap that we may have gotten enough to piece together what the Soviets are doing. The question is, did the Soviets get enough to know what we are doing? Does this mean that I have failed? No, I think that I succeeded. I believe enough of the transmission was disrupted to keep her family from achieving what they wanted. I stopped them. Just in time. Only a quick turn of fate kept the goal from being perfectly attained. Still good, just not perfect. Just that. Close. Close, but no cigar, cowboy. The story of my life.

He drove himself to the restaurant, refusing to take the Federal Protective Service guard, and ordered a good bottle of beer with his lunch. We don't know why he went there, but I presume he received some sort of missive from someone in the family, or maybe the Colombians, that they would meet him there. Maybe it was, like so many things in life, just coincidence, since he ate at that restaurant almost every day. He read the paper while he ate, and when he was finished he went down the dark stairs to the basement, maybe to see if the family had kept its part of the bargain. He probably imagined that if the family did not know what had happened there would still be lists of new account numbers lying under a perfectly folded linen napkin. He probably stopped before the closed basement door at the bottom of the steps, leaving a palm print on the railing, and pulled out his gun, twisting the silencer onto its short black muzzle, which left an almost invisible spot of oiled steel dust on the stair carpet. I imagine he opened the door slowly, but the lights were probably out.

When he flicked the lights on he saw the envelope and paper on the table next to a spinning tape recorder, and probably the shadow of a person leaning against the far wall. He must have been startled at first, but then relaxed back against the wall, leaving bits of fabric on the stucco, and tried to pretend that everything was fine. He lowered the gun, letting the oiled muzzle of the silencer touch the wall, probably realizing that he could not win anymore at this game.

"Well, well, well," the Judge may have said nonchalantly, as he often did when he was trying to convince you that he wasn't surprised or didn't care. "Fancy meeting you here," he would have said. "I don't presume you've come to wish me well."

The shadow of a person would not have responded right away, reaching to push the record button of the tape recorder.

"Let me tell you this" were the first words the Judge said on the recording, his voice on the tape as cracked and leathery as an old saddle. "Give me your gun. Or let me use my own. Let me do this myself."

44.

THE JUDGE was not in his office when we arrived.

I strode down the tiled floor of the main hall at HQ, the secretary of state, Carolyn, Murphy, two assistant undersecretaries sweating with excitement, six men from the Bureau, and old Charlie, the organization's front-door guard, who had insisted on coming along to protect me. We were all given security badges so that the warning bells and lights would not go off when the phalanx trotted after me down the halls, and we pushed our way through the crowds headed for the cafeteria for lunch. It was strange to be back in the building after the past few days. I suddenly felt like an analyst again, after being in the field. Everything was very quiet, the only sounds the hum and wheeze of computers and photocopiers. Everyone was silent as we paraded down the ninth-floor hall, guns drawn and eyes moving across the sea of stunned secretaries and bemused analysts. "What the hell?" some of them mouthed at me. What is this all about? You got to be kidding, man, guns drawn? You're not going to have a shootout at the HQ, are you? Steele, have you finally really lost it?

At dawn a sightseeing helicopter had taken off from Miami, wandered along the coast, and then dashed out to sea and hovered above the gleaming white deck of *The Carolyn* just long enough for five people to be hoisted up into its padded seats. Carolyn, Murphy, Rebecca, Tommy, and I watched the art deco hotels appear along the beach as we swung under a DEA patrol, and, like sightseers, we applauded the first American flag we saw. The helicopter dropped us off at a remote airstrip, where an unmarked Lear jet was waiting for us, and within minutes we were on our way to Washington. The jet landed at the airport near Carolyn's house, and Carolyn, Murphy, and I quickly got into the back of a waiting car, which went straight up along the river to the Watergate, where we knew the secretary had a condominium. James, our now armed housekeeper, and two of his friends drove Tommy and Rebecca to Carolyn's house, where they were given strict instructions on remaining not seen and not heard.

On the way to the Watergate we stopped in Georgetown and picked up a wealthy older lady who was a friend of Carolyn's, and who the afternoon before, after receiving a phone call from Carolyn's assistant, Laura, had arranged to meet the secretary of state and his wife for a late breakfast this morning to discuss paying off his entire campaign debt.

The guards at the entrance of the Watergate had Carolyn's friend's name on their list, but they were suspicious of Murphy and me. Fortunately, the armed doorman recognized Carolyn and agreed to call up to the guard on the secretary's floor, even though the secretary was "working at home" this morning. There was some argument when word came down to meet him at his office at noon, and only after Carolyn insisted on talking to the secretary's wife, who remembered everyone who had ever written a check for one of her husband's campaigns, were we allowed up.

The secretary was still at home, he explained, because he had been up half the night listening to experts tell him exactly how the whole intelligence community was up in arms over so many things that he didn't even know where to begin to explain them all to me.

"I can explain," I said, sounding more confident than I was. "Last night something happened that may well change the world forever."

"All right, Mr. Steele," the secretary said. "Lay it on me."

I told him the whole story, except that I neglected to remember that we had picked Tommy and Rebecca out of the sea. In my version, Carolyn and I were the only lucky survivors. Tommy and Rebecca had gone down with the boat: Rebecca trying to save her transmission and Tommy trying to save Rebecca.

With that simple little omission, I kept my part of the bargain. They would have a new life.

Miraculously, the secretary believed the story we told him, or at least decided to humor us by staging a noon raid on HQ to interview the Judge himself. One of the secretary's minions arrived for his morning briefing, only to be sent to the Bureau to gather up a half dozen good men for the surprise visit. Against everyone's advice, the secretary insisted on going along.

We waited patiently for the FBI internal security men, and then, leaving Carolyn's friend and the secretary's wife behind, we piled into several Bureau cars and raced up the parkway to Fort Meade.

"If we get him," I suggested, the words coming out before I had thought them, "I'm going to quit."

"What?" Carolyn asked, shaking her head.

"If we get the Judge, I'm going to quit the organization. I'm going to raise flowers, raise kids, and spend your money. Maybe I'll become a world famous rosebush grower. Maybe I'll retire and travel the world. Maybe I'll just follow you around all day and engage in pleasant conversation."

"Shut up," Murphy said. "Stop the bullshit."

"You're just tired," Carolyn suggested.

"No, I'm wide awake and, for at least this short moment, vividly sane. I'm through. I've had enough. This really isn't important anymore, even though I've been saying that it isn't important for decades. I'm getting out while the getting is good. I'm splitting. Moving on. Out of here. I'm going to enjoy life. I'm going to . . . to . . ."

Then the words fell from my tongue.

"To adopt a son. Or a daughter. Maybe a half dozen. I'm going to adopt some kids."

In unison, Carolyn and Murphy both pulled away from me, wedging themselves up against the car doors, and stared at me. I simply smiled.

"Not this again," Carolyn said.

"Could you repeat that for the jailer we're going to send for you?" Murphy said. "Did I hear you right?"

"You're the godfather," I muttered to Murphy, and then quickly added, "if Carolyn agrees."

She looked at me for a moment and laughed. "Of course," she said, kissing my cheek. "I agree."

"You agree to what?" Murphy practically screamed. "I don't know what is more crazy, me being a godfather or you having a kid. The stress has damaged your brain, buddy. You are totally bananas, boss. You are gone, gone."

"But you'll agree?" I asked again, loving the game.

"Oh hell, if it will make you happy. Yes, I'll be the goddamn godfather of this made-up kid you'll never have. Now just shut up about it."

Then we were there, swinging into the garage and flashing our badges to the Federal Protective Service guards and striding through the long halls covered with the brightly colored murals and up the elevator to the ninth floor, where behind one of the mahogany doors was the Judge's giant corner office. When we got to the closed door everyone stopped and looked at me. I thought about knocking, but then realized that it would be silly and might give him time to do something. No, I thought with a smile, I'll just punch the ten buttons of the secret cipher code, let the door swing open, and let him see me, which might give him a fatal heart attack. A ghost come back to haunt him. Someone he assumed was dead suddenly reappearing.

"Mr. Steele," the Judge's secretary said, "the Judge is—"

I nodded at the gunmen, who stepped back from the line of fire, their pistols raised and cocked, as I punched the cipher code on the lock and pushed the door open. The group of men swarmed over me into the room, pushing me against the wall as they aimed at everything and found nothing to shoot at.

"At lunch," the small voice of the Judge's secretary said behind me. "He went by himself to the café on the parkway about an hour ago."

His empty chair was turned to face the expansive window with its view of the forest the military wanted to sell, so he could prop his feet up on his credenza to have a smoke. A cigar was still burning in the ashtray on his desk, and we could see two glistening black crows sitting on a tree branch on the edge of the woods, their eyes beaming through the hanging plume of cigar smoke that rose in front of the window.

We raced back down the parkway with our lights flashing and sirens wailing, until we got within a mile of the café. We came up quickly but quietly, and I went in the front of the restaurant with Murphy, Carolyn, and the secretary of state while the Bureau boys went in the back door. The manager fluttered around us when we asked for the Judge, and he pointed to the door to the basement room, unable to speak at the sight of so many armed men in his quiet little restaurant. We met the Bureau boys and the assistant undersecretaries in the hallway to the basement, and they all followed me down the dark stairs to the closed basement door. Murphy moved in front of me and motioned all of us to edge up against the wall. When we were all out of the firing line and lined up the stairs, he swung the door open.

The Judge sat alone at the table in the middle of the room, his back to us, one hand on an envelope on the table. There was a red stain on the tablecloth that looked like spilled spaghetti sauce from lunch.

"Judge?" I said quietly to his back. "It's Steele."

He didn't move, and for a moment I wondered whether my voice had given him a heart attack.

"It's Steele," I repeated. "I'm back."

I stepped into the room, and the gunmen and Murphy followed me. I went directly to him without scanning the room, but when I went around the chair I stopped breathing.

There was a bullet hole in the middle of his forehead. A single line of blood trailed down his starched white shirt and puddled in his lap, where his handgun and silencer lay in one hand. The spaghetti sauce on the tablecloth was blood from his other hand, which lay next to the envelope.

The forensic experts argued among themselves for weeks about whether he had actually killed himself. The gun bore his fingerprints, and the trajectory of the bullet was consistent with shooting himself. But how did the gun land so neatly in his lap and his other hand extend so poetically out onto the table where his suicide note lay in a neatly sealed envelope? After more debate, someone finally suggested that maybe he did shoot himself, but then someone else cleaned him up, twisting the smile on his face and putting his hands in a position that would hold his body upright in the chair. There were no fingerprints in the room except for the Judge's. The room had been wiped clean before the Judge entered.

The note in the envelope was simple and to the point:

> Steele—You will find in a compartment in my second desk drawer on the left a letter that explains what I did and why. I didn't address that letter to anyone, but it seems fitting that it is to you. After John X's note, I'm tempted not to say anything, since these things always come

out badly. But that would be wrong. While suicide seems like the coward's way out, I want you to know that the humiliation of an investigation or a trial—of my honesty, my patriotism, my integrity being questioned—is too much for me to even contemplate, let alone bear. Particularly, as you'll understand when you read the letter, if the time I have left is so short. This way is better. Neater. More American, don't you think?

Promise me this, my fishing partner: Take care of Helen and the kids. I want you and Carolyn to make sure that they never need anything. I don't want them to know what happened. Tell them I was shot in the line of duty. Tell them that you can't tell them anything else. Tell them to bury me in Texas under the boot tree—they'll know which one I'm talking about. Tell them that I ordered new tires for that old truck on Dad's ranch and to make sure that the dogs get their heartworm pills. Then again, they've heard enough of my nagging. I'm just writing to avoid doing now. Thinking that as long as this old pen keeps gliding across this page I don't have to pick up that gun and get it over with. But you're the storyteller, Steele. You keep the pen.

Then he scrawled "TOP SECRET UMBRA/HANDLE VIA COMINT CHANNELS ONLY" on the top of the page, the dernza until the end.

"I don't think he shot himself," Murphy said as we stood around the lifeless body and the Bureau boys scrambled around the building and called out an army of support people. "But who did it then?" the secretary of state kept asking while we all looked at each other.

"Someone cannot be killed in the middle of—of Maryland," the secretary said. "Not here of all places. The head of thc damn National Security Agency cannot just be shot in the basement of a restaurant."

"I'll call the house and check the whereabouts of our red-haired friend," Carolyn whispered to me.

"What?" the secretary of state said to us. "What do you know about this?"

"Make sure she's been there the entire time," Murphy said to Carolyn as she left the room, speaking so quietly that he was only mouthing the words. "Make sure that every minute of her time has been accounted for."

"Mr. Secretary," I said over Murphy's whisper, our voices mixing in a frenzy of sound as everyone tried to figure out what was going on. "I don't know anything about this, but there are some people that might. I cannot reveal their names to you, but—"

"What did he say?"

"While we were sitting around the Watergate for damn hours," Murphy mumbled to me. "She slipped in here and—"

I kept talking, pretending that Murphy wasn't saying a thing. "I will talk to them and get answers quick. We need a full investigation. This means that there is someone out there who may know the whole story we've told you. Someone else—"

"Of course she would know how to get in," Murphy mumbled to himself. "This is how they met to plan the whole goddamn thing. She found out that he had gone to lunch. She had planned to transfer something to him here if everything went as planned. Jesus, she had clearance to get into the building. Everybody knew her. Probably banged half the guards."

"What?" the secretary said.

"We need to alert Langley," one of the assistant undersecretaries asserted.

"And the president," I said, to distract everyone from Murphy, who was prowling the room looking for clues.

"Now let's proceed cautiously," the secretary said. "We may want some—"

"Deniability," another of the assistant undersecretaries offered.

"No traces. No press. No waves," another one commented.

"Of course," I agreed, trying to keep my eyes off Murphy, who was prying up paper napkins with a pen, not touching anything, but moving too fast to be in control.

"Let's get this thing under control first," the secretary said. "And then—"

And then I saw it. Maybe someone moved and changed the light in the small dark room, but my eyes fastened on a brass bookend inches from the end of a shelf of cookbooks. Between the metal mane of the art deco horse's head that formed the bookend and the thick leather of a never-opened French sauce book was a single long hair. I moved toward it as everyone around me spoke, their voices receding into the background, and my eyes zeroed in on the hair.

"And the Joint Chiefs of Staff."

"Let's get a meeting right away so Steele can tell this story."

"Who's going to notify his wife?"

As I got close I saw that the hair was red. A deep, well-sunned auburn. As lush as Rebecca's long, smoldering hair.

"Steele?" the secretary asked. "Are you okay?"

I shook my head, grabbed the hair while my back was to the rest of the room, and put it in my pocket. "Yes," I said, turning. "It's just . . . he was a friend. A good friend."

Then I paused with true emotion, as if I had just realized that my friend, the best spy and the best traitor I had known, was dead.

"Of course," someone said.

"Of course," another echoed, as Carolyn came back into the room.

"Well?" Murphy asked, all eyes trained on him and Carolyn.

She looked nervously at me, and I nodded approval that she could go ahead and talk, since I had guessed that we would have to explain everything to the secretary now. I would have to tell him that Rebecca was alive. That somehow we had screwed up and let her have a chance to get the Judge. We had been stupid enough to believe her. To trust her.

But Carolyn simply said, "Every minute accounted for. She's been there every minute. Watched every minute. She hasn't moved. She didn't do it."

"What?" I asked incredulously, touching the hair in my pocket. She had cut her hair short at the lodge, I suddenly remembered. This hair must have been from sometime before.

"She never left the house," Carolyn repeated. "She has been sunning all morning. They were all worried about us. I didn't tell them what happened."

"Who are we talking about?" one of the secretary's boys asked, obviously annoyed.

"No one," I said. "If they couldn't have been involved, then no one."

"I demand to know who—" another one of the assistant under-secretaries began to say. He was cut off by the secretary of state.

"Let's get out of here," he ordered, with a smile at Carolyn. "I'm sure that Mr. and Mrs. Steele will write a full report that will clear up all of these details, won't you?"

"Of course," I said.

"And, Carolyn, will I see you over at the Robinsons' next week?" The Robinsons were having a dinner party that was a thinly veiled fundraiser for the secretary of state's campaign debt.

"Of course," Carolyn said, taking his hand and holding it longer than was needed.

Then we all left the Judge to the Bureau boys, coming out of the dark basement to the bright light of literally hundreds of men surrounding the restaurant and interviewing everyone who was there while dozens of others combed the woods around the restaurant. I took Carolyn's hand as the men parted for us and the secretary of state. As we got into the car to go back up to Fort Meade, I watched the men walking slowly through the lush carpet of bramble under the trees that surrounded the parking lot, their eyes fastened on the ground in front of them. In two weeks they found not a single clue. In my pocket I had the only red hair.

Rebecca's hair must have been left between the bookend and cookbook for months: a relic from an earlier visit and not just the last trace of a visit to the Judge that morning. The boys in the lab were able to identify the hair as hers, but they couldn't tell me anything about its age, other than it had fallen out within the last two months. Of course, Rebecca admitted knowing all about the Judge's basement room and meeting him there several times over the past months. Of course, I remember saying to myself, it was not so surprising that she would leave a single strand of auburn hair behind.

Of course.

45.

AS YOU ALL KNOW, my fellow bureaucrats and government leeches, I turned down the president's offer of the Judge's job as head of the organization. The president called me himself, and when I turned him down, feeling a pang of patriotic guilt, he asked me to stay involved with the investigation until we knew more about what had happened. We talked about our alma mater, and I promised him a full report in eight weeks.

I spent all my time either at the organization, monitoring the rumblings all over the world, or talking to Carolyn's lawyers about adoption. The day I gave my final report to the president and the Joint Chiefs of Staff the lawyer called me and told me to come by the hospital with Carolyn around four that afternoon. "By the way," the man on the phone said casually, "you might want to bring a blue blanket. It's a boy."

I couldn't concentrate in that dark wood-paneled room with the dozens of somber faces staring at me. They were all concentrating on me, and, like a teenager with a new convertible waiting in the school parking lot, I just wanted to be done and out of there.

About three-fourths of the transmission had gotten through, I told the assembled crowd. I agreed to summarize my report, but I suggested that they might get a kick out of reading it, since the truth was stranger than fiction. This is the essence of that report.

The United States had received most of the information on the Soviet Union, and all of it on Eastern Europe. We knew the military capability and state secrets of East Germany, Poland, and Czechoslovakia better than our own. We got most of the transmission on Romania, and some of it on Yugoslavia. South Korea had gotten nearly everything on North Korea, but we had gotten very little. Israel had received a good portion of the information on Saudi Arabia and Iran, but no one got very much on Israel. Iraq claimed to have more than we thought they had, but I predicted that there would be trouble in the region even in that early meeting.

We had received virtually nothing on China, so they remained as isolated and isolationist as before. However, South Africa's information went to everyone, as did the information on every South American country. Ethiopia, Libya, and Afghanistan were all almost completely transmitted and traded. I recommended that we move quickly to encourage South Africa to liberalize while we had a bargaining chip. For example, releasing Mandela might be a good trade for not telling their neighbors how to disable South African tanks with nothing more than a screwdriver. We had already backed the Soviets into a corner on East Germany and secured the reunification of Germany. Now, with Gorbachev forced to accede to our every wish, it was just a question of time, in my view, before he began losing power. Several analysts had predicted that without any ultimate military power the nationalist states that made up the Soviet Union would immediately seek to become independent and the Soviet Union, once the strongest military power on the globe, would fall apart.

As I looked at my watch, my mouth moving without my brain attached, I predicted that the cold war would be over within months if we used the information quickly and let the Soviets know that they had to retreat from Eastern Europe and their circle of fascist states around the globe. They allowed the Wall to fall while I was preparing my report, because we had made it clear that with the information we had they were no longer a threat.

We must encourage change immediately before the information we had was outdated. We could change the face of Africa within years, and South America could be coaxed toward true market economies, I argued. The Middle East would be subject to yet another historical accident, since the limited amount of information transmitted would probably just destabilize the region rather than bring peace. China would remain alone, aloof, a mystery to us all.

"You see, I have this theory," I said, but then I looked at my watch and up at the president of the United States of America, now without question the most powerful man in the most powerful country in the world, and said, "but I'm sorry, that will have to wait. I've got to pick up my son."

SIX

THE RESURRECTION

Then he took them out as far as the outskirts of Bethany, and lifting up his hands he blessed them. Now as he blessed them, he withdrew from them and was carried up to heaven. They worshipped him and then went back to Jerusalem full of joy; and they were continually in the Temple praising God.

—Luke 24:50

46.

It came to me who the eighth disciple was one day more than a year later. As I stood next to him on top of a grassy hill that we had hiked up, still panting and laughing from a joke he had told, I simply asked him out of the blue.

"You're the eighth one, aren't you? The eighth disciple?"

He pulled a long piece of dried grass up from the ground and chewed on the end of it as he stared out over the rolling Virginia landscape, which stretched out in front of us like one of his wife's giant paintings. Big bunches of clouds rumbled by in the sky like herds of massive white animals. I felt so light with the sudden burst of inspiration that I believed I could simply step up into the air and ride the clouds over the acres of flowing grass.

"It's you, isn't it?" I asked. "I've found all of them but you."

The eighth disciple was the doubter and was often skipped over in the family's plans. Some members of the family even doubted he existed. He was the adopted grandson of the rebel member of the family—the one brother who doubted the worth of their family enterprises and refused to take part in the business. When his grandson, adopted by his daughter, was growing up in a little town in the Midwest, sometimes even the grandson doubted he was a member of the family. He doubted because the whole story of the family seemed so unreal, so fantastic to a kid growing up in a small, uneventful town. A secret story of his mother's father's brothers and sisters, all fantastically wealthy, all involved in dark, clandestine conspiracies that could not be explained. A story that not only his father didn't believe, and that he was not allowed to talk about in front of his father but that his mother told him his grandfather, long dead now, had never even approved of her telling.

And yet his mother insisted on telling him the story, beseeching him to believe, not in words, but in the act of her whispered telling.

Over his father's constant objections, his mother insisted that he learn how to defend himself. She managed to turn him into an ace shot, solid runner, and winning wrestler. But his mother's constant attempts to make him fit some ideal she had in mind made him feel that he didn't belong—as if he had a secret that he could not share with any of the people he went to school with or who lived nearby. She read him stories when he was very young that were designed to expand his logic abilities, and told him that someday, regardless of his father's protests, he would meet the rest of her family. His reaction was to withdraw from those around him, terrified that he might somehow accidentally let go of the secret he could tell no one.

His mother finally explained the family to him after his father was killed. She explained that his father had doubted out loud about the motives and plans that the family had, so the family had had him eliminated. They had made it look like an accident, but she knew that the family had arranged to have his father die in a barn fire. She did not complain about the family's decision, but simply told him that someday the family would find someone for him to marry and then he would understand. Because he was adopted, his mother told him, he would have to marry into the family. And then maybe he would not doubt.

When he was older he began to hate what his mother had done to him, virtually poisoning his childhood with her constant ominous stories about her family. When he was sixteen he quizzed her on why his grandfather and his father had disapproved so of the family, and she couldn't answer him. So he too began to doubt the veracity of his mother's stories. Was she simply crazy? He never really knew.

His mother died young when he was in college, and the funeral was attended by a few of her relatives whom he had never met. They simply appeared at the funeral, introduced themselves by their relationship to him without mentioning their names, and then left. An older man who introduced himself as his uncle gave him an envelope and tipped his hat as he left. They did not show up at the funeral home or stop at the church for the lunch after the funeral. They were simply there, dressed all in tailored black, and then gone. Inside the envelope were two hundred and fifty one-hundred-dollar bills. The doubter in him began to believe.

Years later, he told me, kicking the grass on the Virginia hill, one of his mother's oldest friends arranged to have him meet the daughter of a friend when he was in graduate school. She seemed interesting, but maybe a bit too old for him, and he didn't realize that she was the woman he was supposed to marry until weeks after they had become friends. The man who had introduced himself as his uncle simply appeared at his apartment one evening and asked if he could sit down and talk. His uncle told him that he had a choice: He could marry this woman or he could simply forsake the family and never hear from them again. It was his choice. Either way, there were no hard feelings. The uncle handed him another envelope and said, "But there is one condition. This woman cannot know that you are a member of the family. You cannot tell her. She must come to her own conclusion that she wants to marry you. We want her to be happy, after all."

He walked around me as he talked, watching his feet leave a path in the tall, dry grass. He was nervous when he talked about the woman. Talking about her, about how he felt about her in those early days, seemed to trouble him. As if there was something not yet completely resolved.

He felt the thickness of the envelope, he told me, and began to believe even more. He handed the envelope back to his uncle and told him that he couldn't be bought or paid to marry someone, no matter how much was in the envelope. He liked her. Liked her quite a bit, he remembered telling his uncle. "Let's just see what happens. Maybe everything will work out. If it works out," he told his uncle, "then it was meant to be. If it doesn't work out, then I'll just go on living my life."

He never asked the woman if she knew that he was merely part of a family plan. Maybe she was merely pretending to be in love with him, he wondered. After a while he stopped worrying about the truth of her passion and lost himself in enjoying it. The lines between fiction and reality seemed meaningless when he became involved with her family—everyone was playing so many roles that he forgot what the truth was. Did they all know that he was part of the family? Was that why they were so willing to welcome him into the family, to tell him their plans, even in a time of crisis? Within weeks he decided that there was no truth; there were only plans. He was part of a plan bigger than himself, and the feeling of belonging was comforting and gave him strength. He had, after all, really always been married to this woman. It had been foreordained and arranged by the family years ago as a way to bring the line of the doubting eighth disciple back into the family. The only question was whether he would acquiesce. When he kissed her the first time, he knew the answer was yes.

But he had no one to answer his many questions. He had no idea where his relationship with this woman was going. He really hadn't planned to marry until he was older, and there was something vaguely unsettling about not knowing what she had planned, but knowing that she did have an agenda that she was not sharing. Sometimes he doubted whether he was being smart by playing along as if he knew nothing about the family, or was being ridiculously stupid by putting himself in positions where he was in danger. He knew only about the history of the family, not what their current agenda or makeup was all about. He had no idea about their big plan. He knew only that he had stumbled into something that was much bigger than his little game. He was simply playing a role in a drama much bigger than any one member of the family, all of whom seemed to scheme about the other members of the family.

Then all of a sudden I appeared and whisked him into a whole different world of mental chess and the contortions of professional intelligence operatives. All he knew when Carolyn and I picked him up, he told me, looking me straight in my squinting eyes, was that he had to get back to Rebecca as quickly as possible. Whatever she was up to, and he really didn't know what her plan was, he knew that he had to be with her, because she was planning on dropping out of sight. Regardless of the risks he had to take by going along with my crazy plans, they were less risky than not being with her. So he continued to play along. Never lying, since no one had ever asked him if he was part of the family. No one asked if he had known anything about the family before he met this woman. Everyone simply assumed that he was without knowledge, an innocent thrown into an incredible situation.

They were right, he told me later, standing on that hill in Virginia, that it was an incredible situation and that he doubted the veracity of most of what he was told. The game seemed to exist on so many levels that he often got confused as he moved from one to another. He kept allowing himself to be put in dangerous situations because he couldn't figure out any better alternatives. He was afraid that if she knew he was part of the family she would leave him, she wouldn't trust him, which was exactly what happened when she thought he was brainwashed by me. But as each hour passed, he told me, he found that he was more carried along by events outside his control. He was trapped in one version of reality because he couldn't tell her what he really knew.

But it was not until he sat with a gun in his hand at the small table in the restaurant's basement, across from the Judge, that he truly stopped doubting whether his mother was right. Only then did he truly belong.

"You're part of the family," the Judge had said to him and into the tape-recorded cassette, which he had kept in case there were ever any questions about what had happened. He had taken photographs and a blood sample in case anyone ever questioned whether he had fulfilled his obligation. He remembered rolling the Judge's words around in his mind, wondering if they were a statement or a question.

"I am," he had responded, adding the word "now" in his mind. I am now a member of the family. "And you have betrayed us."

"Yes," the Judge agreed. "Tried to outsmart you and boxed myself in a corner. But does it really matter? Isn't the family over? Haven't you accomplished everything and gone out of business, so to speak?"

"Almost everything," he said, his voice distant and weary. "You are the only loose strand."

"I see," the Judge said with a sigh. "Let me just write a little note here and I'll get on with it. Who should I write it to? I mean, who will find me here?"

There was a pause on the tape.

"Steele," he answered flatly.

The Judge chuckled. "I should have guessed. I should have known."

He remembered watching the Judge write slowly, the words scrawled across the paper in big loops that quivered with the Judge's shaking hand. The veins on the Judge's forehead bulged as he struggled to find just the right words for the letter. There was the overpowering smell of sweat from the two of them in such a small place, he remembered as we stood on that grassy hill and looked out over miles of emptiness. There had been so much death that he wasn't sure he could stand the sight of one more dead body, he told me, but he hoped this was the end. After this it would all be over, he remembered telling himself, like a man waiting for the inevitable pain that he knew would come and that he knew would be a shock despite all the expectation and preparation.

When the Judge was finished writing he put the short note in the envelope and licked it closed. The older man looked up at him, and their eyes met for a long time.

"I'm sorry," he said to the Judge. "I need to record this, and then take a few photographs just to prove that—"

He thought the Judge was going to say something, but the Judge simply picked up the gun, put it to his furrowed forehead, and pulled the trigger. Blood spattered over the white tablecloth and left a faint, sticky spray on his own face, only feet away. He remembered, he told me, standing on that hill watching the sun play with the herd of clouds, how he wiped off his face, then the Judge's face, and then straightened the Judge's arms and pulled him up in the chair so that he would look better in the photographs: nobler, calmer, more like the soldier he was. The Judge, code-named Judas, was dead.

Peace, he remembered thinking, so often comes only after so much death. He shook his head again as he stood under the expansive sky remembering how he had shook his head in that small basement room, doubting that it was worth it. Doubting, for a moment, that his marriage was worth all this trouble. "But she will never know," he said, first to the stampeding clouds, carrying away the last traces of my memory of the cowboy Judge into the sky, and then to me. "Steele," he said, "you won't tell her, right?"

"I won't tell her," I said, with a slight, meaningless smile. "Let's get back to dinner. They'll be expecting us."

"Yes," he agreed, craning his neck up to watch the big sky. "They'll be expecting us."

The eighth disciple was code-named Thomas. Doubting Thomas, Tommy Wood.

47.

A LITTLE MORE than one year later, on the day the Communist party in the Soviet Union fell, I loaded up our new green Jeep and drove Carolyn and our dark-haired son, Eddie, out to Maryland. Eddie had gotten used to the ride, since we made it virtually every other week. The truck always wheezes at the same place on the hill up the country lane where Teddy and Rachel Smith are building a beautiful new house. Teddy is an architect who grew up in the Midwest and went to Yale. He is now the principal architect for Carolyn's company, but does all his work without ever coming into Washington or New York. His wife, Rachel, spends most of her time with their three-month-old daughter, named Rebecca, who is already showing wisps of her mother's famous auburn hair. Rachel paints large landscapes in the studio building and collects antiques for the new house. They have a pair of big dogs and two tenant farmers who live with them and are always armed. Sometimes their Uncle Murphy visits them from New York, or their friend Sam flies into the little airport nearby to have lunch and then is just as quickly gone.

Carolyn and I and Eddie go out there and visit the country store with them. We take long walks along the creek that cuts across their property, and Teddy and I play tennis until Teddy's leg hurts. Sometimes I feel as if it is not Eddie who is the son I never thought I'd have, but Teddy, with his arm slung over my shoulder and beer on his breath. He'll pat me on the back and talk quietly about old times. About excitement that we could never forget. We'll laugh at our wives and get down on our hands and knees to play with our kids. I've settled any doubts I ever had in my mind about right and wrong and Teddy and Rachel. Somehow, without knowing when or why, we have all become a family, in the sense that we share an unquestioning, forgiving bond that makes right and wrong simply seem out of place.

When I am out in Maryland, visiting the Smiths, who appeared one day virtually out of thin air, I sometimes feel like a grandfather instead of a father, and this strange, warm dislocation comes over me like the gentle happiness of wine. What time is it? How old am I? Can we live like this for ever and ever?

The whole world has changed. Capitalism and democracy are breaking out all over without the Russians in their commonwealth raising an alarming voice, let alone a hand to stop it. Democracy is as infectious as the common cold. Only those of us sitting around the dinner table out in the country, and a couple of dozen leaders around the globe, really know what kept the Soviets from sending tanks into Czechoslovakia. Only a hundred people in the world know why the Soviets let East Germany, their crown jewel, reunite with the West. Only a few more know why the coup in the Soviet Union, and then the Soviet government itself, really failed.

"I have this theory about love and life and the power of information," I begin to say through the laughter at the dinner table, but they boo me quiet and go back to talking about the kids. The four of us, I think, smelling the musty fragrance of the glass of wine in my hand, have married out of trouble and into this earthly bliss.

Over the candlelight of a late dinner after the two children are both asleep, Teddy and Rachel tell us they are going to have a second child. We laugh and cry and have a toast to them, and then to friends lost but not forgotten. If it's a girl, they will name her Carolyn. If it's a boy, they will name him Steele. Immortality by not another name.

Theory number 1: Life goes on. Not like the undertow of a ceaselessly rushing river or the overreach of a human voice simply answering yes, but by building, growing, learning from what happened the day before. Every day, after all, is a Second Coming.

ACKNOWLEDGMENTS

THEORY NUMBER 22: Every story is stolen and every writer is a thief. Every story is the amalgamation of borrowed bits of other people's lives that the teller has absorbed like a sponge, or mopped up like a kleptomaniac cleaning lady, as he or she wanders through this messy life. This book is more love story than spy exposé, and therefore I owe more to the intelligent, passionate comments and poetry of my wife, Anne Slaughter Andrew, than to any sources within America's secret agencies. I also owe a debt to the friends and family who read this story as it was being told, to my friend Hayden Schultz for technical advice, to my editor, Gary Luke, and to my agent, Diane Cleaver, for her elegant edits and enduring faith.